Tom, Dick and Harry

Talbot Baines Reed

Contents

TOM, DICK AND HARRY

BY

Talbot Baines Reed

CHAPTER ONE.
WHO SHOT THE DOG?

A shot! a yell! silence!

Such, Fas soon as I could collect myself sufficiently to form an idea at all, were my midnight sensations as I sat up in my bed, with my chin on my knees, my hair on end, my body bedewed with cold perspiration, and my limbs trembling from the tips of my fingers to the points of my toes.

I had been peacefully dreaming--something about an automatic machine into which you might drop a Latin exercise and get it back faultlessly construed and written out. I had, in fact, got to the point of attempting nefariously to avail myself of its services. I had folded up the fiendish exercise on the passive subjunctive which Plummer had set us overnight, and was in the very act of consigning it to the mechanical crib, when the shot and the yell projected me, all of a heap, out of dreamland into the waking world.

At first I was convinced it must have been the sound of my exercise falling into the machine, and Plummer's howl of indignation at finding himself circumvented.

No! Machine and all had vanished, but the noises rang on in my waking ears.

Was it thunder and storm? No. The pale moonlight poured in a gentle flood through the window, and not a leaf stirred in the elms without.

Was it one of the fellows fallen out of bed? No. On every hand reigned peaceful slumber. There was Dicky Brown in the next bed, flat on his back, open-mouthed, snoring monotonously, like a muffled police rattle. There was Graham minor on the other side, serenely wheezing up and down the scale, like a kettle simmering on the hob. There opposite, among the big boys, lay Faulkner, with the moonshine on his pale face, his arms above his head, smirking even in his sleep. And there was Parkin just beyond, with the sheet half throttling him, as usual, sprawling diagonally across his bed, and a bare foot sticking out at the end. And here lay--

Hullo! My eyes opened and my teeth chattered faster. Where *was* Tempest? His bed was next to Parkin's, but it was empty. In the moonlight and in the midst of my fright I could see his shirt and waistcoat still dangling on the bed-post, while the coat and trousers and slippers were gone. The bed itself was tumbled, and had evidently been lain in; but the sleeper had apparently risen hurriedly, partly dressed himself, and gone out.

If only I could have got my tongue loose from the roof of the mouth to which it was cleaving, I should have yelled aloud at this awful discovery. As it was I yelled silently. For of all terrors upon earth, sleep-walking was the one I dreaded the most. Not that I had ever walked myself, or, indeed, enjoyed the embarrassing friendship of any one who did. But I had read the books and knew all about it. I would sooner have faced a dozen ghosts than a somnambulist.

I had no doubt in my mind that the Dux's empty bed was to be accounted for in this uncanny manner, and that the shot and yell were intimately connected with his mysterious disappearance. Now I thought of it, he had not been himself for some time. For a whole week he had not licked me. Ever since he had got his entrance scholarship at Low Heath he had been queerer than ever. He had not broken any rule of importance; he had been on almost friendly terms with Faulkner; he had even ceased to plot the assassination of Plummer. He was evidently in a low state, and suffering from unusual nervous excitement, thus violently to interrupt the usual tenor of his way; and, as I knew, such a state lends itself readily to the grisly practice of somnambulism.

What was to be done? Yell? I couldn't do it for the life of me. Get up and look for him? Wild horses could not have dragged a toe of me out of bed. Stay where I was till the unearthly truant returned? No, thank you. At the bare notion my rigid muscles relaxed, my erect hair lay down, and I collapsed, a limp heap, on to the pillow, with every available sheet and blanket drawn over my tightly closed eyes.

And yet, in my unimpassioned moments, I do not think I was a notorious coward. I had stood up to Faulkner's round-arms without pads, and actually blocked one of them once, and that was more than some of the fellows could say, I could take my header into the pool from the same step as Parkin. And once I had not run away from Hector when he broke loose from his kennel. Even now, but for the dim recollection of that awful automatic machine, I might have pulled myself together sufficiently to strike a light and jog my next-bed neighbour into wakefulness.

But somehow my nerves had suffered a shock, and since there was no one near to witness my poltroonery, and as, moreover, the night was chilly enough to warrant reasonable precautions against cold, I preferred on the whole to keep my head under the clothes, and drop for a season, so to speak, below the surface of human affairs.

But existence below the sheets, when prolonged for several minutes, is apt to pall upon a body, and in due time I had to face the problem whether, after all, the vague terrors without were not preferable to the certain asphyxia within.

I had put my nose cautiously outside for the purpose of considering the point, when my eyes, thus uncovered, chanced to fasten on the door.

As they did so paralysis once more seized my frame; for, at that precise moment, the door softly opened, and a figure, tall, pale, and familiar, glided noiselessly into the dormitory.

It was Tempest. He stood for a moment with the moonlight on him, and glanced nervously round. Then, apparently satisfied that slumber reigned supreme, he stepped cautiously to his deserted couch. My eyes followed him as the eyes of the fascinated dove follow the serpent. I saw him divest himself of his semi-toilet, and then solemnly wind up his watch, after which he slipped beneath the clothes, and all was silent.

I lay there, moving not a muscle, till the breathing of the truant grew long and heavy, and finally settled down to the regular cadence of sleep. Then I breathed once more myself; my staring eyes gradually drooped; my mind wandered over a large variety of topics, and finally relapsed into the happy condition of thinking of nothing at all.

When I awoke next morning, in obedience to the summons of the bell, the first thing I was aware of was that Tempest was complacently whistling a popular air as he performed his toilet.

"Poor Dux!" thought I, "he little dreams what a terrible night he has had. Good morning, Dux," I said deferentially.

Tempest went on brushing his hair till he had finished his tune, and then honoured me with a glance and a nod.

Something in my appearance must have attracted his attention, for he looked at me again, and said, "What makes you look so jolly fishy, eh, youngster?"

"Oh," said I, a little flattered to have my looks remarked upon, "I had a nightmare or something."

"Comes of eating such a supper as you did," replied the Dux.

"Wouldn't he open his eyes," thought I, "if I told him what the nightmare was! But I won't do it."

I therefore relapsed into my toilet, and, as time was nearly up, left the unconscious sleep-walker to finish his in silence.

Dr Hummer's "select young gentlemen" only numbered thirty, all told-- chiefly sons of the trading community, who received at the establishment at Hampstead all the advantages of a good commercial education, combined with some of the elegances of a high-class preparatory school. Tipton's father, who was an extensive draper in an adjoining suburb, was rather fond, I believe, of telling his friends that he had a boy at Dangerfield College. It sounded well, especially when it was possible to add that "my boy and his particular chum, young Tempest, son of the late Colonel Tempest, you know, of the Guards, did this and that together, and might perhaps spend their next holidays together at Tempest Hall, in Lincolnshire, if he could spare the boy from home," and so on.

It was an awful fascination for some of us to speculate what the "Dux" would have to say if he could hear this sort of talk. We trembled for Tipton's father, and his shop, and the whole neighbourhood in which he flourished.

Tempest's presence at the "College" did, however, add quite a little prestige to the place. No one seemed to suppose that it had anything to do with the fact that the terms were exceptionally moderate, and that his gallant father had left very slender means behind him. Even Dr Plummer had a habit, so people said, of dragging his aristocratic head pupil's name into his conversation with possible clients, while we boys mingled a little awe with the esteem in which we held our broadbacked and well-dressed comrade.

Within the last few weeks especially the school had had reason to be proud of him. He had taken an exhibition at Low Heath, one of the crack public schools, and was going up there at Midsummer. This was an event in the annals of Plummer's which had never happened before and in all probability would never happen again.

To do the Dux justice, he set no special store by himself. He believed in the Tempests as a race, but did not care a snap whether anybody else believed in them or not. Any boy who liked him he usually liked back, and showed his affection, as he did in my case, by frequent lickings. Boys he did not like he left severely alone, and there were a good many such at Dangerfield.

As to the exhibition, that had been entirely his own idea. He had not said a word about it to Plummer or any of us, and it was not till after he had got it, and Plummer in the fulness of his heart gave us a holiday in celebration of the event, that we had any of us known that the Dux had been in for it.

The second bell had already sounded before I had completed my toilet, the finishing touches of which, consequently, I was left to add in solitude.

When I descended to the refectory I was struck at once by an unusual air of gloom and mystery about the place. Something unpleasant must have occurred, but what it was nobody appeared exactly to know, unless it was the principal himself. Dr Plummer was just about to make a communication when I made my belated entry.

"Jones," said he, as much in sorrow as in anger, "this is not the first time this term that you have been late."

It certainly was not.

"What is the reason?"

"Please, sir," said I, stammering out my stereotyped excuse, "I think I can't have heard the first bell."

"Perhaps the first six sums of compound proportion written out ten times will enable you to hear it more distinctly in future. We will try it, if you please, Jones."

Then turning sternly to the assembled school, he said, "I was about to say something to you, boys, when this disturbance interrupted me. A shameful act has been done by some one in the night, in which I sincerely hope no one here has had a hand. The dog has been killed."

A whistle of consternation went round the room. What? Hector killed?-- Hector the collie--the beast--the brute--the sneak--the traitor--the arch-enemy of every boy at Plummer's? Hector, who was reported to be worth thirty guineas? Hector, the darling of Mrs P. and the young P.'s? Hector of the teeth, and the snarl, and the snap, the incorruptible, the sleepless, the unforgiving?

What miscreant hero had dared perform this sacrilegious exploit? "Perish Hector!" had been an immemorial war-cry at Plummer's; but Hector had never yet perished. No one had been found daring enough to bell the cat--that is, to shoot the dog. To what scoundrel was Dangerfield College now indebted for this inestimable blessing?

Dead silence followed the doctor's announcement. Boys' faces were studies as they stood there rent in twain by delight at the news and horror at the inevitable doom of the culprit.

"I repeat," said the head master, "Hector was found this morning shot in his kennel. Does any boy here know anything about it?"

Dead silence. The master's eyes passed rapidly along the forms, but returned evidently baffled.

"I trust I am to understand by your silence that none of you know anything about it. There is no doubt whatever that the guilty person will be found. I do not say that his name is known yet. If he is in this room,"--here he most unjustifiably fixed me with his eye--"he knows as well as I do what will be the consequence to him. Now go to breakfast. I shall have more to say about this matter presently."

If Dr Plummer had been anxious to save his tea and bread-and-butter from too fierce an inroad he could hardly have selected a better method. Dangerfield College was completely "off its feed" this morning. Indeed, Ramsbottom, the usher, had almost to bully the victuals down the boys' throats in order to get the meal over. The only boy who made any pretence to an appetite was the Dux, who ate steadily, much to my amazement, in the intervals of the conversation.

"It's a bit of a go, ain't it?" observed Dicky Brown, who, despite his educational advantages, could never quite master the politest form of his native tongue.

"Rather," said I--"awkward for somebody."

Then, as my eyes fell once more on Tempest, complacently cutting another slice off the loaf, an idea occurred to me.

"You know, Dicky," said I, feeling that I was walking on thin ice, "I almost fancied I heard a sound of a gun in the night."

Dicky laughed.

"Trust you for knowing all about a thing after it's happened. It would have been a rum thing if you hadn't."

This was unfeeling of Dicky. I am sure I have never pretended to know as much about anything as he did.

"Oh, but I really did--a shot, and a yell too," said I.

"Go it, you're getting on," said Dicky. "You can pile it up, Tom. Why don't you say you saw me do it while you are about it?"

"Because I didn't."

"All I can say," said the Dux, buttering his bread liberally, "I'm precious glad the beast is off the hooks. I always hated him. Which of you kids did it?"

We both promptly replied that he was quite under a wrong impression. We were pained by the very suggestion.

"All right," said he, laughing in his reckless way, and talking quite loud enough for Plummer to hear him if he happened to come in, "you've less to be proud of than I fancied. If you didn't do it, who did, eh?"

That was the question which was puzzling every one, except perhaps myself, who was undergoing a most uncomfortable mental argument as I slowly recalled the events of last night.

"Give it up; ask another," said Faulkner. "I'm precious glad I've not got a pistol." Here the Dux coloured a little, and relapsed into silence. He disliked Faulkner, and objected to his cutting into the conversation.

"One comfort," said I, endeavouring to change the topic: "we may get off that brutal Latin exercise if Plummer takes on hard about this affair."

"Poor old Hector!" said Dicky. "If that's so, we shall owe him one good turn at least--eh, old Compound Proportion?"

This pointed allusion to my misfortunes disinclined me to hold further conversation with Richard Brown, and the meal ended in general silence.

As we trooped back to the schoolroom I overheard Faulkner say to another of the seniors--

"I say, did you see the way Tempest flared up when I said that about the pistol just now? Rather awkward for him, I fancy, if he's got one."

"What's the odds if he didn't shoot the dog?" was the philosophical reply.

For all that, I had observed the Dux's confusion, and the sight of it made me very uncomfortable on his account. Faulkner was right. It would be precious awkward for any one who might be discovered to possess a pistol. The fact that firearms were expressly forbidden at Dangerfield College was itself, I am sorry to say, a strong presumption in favour of Tempest having one. Besides, I had myself once heard him speak about shooting rooks at home with a pistol.

Oddly enough, chance was to put in my way a means of setting my mind at rest almost immediately.

"I say, kid," said the Dux, as I entered the schoolroom just before the time, "I've left my Latin grammar in my locker upstairs. Look sharp, or you'll be late again and catch it."

That was his style all over--insult and injury hand in hand. He only practised it on fellows he really liked, too.

"I say, I can't," pleaded I. "Plummer will give it me hot if he catches me again. I've got it pretty bad as it is."

"I know you have; that's why I tell you to look sharp." It was no good arguing with Tempest. I knew he would risk his neck for me any day. That would be much less exertion to him than running upstairs. So I went.

The Dux's locker, I grieve to say, was a model of untidiness. Cricket flannels, eatables, letters, tooth-powders, books, and keepsakes were all huddled together in admired disorder to the full extent of the capacity of the box. The books being well in the rear of the heap, and time being precious, I availed myself of the rough-and-ready method of emptying out the entire contents at one fell swoop and extracting the particular object of my quest from the *debris*.

I had done so, and was proceeding to huddle up the other things into a compact block of a size to fit once more into the receptacle, when something fell from the pocket of one of the garments with a clatter to the floor. It was a pistol!

With a face as white and teeth as chattering as if I had seen a ghost, I instinctively pounced upon the tell-tale weapon, and whisked it, with a shudder, into my own pocket. Then, with decidedly impaired energy, I punched the bundle back into its place, slammed down the lid, and returned to the schoolroom just in time to regain my place before Dr Plummer made his entry.

"You'll give yourself heart-disease if you rush up and down stairs like that," said Tempest as I handed him the book. "You look fishier than ever."

"Latin grammar, juniors," announced the doctor. "Close books. Jones, stand up and decline *gradus*."

I declined, and fell. The excitements of the past six hours had demoralised me altogether. I could not remember who or what *gradus* was--whether it was an active noun or a feminine verb or a plural conjunction, or what. In vain the faithful Dicky prompted me from behind and Graham minor from the side. As they both prompted at the same time, and each suggested different things, I only floundered deeper. I felt myself smiling vacantly first at one, then at the other, then at the doctor. I moved one hand feebly behind me in token of my despairing gratitude to Dicky, and the other I laid convulsively on the collar of Graham's coat. It was all of no avail, and finally, when I had almost reached the stage of laughing aloud, my mother wit came to my rescue and I sat down.

This was the beginning of a tragedy of errors. With the ghost of Hector haunting us, none of us, except the Dux, who always kept his head, could do anything. The doctor's favours were lavishly and impartially distributed. Watkins, the "baby" of the class, made an ingenious calculation that if all the "lines" which were doled out as the result of that morning's work were to be extended in one unbroken length, they would reach exactly from Plummer's desk to the late Hector's kennel. Hector again! Every one's thoughts veered round to the unlucky quadruped and the storm that was brewing over his mangled remains.

Morning school passed, however, without any further official announcement on the subject. When class was dismissed half an hour earlier than usual, it was tacitly understood that this was in consequence of the obsequies of the late lamented, which were attended by the Plummer family and the errand boy, not indeed in crape, but amid every sign of mourning.

We young gentlemen were not invited. Had we been, it is doubtful whether the alacrity with which some of us would have obeyed the summons would have been altogether complimentary to the memory of the deceased.

As it was, we loafed about dismally, discussing the topic of the hour in corners, and wished the storm would break and be done with.

We had not long to wait!

CHAPTER TWO.
A CONSPIRACY OF SILENCE.

As for me, I was very poor company for any one that afternoon of Hector's funeral. Something was burning a hole in my pocket, and I felt myself in a most uncomfortable fix.

"It's all up with old Dux," said I to myself, "if it's found out. But suppose it's found on me? Still more precious awkward. I'd either have to lump it or let out. Don't see much fun in either myself. Seems to me the sooner I get rid of the beastly thing the better. Fancy his letting it lie about in his locker! He'd give me a hiding for interfering, I know, if he only knew. But I wouldn't for anything he got lagged. Old Dux is one of those chaps that has to be backed up against himself. Sha'n't be my fault if he isn't."

The reader will have judged by this time that I belonged to the species prig in my youthful days. Let that pass; I was not a unique specimen.

Full of my noble resolve of saving the Dux from himself, I went out to take the air, and strolled aimlessly in the direction of the pond. A professional burglar could not have ordered his footsteps more circumspectly. I perambulated the pool, whistling a cheerful tune, and looking attentively at the rooks overhead. Not a soul was in sight. I began to throw stones into the water, small to begin with, then larger, then bits of stick about six inches long. Then I smuggled the unlucky pistol out of my pocket in my handkerchief, and whistled still more cheerfully. Although no one was looking, it seemed prudent to adopt an air of general boredom, as if I was tired of throwing sticks into the pond. I would only throw one more. Even that was a fag, but I would do it.

What a plump, noisy splash it made, sending out circles far and near, and gurgling in a sickening way as it sank in a very unsticklike fashion to the bottom.

My whistling ceased, my air of dejection increased. I must be unsociable no longer. Let me rejoin my dear schoolfellows, making a little *detour* in order to appear to reach them from the direction not of the pond but of the orchard.

I was sheering off by the lower end of the pond, when, to my horror, I perceived a boy groping on the grass on all fours, apparently digging up the ground with a trowel.

On closer inspection I found that it was Dicky.

"Oh, it's you, is it?" said he, as I came upon him. "Have you done chucking things into the pond?"

"Why," said I, taken aback; "why, Dicky, what on earth are you up to?"

"Never mind--an experiment, that's all. I'm glad it's only you. I was afraid it was some one else. You must be jolly hard up for a bit of fun to come and chuck things into the pond."

"Oh!" said I, with tell-tale embarrassment, "I just strolled down for the walk. I didn't know you'd taken to gardening."

"There goes the bell," said Dicky. "Cut up. I'll be there as soon as you."

I obeyed, mystified and uncomfortable. Suppose Dicky had seen the pistol! I found the fellows hanging about the school door waiting to go in.

"Been to the funeral, kid?" said the Dux, as I approached. I wished he would speak more quietly on such dangerous topics when Plummer was within earshot.

"No, I've been a stroll," said I. "It's rather hot walking."

"I guess it will be hotter before long," said some one. "Plummer looks as if he means to have it out this afternoon."

"I hope he won't go asking any awkward questions," said Dicky, who had by this time joined us.

"What's the odds, if you didn't do it?" demanded the Dux.

"Look out," said Faulkner; "here he comes. He's beckoning us in."

"Now we're in for it!" thought we all.

Plummer evidently meant business this time. The melancholy ceremony at which he had just assisted had kindled the fires within him, and he sat at his desk glowering as each boy dropped into his place, with the air of a wolf selecting his victim.

As I encountered that awful eye, I found myself secretly wondering whether by any chance I might have shot the dog in a fit of absence of mind. Brown, I think, was troubled by a similar misgiving. Some of the seniors evidently resented the way in which the head master glared at them, and tried to glare back. Faulkner assumed an air of real affliction, presumably for the departed. Tempest, on the other hand, drummed his fingers indifferently on the desk, and looked more than usually bored by the whole business.

"Now, boys," began Plummer, in the short sharp tones he used to affect when he was wont to administer justice; "about Hector."

Ah! that fatal name again! It administered a nervous shock all round, and the dead silence which ensued showed that every boy present was alive to the critical nature of the situation.

"I have already told you what has occurred, and have asked if any one here knows anything about the matter," said the doctor. "I repeat the question. If any of you know anything, let there be no hesitation in speaking up."

No reply. Boys looked straight in front of them and held their breaths.

"Very well," said the doctor, his voice becoming harder and sterner, "I am to understand no boy here is able to throw any light on the mystery. Is that so?"

If silence gives consent, no question was ever more emphatically answered in the affirmative.

"I hoped it would be unnecessary to ask the question twice," said Dr Plummer. "I decline to accept silence as an answer. Let the head boy come forward."

Tempest left his place and advanced to the desk.

"Tempest, do you know anything of this matter?"

"No, sir," said Tempest.

I felt the skin on the top of my head grow tight, and my breath catch in my throat. Never had I known the Dux to tell a he to any one. What was I to do when my turn came?

"Go to your seat. The next boy come forward."

Parkin obeyed, and answered the question with a clear negative.

"The next boy."

The next boy was Faulkner, who I suspected would fain have been able to say he knew anything. But for once he was at fault, and had to reply with an apologetic "No."

In due time it was Dicky's turn.

"Do you know anything of the matter, Brown?"

"No, sir," said Brown, almost noisily.

The doctor looked at him keenly, and then ordered him to his place.

"Jones, come forward."

I felt the blood fly out of my cheeks and my heart jump to my mouth as I obeyed. As I passed up the room I glanced nervously at the Dux where he sat listlessly regarding the scene. But he took no notice of me.

"Jones," said the doctor, "do you known anything of this matter?"

The words would not come; and I glanced around again for succour.

"Turn your face to me, sir," thundered the doctor, "and answer my question."

What could I say? Where could I look? The question was repeated once more.

"I only know I fancy I heard a shot in the night." I stammered at last.

A flutter of interest went round the room. Failing all other clues it evidently seemed to be something to most of those present to elicit even this.

"Why did you not say so when you were asked this morning?"

No answer.

"Do you hear me, sir?"

"Please, sir, I couldn't be sure I had not been dreaming."

"When did you hear this sound?"

"I don't know what time, sir; I had been asleep."

"Was it light or dark?"

"Dark."

"Is that all you heard?"

"I thought I heard a yell, too."

"Did you get up or wake any of the others?"

"No, sir."

"Did you do nothing at all?"

"I was frightened, sir, and hid under the clothes."

"Is that all?"

Wasn't it about enough? I thought.

"Yes, sir."

I staggered back to my seat like a wounded man after a fray. I knew I had lost caste with the fellows; I had seriously compromised myself with the head master. At least, I told myself, I had escaped the desperate fate of saying anything against the Dux. For the sake of that, I could afford to put up with the other two consequences.

The grand inquest came to an end. One candid youth admitted that all he knew of the matter was that he was very glad Hector was dead, and for this impious irrelevance he was ordered to write an appalling imposition and forfeit several half-holidays. But that, for the time being, was the worst thunderbolt that fell from the doctor's armoury.

The Dux was kindly waiting for me outside. If he was grateful to me he concealed his feelings wonderfully; for he seized me by the coat collar and invited me to step with him to a quiet retreat where he administered the soundest thrashing I had had that term without interruption.

Explanation, I knew, would be of no avail. Tempest made a point of always postponing an explanation till after the deed was done.

When at length I gathered myself together, and inquired as pleasantly as I could to what special circumstances I was indebted for this painful incident, he replied--

"For being an idiot and a sneak. Get away, or I'll kick you."

Brown, whom I presently encountered, put the matter rather more precisely.

"Well," said he, "you told about as much as you could. How sorry you must have been not to tell more!"

"Don't, Dicky;" said I; "I--I--"

"You're almost as big an ass as you look," said Dicky, "and that's saying something. Come and see my experiment."

I was not in a scientific mood, but anything was welcome to change the subject. So I took Dicky's arm and went.

Dicky was a queer boy. He was of an inventive turn of mind, and given up to science. His experiments rarely succeeded, and when they did they almost invariably landed him in disgrace. Still he persevered and hoped some day to make a hit.

He explained to me, as we walked down the garden, that he had lately been taking an interest in the pond.

It was all I could do to appear only moderately interested in this announcement. Had not I an interest in the pond too? What followed was even more uncomfortable.

"You know Lesseps and all those chaps?" said he.

"He left before I came, I think," said I.

Dicky laughed unfeelingly.

"I mean the chap who cut the Suez Canal," said he.

"Oh! I beg your pardon," said I. "No, I don't know him."

"Well, I've been having a go in at the same kind of job," continued Dicky. "You know what a drop there is at the end of the pond, where you saw me yesterday, in the shrubbery? Well, it struck me it wouldn't take much engineering to empty it."

"What!" I exclaimed, "empty the pond! You'll get in an awful row, Dicky. Don't think of it."

"Think--it's done, I tell you," said the man of science. "That was what I was at when you saw me."

"I thought you were digging up primroses."

"Digging up grandmothers! I was letting in a pipe to drain it. It was a rare job to shove it in from the bottom corner of the pond through the bank into the shrubbery. But I managed it. It was coming through like one o'clock when I left. I expect the pond will be empty by this time."

I quailed with horror. If so, I should be discovered. I was tempted to turn tail: but that would be even worse. The only thing was to stay and see it through.

I confronted myself with the reflection that Dicky's experiments so rarely succeeded, that in all probability the pistol still lay safe under four feet of water. If not--

"Hooray!" exclaimed Dicky, as we came in sight of the place; "it's done the trick this time. See, Tom!"

I did see. In place of the water I left there in the morning was a large empty basin of mud, with a few large puddles of water lying at the bottom, and a few hillocks of mud denoting the places which had once been shallows.

My quick eye hurriedly took in the dismal landscape. For a moment my spirits rose, for I could nowhere discern the compromising object I dreaded to see. It was no doubt buried in the mud, and as safe as if the pond were full to the brim.

"Isn't it ripping?" said Dicky. "It wasn't easy to do, but it only wanted a little management. I mean to go in for engineer-- Hullo, what's that rummy stone out there? or is it a stone, or a fish, or-- I say, Tom," he added, clutching my arm, "I'm bothered if that's not a pistol!"

My white face and chattering teeth made reply unnecessary. There, snugly perched on a little heap of stones, as if set up for inspection, lay the unlucky pistol, gleaming in the afternoon sun.

Dicky looked first at the pistol, then at me; and began slowly to take in the state of affairs.

He took a cautious step out in the mud in the direction of the weapon, but came back.

"I thought you could hardly be chucking in all those things for fun," said he presently.

I stood gaping in an imbecile way, and said nothing.

"I know whose it is. He had it up here once before."

"I say," gulped I, "can't you let the water in again?" Dick had not considered this. His triumph had been letting the water out. However, he would see what could be done.

We went down into the shrubbery. About a foot of water lay on the ground, promising great fertility some day, but decidedly muddy-looking to-day.

"The thing will be to bung up the hole first," said Dicky.

So we set to work to hammer up the end of the zinc pipe and stuff the aperture round with sods and stones. I even sacrificed my cap to the good cause.

The bell began to ring before we had well completed the task. "That ought to keep any more from running out," said Dicky. "If we're lucky, the water will come in on its own hook at the other end."

The theory was not exactly scientific, for scientific men do not believe in luck. Still, it was the best we could think of as we turned to go.

"Stop a bit," said I, as we were leaving. "May as well tidy up a bit in there before we go, eh?"

"In there" was the bed of the pond.

"It might look better," said Dick, turning up his trousers. We decently interred the pistol in the mud, and raised a small heap of stones to keep it down; and then cautiously obliterating our footsteps in the mud, we made for **terra firma**, and scuttled back to school as fast as our legs would carry us.

Fortunately we entered unobserved, and disencumbered ourselves of our muddy boots without attracting attention to their condition. Ten minutes later we were deep in our work in the big schoolroom.

Preparation that night was a solemn and gloomy ceremony. Dicky and I kept catching one another's eyes, and then glancing on to where the Dux, cool as a cucumber, sat turning over the leaves of his lexicon.

"He's got a cheek of his own, has Dux," said I to myself.

"If I didn't know it was him," signalled the ungrammatical Dicky across the room, "I should never have believed it."

"You may make as many faces as you like at young Brown," glared Tempest at me, "but if I catch you making any more at me, your mother will need some extra pocket-handkerchiefs."

"Jones," observed Dr Plummer aloud, "a double **poena** for aggravated inattention."

All right. I was getting pretty full up with engagements for one day, and began to think bed-time would be rather a relief.

It came at last. In the dormitory Ramsbottom successfully interfered with conversation by patrolling the chamber until the boys were asleep. No one doubted that he had been set to the task by the head master, and it augured rather badly for the resumption of the inquest next day.

However, even patrols go to sleep sometimes, and when I woke early next morning the usher had vanished to his own chamber. My first thought was not Hector, or the doctor, or my **poenas**, or the Dux, but the pond.

How, I wondered, was it getting on?

I routed up Dicky, and very quietly we dressed and slipped out. I knew that my early rising, if it were discovered, would probably be set down to my zeal for discharging impositions. But even they must wait now till we were sure about the pond.

For Dicky and I stood liable to as big a row as the assassin of Hector himself if anything went wrong with our experiment in engineering. Luckily very few fellows haunted this particularly muddy corner of the grounds, and now that Hector was above a daily bath, there was little chance of Plummer himself discovering the remarkably low tide on his premises--still less of his poking about among the stones in the bed of the pool.

To our great relief we found that our dam at the foot was holding out bravely, and that comparatively little water was trickling through the bank into the shrubbery. The flow at the upper end, however, was distressingly small, and though a whole night had passed we could still see the heap of stones under which the pistol was buried rising up from the shallow puddles around it, inviting investigation.

With astounding industry we worked away that morning, widening and deepening the little channel along which the rivulet made its way to the pond. And before we had done we had the satisfaction of seeing a fairly brisk inflow. We would fain have waited to see the fatal little island disappear below the surface. But the first bell was already an sounding when the water completed the circle, leaving it standing up more prominent than ever.

To our horror, at this precise moment Tempest strolled down.

"Hullo! what are you two after? Fishing? One way to catch them, letting all the water out."

"It was an experiment," said Dicky, who, like myself, was very pale as he looked first at the Dux, then at the guilty hillock in the pond.

"So it seems. In other words, you're making a jolly mess, and are enjoying yourselves. I hope you'll enjoy it equally, both of you, when Hummer sees what you've done."

"Shall you tell him?" I asked, somewhat breathlessly. The Dux laughed scornfully.

"You deserve a hiding for asking such a thing. Come here! Jump out on to that little island there, and stay there till I tell you."

"Oh, Dux, please not," said I, in a tone of terror, which was quite out of proportion to the penalty. The pistol was only two inches below the surface!

"Do you hear? Look sharp, or I'll chuck you there."

That might be worse. It might hurt me and cut up the soil. So I jumped gingerly out, and stood poised with a foot in the water on either side, dreading at any moment to see the stones slip and the tell-tale gleam of the buried weapon.

"If you don't stand properly," said the Dux, "I'll make you sit down. Come along, young Brown, it's time we went up to school."

"How long am I to stay, please?" I inquired.

"Till you're in water up to the knees," said the Dux, as he turned away, with the faithless Dicky beside him.

Up to the knees! I stood loyally for five minutes, during which the water gained about an eighth of an inch up my ankles. Then the second bell rang, and things became desperate.

Accordingly I knelt in the water until I could confidently assert that I was wet, very wet indeed, up to the knees; which done, I posted as fast as my ill-used legs would carry me to morning school.

CHAPTER THREE.
"WHEN SHALL WE THREE MEET AGAIN?"

Once more Dr Plummer reserved himself for the afternoon. Perhaps it was the haunting tyranny of the defunct Hector; perhaps it was pique at being baffled, so far, in finding the culprit; whatever may have been the reason, he was in an ominously uncompromising mood when at last he returned to the fateful question.

"Come up, the first boy," said he abruptly.

The Dux was evidently getting tired of all this business (and no wonder, it seemed to me), and obeyed the summons not in the best of humours.

"Tempest," said the doctor, "I repeat my question of yesterday. Do you know anything whatever of this matter?"

"No, sir--I said so," replied the Dux, in a clear voice.

Dr Plummer scowled somewhat at this tart reply. He rather liked his head boy, and was not prepared to find him, of all others, recalcitrant.

"I do not ask what you said, sir; I ask what you say," said he.

"I said No. I'm not a liar," replied the Dux rather fiercely.

The doctor received this rather more meekly than most of us expected, and proceeded with his next question.

"Have you the slightest reason to suspect any one of having done it, or of knowing anything about it?"

Tempest remained silent, with flushed and angry face.

"Do you hear me, sir?" asked the doctor, now thoroughly roused.

"Yes, sir."

"Then why don't you answer at once?"

"I would not answer the question if I could," said the Dux defiantly.

Dr Plummer stared at the boy as if he had been a wild beast.

"How dare you say such a thing to me?" he demanded. "You heard my question. Have you the slightest grounds for suspecting any one?"

The Dux bit his lips and remained silent.

"Do you hear, Tempest?"

No reply.

"Go to your seat, sir. I will speak to you presently."

Tempest obeyed, with head erect and a red spot on either cheek.

We gazed at him in amazement. We had always given him credit for hardihood, but we had never believed him capable of mutiny of this kind; especially--

"Seems to me," whispered Dicky, "he might as well tell right away. He'll get expelled either way. Anyhow--"

"Brown, come forward."

Dicky started as if he had been detected in the act of holding a pistol to Hector's head. He was not in the least prepared to be summoned thus out of his turn; and morally he went to pieces as he rose to obey.

"Mum's the word!" whispered I, encouragingly, as he started for the front.

The doctor was on the alert with a vengeance to-day!

"Jones, come forward too," said he.

It was my turn to jump now.

"Now, sir, what was that you said to Brown just now?"

My back went up instinctively at his tone.

"I said, 'Mum's the word,'" I replied as doggedly as I could.

The doctor changed colour. This was getting serious. He had no precedents for such a case at Dangerfield, and for a moment was evidently at a loss how to proceed.

Perhaps he regretted for once in a way the policy of believing a boy guilty till he can prove himself innocent. Whether he did or no, it was too late to surrender it now.

"Go to your seat, Jones; I shall deal with you presently."

I marched off, with all the blood of the Joneses tingling in my veins. The ingenuous Dicky was left to his ordeal single-handed.

"Now, Brown," said the doctor, "you have heard the question, to which I mean to have an answer--and I caution you before I repeat it, to be careful--I shall know what interpretation to put on any attempt to prevaricate. Tell me, Brown, do you know anything at all of this matter, or have you grounds for suspecting any one of being concerned in it?"

Dicky shut his mouth with a snap, and looked as if he wished devoutly some one could turn a key on it and keep it so.

"Speak, sir," said the doctor, coming down from his desk.

By one of those strange freaks of perversity which are so hard to account for, Dicky's spirits went up higher every moment, and when the doctor stood over him and repeated the question a third time, he almost, I believe, enjoyed himself. He had never imagined courage was so easy.

To his surprise Dr Plummer did not strike, but returned quietly to his desk.

"Brown," said he, "you may go. Tell the housekeeper to pack your box in time for the early train to-morrow."

"What!" exclaimed poor old Dick, fairly electrified into speech; "am I expelled, sir?"

"You will be unless you speak at once. I give you a last chance."

Dicky looked up at the doctor, then down at the floor. I knew the struggle in his mind: the thought of his people at home, of the disgrace of being expelled, of the suspicions he would leave behind. Then I could see him steal a doubtful glance at the Dux and at me, and then pass his eye along the rows of faces eagerly waiting for his decision.

Then he held up his head, and I knew dear old Dicky was as sound as a bell. No one had the right to make him turn sneak--and no one should do it! "I'll go and pack," said he quietly, and turned to the door.

Neither the Dux nor I saw the last of poor Dicky Brown at Dangerfield. We were otherwise engaged when he departed home in a four-wheeled cab in charge of Mr Ramsbottom that evening. We were, in point of fact, in durance vile ourselves, with every prospect of speedily requiring the services of two more four-wheeled cabmen on our own accounts.

The Dux's fury at Dicky's summary expulsion had been quite a surprise even to me.

"It's a shame," he had shouted as the door closed; "a caddish shame!"

"Who said that?" asked Dr Plummer.

"I did. I say it's a caddish shame!"

"So do I!" yelled I at the top of my voice, and quite carried away by the occasion.

This was getting very embarrassing for Plummer. Perhaps he behaved in the best way open to him under the circumstances. He ignored us both, and proceeded to call up Faulkner to answer his precious questions.

Much depended on Faulkner then. If he had refused to answer, as the Dux had done, and Brown had done, and others were prepared to do, Plummer might have seen that his case was hopeless, and have given it up. Faulkner was nothing like such a favourite with the head master as Tempest, nor had he such a following among the boys. Still, he led his party, and if he chose now to leave us in the lurch Plummer was saved and we were lost.

"I know nothing of the matter, sir," said Faulkner, "and I have no reason at all to suspect any one."

It sounded a simple answer, but it was rank treason. For it was as good as saying Plummer had a right to ask these questions, and that he, Faulkner, would inform if he only knew who the culprit was.

After that it was evident the game, the Dux's game and mine, was up. Boy after boy was called up and interrogated, and one by one they followed Faulkner in his submission. A few--like Graham junior-- attempted to hold out, but broke down under pressure. A few feebly compromised by explaining that had they known the culprit they would not have answered; but as they did not they saw no reason for not saying so.

"It comes to this, then," said the doctor: "that out of the entire school, three boys, and three only, are silent. The only conclusion I can draw from their conduct is that they dare not deny that they know something of this shameful outrage. Tempest, you are the head boy. I have always looked on you as a credit to the school, and a good example to your youngers. You see your present behaviour involves trouble to others than yourself. I do not wish to be hasty in this matter, and am willing to give you one more opportunity of answering my question. Do you know anything of this affair, or have you any grounds for suspecting any one of being connected with it?"

The Dux flushed with indignation, glared straight at the head master by way of reply, and closed his lips.

"Very well, sir. Jones, I now repeat the question to you. You are a little boy, and there is more excuse for you, as you were led astray by the bad example of a senior. I caution you now to do as the others have done, and give me a plain answer to a plain question. Otherwise you must take the consequences."

I am afraid I blushed and looked far less determined than I would have liked. But I did my best to glare back and tighten my lips like the Dux.

"Very well. Tempest and Jones, go to my study and remain there till I come."

We had not long to wait for our doom. The doctor was in the study almost as soon as we.

We stood there while he wrote some letters and put away some books on the shelves. Then he rang the bell, and handed the letters to the servant to post. After that he sat in his chair for a quarter of an hour in silence, evidently ruminating.

At last he deigned to notice our presence.

"Tempest," he said, "I am very grieved at this. I had hoped better things of you. You know what the consequence must be to you?"

"I'm to be expelled, I know," said the Dux. "The sooner the better."

The doctor raised his eyebrows. There was no dealing with a reprobate like this.

"I have written to your grandfather to say you will return home to- morrow."

"I'm sorry it's not to-night," said the Dux.

"And you, Jones," said the doctor to me, not heeding the last speech,--"I am more sorry for you. You are a foolish, misguided boy. Even now, if you atone for your fault by replying to my questions, I am willing to spare your mother the misery you seem bent on bringing upon her."

This was a cruel thrust. The thought of my mother had crossed my mind once or twice already, and almost brought the tears to my eyes. It would be hard to explain all to her--and yet, and yet, anything was better than turning sneak.

"I won't answer," said I. "I'd sooner be expelled."

"Your desire shall be gratified," said the doctor drily; "to-morrow you will go too."

"Thank you, sir."

"Tempest, you will remain here for the rest of the day--Jones, you will go to the dormitory and remain there. I forbid you, either of you, to hold any communication with your late schoolfellows while you remain here."

Next morning after breakfast we were finally brought up before the whole school and harangued publicly by the head master. Our punishment, he told us, we had deliberately brought on our own heads. Aggravated insubordination like ours was not to be tolerated in any school. He was sure we should soon regret and be ashamed of our conduct, if we were not so already. For his own part he would try to forget the unfortunate affair, and to think kindly of us both. Mr Ramsbottom would see Tempest to the station, and the matron would escort me.

"Good-bye, Tempest," said he, holding out his hand.

"Good-bye," said the Dux, not heeding the hand, and walking to the door.

"Good-bye, Jones."

I shook hands. After all, Plummer, I thought, meant to be kind, though he took an odd way of showing it. I was thankful when the ceremony was over, and the Dux and I found ourselves with our luggage in the hall waiting for our cabs.

All at once the old school we were leaving seemed to become dearer than I had thought.

The hall where we stood was full of the memory of jolly comings and goings. The field out there seemed to echo with the whizzing of balls and the war-whoops of combatants. The very schoolroom we had just left, from which even now came the hum of work in which we were no more to join, had its pleasant associations of battles fought, friends gained, difficulties mastered. How I would have liked to run down to get a last look at the pond, or upstairs for a farewell glance round the dormitory! But now we were out of it--Dux and I. The place belonged to us no more. We were outsiders, visitors whose time was up, and whose cabs were due at the front door at any moment.

And what was it all for?

"If it hadn't been for that beast Hector," said the Dux rather dismally, "we shouldn't have been out here, Tommy."

He rarely called me by my Christian name. It was always a sign he was out of sorts.

"I do wish you'd missed him," said I.

"Missed him! What on earth do you mean?"

"Not made such a good shot--that's what I mean."

"Shot! Young Brown, are you crazy?"

"Most likely," said I, beginning to get hot and cold at the same time. "Why, do you mean to say you didn't, then?"

"Didn't what?"

"Shoot him."

"Shoot him? Me shoot? I no more shot the beast than you did."

The perspiration started to my forehead.

"But the pistol. Dux?"

"What pistol?"

"The one I found in your locker, when I went to get your book, you know."

"That thing? It's been there all the term. It hasn't even got a trigger!"

"It's not there now. It's at the bottom of the pond."

The Dux looked at me as if he were about to eat me up, I looked back as if I were ready for it.

"You didn't shoot Hector, then?" I faltered.

"What do you take me for, you young ass? Of course not."

"Then Brown and I have both--"

"Brown? What about him? He didn't think I'd done it?"

"He wouldn't have been expelled if he hadn't."

The Dux gave a whistle of mingled dismay and fury.

"You know," said I, "I saw you come in that night, just after I'd heard the shot, and made sure--"

"Oh, you--you beauty!" cried the Dux, with a bitter laugh. "Why, I'd just gone down for my watch, which I'd left in my blazer, so as to wind it up--and you--you actually go and set me down as a murderer!"

"Oh, Dux, I'm so awfully sorry! Let me go and tell Plummer."

"If you do, I'll wring your neck. I wouldn't stay in this hole another day if he came on his knees and asked me. What right has he to want to make sneaks of us? Do you mean to say you and young Brown thought all along I had done it, and that I was telling lies when I said I didn't?"

"I thought perhaps you'd done it in your sleep, and didn't know."

He laughed scornfully.

"That's why you two were mum?" asked he. "Didn't want to let out on me?"

"Well, yes, partly. I'm awfully sorry, Dux. Will you ever forgive me?"

"Forgive you, kid! If I'd time I'd thrash you within an inch of your life for being such a fool, and then I'd thank you for being such a trump--you and Brown too."

"Is it too late to do anything now?" asked I again.

"Not for me--nothing would keep me here. But I don't see why you should be expelled. I'll tell Plummer it was a mistake."

"No, you won't," said I, catching his arm. "I wouldn't stay here now for worlds."

"It's rough all round," said Tempest, looking profoundly miserable, as the rumble of a cab came up to the hall door.

"What will your mater say, kid?"

"She'll understand. I hope she won't send me back though."

"Get her to send you to Low Heath."

"She couldn't afford it. You'll write to me, Dux?"

"Most likely. Tell Brown how sorry I am."

"Now, Tempest, ready?" said Mr Ramsbottom.

"Good-bye, kid. I sha'n't forget you."

Next minute he was off, and I was left alone.

I do not deny that for a moment or two I found it convenient to rub my eyes. It was a hot day, and the light through the window was dazzling, I think.

Then to my relief up came my cab, and under the stalwart escort of Mrs Potts, the matron, I quitted Dangerfield for good.

My journey home was, as may be imagined, not a festive one. What would my mother say, or my guardian? What version of the story had Plummer given them? It consoled me to work myself up into a fury as I sat in the corner of the railway carriage, and prepare an indictment of his conduct which should make my conduct appear not only justifiable, but heroic.

Alas! heroism can rarely endure the rattle of a long railway journey. Long before we reached Fallowfield my heart was in my boots, and my fierceness had all evaporated.

But a year ago my father had died, leaving me, his only child, to be the comfort and support of my mother. What message of comfort or support was I carrying home to-day? What would my guardian, who had given me such yards of stern advice about honouring my betters, say when he heard? Should I be sent to an office to run errands, or passed on to a school for troublesome boys, or left to knock about with no one to care what became of me?

With such pleasant misgivings in my mind I reached Fallowfield, and braced myself up for the interview before me.

CHAPTER FOUR.
BRUSHING-UP THE CLASSICS.

My guardian, I am bound to say, disappointed me. I had rather hoped, as I travelled home, that I would be able to put my conduct before him in such a way that he would think me rather a fine young fellow, and consider himself honoured in being my guardian. That my mother would take on, I felt sure.

"Women," said I to myself--I was thirteen, and therefore was supposed to know what women thought about things--"women can't see below the surface of things. But old Girdler was a boy himself once, and knows what it is for a fellow to get into a row for being a brick."

My sage prognostications were falsified doubly. My mother, though she wept to see me come home in this style, did me justice at once. To think I could ever have doubted her!

"Of course, sonny dear," said she, kissing me, "it was very hard. Still, I am sure it would have been a shabby thing to tell tales."

"I wasn't going to do it, at any rate," said I, growing a little cocky, and deciding that some women, at any rate, can see more than meets the eye.

But Mr Girdler, when he called in during the evening, was most disappointing.

"So this is what you call being a comfort to your mother?" began he, without so much as giving me a chance to say a word.

"Oh, but you don't understand, sir," began I.

"Don't understand!" said he. "I understand you are a naughty little boy"--to think that I should live to be called a little boy!--"and that the mischief about your schooling is that you've not been smacked as often as you ought. Understand, indeed! What do you suppose your mother's to do with a boy like you, that's wasted his time, and then tells people they don't understand?"

"I don't think Tommy meant--" began my mother; but my guardian was too quick for her.

"No, that's just it. They never do, and yet you pay fifty pounds a year to teach him. It doesn't matter to some children who else is troubled as long as they enjoy themselves."

Children! And I had once caught Parkin at cover-point! "Go up to bed now," said my guardian. "Your mother and I must see what's to be done with you. Don't I understand, indeed?"

The conceit was fairly taken out of me now. To be called a little boy was bad enough; to be referred to as a child was even worse; but to be sent to bed at a quarter to eight on a summer evening was the crowning stroke. Certainly, Plummer's itself was better than this.

What my mother and guardian said to one another I do not know. My mother, I think, had great faith in Mr Girdler's wisdom; and although she tried not to think ill of me, would probably feel that he knew better than she did.

I knew my fate next morning--it was worse than my most hideous forebodings.

I was to work at my guardian's office every morning, and in the afternoon I was to go up and learn Latin and arithmetic at--oh, how shall I say it?--a girls' school!

For an hour after this discovery I candidly admit that I was sorry, unfeignedly sorry, I had not turned sneak and informed against Harry Tempest. I think even he would have wished me to do it rather than suffer this awful humiliation.

I had serious thoughts of running away, of going to sea, or sweeping a London crossing. But there were difficulties in the way; the chief of them being my mother.

"You mustn't worry about it, Tommy," said she. "Mr Girdler says it will be the best thing for you. It will be good for you to learn some business, you know, and then in the afternoon you will find Miss Bousfield very nice and clever."

"It's not the work I mind, mother," said I; "it's--it's going to a girls' school."

"There's nothing very dreadful about it, I'm sure," said my mother, with a smile. "I was at one myself once."

"But," argued I, "you are only a--"

No--that wouldn't quite do to one's own mother. So I stopped short.

"Besides," said she, "Mr Girdler thinks it the best thing, and he is your guardian."

This was unanswerable, and I gave it up.

But I was not at all consoled. The bare idea of Tempest, or Brown, or any of the other fellows getting to know that I, Thomas Jones, aged thirteen, who had held my own at Plummer's, and played in my day in the third Eleven, was going to attend a girls' school, and be taught Latin and sums by a--a female, was enough to make my hair stand on end. How they would laugh and wax merry at my expense! How they would draw pictures of me in the book covers with long curls and petticoats! How they would address me as "Jemima," and talk to one another about me in a high falsetto voice! How they would fall into hysterics when they met me, and weep copiously, and ask me to lend them hairpins and parasols! I knew what it would be like only too well, and I quaked as I imagined it.

My one hope was that at Fallowfield nobody knew me; at least, nobody who mattered.

"At least," said I to myself, "if I am to go and herd with a parcel of girls, I'll let them see I'm something better than a girl myself."

When I presented myself at my guardian's office on the appointed morning in order to start on my commercial career, I met with a reception even less flattering than I had pictured to myself.

Mr Girdler was out, and had left no instructions about me. So for two hours I sat in the waiting-room, balancing my cap on my knee, and trying to work up the spots on the dingy wall-paper into geometrical figures.

When at last he came, so far from commending my patience, he had the face to reproach me for sitting there idle instead of getting some one to set me to work.

"You are not at school here, remember," said he, by way of being sarcastic; "you come here to work."

"I worked at school," said I meekly.

"So I hear," said he. "Now go to Mr Evans, and tell him you want a job."

Whereupon my genial guardian quitted me. But he came back a moment after.

"Remember you are to be at the girls' school at 2:30. Tell Miss Bousfield you are the little boy I spoke to her about, and mind you behave yourself up there."

Was ever a young man in such a shameful disgrace?

Three days ago I had imagined myself everybody; two days ago I had at least imagined myself somebody; yesterday I had discovered with pain that I was no-body; and to-day I was destined to wonder if I was even that.

Mr Evans raised his eyebrows when I delivered my message to him.

"Are you the governor's little ward," he inquired, "who's just finished his edu-cation? All right, my little man, we'll find a job for you. Run up High Street and bring me the time by the market clock, and here's a halfpenny to buy yourself sweets on the way."

It occurred to me as odd that Mr Evans should want to know the time by a clock which was quite ten minutes' walk from the office. Still, perhaps he had to set the office clocks by it, so I set off, wondering whether I ought to take the halfpenny, but taking it all the same.

I decided that the dignified course would be to buy the sweets, but to take them all back to him, so as to impress him with the fact that I was not as devoted to juve-nile creature comforts as he evidently thought me.

"Is that all you have left?" said he, when, after accomplishing my errand, I presented them to him. "My eye! you've made good use of your time, and no mis-take."

"I've not eaten a single one," said I.

"It would have been better for your digestion if you had only eaten a single one, instead of swallowing half the lot. I know the ways of you boys. Well, what's the time?"

"It was twenty-five past ten."

"I didn't ask you what it was--I want to know what it is."

It then occurred to me for the first time that Mr Evans was a humourist. It seemed to me a feeble joke, but he evidently thought it a good one, as did also the other clerks to whom he communicated it.

The worst of it was that the more I tried to explain that, not having a watch of my own, I could not answer for the time by the market clock at any moment but that at which I saw it, the more they seemed to be amused. Some suggested I should go back with a bag and bring the time in it. Others, that I should put it on ten minutes, and then come back, so as to arrive at the exact moment it was when I left it. Others were of opinion that the best way would be for me to go and fetch the market clock with me.

Mr Evans, however, decided that my talents were not equal to the task of bringing the time in any shape or form, and that the best thing I could do was to sit down and lick up envelopes. Which I accordingly did, feeling rather small. I cut my tongue and spoiled my appetite over the operation, and was heartily glad when, after a couple of hours, Mr Evans said--

"Master Tommy, we're going to lunch. You've had yours, so you can stop here, and keep shop till we return."

"I have to go to Miss Bousfield's at 2:30," said I.

"To go where?" they all inquired. And as I blushed very red, and tried to explain myself away, they made a great deal out of my unlucky admission.

"You're young for that sort of thing," said one. "I didn't go courting myself before I was fifteen."

"I'd made up my mind Sarah Bousfield was going to be an old maid," said another. "Heigho! it's never too late to mend."

"I hear she keeps sugar-plums for good little girls," said another.

"And the bad little ones get whipped and put in the corner."

"He mustn't go like that, anyhow," said Mr Evans, who, for a responsible head clerk of a big business, was the most flippant person I had ever met; "look at his hair--all out of curl! Come here, little girl, and be made tidy."

Once at Hummer's I had come in second for the half-mile under fourteen, and been captain of my side in the junior tug of war! Now I was to have my hair curled publicly!

It was no use resisting. I was held fast while Evans with a long penholder made ringlets of my back hair, and Scroop, with his five fingers, made a fringe of my front. My hat, moreover, was decorated with quills by way of feathers, and a fan made of blotting-paper was thrust into my hands. Then I was pronounced to be nice and tidy, and fit to go and join the other little girls.

I fear that the energy with which, as soon as I was released, I deranged my locks and flung the feathers from my hat, amused my persecutors as much as it solaced me. I was conscious of their hilarious greetings as I strolled up the street, trying to walk in a straight masculine way, but hideously conscious of blushing cheeks and nervous gait. I so far forgot myself that, in my eagerness to display my male superiority, I jostled against a lady, and disgraced myself by swaggering on without even apologising for my rudeness--when, to my consternation, the lady uttered my name, "Tommy."

It was my mother! I was still within sight of the office. How Evans and his lot would make merry over this *contretemps*! They wouldn't know who it was who was putting her hand on my shoulder. And yet I am glad to say that I was spared that day the disgrace of being ashamed of my own dear mother. Let the fellows think what they liked. If they had mothers like mine they wouldn't be the cads they were!

So, with almost unnecessary pomp, I raised my hat to my parent, and put my hand in her arm.

"You're going up to Miss Bousfield's," said she; "I thought I should meet you. What a hurry you were in!"

"Yes; I'm sorry I knocked against you, mother."

"I'm glad you did. I'm longing to hear how you got on to-day."

"Oh, pretty well."

"Was it very hard work?"

"Not particularly."

"You'll soon be quite a man of business."

It occurred to me that if my business career was to be based on no better experience than that I had hitherto had in my guardian's office, I should not rank as a merchant prince in a hurry.

"Would you like me to go with you to Miss Bousfield's?"

"If you like, mother. But I can go alone all right." She was a brick. She guessed what I hoped she would say, and she said it.

"Well, I'll be looking out for you at tea-time, dear boy," said she. And she patted my arm lovingly as I started on.

I wished those fellows could have heard her voice and seen her kind face. *She* treated me like a man--which was more than could be said for them.

I went on my way soothed in my ruffled spirits. But my perturbation revived when I stood on the doorstep of the Girls' High School, and rang the head mistress's bell. It was a bitter pill, I can tell you, for a fellow who had once been caned by Plummer for practising on the horizontal bar without the mattress underneath to fall on.

Miss Bousfield was a shrewd, not disagreeable-looking little body, who saved me all the trouble of self-introduction by knowing who I was and why I came.

"Well, Jones," said she--I liked that, I had dreaded she would call me Tommy--"here you are. How is your mother? Why, what a state your hair is in! I really think you'd like to go into the cloak room; you'll find a brush and comb there. It looks as if your hair were standing on end with horror at me, you know."

Little she knew what my hair was on end about. I was almost grateful to her for the way she put it, and meekly retired to the cloak room, where--I confess it--with a long-tailed girl's comb, and a soft brush, and a big looking-glass, I contrived to restore my truant locks to their former masculine order.

When I returned to the room. Miss Bousfield was sitting at a table, at which was also seated a young lady of about twenty, with an exercise book and dictionary in front of her.

Was it a trap? Was I to be taught along with the girls after all? Miss Bousfield evidently divined my perturbation and hastened to explain.

"Miss Steele, this is Master Jones, who is going to read Latin with us. Miss Steele is one of my teachers, Jones, and we three are going to brush up our classics together, you see."

Oh, all right. That wasn't so bad. I had no objection to assist Miss Steele, or Miss Bousfield, for the matter of that, in brushing-up their classics, as long as the girls at large were kept out of the way.

I acknowledged Miss Steele's greeting in a patronising way, and then looked about for a chair. I wished Mr Evans and his lot could see how far removed I was from the common schoolgirl; here were two females actually going to pick my brains for their own good. If women must learn Latin at all, they could hardly do better than secure a public schoolboy to brush them up.

"Now, let us see," said Miss Bousfield, "how far we have all got. Miss Steele, you have read some Cicero, I know, already."

Cicero! That girl read Cicero, when I had barely begun Caesar! This was a crusher for me. How about the brushing-up now?

"And you, Jones, have you begun Cicero yet?"

"Well, no," I said, "not yet."

"Caesar, then; I think we shall both be ready to take that up again. How far were you--or shall we begin at the beginning?"

"Better begin at the beginning," said I, anxious not to have to confess that I had not yet got through the first chapter.

But before we had gone many lines, Miss Bousfield, I could see, began to have her doubts about my syntax; and after a little conference about syntax, the question of verbs came up, unpleasantly for me; and after deciding we had a little brushing-up to do there, the conversation turned on declensions, a subject on which I had very little definite information to afford to these two females in distress.

I verily believe we should have come to exchanging views on the indefinite article itself, had not Miss Bousfield taken the bull by the horns, and said--

"I think the best thing, Jones, will be for us to assume we know nothing, to begin with, and start at the beginning. We shall easily get over the ground then, and it will be all the better to be sure of our footing. Let us take Exercise 1. in the grammar."

Miss Steele pouted a little, as if to indicate it was hardly worth her while, as a reader of Cicero, to waste her time over "a high tree," "a bad boy," "a beautiful table," and so on. But I felt sure the exercise would do her good, and was glad Miss Bousfield set her to it.

She irritated me by having it all written down in a twinkling, and going on with Cicero on her own account, while I plodded on up the "high tree" and around the "beautiful table." I hoped Miss Bousfield would rebuke her for insubordination, but she did not, and I began to think much less of both ladies as the afternoon went on.

It did not add to my satisfaction to get my exercise back with fifteen corrections scored across it in bold red pencil--whereas Miss Steele's was not even looked at.

I thought of suggesting that it would be only fair that she and I should be treated alike, when Miss Bousfield capped all by saying to her governess--

"Perhaps, Miss Steele, you will go through the exercise with Jones and show him where he has gone wrong. Then he can write it out again for you, and try not to have any mistake this time."

This was really too much! To be passed on to a girl who was learning Latin herself, and for her to score about my exercises! It was a conspiracy to degrade me in the eyes of myself and my fellow-mortals.

But protest was rendered impossible by Miss Bousfield quitting the room and leaving me to the mercies of her deputy.

"Why," said Miss Steele, not at all unkindly, but with a touch of raillery in her voice--"why were you such a goose, Jones, as to pretend you knew what you didn't?"

"I didn't; I forgot, that's all," said I.

"Well, look here, Jones," said she, in a friendly way--and, by the way, she was not at all bad-looking--"if you really want to get up Latin, and mean to work, I'll do my best to coach you; but if you're only playing at learning, I've something better to do."

"I'm not playing," said I. "I don't know why I've got to come and learn Latin at all."

"I suppose you are going to a school some day, aren't you?"

"I've been to one, and I've left," said I.

"Left?" said she, with a little laugh.

"Well, then, I was expelled," said I.

"Tell me all about it."

And I did, and found her not only interested and sympathetic, but decidedly indignant on my account.

"It was a great shame," said she, "especially as your friend never shot the dog at all."

"He's all right, lucky chap," said I; "he's got an exhibition to Low Heath, and is going there after the holidays."

"Why don't you get an exhibition too, Jones?"

The question astounded me. I get an exhibition! I who had been licked once a week for bad copies, and had been told by every teacher I had had anything to do with that I was a hopeless dunce.

"Why not?" said the siren at my side. "You're not a dunce. I can tell that by the way you picked up some of the Caesar just now. You're lazy, that's all. That's easily cured."

"But I'd have no chance at Low Heath. Tempest was a dab at lessons."

"He's older than you. Besides, the junior exhibitions are not as hard to get. When will you be fourteen?"

"July next year."

"Just twelve months. Why not try, Jones? I'll back you up. I've coached my young brother, and he got into Rugby. You needn't tell any one--so if you miss nobody will be any the wiser. It will make all the difference to have an exam, to aim at."

I stared in wonder at Miss Steele. That young woman could have twisted me round her finger.

"I'll try," said I.

"Not unless you mean to work like a horse," said she.

"All serene," said I; "honour bright."

"Then it's a bargain. Mark my word, we'll pull through."

Whereat we fell hammer and tongs on Exercise Number 1. of the grammar.

CHAPTER FIVE.
A "COACH" DRIVE!

If any one had told me two days ago that it would be reserved to an assistant teacher in a girls' school to inspire me with an ardent interest in Latin and arithmetic I should have laughed him to scorn.

Miss Steele, however, succeeded in achieving the impossible. I am bound to confess that my new-born ardour was not mainly due to affection for the dead language in question, or even to esteem for my preceptress. But the idea of taking Low Heath, so to speak, by storm, had fairly roused my ambition. The glory of rising superior to my fate, of shaking off the ill-tutored Mr Evans and his works, and rejoining my old school-comrade with all the prestige of a fellow-exhibitioner, captivated my imagination and steeled me to the endurance of hardships of which I had hitherto conceived myself utterly incapable.

Miss Steele had no notion of letting me off my bargain. She procured particulars of the examinations, and very formidable appeared the list of subjects as we conned them. Still she was firm in her belief that I could do it if I only worked, and since her eagerness fully equalled my own, there was not much chance of my work dropping slack.

If any other incentive was wanted it was the supreme discomfort of my position at my guardian's office.

My comrades there persistently misunderstood me.

They put me down as an opiniated young prig, with whom all sorts of liberties might be taken, and out of whom it was lawful, for their own amusement, to take unlimited "rise."

I was, of course, unmercifully chaffed about the girls' school.

"He's getting on," said one of them, on the very morning after my *debut*.

"They walk out together."

"That was not Miss Bousfield you saw me with at all," I explained. "That was my mother."

"Quite time she came to look after you, too. How did she like your curls? You should put them in papers overnight, then we shouldn't have to do them every day."

Where upon I was seized, and had my locks tied up in wads of blotting- paper, and ordered to sit down and lick envelopes, and not dare to put my hand to my head till leave was accorded me from headquarters.

In this plight my guardian came in and discovered me.

"Please, Mr Girdler--" said I, not waiting for him to remark on my curious appearance.

But Mr Girdler, who was not ordinarily given to mirth, abruptly left the room with a smile on his face before I could proceed.

When he re-entered he was stern and severe.

"Make yourself decent at once, sir," said he. "No, I don't want any of your explanations. No doubt they are highly satisfactory. I begin to understand now why you were sent away from school. It strikes me an idiot asylum is the proper place for you."

I dismally tore my curl-papers out of my hair and went on with my work till the blessed hour of release came.

Then I hied straight to the nearest barber.

"I want my hair as short as you can cut it," said I.

"Very good, sir; we can give you the county crop, if you like."

"Is that the shortest you do?" inquired I, not knowing what the "county crop" was.

"Well, sir, we ain't asked to take more off as a rule, unless it is a clean shave you want."

"No, the county crop will do," said I.

And, to do the barber justice, I got it. I barely knew myself in the glass when the operation was over. I had some misgivings as to the remarks of Evans & Company in the morning--at any rate, they wouldn't curl my hair any more.

Miss Bousfield and Miss Steele regarded me with something like dismay when they saw me, but were polite enough to make no remark beyond giving me permission to wear my hat if I felt a draught.

"Miss Steele has been telling me of your plan of work," said Miss Bousfield; "and I fully approve, on the understanding you are serious about it. I am not so sanguine as Miss Steele is; still, I do not wish to discourage you, Jones. But understand, it means a year's hard work."

I assured her I was prepared for any amount of work, and Miss Steele, whose ambition was as keenly aroused as mine, gave a general promise on my behalf that I would work like a horse.

"Now," said she, when Miss Bousfield had left us, "you're in for it, Jones. If you don't work, mind, it will be a disgrace to me as well as you."

I fear, during the months that followed, this ardent young "coach" was frequently on the point of disgrace. For a week or two I surprised myself with my industry. Then I caught myself wondering at odd times whether I was really as sure of passing as I fancied, and whether, if I failed, it would not be a horrible sell to have worked so hard for nothing.

Then for a day or so I came in a little late, and took to grumbling over my tasks.

"Now, look here, Jones," said she, one day, "you were five minutes late on Monday, ten minutes late on Tuesday and Wednesday, and a quarter of an hour late to-day. How much is that in the week?"

"Forty minutes," said I; mental arithmetic was a strong point with me.

"Very good; there's forty minutes lost. The examination may turn on the very lesson you might have learned in that time. Now, I'm not going to threaten you, but what should you say if I were to call at the office and fetch you every day?"

I nearly jumped out of my chair.

"Oh, don't, please don't, Miss Steele!" said I. "I'll be here to the second, in future, I promise."

"All right," said she, with a smile, and the subject dropped.

This dreadful threat kept me up to the mark for the next few weeks, but even it lost its terrors in time, and my preceptress had to apply the spur in other ways as the time went on.

Once, after I had been particularly slack, and had, moreover, been so rude to her that she ended the lesson abruptly, I thought it was all up. For, when I presented myself next day, I was informed by the servant that Miss Steele was busy, and had no time to see me.

I was locked out! My dismay knew no bounds. Suppose she had "chucked" me altogether, what would become of my chance of getting into Low Heath?

I retired home in great perturbation, and confided the state of the case to my mother, who advised me there and then to sit down and write an apology.

I had never done such a thing in my life. Once I had verbally begged Tempest's pardon for some error; but to commit myself in writing to a girl!

"My dear Miss Steele," I wrote,--"I'm sorry. Yours truly, T. Jones."

"That will do very well," said my mother. "It's not too long, at the same time it says what you want to say."

I wasn't altogether pleased with it myself, but allowed the maid to take it up to the school, with instructions to wait for an answer.

In due time she returned with a missive from Miss Steele.

"My dear Jones,--To-morrow as usual. Yours truly, M. Steele."

I am sure no model letter-writer ever said as much in as few words.

This little correspondence cleared the air for the time. No reference was made to it when I turned up as usual the next day; but from the way I worked, and the way she taught, it was evident we had both had a shake.

My next relapse was even more serious. It came early in the spring, after our work had proceeded for about nine months.

I really had made good progress all round. Not in Latin only, but in Greek grammar, arithmetic, and English, and was naturally inclined to feel a little cocky of the result.

"Don't crow, Jones," she said; "you've a lot to do yet."

But I did not altogether agree with her, and was inclined to indulge myself a little of an evening when I was supposed to be preparing my work. In an evil day I fell across an old book-shop, and found two books, which helped to undo me. One was a rollicking story of a pirate who swept the Western Main, and captured treasure, and seized youths and maidens, and ran blockades, and was finally brought to book in a sportsmanlike manner by a jolly young English middy, amid scenes of terrific slaughter amidships. That was one purchase. The other was even more disturbing. It was a "crib" to the arithmetic I was doing, with all the sums beautifully worked out and the answers given.

So--I must make the confession--I astonished Miss Steele greatly for a while by my extraordinary proficiency in arithmetic, and during the same time spent my evenings in imagination on the high seas, flying aloft the black flag, and shooting across the bows of Her Majesty's ships wherever I sighted them.

This career of duplicity could not be expected to last long. One afternoon Miss Steele brought matters to a crisis by calling upon me to work a sum on the spot which was not in the book.

I failed egregiously.

"That's singular," said she; "it's far simpler than those you brought with you to-day. How long did it take you to do them?"

I looked hard at Miss Steele, and she looked hard at me. The pirate game was up at last.

"About two minutes each," said I.

" *Two* minutes?"

"Yes--as fast as I could copy them out of the crib. I'm sorry, Miss Steele."

She shut up her book abruptly.

"I didn't expect it of you, Jones," said she; "you've been making a fool of me. I've lost confidence in you; now you can go."

"Oh, I say. Miss Steele, I'm so awfully--"

"Be quiet, sir, and go!" said she, more fiercely than I had ever known her.

I took up my cap and went. She was in no humour to listen to explanations, but it was clear I had done for myself now. After what had happened she was not likely to give me another chance.

I did not care to tell my mother how matters stood this time. It would be difficult to put my case in a favourable light, and I was quite sure my mother could not help me out of my difficulty.

I solemnly burned my crib that night in the parlour fire, after every one was in bed. It took ages to consume, and nearly set the chimney on fire in the operation. But when that was done I was as far off a solution of my difficulty as ever.

I hardly slept a wink, and in the morning my mother added to my discomfort by remarking on my looks.

"You're working too hard, dear boy," said she. "I must ask Miss Steele to give you a little holiday, or you'll be quite knocked up."

"Please don't," said I. "I'm all right."

Here the postman's knock caused a diversion.

"A letter for you, Tommy," said my mother.

It was from Tempest, of all people--the first he had condescended to write me since we had parted company in Plummer's hall nearly a year ago.

It was a rambling, patronising effusion, in his usual style; but every word of it, in my present plight, had a sting for me.

"It's a pity you're not here," wrote he; "it's a ripping place. Everything about the place is ripping except the drilling master and the dumplings on Mondays, which are both as vile as vile can be. I'm in the upper fifth, and shall probably get my ribbon and perhaps my house after summer. Plummer's was regular tomfooling to this. We've a match on with Rugby this term, and I'm on the reserve for the Eleven. I suppose you know young Brown is coming here; though I'm sorry to say as a day boy. His people are going to live in the town, so he'll be able to come on the cheap. I shall do what I can for him, but I expect he'll have a hot time, for the day boys are rather small beer. The exhibitioners have the best time of it. If Brown could get a junior exhibition and live in school, he could fag for me and have a jolly time. But poor Dicky hasn't got it in him. I got rather lammed after I got home from Plummer's; but it was all right when Plummer wrote to say that a burglar had shot the dog, and he was sorry there had been a mistake, and hoped I'd go back. Catch me! It's better fun here--as much cricket as you like, and a river, and gymnasium, and all sorts of sprees. It wouldn't be half bad if you were here, kid; but I suppose you're a young gent with a topper and a bag at your guardian's office. I hope it suits you-- wouldn't me--" and so on.

How this letter made me long to be at Low Heath, and how it made me realise what an ass I had been to go in for that crib! I really felt too bad to go that day to Miss Steele, even if she would have let me! and wandered about cudgelling my brains how on earth I could get her to take me back again.

She wouldn't believe my protestations, I knew; but she might believe deeds, not words.

So I shut myself up in my room and took down my arithmetic, and worked out sum after sum all off my own bat, till my brain reeled and I could hardly distinguish one figure from another. Some I knew were wrong, others I hoped were right; all were ***bona fide***. I stuck to it till nearly midnight, and then, merely writing my name on the top, put them into an envelope, under the flap of which I wrote, "I've burnt the crib. Try me this once," and posted them to my offended teacher.

No answer came for twenty-four hours, which I spent on pins and needles, working away frantically during my leisure hours, and occupying part of my business time in personally avenging an insult offered to Miss Steele's name by one of my guardian's junior clerks. I wished she could have seen me. I got a terrible blow on the eye, but I gave him two, and caused him to regret audibly that he had spoken disparagingly of my cruel fair.

Next morning a note came to my mother.

"Please tell your boy I shall be in this afternoon."

In fear and trembling I presented myself, and confronted not Miss Steele but Miss Bousfield, who addressed me in terse and forcible language, and gave me to understand that I was a person of extremely second-rate character and attainments. I acknowledged it, but hoped for an opportunity of improving her impressions.

"I shall leave it to Miss Steele to do as she thinks best," said the head mistress. "I am sorry indeed her time has been wasted over a worthless pupil. You had better wait till she comes."

I waited grimly, like a culprit for the jury. When she came in and saw, as I suppose, my woebegone face, I read hope in her manner.

"I got your note, Jones," said she.

"Oh! I say, Miss Steele, I'm really frightfully sorry. I know it was a caddish thing to do, especially when you had been so kind. Look here, I did all those sums myself, without help; and here's another batch I've done since; and--and--" (here I resolved to play a trump card) "and I got this black eye sticking up for you."

That settled it. She smiled once more and said, "Well, Jones, I'll say no more about it this once. I had made up my mind it was no use our going on together; but I'll try, if you will."

"Try--I'll kill myself working," said I, "to make up."

"That wouldn't do much good," said she; "but I'll try to forget all this ever happened, and we'll go on just where we left off."

"That was page 72," said I eagerly; "and, I say, Miss Steele, you remember my telling you about Tempest, and Dicky Brown, you know; well--"

"Is that on page 72, or is it something which we can talk about when work is done?"

So I got my chance once again, and this time I stuck to it.

The nearer the time came, the more desperately we worked. Sometimes Miss Steele had positively to hunt me out for a walk, or, if I would not go alone, to drag me along with her to some place where, regardless of our possible detection by Evans and his friends, we could combine fresh air and education.

The fatal day came at last when I had to go off to my ordeal. I was obliged at the last moment to disclose my well-kept secret to my mother and my guardian. The former fell on my neck, the latter grunted incredulously and embarrassed me by presenting me with a five-shilling piece.

Miss Steele came down to see me off at the station. "Keep cool," said she; "sit where you can see the clock, and don't try to answer two questions at once."

Never did tyro get better advice!

I was too excited to heed much of the big stately building I was so eager some day to claim as my own school. It was holiday time, and only a little band of combatants like myself huddled into one corner of the big hall, and gazed up in an awestruck way at the portrait of the Jacobean knight to whom Low Heath owed its foundation.

To me it was all like a dream. I woke to discover a paper on the desk before me; a paper bristling with questions, each of them challenging me to get into the school if I could. Then I remember dashing my pen into the ink and beginning to write.

"Keep cool. Keep your eye on the clock. Try one question at a time," echoed a voice in my ear.

How lonely I felt there all by myself! How I wished I could turn and see *her* at my side!

The clock crawled round from eleven to three, and I went on writing. Then I remember a hand coming along the desk and taking the papers out of my sight. Then a bewildered train journey home, and a hundred questions at the other end.

I went on dreaming for a week, conscious sometimes of my mother's face, sometimes of Miss Steele's, sometimes of Mr Evans's. But what I did with myself in the interval I should be sorry to be called upon to tell.

At last, one morning, I woke with a vengeance, as I held in my hand a paper on which were printed a score or so of names, third among which I made out the words--

"Jones, T.--(Miss M. Steele, High School, Fallowfield): Exhibition, L40."

So I was a Low Heathen at last!

CHAPTER SIX.
UP TO FORM.

I have reason to fear that for a fortnight after I received the astounding news of my scholastic success I was an intolerable nuisance to my friends and a ridiculous spectacle to my enemies.

I may have had some excuse. I had worked hard, and got myself into a "tilted" state of mind altogether. Still, that was no reason why I should consider that the whole world was standing still to look on at my triumph; still less why I should patronise my mother and Miss Steele and Miss Bousfield as three well-intentioned persons who had just had an object-lesson in the inferiority of their sex.

My mother and Miss Steele were too delighted to mind my airs. They were really proud--one to be my mother, the other to be my "coach." And when I strutted in and talked as if they barely knew how honoured they were by my company, they laughed good-humouredly, and said to one another,--

"No wonder he's pleased with himself, dear boy."

Miss Bousfield was less disposed to bow the knee.

"I hope you won't forget what you owe to Miss Steele," said she. "I never hoped she could make as much as she did of such unpromising material. It's what I always have said--good teaching can make a scholar of a dunce."

"Ah," said I, "you thought I was a dunce. I determined you should see I wasn't. I am glad your school gets the credit of the exhibition."

"I'll wait and see how you turn out, before I am glad," said she. "I hope the High School will not get a reputation for turning out prigs, Jones."

I couldn't quite understand Miss Bousfield. She was not as cordial as I thought she might be, considering the honour I had brought upon her school.

My guardian's clerks were even less impressed by my distinction than she.

"What's the matter this morning?" said Mr Evans on the day of my triumph, as I sat smiling inwardly at my desk.

"Nothing particular," said I.

"It looks as if it was bad stomach-ache--I'd try camomile pills, if I were you."

"Thank you--I don't require pills. If you want to know, I've been up for an exam, and passed."

"Been up where?"

"Up for an exam.--an examination," said I, surprised at their density.

"Where, at the girls' school?"

"Girls' school, no; at Low Heath." Mr Evans looked grave, and beckoned his comrades a little nearer.

"Awfully sad, isn't it?" said he, with a seriousness which surprised me.

"Yes. It's a good institution, though. My uncle tried to get a case in there once, but failed." I wasn't surprised to hear that.

"They only let the *very* dotty ones in," said Mr Evans. "Besides, it'll be a part payment case--at least, I should think the governor will plank down something."

"It's worth L40 a year for four years," said I, understanding very imperfectly the drift of these remarks, but pleased at least to find I had succeeded in impressing my fellow-clerks.

"Ah, so much?--they can't treat cases like yours for nothing. When are you going in?"

"In September. It's a splendid place--five hundred fellows there."

"So many! It's rather sad to think about, isn't it, Hodges? Five hundred! What a lot of trouble there is in the world, to be sure!"

"I can't say I shall be sorry--I know one or two chaps there already."

"Very likely, if it runs in the family at all."

"What runs?" said I, not taking him.

Mr Evans tapped his forehead.

"Never mind," said he, "it's not your fault. I expect four years will do marvels with you. We'll come and see you sometimes, on visiting days."

"Ah, I don't suppose there are visiting days, except for parents," said I.

"I know one or two of the staff, though," said one of the party. "I shall be able to hear about you from them."

"Oh, all right," said I. "I hope things here will go on all right when I'm at school."

"School?" said Mr Evans, stooping with his hands on his knees, and looking into my face. "Did you say school? Is Low Heath a school?"

"Rather. What did you think it was?"

"We thought it was an idiot asylum," said Mr Evans. And a shout of laughter at my expense confirmed his statement.

I did not deign to explain; and for the few days I remained at the office I made no further reference to my academic triumphs, though my comrades rarely failed to make merry over the asylum.

At the end of a fortnight I began to come to myself, and realise that I had not exactly borne my honours blushingly. And I was glad when my mother proposed a week or two at the seaside, to brace up before plunging into the ocean of public school fife.

My guardian, who had of late grown fairly civil to me, in the prospect of getting me off his hands, was good enough to release me from the office; and I shook the dust of that detestable place off my feet with unfeigned thankfulness.

Mr Evans wanted to get up a farewell supper for me, and I was very near allowing myself the honour, when I accidentally discovered that all the provisions were to be ordered in my name and the bill sent to me. Whereupon I declined the invitation with thanks, and regretted that a previous engagement would prevent my having the pleasure of joining their party.

Once in the quiet of the seaside, with my mother for companion, I recovered my proper frame of mind, and began to take sober views of the prospect before me.

I wrote to Tempest--rather a cocky letter, perhaps, but one full of delight at the prospect of joining him at Low Heath, and claiming his patronage and support.

His reply was characteristic to say the least.

"The examiners for exhibitions here are the biggest muffs out. They plough the only men worth having and let in no end of scugs. The consequence is. Low Heath is packed full of asses, as you'll find out. I'm glad they let you in, though, as it will be sport having you here and making you sing small. I do hope, though, it won't get out that you've been coached by a female, or there'll be a terrific lark. I'm getting quite a dab at photography, and shall have my camera up next term. Mind you get the right-shaped boiler, or I shall cut you. The kids are to be stopped wearing round tops like their betters, so you'd best cut yours square. Brown was too 'cute to try for an exhibition. It's bad enough for him to be a day boy, but it would be a jolly sight worse to be an exhibitioner as well. When you come up, mind you're not to collar me. It's bad form for a kid to collar a senior. Wait till I speak to you, or else get some chap to bring you and introduce you. Fellows who shirk form get jolly well lammed; so you'd better go easy at first. Bring plenty of pocket-money, and some thick boots for kicking chaps back.--Yours truly, H.T. Tempest."

This letter both gratified and perturbed me. It was pleasing to be hailed as one of the inner circle of a fellow like Tempest; but it made me suspect that I should not be taken into the fold at my own valuation, but that of my betters, which in a public school is a very different thing. The little details, too, about dress and manners rather startled me. For supposing I had gone up not knowing these things, what mistakes I should have made! Suppose, for instance, I had gone up in a billycock with a round instead of a square top; or suppose I had hailed Tempest without his first speaking to me, what would have become of me? I trembled to think of it, and was glad to feel I had a friend at court who would see I didn't "shirk form."

What made me still more uneasy was the reference to my connection with a girl's school. The prize list had made it appear, to any one who did not know better, that I was a pupil from Miss Steele's, High School, Fallowfield. Suppose this list should get into the hands of any of the fellows, or that some other new boy should carelessly leave his copy about! I wished I had had more sense than to mention the High School at all. This came of my chivalrous desire, said I to myself, to give Miss Steele and her principal the benefit of my distinction. Now I might have to thank them for endless trouble. I did my best to hope the worst would not happen.

"Fellows never read prize lists of exams, they've not been in for," thought I; "and when they have been in, they never trouble themselves about any one's name but their own. Why, I haven't even noticed where a single other chap comes from. They may all be girls' schools, for all I know. It's not likely any one has noticed mine."

And to avoid all accident I dropped mine into the fire, and had to stand my mother's reproaches for destroying a document she had intended to treasure till her dying day.

As the time for my going to Low Heath approached, I began to turn my attention seriously to my *trousseau*.

My first care was to get the square-topped boiler, and a rare job I had to procure it. None of the hatters in Fallowfield knew of such a shape in young gents' hats; and the shopkeepers in Wynd, whither I went over on purpose, were equally benighted. My mother, too, protested that she had never heard of such a kind of hat, and that it would be hideous when I got it.

That was no fault of mine. It was the Low Heath form, and that was enough for me.

At length I heard of a hat of the kind at Deercut, five miles off, and walked thither. It had been made, said the hatter, for a young sporting party who attended to a gentleman's stables, and knew a thing or two. He had got into trouble, it was explained, and was "doing his time on the circular staircase," which I took to mean the treadmill. That was the reason the article had been thrown on the maker's hands. It seemed just the thing Tempest described. The top was as flat as the lid of a work-box; indeed, it was precisely like a somewhat broad-brimmed chimney-pot-hat cut down to half height; and after a little pinching in at the sides fitted me beautifully. The maker was delighted to be able to suit me, and smiled most graciously when I paid him my five shillings and walked out of the shop with my junior exhibitioner's "boiler" on my head.

I set down to envy or ignorance the jeers of the village youths who encountered me on my way home. Some people will laugh at anything they do not understand. My mother's protests, when she saw me, however, were not so easy to dispose of.

"Why, Tommy, it makes you look like a common cheap-jack," said she. "It's not a gentleman's hat at all. I'm sure they would not tolerate it at Low Heath."

"On the contrary," said I, "it's the form there. You might say the same of mortar boards or blue-coat dresses. It all depends on the school."

"But are you sure Tempest was not exaggerating?"

"Tempest is the most particular chap about form I know," said I.

"Well, dear, promise me you won't wear this dreadful hat till you go to school. Wear your nice cap that suits you so well till then."

I humoured her. Indeed, I was a little shy myself of meeting Mr Evans, or any of that set, in my new garb. They would be sure to pass their nasty personal remarks upon it. It would be better to preserve it in its virgin purity for my entrance to Low Heath.

I took the precaution to write to Tempest and mention that I had got it, appending to my letter a rough sketch of the hat, so that, if there were anything wrong about it, he would be able to correct me.

He wrote back in great good spirits.

"Just the thing, kid. It'll take the shine out of all the boilers up here. Did I tell you about gloves? The knowing ones mostly sport lavender; but the outsiders don't wear any, except at the first call- over in the term, when of course it's compulsory. One muff last term got pretty well lammed because he only had two-button gloves instead of six. I believe one or two others were just as bad, only they didn't get kotched; but it was a lesson to them. I wonder if young Brown will be up to the tips, or whether he'll turn up in black boots instead of tan. I sha'n't write to him, because he's a town-boy, and it would be low. Ta-ta. Don't forget to wear your collar outside your great-coat, or I sha'n't speak to you.--Yours, till then, H.T."

I kept this letter carefully from my mother. I knew it would only distress her, and suggest all sorts of difficulties. For, dear soul, it would be so hard to explain to her the exigencies of school form. What would have become of me without old Tempest? I should have come utterly to grief, I felt. My only fear was that he might have forgotten something which it was as important I should be made aware of as the hat, or the six-button lavender gloves, or the tan boots.

I am afraid I must plead guilty to a little duplicity in the matter of purchasing these highly necessary articles of my kit. I had to persuade my mother to allow me to choose my own gloves and boots; and expended the money in such a manner that I could show her an ordinary pair of each, while the special articles were carefully concealed in my box. She thought the cheap black shoes and dog-skin gloves I paraded before her dear at the price; but she little knew that I had safely stowed away an elegant pair of light lavender gloves and a pair of tan boots of the most fashionable appearance.

I had some difficulty about the former. For six-button gloves for young gents was not a "stock-line" in any of the shops. I had finally to get a lady's twelve-button pair and cut them down to suit my requirements. The tan boots were more easily procured, although it grated somewhat against my feelings to be sent over to the ladies' side of the shop to get them, as they were not kept for boys on the men's side. As it was, I feared they did not come up to Tempest's description of "thick boots for kicking back in," but they were the thickest I could procure.

At length my preparations were all complete. My mother had been an angel about them all. She had let me have my own way, and forborne criticism when my taste--or rather my conjecture as to what the Low Heath form might demand--ran counter to hers. On this account she made no remark about my check shirts, or the steel chain which, after the most approved fashion, came out from under the side of my waistcoat and supported the weight of my keys in my side trouser pocket. I confess it was an inconvenient arrangement. It was impossible to unlock my portmanteau without either half undressing, or kneeling down so as to bring the end of the chain on a level with the keyhole, or else standing the portmanteau on a chair or table to bring it up to the key. But it was undoubtedly the smart way of carrying keys. So the tailor said, and so one or two friends in whom I confided also assured me.

I was really quite glad when I had sat down on the floor beside my trunk for the last time, and knew I should not have to perform with the key again till I was unpacking at Low Heath.

My handbag, for certain reasons, I carried with me unlocked. It contained, to tell the truth, the hat and gloves and tan boots and other ***articles de rigueur*** which I did not exactly like to start off in, but which I was resolved to don during the journey, so as to dawn on the Low Heath horizon altogether "up to Cocker," as Tempest would say.

At the last moment my spirits failed me a little. I had been so taken up with my own plans that I had almost forgotten I was leaving my mother solitary, and turning my back on the sunshine of affection which during the last year had come to be such a natural and soothing feature of my surroundings.

"Don't forget the old home, Tommy," she said. "God bless you and keep you good, and innocent, and honest! Don't be led astray by bad companions, but try to help others to be good. And, Tommy dear, don't try to be a man just yet--be the dear boy you are--don't try to be anything else, and--" But here the train began to move, and there was barely time for a farewell kiss.

What she said ran rather in my head, especially the last exhortation, which I was sorry she had uttered. For I was quite sure she was referring to my nervous desire to do everything correctly at the new school; and it grieved me that she should speak of it as trying to be something I was not.

Of course I would remember all she said. There was not much fear of my being led astray; it was much more likely that I, as an exhibitioner, would be looked up to by some of the ordinary small boys to show them a lead. What with Tempest to befriend me at headquarters, and my prestige as a scholar, and the fact that I knew a pretty good deal about school already, it was as likely as not I might be instrumental in helping one or two lame dogs over the stiles of their first term.

My only travelling companion was a motherly sort of person of the farmer class, who eyed me affectionately--too affectionately to please me--and attempted to condole with me on the sorrow of leaving home.

"Never mind, dearie," said she--Cheek! for a stranger to call a chap "dearie."

"You'll be a bit lonely at first, so you will; but you'll get used to it, and it won't be so long to holiday time, and then you'll see mamma again."

I wished she wouldn't. She misunderstood me. I wasn't thinking about the holidays at all. The fact was, I was thinking about my boots and hat in the bag, and wondering when I should put them on.

Bother it! Why should I mind her or her remarks? Some other new chap might get in at the next station, and I couldn't change before him. I'd better get myself up to form now, and so be ready.

So, to the old lady's surprise, I proceeded to take off my shoes and put on the thick tan boots in their place. She watched me in mingled admiration and surprise--no doubt the fresh yellow was very imposing, and made me look as if I was shod in gold. But the High Street at Low Heath would presently be sparkling with a hundred pairs of such boots, so what mattered an old lady's temporary astonishment? It was the same about the hat--indeed worse. For at the sight of that particularly sporting adornment, she threw up her hands and exclaimed,--

"What a funny little fellow, to be sure!"

I tried to look grave, and as if I had not heard her, but I felt very conscious of the hat all the same, and only hoped another new boy would get in presently, so that she might see that a thing might be the fashion and yet she not know it.

I was a good deal perplexed about the lavender gloves. Of course, I had not to wear these until call-over that afternoon, or possibly next morning. But I might as well try them on now. And the difficulty was that it was very difficult to button the six buttons all the way up without baring my arm half-way at least to the elbow. I made a feeble attempt, but it presented so many difficulties, and evidently so seriously perturbed my companion, that I abandoned the attempt, resolving to try them on under the bedclothes that night.

At the first station a youth of about my own age, with a hat-box and bag, got into the carriage. Was he, I wondered, a Low Heath chap? Evidently not. He wore a straw hat, and boots of the ordinary colour, and--Whew! what a lucky thing I had not forgotten it! He wore his white collar inside the velvet of his great-coat. And so should I have continued to do, had not the sight of him called Tempest's injunction to wear it outside to my memory. I availed myself of the next tunnel to rectify this serious omission, and had the satisfaction, when we emerged into daylight, of noticing that neither of my fellow-travellers appeared to pay much heed to the change. They both stared at me now and then; but the boy evidently grew tired of that, and curled himself up in a corner of the carriage and read a **Boy's Own Paper**.

I presently followed his example, and what with reading, and speculating on my coming entry into Low Heath, and an occasional thought for the little home at Fallowfield, the time went quickly by.

"Is this Low Heath station?" inquired I, as the train began to slacken speed.

"Yes," said the boy, regarding me from head to foot with evidently increased curiosity. "Are you a new kid at the school?"

"Yes," said I.

"Oh my! What a lark!" said he.

I was glad he thought it so.

"Are you at the school?" inquired I.

"Looks like it," said he, getting together his traps hurriedly, and bounding from the carriage with what I fancied was a broad grin on his face.

So here I was at last!

CHAPTER SEVEN.
COMING DOWN A PEG OR TWO.

I had half hoped Tempest would be down at the station to meet me. But he was not: and I had to consider on the spur of the moment how to make my entry into Low Heath.

Either I might walk, as I noticed a good many of the fellows who got out of the train did, or I might charter a private fly, as a few of the swells did, or I might go up in one of the school omnibuses, which was evidently the popular mood of transportation. I was so earnestly desirous to do the correct thing, that I was nearly doing nothing at all, and finally found myself standing almost alone on the platform with the last omnibus ready to start.

Surely they might make some arrangement, thought I, for meeting exhibitioners and taking them up. How did I know this omnibus was not a town-boys' vehicle, or one dedicated to the service of the inferior boys? Perhaps it would be better--

"Right away, Jimmy; off you go!" called one of the youths on the knifeboard, whom I recognised as my late travelling companion.

At this point I decided I would risk it, and go up by omnibus after all.

"Wait!" I called. "I'm coming too."

"Fire away, Jimmy. Cut along!" shouted the youth. They could not have heard me, surely. The omnibus was actually moving!

"Hi!" called I, beginning to follow, bag in hand; "wait for me."

"Lamm it on, Jimmy," was the delighted cry from the knifeboard, as a score of heads craned over to witness the chase. The spectacle of an ordinary youth giving chase to an omnibus crowded with roystering schoolboys is probably amusing enough; but when that youth has his white collar outside the collar of his greatcoat, and wears brilliant tan boots and a flat-topped billycock, it appears, at least so it seemed to me, to be exceedingly funny for the people on the omnibus.

"Put it on," called one or two, encouragingly; "you're gaining!"

"Forge ahead, Jimmy; here comes the bogey man!" cried another.

"Whip behind!" suggested a third.

"Anybody got a copper for the poor beggar?" asked a fourth.

By a desperate effort, at last I succeeded in coming up with the runaway omnibus, when to my disgust I discovered that it was one of those forbidding vehicles of which the step disappears when the door is closed. So that I had nothing to hold on to, still less to climb on to; and to continue to run with my nose at the door, like a well-trained carriage dog, suited neither my wind nor my dignity.

So I gave up the chase and dropped behind, covered with dust and perspiration, amid frantic cheers from the knifeboard and broad grins from the passengers on the pavement.

In such manner, I, an exhibitioner and a living exponent of the latest "form," entered Low Heath! I was almost more grieved for the school than for myself. Those fellows on the omnibus evidently didn't know who I was. To-morrow, when they found out, and saw me arm-in-arm with Tempest, they would be sorry for what they had done.

I confess that, as I walked up the steep street, and caught sight at last of the chimneys of the school peeping up over the trees, I half wished myself back at home with my mother. I hadn't expected to feel so lonely. I had indeed looked forward to a little pardonable triumph in being recognised at once as the fellow who had taken the entrance exhibition, and who evidently knew what was what. Of course it was foolish, I told myself, to expect such a thing. Fellows could hardly be expected to know who I was until they were told. Still it was a little--just a little--disappointing, and I could not help feeling hurt.

I tramped on, till presently I came to the bridge, and loitered for a moment to rest and watch the boats flitting about below. There went a four, smartly manned by youngsters no older than myself. There lolled a big fellow in a canoe. There swished by a senior in a skiff, calling on the four-oar to get out of the way as he passed. There, too, stood a master in flannels, with the Oxford Blue on his straw, talking to a group of boys. I wish I could have overheard what they were saying. Perhaps they were discussing the merits of some of the new boys.

I strolled on, passing on the way inquisitive stragglers who stared hard at me, till I came to where the road skirts the cricket field. Here, at a broken paling, I stood a moment and glanced in. Fellows were bowling and batting at the nets, others were strolling arm-in-arm up and down, hailing new arrivals; others were enjoying a little horseplay; others were critically examining the last season's pitch; others, impatient of the seasons, were punting about a brand-new football.

How out of it I was! and yet how sure I felt that if some of those fellows only guessed who was on the other side of the palings they would feel interested!

I strolled on farther, and began now to pass the outbuildings. There was a lecture room, empty at present. Should I be there to-morrow? I wondered, answering to my name and seeing fellows open their eyes as they heard it.

There was the gymnasium, I supposed--the place presided over by the drill master whom Tempest so much detested. I meant to back Tempest up in that feud.

Ah, there was the Lion Gate, standing open to receive me. Little I had expected, when once before I entered it on my way to examination, that I should so soon be coming back, so to speak, in triumph like this.

It took some little self-persuasion, I must confess, to feel that it really was a triumph. I did think Tempest might have been on the look- out for me. I did not know where to go, or of whom to inquire my way. The boys I met either took no notice of me at all, or else stared so rudely at my hat and boots that I could not bring myself to accost them. At length I was beginning to think I had better march boldly to the first master's house I came to, when, as luck would have it, I stumbled up against my old travelling companion, who, having safely arrived a quarter of an hour before, was now prowling about on the look-out for old acquaintances.

"Please," said I, "would you mind telling me the way to Mr Sharpe's house?"

"Are you a Sharper then?" he inquired. "My word! what are we coming to? Why didn't you come up by the 'bus?"

"I tried to," said I; "you wouldn't stop."

"Jim's horses were a bit shy," said he, with a grin. "They can't be held in when they see a moke. You should have got in quietly, without their spotting you."

I didn't like this fellow. He appeared to me to think he was funny when he was not.

"Do you know if Tempest has come?" said I, hoping to impress him a little.

"Who?"

"Tempest--Harry Tempest. He's at Sharpe's too."

"What sort of looking chap is he?" demanded the youth, who, I suspected, could have told me without any detailed description.

"He's one of the seniors," said I; "he was in the reserve for the Eleven last term."

"Oh, that lout? I hope you aren't a pal of his. That would about finish you up. If you want him, you'd better go and look for him. I don't know whether every snob in the place has come up or not."

And he departed in chase of a friend whom he had just sighted.

This was depressing. Not that I believed what he said about Tempest. But I had hoped that my acquaintance with my old schoolmate would redound to my own dignity, whereas it seemed to do nothing of the kind.

Presently I encountered a very small boy, of chirpy aspect, whom I thought I might safely accost.

"I say," said I, "which is Mr Sharpe's house?"

"Over there," said he, pointing to an ivy-covered house at some little distance higher up the street. Then, regarding me attentively, he added, "I say, you'll get in a jolly row if he sees you in that get-up."

"Oh," said I, feeling that the youngster was entitled to an explanation, "I'm an exhibitioner."

"A who? All I know is he's down on chaps playing the fool. You'd better cut in on the quiet before they bowl you out in that thing," said he, pointing to my hat.

That thing! True, I had not observed many hats like it, so far, at Low Heath; but that was probably because I had not encountered any other fellow-exhibitioner. Tempest knew more about the form than this kid.

"Thanks," said I. "Mr Sharpe will know who I am."

"Oh, all right," said he; "don't say I didn't tell you, that's all."

"I say," said I, feeling that enough had been said on a matter on which we evidently misunderstood each other, "do you know Tempest?"

"Rather. He's in our house. You'll get it pretty hot from him if you cheek him."

"Oh, I know him well; he's an old chum."

The boy laughed incredulously.

"He'd thank you if he heard you say so. Oh my! fancy Tempest-- Hullo, I say, there he is. Cut away, kid, before he sees you." And the youth set me a prompt example.

I was sorry he had not remained to witness the fact that I was not quite the outsider he took me for.

Tempest was strolling across the road, arm-in-arm with a friend. He certainly was not got up in the "form" which he had prescribed for me. He wore a straw hat on the back of his head, and boots of unmistakable blackness. But then, though an exhibitioner himself once, he had now attained to the dignity of a senior, and was probably exempt from the laws binding on new boys.

As he approached I crossed the road to meet him, full of joy at the prospect of encountering at least one friend, and marching under his protection into my new quarters. But I was doomed to a slight disappointment. For though for a moment, when he looked up, I fancied he recognised me, he did not discontinue his conversation with his friend, but drew him out into the middle of the road. They seemed to be enjoying a joke between them. His companion looked round once or twice at me, but Tempest, who was looking quite flushed, apparently did not take me in, and walked on, looking the other way.

It was a little shock to me, or would have been had I not remembered his friendly warning about the etiquette of a junior not accosting a senior till the senior accosted him. I wished he had spoken to me, for just then his help would have been particularly patronising. As it was, I was tantalised by seeing him pass by close to me, and yet being unable, without "shirking form" in a reprehensible way, to bring myself to his notice.

In due time I reached Mr Sharpe's house. To my dismay the door stood wide open, and the hall was crowded with fellows claiming their luggage as it was being deposited by the railway van. As I arrived there was an ominous silence, in the midst of which I stood on the step, and carefully rung the bell marked, not "servants," but "visitors." No one came, so after a due interval, and amid the smiles of the onlookers, I mustered up resolution to ring again, rather louder. This time I had not to wait long. A person dressed as a sort of butler, very red in the face, emerged from a green baize door at the end of the passage and advanced wrathfully.

"Which of you young gents keeps ringing the bell?" demanded he. "He's to be made an example of this time. Oh, it was you, was it?" said he, catching sight of me.

"Yes," said I. "Is Mr Sharpe at home?"

"At home?" demanded the official, redder in the face than ever. "You seem to be pretty much at home." Then, apparently struck by my appearance, he pulled himself up and honoured me with a long stare in which all the assembled boys joined.

"Who is it?"

"One of the porters from the station, I should say, from the looks of him," suggested a boy.

"Whoever it is, don't you ring that visitors' bell--do you hear?" said the man-servant. "If you want anything, go round to the side door and don't interfere with the young gentlemen."

"But I'm a new boy," said I. "I'm--I'm an exhibitioner;" at which there was a great roar of laughter, which even my self-satisfaction could hardly construe into jubilation.

I began to have a horrible suspicion that I had committed some great *faux pas* by ringing the visitors' bell, and blushed consciously, to the increased amusement of my fellow "Sharpers."

"Can I see Mr Sharpe?" I inquired, thinking it best to take the bull by the horns.

"Can't you wait?" said the servant. "Do you suppose the master has nothing to do but run out and see--wild Indians?" Here followed another laugh at my expense. "He'll see you quite soon enough."

Here a shove from behind precipitated me into the bosom of the speaker, who returned me with thanks, and before I could apologise, into the hands of the sender. Thence I found myself passed on by a side impetus to a knot of juveniles, who, not requiring my presence, passed me on to a senior standing by, who shot me back to a friend, who sent me forward among the boxes into the arms of the matron, who indignantly hustled me up the passage, where finally I pulled up short in the grasp of a gentleman who at that moment emerged from the green baize door.

In the confusion I had lost both my hat and my presence of mind. I was far too confused to observe who the new-comer was, and far too indignant to care. All that I called to my mind as I reeled into his clutches was Tempest's directions about kicking back, which accordingly I proceeded to do, with all the vigour of which my new tan boots were capable.

Mr Sharpe suffered this assault meekly for a second or two, then he held me out stiffly at arm's length, like a puppy in a fit, and demanded,--

"What do you mean, sir, by behaving like this?"

I was bound to admit that it was a natural inquiry from a person whose shins had been considerably barked by my new boots. I felt as if I owed Mr Sharpe an apology.

"Please," said I, "I didn't mean to do it. The boys shoved me, and I didn't know where I was going, really, sir."

Mr Sharpe seemed inclined to believe me. He was a florid-looking, spectacled young man, with sandy whiskers, and a grip--oh that grip!-- that could have lifted me easily over the Lion Gate.

"Boys," said he, "let us have none of this nonsense, or I must set a house theme. Is Mrs Smiley here?"

Mrs Smiley, looking anything but the "moral" of her name, appeared in due course.

"Mrs Smiley, will you please take charge of this new boy and keep him out of trouble? Run away with Mrs Smiley, my little man; and you, boys, as soon as you have claimed your boxes, clear out till register bell."

What I did my ears deceive me? Was I, an exhibitioner, a scholar who had come up to Low Heath in all the *eclat* of the latest "form," the friend of Tempest, the fellow who had made things too hot for himself at Dangerfield--was I, I say, to be handed over to a sort of washer-womanly person to be kept out of mischief, and called "my little man" in the presence of the whole house? Was this my triumphant entry then?

No sooner had Mr Sharpe retired, than greetings of "My little man," "Spiteful Sarah," "Run along with his Smiley, then," beset me on all sides. I would fain have explained and corrected any wrong impression, but they only laughed when I tried; finally, when Mrs Smiley grabbed at my hand and walked me off the scene like a baby, my humiliation was complete.

Mrs Smiley, who was far too busy with the young gentlemen's luggage to relish the extra duty put upon her by Mr Sharpe, had a very summary way of dealing with cases of my kind.

"Sit down there, and don't move till you're told," said she, pointing to a little three-legged stool in a corner in the box-room.

"But--" began I.

"Hold your tongue; how dare you speak to me?" she retorted.

"I only--"

"Stand in the corner, with your hands behind you, for disobedience," said she.

This was getting serious. The little three-legged stool would not have been exactly luxurious; but to be stood in the corner with my hands behind me by a person of the feminine gender called Smiley, was really too bad. The worst of it was that if I made any further protest I might be smacked in addition, and that possibility I hardly dared risk.

So, rather to my own surprise, I found myself standing in the corner, with my hands at my back, scrutinising a blue and pink rose on the wall- paper, and wondering whether it would not be worth my while to write to the *Times* about the whole business. I could not help thinking that Mrs Smiley did not hurry herself on my account. I was conscious of box after box being dragged to the front, emptied of its contents and put back, to be removed presently by a porter, who probably looked at me every time he came in, but, I am bound to say, received very little encouragement from my studiously averted head.

After nearly an hour I began to get tired, and the blood of the Joneses began to rise within me. I was seriously meditating mutiny, or at least a definite explanation with Mrs Smiley, when at last she broke silence.

"Now, young gentleman, this way, please."

And she led me to a small comfortable-looking apartment, which I surmised to be her particular sanctum.

"What's your name?"

"Jones," said I.

"Ah--you're the boy who's brought down a rubbishy speckled waistcoat and loud striped shirts--eh?"

"Well, yes," said I.

"Did your mother buy them for you, or did you buy them?"

"I did."

"I can see your mother's a lady by the way she has everything else done. You'll find your own trash just where you put it, in the bottom of your trunk. You will not be allowed to wear it. We expect our boys to dress like young gentlemen, whether they are such or not. What's that in your hand, Jones?"

"My hat," said I, hoping I was coming in for a little credit at last.

"Hat!" Here she was rude enough to laugh. "What made you bring a thing like that here for a hat?"

"But," said I, "I'm an exhibitioner."

"All the more shame on you not dressing like a gentleman. Look at those boots; I am sure your mother did not buy them for you. Take them off at once, sir--and put on your proper ones."

"Aren't they--isn't it the thing, the form, you know, for--"

"Form! Fiddlesticks. The thing at Low Heath is to behave and dress like gentlemen, not like vulgar, public-house potmen," said she, with an access of indignation which surprised me. "To think that you, with a nice mother like yours, should come up here a fright like that! There, put the shoes and hat in the trunk with the speckled waistcoat and shirts, and get yourself up decently, and then I'll speak to you."

I was under the impression she *had* spoken to me--pretty strongly too. This, then, was the end of my elaborately prepared toilet!

A horrid suspicion began to come over me at last, not only that Tempest had been having a little joke at my expense, but that I had lent myself to it with an alacrity and eagerness which had almost--nay, very nearly wholly--been ridiculous.

What does the reader think?

My further conversation with good Mrs Smiley, after I had, to use her own expression, made myself decent, only tended to confirm the painful impression. I even went to the length of adding, of my own accord, my six-button lavender gloves to the pile of sacrificed finery which strewed the bottom of my trunk. And when in due time a bell rang, and Mrs Smiley said, "There now, go down to call-over, and don't be a silly any more," I obeyed with a meekness and diffidence of which I could hardly have believed myself capable, had I not been quite sure of the fact.

CHAPTER EIGHT.
TEMPEST TALKS TO ME LIKE A FATHER.

As I entered the hall, in which were already assembled most of my fellow "Sharpers," the first idea which occurred to me was that Low Heath was not such a big place after all. I had expected to encounter the whole school, instead of some fifty boys of my own particular house, and it was a relief to me to find that, for the present at any rate, I was to blush before only a limited company.

The next thing that struck me was that these fellows evinced wonderfully little interest in my appearance; which, considering the active interest they had shown in me not long since, was quite a shock. I had made up my mind to be howled at and laughed out of countenance. Instead of which they contented themselves with a half-glance to see who the new- comer was, and then went on talking together as if nothing had happened.

The conceit was already sufficiently knocked out of me to enable me to take this indifference in good part. Possibly when my name was called reference would be made to my exhibition, which would make a few of them look twice at me; but for the present I was glad to be left alone.

At first I could distinguish nobody; but in a little I caught sight of Tempest's head among the seniors of the house. He did not see me, nor did he appear to be looking out for me.

Suddenly some one called "Seats!" an order that was so promptly obeyed that it left me standing alone near the door at which I had entered.

"Seats--can't you hear?" said some one near me. I made promptly for the first empty desk I could see. The youth at the end of the row had his back partly turned, and it was necessary to push vigorously past him to arrive at my destination.

"Look out, you mule!" said he; "you trod on my-- Hullo, Sarah, how are you?" and a friendly kick on the shins helped me wonderfully on my way.

It was my old acquaintance of the railway carriage; and next to him was the small youth who had been so terribly concerned about my costume in the morning.

He put his feet up on the desk in front, and gave me the option of climbing over or crawling under. He was about three-quarters my size; but he had such an air of authority about him, that I hardly liked to suggest a third alternative, namely, that he should put down his feet and let me pass. So I climbed over, much to his indignation (which he expressed by sticking a nib into me as I passed).

"I say," he began, "you'll catch it. That's not your desk."

I was aware of that, and devoutly hoped the real owner would not arrive on the scene.

"If Tinker kotches you-- Hullo, what *have* you done with your patent boots?"

"I've changed them," said I; "but do you think Tinker's coming?"

"We'll keep him out if he does--"

Just then one of the seniors on the front form, who had been talking to Tempest, leant back, and said in a loud whisper to the boy at the end of the form in front of ours--

"White, see all the new kids have their gloves on properly."

Gloves? I felt my teeth begin to chatter in my head.

Had I not flung my gloves along with my hat and boots into my trunk, thinking they would not be needed? I had considered them as part of Tempest's little joke. But evidently I had made a fearful mistake. For the senior who had given the admonition was not Tempest at all, but his next neighbour; and the fact that it was not given to me but to a monitor made it clear that, however I had been humbugged over the other details of "form," gloves were the order of the day for new boys at first call-over.

In a panic I rose and tried to go out, with the wild idea of rescuing my gloves from my trunk. But it was impossible to escape. Not only had my companion his feet up more uncompromisingly than ever, but my sudden movement called down upon me general remarks.

"Shut up I sit down, can't you?" said my neighbour. "What are you up to?"

"My gloves--I've--I've left them upstairs."

"Your what?"

"Gloves. I thought it was a mistake about new boys having to wear them, and didn't bring them."

The boy looked grave.

"Oh, you'll catch it! You can't go now. There's Sharpe coming in. Haven't you got any at all?"

"Only my ordinary gloves."

"What colour?"

"Yellow."

"Stick them on then."

"But they've only two buttons."

"Can't be helped. You're bound to catch it, but they're better than nothing."

So, in dire agitation, I drew on my new dog-skin gloves. The smiles of the boys near me I interpreted as a grim recognition that I had "shirked form" and did not know any better. I longed to explain that I did, and that I had not come to Low Heath as ignorant as they supposed. But it was impossible. Mr Sharpe was already in his place, and "register" had begun.

Register, a ceremony with which I was destined to become painfully familiar in time, consisted in the calling over of the names of all the boys in the house, in order of place, by the minor prefect, who took his stand at the side of the master's desk for the purpose. Instead of answering "Here" or "Adsum," in the usual way, the boy whose name was called stood in his place and held up his hand.

I had been so preoccupied with the lack of my six-button lavender gloves and the remarks of my two left-hand neighbours, that I had failed altogether to observe the boy on my right, who now quietly nudged me, and presented to my astonished gaze the serene and serious countenance of Dicky Brown.

"What have you got your gloves on for?" inquired he, as if he had seen me daily since we parted.

"It's the form. Haven't you got any? I say, you'll get in a jolly row," said I, quite delighted to be able to lord it a little over an inferior.

"Why--who told you?"

"Tempest."

"Tempest's a regular humbug. He tried to stuff me up by making me bring a cheese-cutter cap. But I wasn't such a fool as I look."

Alas! it was my turn to colour up. Had Dicky, I wondered, seen my square billycock?

At that moment Tempest's name was called, and we saw our old Dux rise complacently in his seat and hold up his hand.

It was difficult to feel angry with him. He looked so cool and determined, his shoulders were so square, and the year that had elapsed since we met had added three good inches to his stature. It was a feather in a fellow's cap to know Tempest, even if he did have his little joke at one's expense now and then.

I came to the conclusion that Dicky and I must be the only two new boys in the house, for none of the numerous hands, grimy and otherwise, which went up were cased in anything but their native skin.

Presently the register clerk came to an end of his list, and I was beginning to congratulate both myself and Brown on our probable escape from detection when Mr Sharpe said--

"New boys, come forward."

My left-hand neighbour interposed no obstruction now, as, followed by Dicky, I sidled out of my place and advanced along with five other youths to the front. I was conscious of smiles as I went past the desks, some of recognition of the late owner of the tan boots, some of appreciation of my blushes, and others, as I supposed, of the greenness which had led all my companions to commit the fatal error of not appearing in gloves, and of my error, though in a smaller degree, of appearing in bright yellow two-button goods instead of lavender of the regulation half-dozen.

I exchanged glances with Tempest, among others, who looked very serious, and was evidently chagrined that after all his kind trouble on my behalf I should now land myself in this dilemma. Good old Tempest! It wasn't his fault.

"Answer to your--" began Mr Sharpe, when, suddenly catching sight of me, he said--

"Why, sir, what nonsense is this? What do you mean by wearing those gloves?"

"I beg your pardon, sir," I faltered, and felt that not a word of my speech was being lost by the assembled house; "I've left my lavender six-button gloves in my trunk."

Mr Sharpe's mouth curled at the corner in a curious way, and a general titter greeted my explanation from the benches behind.

I was fully convinced now that, after all my care, the very solecism I had planned so carefully to avoid had tripped me up at last.

"Take them off at once, sir, and let me have no more of this foolishness. You are making a bad start. Were you not the boy I had to speak to in the hall this afternoon?"

"Yes, sir. I am sorry I kicked your shins. I hope I didn't hurt much. I thought you were one of the boys."

I am sure I meant no harm by it, but he seemed to regard this as a studied insult, and visited me with his wrath not only for it but for the smiles from the boys behind which accompanied it.

"What is this boy's name?" he inquired severely, looking round.

I wondered who would answer the question; it was evidently not intended for me. It astonished me that Mr Sharpe should not apply at headquarters; I am sure I could have told him. "I think," said a voice which I recognised as Tempest's, "his name is Jones, sir."

Think! Surely Tempest might have had a little more confidence than that.

"Perhaps you will see what you can make of him presently, Tempest. If he has any intelligence at all," (nice, wasn't it, for an exhibitioner?) "you may be able to make him understand some of the rules of the place. If not, I am afraid we shall have to put him down as a silly little boy, and bear with him accordingly. Go to your seat now, sir, and report yourself to Tempest after register."

It was not a very dignified end to the interview. Still, I felt myself lucky to be handed over to the tender mercies of my old comrade, and retired to my place a puzzled but not an amused boy.

What perplexed me most was to notice that Brown and the other new boys who had no gloves at all, and did nothing but answer the questions put to them in the plainest possible way, not only passed muster, but received words of approval and encouragement from the master such as I would have given a great deal to have got myself. But such is life. The fellows who take the most pains and deserve most, get least; and the fellows who have least to boast of receive more than they expect.

I was glad when register was over and the time came for me to have an explanation with Tempest.

"Look here," said the candid youth next to me, "you'd better sit up when you go to Tempest, I can let you know. He's cock of our house this term, and he's not over-tender with idiots, I can let you know."

"What, has he been down on you?" I inquired meekly.

The only reply I got was a touch on the calf which made me exclaim "Oh!" rather more loudly than I should have chosen to do under ordinary circumstances. Luckily the general movement of the class somewhat deadened the sound, and if Mr Sharpe heard me, he did not consider it worth his while to deprive Tempest of the task of elucidating the reason of it.

I kept my man carefully in view, and followed him upstairs into a little study about the size of a commodious sentry box, with a window, book- case, sofa, table, chairs, and all the requirements of a single man of few needs. It seemed to me a delightful little sanctum; and for a moment I began to wonder whether, being an exhibitioner, I might not be entitled to one like it for myself--perhaps this *was* mine.

Tempest soon disabused me of that notion.

"Light the fire, and stick on my kettle, kid," said he--they were the first words after more than a year--"and cut and get us a muffin from the shop."

"I say," said I, longing for rather more cordial a recognition, "I am jolly glad to see you again, Tempest."

Just then another senior popped his head in.

"Have tea with me. Tempest? Come on, Wales is coming too."

"Is Crofter coming?"

"No."

"All right, I'm on; thanks, Pridgin. Blow that fire out, kid."

"Is that kid your fag?"

"Not likely."

"Is he all there? Sharpe seemed to doubt it."

Tempest shrugged his shoulders.

"How soon? Ten minutes?"

"Yes--not longer."

"Now, kid," said Tempest, when we were left alone, "how long are you going to play the fool? Take your time; but let us know when you've done, that's all."

"Really, I'm not fooling; I know I ought to have had on the lavender--"

Tempest laughed. A jolly laugh it was, though it frequently preceded a licking.

"You mean to say you sucked in all that rot? I thought I'd just see how far you'd let yourself be humbugged; I'm sorry I didn't tell you to stand on your head. I don't doubt you'd have done it."

I had painful reason to think he might be right.

"Why, even Dicky Brown was too old a bird for that sort of chaff," said Tempest; "he twigged it at once--and he's a day boy. Hand me that cane out of the cricket box, there's a good fellow, and hold out your hand. Don't yell; only muffs do that."

"What?" I exclaimed, "am I to be licked, Dux?"

"Don't call me Dux here. Yes, rather--three on each hand."

"But Mr Sharpe only said--"

"Sharpe--what's he got to do with it? Come on, look alive, or I shall be late for tea."

I could barely be angry with him. He didn't seem to be able to see the matter from my point of view at all, and was so genuinely friendly with it all.

"The third will be a hot one," said he, as I held out my hand; "but I don't want to break the cane--it's a good one."

The third *was* a hot one.

"Hurt you much?" said Tempest, carefully examining his weapon.

"Middling," said I.

"Now the other hand. I suppose you've not got to know many chaps yet? Did you get any cricket in the vac.?"

"No," said I, extending my left in a deprecating way.

"We did," said he. "We were jolly near licking--"

"Ow!"

"Feel that much? Good cane, isn't it? Now the other two will be easy."

To do him justice they were, or would have been had they not fallen uncomfortably near the site of the first.

"Stick the cane back," said he,--"and look here," he added in the old friendly way which always captivated me, "if you'll take any advice you'll drop playing the fool. It may be funny, but it doesn't pay. Fellows get bored by it."

"But I really--"

"I know you can't help it. Your best dodge is to lie low for a bit, and keep out of everybody's way."

"I never meant--"

"Of course you didn't. You can't help being an ass, but don't swagger or brag about it. Go easy--and, by the way, whatever you do, forget you're an exhibitioner. It's not your fault, I know, but it's a sort of thing to be lived down up here. Be nobody, that's the rule! then you'll worry through."

"But *you* were an exhibitioner, Tempest," I suggested, "weren't you?"

"Yes, but I kept it dark. Do you know the chap who asked me to tea?"

"No."

"He's Pridgin--in the Eleven--makes beastly bad jokes, but not a bad chap. You'll like fagging for him."

"What--am I to fag?" said I, undergoing another shock. I had made quite sure exhibitioners were exempt from that indignity.

"There you go again. What did I tell you?" said Tempest, in tones of mild menace; "you're putting it on again already. You'd better fish out that cane again, there's a good chap."

"Oh, please don't--I didn't mean, Tempest! All right, I'll fag for him."

Tempest regarded first me, then the cricket box where the cane lay, doubtfully.

"I tell you he's not half a bad chap. Bother it," added he, picking up the cane, "I must do it, kid. Awfully sorry, but it would be low to let you off because I know you. Look alive. One, middling warm, on each hand, that's all. Thanks."

He was quite unnecessarily grateful. His idea of middling warm, I could not help thinking, was not very different from hot. And yet I felt I could stand it better from him than from most.

"Some chaps," said he, after returning me the cane to put back in its place, "would say that this sort of thing pained them more than it does you. It didn't me. I fancy you felt it more than I did. Anyhow, you'll remember what I said, won't you? Pridgin's not half a bad chap."

"If you want any one to fag for you. Tempest--"

I began.

"Oh, I've got one--a beauty--young Trimble; he sat next to you at register to-day. You'll hit it off with him to a T. Talking of tea, by the way, it's time we showed up at Pridgin's. Come along, and I'll introduce you."

The reader may not believe it, but my interview with Tempest helped to knock the nonsense out of me more than any treatment I had yet undergone. It was not so much the caning (which, by the way, I afterwards discovered to be a wholly unauthorised proceeding on my old comrade's part), but his plain advice, and the friendly way in which it was all given. It made me realise that he really meant to stick by me and pull me through my troubles, and the sense of his interest in me made up wonderfully for the loneliness which had been growing on me ever since I entered Low Heath that morning.

Pridgin, as became a member of the Eleven, received me with dignity quite devoid of curiosity. He informed Tempest that he considered it was playing it pretty low down on him to let an idiot like me loose on him. Still, times were bad, and one must put up with what one could get.

Whereat I had the good sense to grin appreciatively, and was thereupon permitted to boil my new master's eggs and stand by the kettle until it was ready for the tea.

CHAPTER NINE.
ACQUAINTANCES, HIGH AND LOW.

I was at first too much concerned in my important culinary occupations to bestow much attention on the company. It was only when the eggs were boiled and the teapot filled that I had leisure to make a few observations.

The host, Pridgin, my new master, was not a very formidable sort of person at first blush. True he was in the Eleven and a fine all-round athlete. True he was fairly well up in the Sixth, and one of the boys Low Heath was proud of. These things did not strike one in beholding him. What did strike one was his air of lazy humour, which seemed to regard life as a huge joke, if only one could summon up the energy to enjoy it. Pridgin did indeed enjoy his share of it, but one could not help feeling that, were he to choose, that share would be a great deal larger than it really was.

It was plain to see he was fond of Tempest; a weakness which reconciled me to him from the first. Tempest, however, seemed, if anything, to prefer the third member of the party present, who was in every way a contrast to his genial host.

Wales struck one as a far more imposing person than Pridgin, but not quite as attractive. He was dressed in what seemed to me the top of the fashion, and had the appearance of a youth who made a point of having everything of the best. He had the reputation, as I discovered afterwards, of possessing the most expensive bats and racquets, the best-bound books, the best-fitting clothes, of any one in Low Heath. It was also rumoured that he spent more than any boy in the town shops, and gave the most extravagant entertainments in his study. Fellows were a little shy of him for this very reason. He forced the pace in the matter of money, and there were only a few fellows who could stand it.

Tempest was not one of these, and yet he seemed very thick with Wales. It was certainly not for the sake of his money, for Tempest was one of those fellows who never care for a fellow for the same reason that any one else would. He had begun by being amused with Wales's dandyism and extravagance, and had ended in encouraging him in them.

"I expect," said Wales, as the three heroes sat discussing their tea, "we're in for a pretty lively term, if it's true what I hear, that Redwood is to be captain."

"Why shouldn't he be?" asked Pridgin; "he's a hot man in the fields, as well as in classics."

"My dear fellow, he's a town-boy."

"What of that?"

"What of that? First of all, the town-boys are most of them snobs. Sons of hard-up people who come to live at Low Heath so as to get them into the school cheap. Then they can't possibly keep up with what goes on in school when they are away every evening."

"There's more in the second objection than the first," said Tempest. "I don't see why a fellow should be out of it because he's poor. If so, I can cut my lucky here. But it does seem a swindle to stick a town-boy over all of us."

"I don't see it," said Pridgin. "He's one of us. The only difference is, he goes home to sleep instead of tucking up in a cubicle here. No, what seems to me the cool thing is this talk of a town-boys' club, that brags it's going to lick the school clubs into fits. I hope it's not true, for if it is, we shall have to sit up, and I loathe sitting up."

His guests laughed. It was notorious that Pridgin when he did bring himself to "sit up" was a person worth reckoning with.

"For the matter of that," said Wales, "Redwood's not likely to trouble himself much. He'll take all the glory and do none of the work. The captain of Low Heath ought to have his hand in everything, and not let everything slide."

"You'll find Redwood can be awkward enough when he chooses. You can never tell how far he'll let things go on. But when his back once gets up he'll stiffen pretty hard."

"All I can say is," said Tempest, "if I'm to be cock of this house this term--and I've no right to be--"

"Yes, you have, old chap," said Pridgin.

"You know you purposely ran for second place last term, so as to get out of the fag of cocking the house," retorted his friend. "Anyhow, if I **am** to be cock, I mean to stand up for our rights, and see we're not done out of them by town-boys, of all people."

"Hear, hear," said Pridgin; "stick up for your rights. I don't exactly know what rights we're got more than any other Low Heathens, but stick up for them certainly. Nothing like having a grievance, if you can only find one."

"What do you say to Jarman for one?" said Wales.

The faces of all three clouded at the mention of this name.

"Ah, I'd forgotten about that. Is it true he's to be a sort of general discipline master, and have the right of pulling up any fellow, senior or junior, without even saying a word to his house prefects?"

"He won't do it here, if I can help," said Tempest, with a frown.

"Well, have some more tea," said Pridgin, "before you begin operations. Here, kid, make a fresh brew, sharp, and then cut."

What I had heard had been quite enough to satisfy me that things were not running altogether smoothly at Low Heath, and that Tempest was not beginning his new duties as head of his house in the best of tempers. I confess I felt a little uneasy. For I knew my old chief's impulsive, generous nature well enough to be sure that he might easily get himself into trouble for the sake of other people. His friends were evidently glad enough to let him fight their battles, but were not likely, at least so it seemed to me, to take much trouble to help him through with them.

I was wandering rather disconsolately down the passage when it occurred to me I did not know what I was expected to do or where I was expected to go.

I therefore ventured to accost a senior who was lounging about at the head of the stairs.

"If you please," said I, "I'm a new boy--can you tell me where to go?"

The senior, a bland, good-looking sort of youth, surveyed me carefully and replied--

"To bed, I should say."

"All right, thanks," said I; "which way is that?"

He laughed pleasantly.

"What's your name?"

"Thomas Jones."

"You needn't mind about the Thomas up here. Where have you come from?"

"Do you mean, where do I live, or where have I been just now?" I inquired, anxious to avoid any misunderstanding.

"Look here," said he, "hadn't you better take a seat, if you want to tell me all your family history? I'm sure it's very interesting, but it's rather late in the day to begin now. Where have you come from, not originally, but just now?"

I flushed up very much at this polite rebuke. Whatever made every one so anxious to assume that I was an ass?

"Pridgin's," said I. "I'm his fag, and he's having a tea party."

"Oh," said the youth; "who's there?"

"Only Tempest and Wales," I replied, feeling more at my ease.

"No one else?"

"No," I answered. Then, guessing he might have the same antipathies as Tempest, I volunteered--

"Crofter's not asked."

My companion opened his eyes. "Indeed--why?"

"I don't know. Only I know Tempest wouldn't have gone if he had been. Please which way do I go?"

"What objection has Tempest to Crofter?"

"I don't know--I suppose he's a beast. Tempest hates beasts."

The boy laughed.

"He must be very fond of you," said he.

"Yes," said I, "we're old chums; we were at Dangerfield together, and both got ex--"

There I was, after Tempest's warning about keeping my exhibition dark.

"Both got what? *Expelled*?" inquired the senior, with interest.

"Well--yes," said I, thinking that the best way of getting out of it. "It was this way--"

"Really, Jones, it's getting late," said the senior; "I've no doubt it's an interesting story. There, go and inquire in the fourth room on the left. They'll show you the way to bed."

And he departed.

I was very sorry he had not given me time to explain the little matter at Dangerfield. It would be a pity for any one to get a wrong impression about it. Still, what a lucky escape I had had from blabbing about my exhibition! The fellow, too, seemed a nice sort of chap, and disposed to be friendly, so there was no harm done after all.

I could tell, long before I reached it, that the room which had been indicated to me as the place where I might get the information for which I thirsted was, to say the least, inhabited--for the noise which penetrated through the keyhole and the cracks of the door was appalling. Either, thought I, a free fight is going on within, or there is a steam engine at work, or the builders are shooting bricks through the window. I was mistaken. It was only five boys of about my age talking.

The silence which greeted my appearance was rather more formidable than the noise which had preceded it. In the midst of it, however, I observed the form of Master Trimble, also that of my travelling companion of the morning, and concluded therefore that I had come to the right place for information.

"Full up! cut!" was the cordial greeting of the company generally.

"Hullo, it's Sarah!" cried my travelling companion. "What a lark! Collar him, you chaps. That's the idiot I was telling about. He came down in the train with his ma--"

"She wasn't," said I; "she was no relation."

A loud laugh greeted this disclaimer.

"Well, his nurse, or aunt, or washerwoman, or something."

"No, she wasn't."

"Shut up, and don't tell crams."

"It's *you* who are telling crams," said I, for the blood of the Joneses was getting up.

"Look here; do you mean to call me a crammer?" demanded the speaker, looking very imposing.

"If you say it again I will," said I. "I tell you that woman had no more to do with me than you; there!"

It was a critical situation, and the key to it was in my accuser's hands. If he insisted that the lady in question had anything to do with me, I was committed to call him a crammer. And if I called him a crammer, he was equally committed by all tradition to punch my head. And in the humour I was then in, he was not likely to do that without getting one back for himself.

"I know who it was," suddenly cried Trimble; "of course! Tempest told me last term there was a young ass coming up who'd been at a girls' school, and had got an exhibition or something. Of course this was his old school dame. Good old Sarah!"

At this terrific exposure the spirit leaked out of me. My tell-tale blushes confirmed what was true in the story, and my silence lent countenance to what was untrue. The delight of my tormentors was beyond words. They danced the "mulberry bush" round me, overwhelmed me with endearing expressions, offered me fans and smelling salts and cushions and hairpins, simulated hysterics and spasms, trod on my skirts, and conversed to me in shrill treble till I was sick of the business. Only one course was open to me. It was an unpleasant one, but on it depended, I felt, my future welfare at Low Heath.

I seized the nearest, who happened to be Master Trimble, and pulling him gently but firmly by the nose, demanded if girls generally treated him that way? He kicked vigorously, and ordered me to release the imprisoned member. I declined to do so until I had kicked back, and finally deposited him on the floor, amidst the laughter of his perfidious comrades, who told him it served him right, and that "Sarah" was evidently one too many for him.

This little protest stood me in good stead. It put an end to all direct aspersions on my sex, although it was a long while before I was destined to hear the last of delicate insinuations on the topic. And it advanced me very considerably in favour with the four whose noses I had not been fortunate enough to engage.

"Look here; stop fooling, you chaps," said one of them, when in due time Master Trimble was permitted to regain his feet. "This new kid had better make up our sixth man here. No other faggery would be likely to take him, so we may as well."

I concluded from this remark that the juniors of Mr Sharpe's house were permitted to herd together in half dozens; and on the whole I was disposed rather to bear the ills I had than fly to others I knew not of.

"I don't mind," said I, "if you let me be."

"Who wants to touch you with a pair of tongs? You may as well pull in with us, and help us kick the others. It'll be a change after the girls' school."

"I **wasn't** at a girls' school," said I, "I told you. All I did was to coach with one of the teachers."

"About the same thing, I fancy," said Trimble, blowing his outraged nose somewhat defiantly, "Sarah!"

"If you call me Sarah again," said I hotly, "I'll pull your nose again."

"All right: Miss Jones, then."

"No, not Miss; just Jones."

"All serene, just Jones, then shut up; stick on your lavender gloves, and keep your hair on."

There was a general laugh at this which vastly solaced the aggrieved Trimble, and encouraged him to refer jocularly to my late hat and boots, topics which I had not the spirit to resent.

As soon as these personal matters were disposed of, I was tacitly admitted as a member of the honourable faggery, and invited to express my opinion on a matter which had been engaging the attention of the fraternity before I arrived.

"We were thinking," said my late travelling companion, whom his friends addressed as Langrish, "that it would be a score to get up a Philosophical Society in the school. What do you say?"

"What to do?" I ventured to ask.

"Oh, discussions, and picnics, and larks. What do you suppose we **should** do? There's a senior club of the kind already. They go in for dry rot--science and history, and that sort of thing. Awful slow, and nobody knows what he's talking about. I flatter myself **we** should."

"We ought to draw up some rules, oughtn't we?" said Trimble.

"Rather--forge ahead."

Whereupon we crowded solemnly round the small table and put our heads together.

One of the party, by the way, answering to the name of Purkis, appeared to be the leading spirit, and made the most valuable suggestions.

"Rule 1," dictated he, "That this club be called the Low Heathen Conversation Club."

"Hold on," said Trimble; "you've got club coming twice in the same sentence. Bad grammar."

"Besides, I thought there was to be something about philosophy," suggested Langrish.

"And keeping out the day cads," said Warminster, another of the party.

"Of course, if you make the rule long enough," said Purkis, with lofty contempt, "you can get something in it about the man in the moon."

"But," said I, thinking to make a little joke, just to show I had no ill-feeling, "we don't want him in the club, do we?"

"No," said Langrish, who had evidently been on the look-out for his chance; "no more do we want pretty Sarah's washerwoman; do we, you chaps?"

I subsided gracefully. The time was not yet ripe, evidently, for me to assert myself.

"I tell you what," said Warminster; "what's the use of every one making each rule? Let old Purkis make the first, and I'll make the second, and Langrish the third, and so on. It will be ever so much quicker, and give each chap a fair innings."

It seemed a good idea, and as it allowed Purkis's rule to stand unchallenged, he acquiesced.

So in due time the following wonderful code of rules was drawn up and adopted--

1. That this club be called the Low Heath Conversation Club. (Purkis.)

2. That the object of the club be and are periodical picnics and meetings for the discussion of philosophy, etcetera. (Warminster.)

There was some debate as to whether the ninth word should be "is" or "are." But "are," as agreeing with the plural, was carried by a large majority.

3. That each member bring his own grub, *alias* provisions. (Trimble.)

4. That no day boy be eligible on to the club. (Langrish.)

5. That any member breaking the rules is hereby expelled. (Coxhead.)

6. That the subscription be two shillings a term, payable in advance. (Jones.)

Warminster was anxious for consistency's sake to add the words "and are" after "be," but was overruled.

After which we honourably drew lots for the various posts of emolument and honour in connection with the club.

To my surprise I was drawn for president. At first I was disposed to disclaim the honour on account of my youth and inexperience. But my fellow-Philosophers assured me that was no excuse, and that my name would undoubtedly "draw." I did not exactly see how, but they were probably better judges than I; and perhaps as an exhib--

No, I was bound to keep that dark. At any rate, it would be a nice thing to be able to write home to my mother, that on the day of my arrival I had been appointed president of the Philosophical Conversation Club, with a right to add the initials P.L.H.C.C. after my name. It sounded well, and would give me a better footing in Low Heath than my tan boots.

Langrish was drawn for treasurer, and Purkis for secretary; while, to obviate any cause for jealousy, Trimble was selected as auditor, Warminster as librarian, and Coxhead as registrar.

A levy of subscriptions was made forthwith by the treasurer, and the secretary was ordered to expend part of the amount in a handbill setting forth the object and *personnel* of the society, for distribution through the school. The auditor undertook to check the printer's bill, the librarian to keep a copy of the document among the archives of the club, and the registrar to prepare a book for entering the names of the new members. Altogether it was a most businesslike proceeding, and one which reflected, as it seemed to me, great credit on the young life of Low Heath.

After this, a peremptory summons from the bell dismissed us precipitately to bed. I had the indignity of being conducted to my cubicle by Mrs Smiley, who had the bad taste to adjure me in the hearing of my comrades to behave myself like a good boy and go to sleep directly the lights were out. This was not altogether easy, for my cubicle happened to be between those of Trimble and Langrish, and the partitions were not particularly high. I was, indeed, allowed to undress and say my prayers without interference, which was more than I had hoped for. But no sooner was I in bed, and lights out, than I was favoured with all sorts of missiles pitched over the partitions on either side with extraordinary accuracy. A book from Langrish hit me on the ear, and a wet sponge from Trimble moistened my cheek. And when I sought shelter under the sheets, the butt-end of a fishing-rod in the ribs drew me from my hiding-place, and a clever cast with a hooked pin by Langrish relieved me of my outer covering altogether. The footsteps of the monitor on duty deprived me of the privilege of making an audible protest. All I could do was to send Trimble's sponge quietly over to Langrish, and Langrish's book across to Trimble, and, as well as I was able, recover my abstracted sheet with the aid of the rod. It took a long time, and laid me open to dire penalties for disturbing the public peace. But it had to be done, and fortunately for me a row at the other end of the room called the monitor away in the nick of time.

When he returned, all was still, and I was dreaming that Mr Evans was selling a pair of second-hand six-buttoned lavender gloves to my mother in the hall of Mr Sharpe's house.

CHAPTER TEN.
SPECIAL SERVICE.

My introduction to Low Heath at large next day turned out to be a far less formidable affair than I had anticipated. I had long since given up the notion that the whole school would rise at my appearance and salute me. I had even ceased to expect that they would all stare and make remarks. But I was hardly prepared for the absolute indifference with which I was permitted to answer to my name at "Great register." Not a soul took any notice of me, even when Dr England explained to me publicly that as there were already three other Joneses in the School, I would please answer in future to the title of Jones iv., which I humbly promised to do. Brown, I was not sorry to hear, was to be designated as Brown iii. for similar reasons.

The ceremony being over, the new boys were trooped up to the head master's library, and there told off to their respective forms with a few words of warning and encouragement. It surprised me that, in spite of my scholastic honours, I was entered in the same form as Brown. But on the whole I was more pleased than disappointed, for I loved my old comrade dearly, and after all, if he *was* placed above his merits, it wasn't his fault.

"It's a pity you aren't a day boy," said he, as he walked across afterwards; "we could have larks together."

"It's a pity you aren't in the school," said I.

"Oh, our chaps say it's rather stale to be in the school. I don't see why your fellows should be looked down on, but they are."

"Pooh! you should hear our chaps talk about the day boys. Do you know, Dicky, I'm president of a club, a Philosophical Club; and day boys aren't eligible. I'm awfully sorry; I should have liked to have you in."

"That's just what I thought about the Urbans. They don't let in any fellow who's in the school--only day boys--they're obliged to draw the line somewhere, you know. Do you know Redwood, the captain, is a senior Urban?"

"I know. Our chaps say it's a soak for the school having a day boy for captain."

"Oh! *We* don't think so! I say, do you see that chap there?"

The youth at whom he pointed was the friendly senior of whom I had inquired the way to bed last night.

"Rather; he's a Sharper. Why, and what about him?"

"He's a hot man, they say, and the most popular chap at Low Heath. He's captain of the Rifles."

"What's his name? Do you know?"

"Crofts, or Crofter, or something like that. What's up?"

He might well ask!

"Crofter!" exclaimed I. "My word, Dicky, I've been and done it!"

"Done what?"

"Why, I called him a beast yesterday."

"You did? You're getting on, Jones iv."

"No, without humbug, I did. I didn't know it was Crofter, and I told him Tempest thought he was a beast."

"If Tempest says so, he probably is," remarked the unemotional Dicky.

"But what's to become of me? How was I to know?"

"I don't know. Perhaps you'd better go and tell him you were mistaken."

"I don't like to. I say, what a downer he'll have on me! I half wish I was a day boy, after all."

"It's a pity you aren't. We've a jolly lot in the Urban Minors; quite a literary lot."

"Bother the Urban Minors!" said I, looking dismally after the retreating form of Crofter.

"It'll take you all your time to bother some of them. There's Flitwick, he's--"

"Hang Flitwick! Whatever am I to do, Dicky?"

"I wouldn't advise you to hang Flitwick. Oh, about that fellow Crofter! Oh, it'll be all right. He's plenty else to think about."

It was poor comfort, but the best I could get, and our arrival at our class room cut short further discussion on this most unfortunate incident.

But it weighed on my mind all day. When class was over, I was summoned by my fellow "Philosophers" to come out into the playing fields; I went in fear and trembling, lest I should encounter Crofter. But he was nowhere to be seen.

My companions were evidently hand and glove with most of the juniors in the school, and I was favoured with a bewildering number of introductions, not always of the most gratifying kind.

"What have you got there, Trim? A tame monkey?" asked one gorgeous youth, whose cap bore the badge of Mr Selkirk's house.

"Not exactly," said Trimble; "haven't had time to tame him yet."

"What's his name?"

"Sarah. Allow me. Muskett--Sarah Jones; Jones--Silly Muskett. Now you know one another."

"He's only fooling about my name," said I; "it's Thomas."

"Oh, is it? Delighted to see you, Sarah Thomas."

And before I could put him right he was off, and I was led away by my rejoicing comrades.

"Look here, Trimble," said I, "it's time you knew my name by now."

Trimble laughed, as did the others. They all thought it was high time.

But everybody we met I was introduced to as Sarah.

"Awfully sorry," said Langrish, after the fourth or fifth offence. "I've such a bad memory for names.--Well kicked, sir."

This exclamation was addressed, not to me, but to a senior who had just appeared on the scene, and was kicking about the practice football with a friend prior to a match which was evidently due.

It was a splendid kick, and the author of it was a splendid fellow-- brawny of limb and light of foot, with fair hair and clear blue eyes--as one might picture one of the Norsemen of the story-books. You could see by the way he moved, and the spirit he put even into this practice kicking, that he was a sportsman every inch of him; and his good-natured laugh, as he exchanged greetings with this and that arriving friend, proclaimed him, even before you heard him speak, as good a gentleman as he was an athlete.

"Redwood's in form to-day," said some one. "We'd better stop and see the play."

"Is that Redwood, the captain?" inquired I, in an awestruck way, of Warminster.

"Rather," was the reply, in a tone of pride which convinced me that Low Heath was proud of its chief, even though he had the misfortune to be a day boy.

Just then Redwood turned and waved his hand to somebody near us.

"Look out; he wants you," said Langrish.

"Me?" said I, flabbergasted.

"Don't you see him beckoning? Look alive, or you'll catch it."

I could hardly believe it; and yet everybody near looked round at me in apparent wonder at my delay.

Perhaps Redwood had heard something about me from Tempest and wanted to--

"Go on," said Trimble, giving me a shove. "If he wants to stick you in the Fifteen, tell him it's not good enough."

"Look sharp," called the others, encouragingly, as I started to obey the summons.

By this time Redwood was strolling our way. Mahomet, thought I, is coming to the mountain. So, to save him trouble, I trotted up to meet him.

At first he didn't notice me. Then when I said, "Did you want me?" he stared me over from head to foot as a Newfoundland dog would inspect a pug. It was on the whole a benevolent stare, not unmingled with humour; especially when the cheers of my late comrades called his attention to my ingenuous blushes.

"I didn't," said he; "but you'll do, if you don't mind. Cut home to my house. Number 3, Bridge Street, and ask them to send my leather belt. Look alive, there's a good chap."

This speech, the first really polite speech I had heard since I entered Low Heath, took me by storm, and captivated me at once to the service of the captain of the school. I galloped off, as proud as a non- commissioned officer who has been sent to fetch his regimental flag on to the field of battle. The chaps behind might cheer and jeer and cry, "Gee-up, Sarah!" and "Mad dog!" as much as they liked. They would have been only too proud to be sent on my errand.

It was a good ten minutes' run to Bridge Street, and I was fairly out of breath when I rang at the bell of Number 3. It seemed a long time before any one came, and I was beginning to be afraid I should forfeit the reputation I hoped to acquire, when hurried footsteps announced that my ring had been heard.

Mrs Redwood was out, said the servant, and she had been down the garden with the children.

When I delivered my message, she asked me to wait; and with her little charges evidently on her mind, ran upstairs to fetch the belt.

It was a nice house, although a small one. The garden door was open, and gave a beautiful peep over the little sloping lawn to the river and the woods beyond. I was not sure that, after all, a town-boy might not have a good time of it, living in a place like this, instead of in school.

Suddenly my reflections were disturbed by a shrill scream from the garden, followed by a little girl of five or six crying--

"Annie, Annie! Mamie's tumbled in; Mamie's tumbled in!"

For a wonder I had my wits about me, and divined the truth at once. With a bound I was down the steps and across the lawn, half knocking down the panic-stricken little messenger on the way, and at the river's edge, floundering piteously in about two feet of water, found the unfortunate little Mamie--evidently a twin-sister--more frightened than hurt, but perilously near to getting into deep water.

Her yells redoubled when she found herself grabbed by the sash by a stranger, and lugged most unceremoniously on to *terra firma*.

Scarcely had I achieved this gallant rescue, without even wetting my own shoes, when Annie, as white as a sheet, came flying on to the scene.

"It's all right," said I; "she's not hurt."

Whereupon Annie most inconsiderately leaned up against a post, clapped her hands to her heart, and went or threatened to go off into hysterics. And there was I, a poor unprotected male, left to face the squalling of two infant female children and a full-grown female nurserymaid!

"Look here," said I, appealingly, "Mamie's soaking wet. You'd better take her and dry her, before she gets her death of cold."

This appeal had the desired effect. It stopped the nurse's spasms and let loose her tongue.

"Oh dear, oh my! And I told her not to go through the gate. Oh, you naughty girl you; and you. Miss Gwen, for letting her do it. Come in directly, you little hussies!"

It struck me as grossly unfair of Annie; but I did not venture in her present state of mind to protest, for fear she should call me hussy too. I followed indoors, somewhat guiltily, at the tail of the procession, feeling myself in a very unpleasant situation, in which I would not on any account be caught by Redwood's mother or by Redwood himself. To my delight, on the floor of the hall, where Annie had dropped it, lay the belt, at which I sprang greedily, and not waiting to say thank you, or put in a word for the doomed infants, which would have been quite inaudible in the volume of Annie's philippics, I saved myself (as the Frenchman says), and ran at racing speed with my prize back to the school field.

To my mortification I found the match had just begun, and it would be impossible to deliver my missive till half-time. What would the captain think of me? Would he suspect me of having dawdled to buy sweets, or look over the bridge, or gossip with a chum? I would not for anything it had happened, and felt not at all amiably disposed to Miss Mamie, as the inconsiderate cause of my delay.

However, there was nothing for it but to wait. I resolved not to put myself into the clutches of the Philosophers till my mission was discharged, for fear of accident; so I seated myself on one of the pavilion steps and watched the play.

It was evidently a hot match for a scratch one. As far as I could make out, the remnants of last season's Fifteen, amounting to eleven veterans only, were playing the next Fifteen, who, having the best of the wind, were giving a dangerously good account of themselves. They were acute enough to make all the use they could of the favouring element by keeping open order and kicking whenever they had the chance, whereas of course the other side played a tight game, and ran with the ball. Even for a novice like myself, it was interesting to watch a contest of this kind. The Fifteen evidently hoped to rush the thing and carry their goal before half-time deprived them of the wind, whereas the Eleven were mainly concerned to keep on the defensive and risk nothing by over- haste.

Among the veterans I could distinguish the big form of Redwood, always close to the ball, and near him with a shudder I recognised Crofter working hard, while hovering on the wing of the scrimmage was the genial Pridgin, looking as if he would fain be in bed, but, when the time for action came, making it very uncomfortable for the enemy. On the other side I was not long in finding out Tempest, with the glow of enthusiasm on his cheek as now and again he broke through the ruck and sent the ball into quarters. Wales, too, was there, spick and span as usual, playing neatly and effectively, and withal elegantly.

As time wore on it was evident the veterans were being penned closer and closer by their antagonists. Presently a dangerous scrimmage was formed just in front of their goal. For some minutes the ball was invisible, then by an apparently preconcerted movement the forwards of the Fifteen loosened and let it dart back into the open behind them, where lurked Tempest ready to receive it. He did not wait to pick it up, but ran to meet it with a flying kick. For a moment it seemed doubtful whether it would clear the onward rush of Redwood and his forwards. But it did, and rose steadily and beautifully over their heads, and with the wind straight upon it, reached the goal and skimmed over the bar, amid the loud shouts of every one, conspicuous among which was my shrill voice.

Half-time! Now was my chance; and before the shouting had ceased, or the discomfited Eleven had quite realised their misfortune, I darted into the sacred enclosure, and presented the captain with his belt.

"I'm awfully sorry I wasn't in time," said I. "You'd just begun when I got back."

"Thanks, youngster, it's all right," said Redwood, wonderfully cheerful, as it seemed to me; "here, take care of this for me," and he divested himself of the belt he was wearing and donned the new one.

"You'll have the wind with you now," I ventured to observe.

"Yes," said he with a nod, "I think we shall do the trick this time, eh?"

"Rather," said I; and departed elated, not so much to have been spared the rebuke I expected, but to be talked to by such a hero, as if I was not a junior at all, but a comrade.

My chums when I rejoined them were anxious to prevent my being too much puffed up by my exploit.

"Good old Sarah Toady," cried Trimble, as I approached. "Is he coming?"

"Who? Where?" I inquired.

"I thought you were asking Redwood to tea or something."

"No, I wasn't--I only--"

"There's Jarman," cried Langrish. "Run and cadge up to him. Perhaps he'll pat you on the back too."

Despite these taunts I could not fail to notice the depressing effect of the new arrival on the onlookers generally. Mr Jarman, the gymnasium master, was a ruddy, restless-looking man of about thirty-five, with cold grey eyes, and the air of a man who knew he was unpopular, but was resolved to do his duty nevertheless. If I had heard nothing about him before, I should have disliked him at first glance, and instinctively tried to avoid his eye. And yet, as he stood there, talking to Mr Selkirk, the melancholy master of the reputedly "fast" house at Low Heath, he did not look particularly offensive.

"Look out now; they're starting again."

There was no mistaking the veterans now. Their backs were up, and the order had evidently gone out for no quarter to be given to the audacious Fifteen.

Redwood's kick off all but carried the goal from the middle of the field, and from that moment it never got out of the "thirties," as the imaginary line between the two distance flags was called. To Crofter belonged the honour of first wiping off scores with the enemy. And after him Redwood dropped a goal, first from one side line, then from the other. Pridgin, too, scored a smart run in; but, unluckily, the kick fouled the goal post and saved the Fifteen a further disaster then. But before time was called a fourth goal was placed to the credit of the veterans. The vanquished fought gamely to the end. Once or twice Tempest broke away, but for want of effective backing was repulsed. And once a smart piece of dribbling down the touch line by Wales gave the Eleven's half-backs an anxious moment. But that was all. The match ended, as every one expected, in a slashing victory for the old hands, together with a general verdict that Tempest and Wales, at any rate, had won their laurels and were safe for two of the vacant caps.

In the stampede which followed I missed my opportunity of restoring Redwood's property, as he vanished immediately after the game, and my comrades would by no means allow me out of their sight. Indeed, it was not till after evening chapel that I contrived to elude their vigilance and start on my second run to Bridge Street.

But if I eluded them I was less fortunate with another sentinel. For at the gates

I encountered the forbidding presence of Mr Jarman.

"What are you doing here?"

"Please, sir, this is Redwood's belt, and I promised to give it to him."

"Go back. What is your name?"

"Jones, sir."

"Whose house are you in?"

"Mr Sharpe's."

"Do not let me find you out of bounds again, Jones."

And he fixed me with his eye as if to impress me with the fact that he would certainly know me again.

"But, sir, Redwood--"

"Did you hear me, sir?"

I capitulated, cowed and indignant. I was beginning to understand what the fellows said about Mr Jarman.

"It's all rot," said the Philosophers, when I confided my grievance to them; "it's not out of bounds before 6:30--and if it was, it's no business of his. It's the house master's business, or the house captain's. If you get lagged by them, all right; but *he's* got no right to lag fellows, the cad."

In my present humour I was far from disputing the appellation.

CHAPTER ELEVEN.
CHEAP ADVERTISING EXTRAORDINARY.

I spent a bad quarter of an hour that evening before bed-time in inditing a letter of "explanation" to Crofter. I had come to the conclusion this would be easier and safer than a personal interview, and that the sooner it was done the better. How to do it was another problem. To write a letter in the raggery was out of the question. I tried it, but failed miserably. For either my paper was twitched away from under my pen, or some one looked over my shoulder and pretended to read expressions of endearment which were not there, or some one got under the table and heaved it about tempestuously to the detriment of my handwriting, or some one drew skeleton figures of spider-legged bipeds on the margin of the paper. Worse still, it was evident every word I wrote would be common property, which I did not desire. I had therefore to abandon the attempt till later on; when, finding myself in Pridgin's study, I ventured to inquire if I might write there.

Pridgin was good enough to express admiration of my cheek, but said if I spread one newspaper over his carpet and another over his table-cloth to catch the blots, and didn't ask him how to spell any word of less than four letters, or borrow a stamp, I might.

All which I faithfully undertook to do, and sat down to my delicate task. It took me a long time, considering the result, and I was by no means satisfied with the performance when it was done.

"Dear Crofter," I wrote; but that seemed too familiar, whereas "Dear Sir" from one schoolfellow to another was too formal. So I attempted my explanation in the "oblique oration":--

"Jones iv. is sorry he accidentally told Crofter he was a beast yesterday. He did not know it was him when he saw him, or he would not have told him what Tempest said about him, which was quite unintentional. He also must explain that what he said about his being expelled was in consequence of a dog's death, about which there was a misunderstanding. He hopes Crofter will not tell him he told him, as he would be very angry with him."

"Done?" said Pridgin, who, comfortably ensconced in his easy-chair with his feet upon the window-ledge, was reading a comic paper.

"Yes, thanks," said I, half terrified lest he should demand to read my not too lucid epistle.

"All right. Go and tell Crofter I want him, will you? Look alive, and then cut to bed."

Here was a blow! I had been at all this labour in order to avoid the painful necessity of an interview with Crofter, and here I was as badly off as ever.

"Can't you hear?" said Pridgin as I hesitated.

"If you please, Pridgin," said I, resolved to take the bull by the horns, "I'm awfully sorry, but I don't want Crofter to catch me. The fact is--"

Pridgin's good-humoured reply was to shy a book at me, which I was fortunate enough to miss, but which Tempest, who entered the study at the moment, caught fairly on his forehead.

"Hullo! Are you and the kid playing catch?" said he. "Sorry to disturb you, really; but my fag's skulking somewhere, and I want to borrow yours to take a message to Crofter."

"Was it a plot, or what? I had far better have written in the faggery after all."

"That was exactly the subject about which the kid and I were playing catch just now," said Pridgin. "I asked him to go to Crofter too."

"What, has he been sending you a *billet-doux*?" said Tempest.

"Well, yes. He seems to be sore I didn't ask him to tea yesterday, and says he's afraid some one has been libelling him, though how he knew I had any one here last night I can't imagine."

"That's funny," said Tempest; "he writes to me to say he is sorry I should take the trouble to call him a beast in public. He understands a fellow's right to his private opinion, he says, and would be sorry not to be allowed his about me, but he thinks it imprudent to shout it out for every one to hear. Just his style."

"I was going to send him word to ask him to come in and make himself a cup of tea out of my pot, just to show there was no ill-feeling," said Pridgin.

"And I was going to say that I hope he won't trouble to think better of me in private then I think of him in public. Though for the life of me I can't imagine what he refers to."

"The fact is. Tempest," said Pridgin, putting his feet up on the window-ledge again, "it's just as well to be above board with Crofter. He's a slippery customer, and if he knows what we think of him, and we know what he thinks of us, we shall get on much better."

"If he'd only give a chap a chance of a row with him," said Tempest; "but he won't. The more down on him you are, the more affectionate he is, and the sweeter he smiles. Ugh!"

"But who on earth has been blabbing to him?" said Pridgin; "not Wales?"

"Wales?" said Tempest; "rather not. He's not that sort."

"I don't think he is," said Pridgin; "and yet, old man--the fact is-- I--"

"You don't fancy Wales, I know."

"Hardly that. I don't mind him; but he's more of a pull over you than he has over me. I can't be bothered with his fashions. It's too much grind. But you aren't lazy like me, and--well--you know he runs you into a lot of expense. That picnic last term, for instance. We could have had quite a jolly day for half the cost. Chicken and ham's all very well, but cold boiled eggs are just as good for keeping a chap going."

"But Wales can't stand things not being--"

"Dear!" said Pridgin. "Don't flare up, old chap. You've got your work cut out for you this term, and can't afford to spend all your time paying bills, even if you had the tin."

"All very well for you who've let me in for cocking the house," said Tempest, with a laugh. "Anyhow, you've a right to talk to me like a father. All the same, I fancy you've a little downer on old Wales. He's a good sort of chap, and there's nothing of the eel about him."

"Which brings us back to Crofter," said Pridgin. "Some one has told him that he's not popular in this study, and he doesn't like it. I wonder who our candid friend is."

"It was me," said I, coming out at last with my pent-up confession. "I'm awfully sorry, Tempest. It was this--"

"Take a seat," said Tempest, putting me off in the identical way that Crofter had done yesterday. But I was not to be put off; I took a seat and continued--

"I met him and didn't know who he was, and I mentioned that I'd come from here, and that a tea was going on, and that Crofter was out of it, and the reason was because Tempest thought him a beast. And--I'm awfully sorry, Tempest--I let out to him that we'd been expelled from Dangerfield, and I'd not the least idea it was him."

"He," suggested Pridgin.

"He; and I've just been writing to him to explain."

"Rather a tough job, eh?" said Tempest.

"You may see the letter," said I.

The two seniors read it with a gravity which scarcely seemed genuine.

"I think it may pass," said Tempest, coming out at last with a laugh. "There are only about twelve 'he's' and 'him's' in it, and as it will be absolutely unintelligible it can't possibly do harm."

"If Crofter has the least sense of literary taste, he will frame it," said Pridgin. "I trust no dogs' deaths will occur here."

My confusion was tempered by the relief I felt that they took my indiscretion in such good part, and saw only--what I failed to see myself--the humorous side of the incident.

I begged hard to be allowed to tear up my letter, but this they would by no means allow. On the contrary, I was compelled to address it and stamp it then and there, and place it in the post-box in the hall. Then, with compliments and good wishes, I was dismissed to bed, and left the two friends talking school politics.

I felt a good deal more humbled by the manner in which they had received my confession than if they had, as I had expected, roundly abused me. To be let down easy, as if I was barely responsible for my actions, was not conducive to my vanity; and if that was the object they had in view, it was amply attained. I went to bed on my second night at Low Heath with as little vanity in me as I could decently do with; and even that, as I lay awake for an hour or two, oozed away, and did not return till in a happy moment I fell asleep, and once more, and for a few unconscious hours, became a hero to myself.

The next morning I tumbled out of bed at the call of the bell in no very light-hearted way. First of all, Crofter would receive my letter; secondly, I had still got Redwood's belt; thirdly, I had not done my preparation; and fourthly, I felt concerned about Tempest and his alliance with the expensive Wales. Strangely enough, this last trouble weighed on me most as I dressed.

Tempest, I knew, was not well off. But he was proud, and not the sort of fellow to shirk a thing on account of the cost. I could remember at Dangerfield his spending all his money at the beginning of the term on an absurdly expensive cricket bag, and having to go without spikes in his shoes because he could not afford a set. At Low Heath, where seniors were allowed to run up bills in certain shops, I was certain his ignorance about money matters, added to the friendly encouragements of an exquisite like Wales, would make it all the worse for him. Why, even *I* knew more about money than he did, and could reckon that if I brought thirteen shillings up at the beginning of the term, I should have just a shilling a week to bless myself with till break-up. Whereas he, I verily believe, would consider that he had thirteen shillings a week. And the worst of it was he would never let any one know how hard up he was, or tolerate any remarks, except from a privileged chum like Pridgin, on the subject.

As I joined my comrades in the faggery, in the fond hope of snatching a precious quarter of an hour for my neglected studies, I found great excitement and jubilation afoot. The printer had sent home the handbills of the Conversation Club.

"That ought to do our business," said Langrish, flourishing one of the documents in my face.

I took it, and read it with mingled pride and concern. It ran as follows:--

Under the distinguished Patronage of the Nobility and Gentry of Low Heath:

A Philosophical Conversation Club has been started for conversation on Philosophy, Picnics, and Cross-country Runs. Meetings weekly; to be announced. Subscription: Two shillings in advance; every member to find himself. No town-boys or masters eligible. "Come in your hundreds!!! No questions asked. Evening dress or flannels. The Inaugural Picnic next week. Particulars on receipt of subscription. No connection with any other so-called club in Low Heath! For further particulars apply to the following:

Sarah Jones, Esquire, Pr.Ph.C.C, President.
Ted Langrish, Esquire, S.Ph.C.C, Secretary.
Wilfred Trimble, Esquire, T.Ph.C.C, Treasurer.
Jos. Warminster, Esquire, L.Ph.C.C, Librarian.
Tom Coxhead, Esquire, A.Ph.C.C, Auditor.
Michael Purkis, Esquire, R.Ph.C.C, Registrar.

P.S.--As the membership is strictly limited to 500, early application is advised. No eligible cash offer refused! Our motto is "***Mens sano in corpore sanae***."

I naturally bridled up at the record of my own name.

"Look here," said I; "you've stuck it down wrong again."

"Awfully sorry," said Langrish; "the printer chaps made a little slip over the Christian name, but all the rest seems right. It's wonderful how sharp they are, isn't it?"

"But you're going to have it corrected, surely?" said I.

"Why, it would cost a frightful lot!" protested the company. "We might alter it in ink, but that would only call attention to it. Bless you, no one will notice it. They'll put it down to a printer's error."

I was by no means satisfied, but their delight at the whole performance was so unbounded that it was impossible to be as angry as I felt.

"It'll draw, and no mistake," said Trimble, who had evidently never seen his name in print before. "Jolly well drawn up of you, Lang."

"Oh," said Langrish modestly, "when you know what you want to say, it's easy enough to stick it down."

"That's why you stuck down 'Sarah,' I suppose," said I, rather crossly.

"I never knew such a kid as you," retorted Langrish; "you seem to fancy nobody can think of anything but you and your washerwoman."

The conversation was drifting on to dangerous ground, and Warminster promptly changed the subject.

"The thing now will be to put the papers about. I vote we each take a batch and give them round."

"We might shove them under the fellows' doors," said Coxhead.

"The best way will be to do it in Big Hall," said the more practical Purkis.

"One or two of us can easily get in ten minutes early, and stick one on every chap's place."

"But suppose you stick one on a day boy's place?" I suggested.

"What's the odds? the paper tells him he's out of it," replied Purkis.

It occurred to me that this would not cheer the day boy very much; still, on the whole, Purkis's suggestion seemed the best.

"I tell you what," said Langrish, "I beg to move and second that the President be authorised to stick round the papers."

"I third and fourth that," said Trimble.

"Carried unanimously," said Langrish.

"Look here, one of you had better do it," said I, feeling a little alarmed at this imposing honour; "you know the way better."

"That's where you've the pull," said Purkis; "you're a new kid, they won't interfere with you. Big Hall's at five, and you can easily slide in at a quarter to, and do the trick. Hullo, there's bell."

School that morning went uncomfortably for me. I escaped being "lagged" for my neglect of preparation, chiefly owing to the friendly prompting I received from Dicky Brown. But it was a time of anxiety and trepidation, and my nerves were somewhat strained before it was over.

The shock of the day, however, awaited me as I got outside on my way to the fields.

A small youth of my own size accosted me.

"I say, are you the new chap?"

"What new chap?"

"The new chap that Redwood told to fetch his belt."

"Yes," said I, turning a little pale.

"All right. You've got to go to him, sharp."

"I tried to give it him back yesterday, really I did; but I was stopped," said I. "Do you think I'll get in a row?"

"I wouldn't be in your shoes, that's all I know," remarked the messenger brutally. "It'll be all the worse if you don't cut."

"Where is he?"

"In the captain's room at the School House."

I went off with my heart in my boots. And I had hoped so much to show up well to Redwood! It was all Jarman's fault, and I wrote down yet another grudge against him in my mental book.

The captain was alone, and evidently expecting me, as he rose and came to meet me when I appeared.

"Here you are, then, youngster," said he, in a tone which, if it meant a licking, was a very deceptive one.

"I'm very sorry," said I; "I tried to bring the belt round yesterday evening, but--"

"Hang the belt!" said the captain. "That's not what I want you for. Why didn't you tell me what happened at home yesterday afternoon?"

Then it was another row altogether I was in for! What, I wondered, had I done! Surely he didn't suspect me of having pushed his young sister into the water?

"I didn't like, while the match was on. I didn't know Mamie had tumbled in, or I would have stopped her."

"But you fished her out?" he asked.

"I told Annie to take her and dry her," said I, wondering where the blow was going to fall. "You see, she went upstairs for the belt, and it was when she had gone it happened. I don't think it was her fault."

To my amazement Redwood laughed and clapped me on the back.

"You young donkey, don't you know you saved Mamie's life, and I want to say 'Thank you,' to you?"

This unexpected ***denouement*** alarmed me almost as much as my previous misgivings.

"Oh no, really I didn't," said I; "she was close to the edge."

"Another inch or two and she would have been in six feet of water," said he. Then, with a friendly laugh, he added--

"You may not have meant to save her life; but you did, and must take the consequences. My mother wants you to come to tea to-morrow. Call here for me after evening chapel, and we'll go together. Good-bye now, and thanks, youngster."

I could hardly tell if I was on my head or my heels as I walked back. It had never occurred to me till now that I had done anything out of the common in fishing Miss Mamie out of her muddy bath. Indeed, I still felt I was getting credit I did not deserve, and blushed to myself. As to the invitation for to-morrow, that seemed to me a burst of glory quite past my present comprehension, and I resolved to treasure it as a secret in my own bosom until at least I had made sure it was not a dream.

Before then, however, I had less pleasant work on hand. My comrades did not fail to remind me several times during the afternoon of my "promise," as they called it, to distribute the Conversation Club circulars in Great Hall, and adjured me not to run it too fine. The consequence was that, at a quarter to five, I was convoyed, with the bundle of papers under my arm, to the door of the dining-hall, and gently shoved inside, with all retreat cut off until my task was done.

Some of the servants who were laying the tables objected to my presence, but on my explaining I had been sent to do it, they allowed me without interruption to lay a copy of the precious document on each of the five hundred plates. I had barely concluded this arduous duty when the bell commenced to ring, and the fellows in twos and threes began to drop in. It was all I could do to affect unconsciousness, as from a modest retreat near the door I marked the effect of the announcement on Low Heath generally. At first there was a note of surprise; then, as one after another read on, a titter, and finally a general laugh, which was only checked by the entrance of the masters and the call to grace.

I had--being a stranger to the place--distributed my favours among the masters quite as liberally as among the boys, and presently, with horror, perceived Dr England rise in his place with his copy in his hand.

"Whew!" whistled Langrish, "there's a row on, I fancy."

"Serve you right if there is," said Trimble. "Why ever did you put them on *that* table?"

"How was I to know?" groaned I.

"What boy," said the doctor, when silence prevailed, "what boy has been putting this foolish paper round the hall?"

Oh dear! How I wished I was safe at home!

"Please, sir, I did," said I, rising meekly in my place.

"Your name?"

"Jones iv., please, sir."

"Then come at once, Jones iv., and collect them again, every one, and write out two hundred lines. Let dinner proceed now."

If the object of the promoters of the Philosophical Conversation Club had been cheap advertisement, they must have been amply gratified. Hercules never performed any labour equal to mine that afternoon. The masters handed me up their copies gravely and reproachfully; but the Low Heathens generally made sport of my misery. Scarcely one in ten would part with his rare broadside, and those who did made it manifest that they had the contents by heart. The unfortunate "misprint" of my Christian name, moreover, was the occasion for much ribald comment.

When, finally, I reached the quarters of my own particular comrades, I received more kicks than papers. They were unkind enough to say I had mulled the whole thing, and to promise me untold penalties when they got me in the privacy of the faggery.

At last, when the pudding was almost vanishing, I sat down to my hard- earned meal. But it mattered little, for I could have eaten nothing.

Be that as it may, the Philosophical Conversation Club was able to boast that afternoon that it had attracted the attention and interest of every member of the school, from the headmaster down to the junior fag. And few school clubs can boast as much as that!

CHAPTER TWELVE.
A COMMITTEE OF WAYS AND MEANS.

"Where are you going?" demanded the faggery next afternoon, as I tried to desert them after afternoon chapel. "To take up your lines to England?"

I should have preferred that they had not asked me the question, but having asked it I felt bound to answer.

"No; I'm going to tea at a fellow's."

"Who? The washerwoman's?"

"No; to Redwood's."

I tried to pronounce the name with the unconcern of a man who is in daily communion with heroes, but I fear I betrayed my emotion. At least, their laughter made me think so.

I was instantly greeted with all sorts of mock salutations and obeisances, and, whether I liked it or not, rushed off to the faggery to be tidied up. It was in vain I struggled, and explained that Redwood was waiting for me. They would not be put off.

"You must wash your face for the credit of the Ph.C.C," said Langrish.

"And put on a clean shirt for the credit of your wash--"

Here by a frantic effort I broke loose and made off, followed by the pack in full cry, with shouts of--

"Stop thief!"

"Welsher?"

"Clear the course!" "Hurry up for tea there!" and other exclamations of a similar nature.

It was not certainly a very dignified way of accepting a friend's invitation; still, it would have been worse had I remained in their clutches.

As it was, I only just made the schoolhouse door before Warminster and Cox-head were up to me, and presented myself to my host painfully out of breath and red in the face.

"Been having a trot over?" said he, with a nod.

"Yes, a little," I gasped.

"I'm ready; come along."

My heart sunk within me, as, on reaching the door, I saw my five comrades, all apparently by accident, hovering round to see me go out. They did their best, and very successfully too, to stare me out of countenance, and encourage my blushes by allusions to "Sarah" and my tin sleeve-links, and the smudges on my face, and by cries of "shrimps" and "muffins," and other awkward allusions.

Redwood, as became the cock of the school, affected not to hear their ribald remarks, though he must have caught a word or two, and inquired,--

"Been playing football since you came?"

"No, not yet," said I, painfully aware that Trimble and Langrish were walking behind us critically; "that is, yes, a little."

I was glad when we reached the big gates, and were able to shake off the enemy, who continued audible comments till I was out of earshot, and finally went off on some new quest.

At Number 3, Bridge Street, I found myself, much to my discomfort, quite a hero. Mrs Redwood, a gentle-looking lady, kissed me effusively, so did little Miss Gwen, who having once begun could scarcely be prevailed upon to leave off. The servants smiled approvingly, as did a lady visitor, who shook me by the hand. The only person who did not appear to rejoice to see me was the heroine of the occasion, Miss Mamie, who declined altogether to kiss me, and added I was a naughty big boy to spoil her nice sash, and ought to be sent to bed.

To her mother's protests and brother's encouragement she was quite obdurate. No; she hated me, she said, for spoiling her nice sash, and wild horses would not draw from her a contrary declaration.

After which we were summoned to tea, and I was consoled for this base ingratitude by plum jam and "sally-lunn" and sultana cake and other delicacies, which only a schoolboy, well on in the term, knows how fully to appreciate.

The talk was limited; first because I made it a rule not to talk with my mouth full, and secondly, because, had that difficulty been removed, I had nothing to say. Redwood, fine fellow that he was, did not try to pump me, and the ladies, who kept up most of the talk, most conveniently worded their observations in such a form as not to call for a reply.

After tea, however, I did find myself talking to Mrs Redwood about my mother, and presently to Redwood about Dangerfield and my previous acquaintance with Tempest and Brown.

"Brown iii. is a town-boy," said the captain. "I wish we'd had him in. Is he a member of your wonderful club, by the way?"

I blushed. Of course Redwood had seen that fatal document yesterday!

"Ah--well, you know, that is only for chaps in the school."

"Rather rough on us town-boys," said Redwood, with a laugh.

"I'm sure they'd be delighted to have you," said I.

"Ah, well, our fellows have a club of their own," said he, "although they don't talk philosophy. By the way, is your Christian name correctly printed?" asked he.

"Oh, no," said I; "that was Languish's fault. He says it was a printer's error, but I'm sure he did it on purpose."

"It helps to call attention to the club," said the captain, laughing. "Your lot seems to be fond of its little joke, to judge by the specimens that came to see us off just now."

"I'm awfully sorry," said I; "they do fool about so--I say, I hope you aren't in a wax about it."

He certainly did not look it.

I went up with him to his den, and we had quite a long talk, and somehow without seeming to mean it, he managed to knock a great deal of nonsense out of my head, and incite me to put my back into the work of the term.

"I suppose," said he, "you mean to back up Tempest now he's cock of Sharpe's? You kids can make it pretty hot in a house if you choose."

"Oh, we're all backing up Tempest," said I, "especially now he's got his colours."

"All serene," said the captain; "he'll pull through well, then."

I stayed till it was time for Redwood to go over to the school for a committee of the Sports Club. I did not leave Number 3 without a standing invitation to come in whenever I liked, or without painful apologies for the contumacy of Mamie.

Redwood and I had just reached the bridge when some one confronted us whom I recognised at once as Mr Jarman.

"Ah, Redwood, you've a meeting on. Who's this boy? Ah, I remember-- Jones iv. What did I say to you yesterday, Jones?"

"Jones has been to tea at my house," said the captain, with a flush, and looking less amiable than I had yet seen him.

"It's after hours," said Mr Jarman, coolly. "I cautioned him yesterday. A hundred lines, Jones iv., by to-morrow evening."

"It's not his fault," said Redwood; "I gave him leave, sir."

"We need not discuss this, Redwood," said Mr Jarman, and walked away.

I felt quite sufficiently avenged when I saw the captain's face. He strode on some distance in silence, and then said,--

"I'm sorry, youngster. It can't be helped, though. Jarman's strictly in the right, though it's sharp practice. You'd better cut in now. Good night."

"Good night," said I, making off. But he called me back.

"You'd better do the doctor's lines to-night. Leave Jarman's till the morning."

"All right."

And I departed, not a little impressed with the incident.

The captain had disappointed me a little. I should have liked to see him knock Jarman down, or at least openly defy him; whereas he seemed to back him up, although much against his will. The net result to me was that I had three hundred lines to write on my third day at school, and that, for a well-meaning youth, was tribulation enough.

I took Redwood's advice and wrote the doctor's lines that evening, trusting to a chance next forenoon of satisfying the demands of Mr Jarman. To their credit be it said, some of the faggery helped me out with my task, and as we all wrote in the same style of penmanship, namely, a back-handed slope spread out very wide to cover as much ground as possible, it was very difficult when all was done to believe that the performance was a co-operative one.

Before going to bed I told Tempest of my adventure, and had the satisfaction of receiving his complete sympathy.

"That's the worst of Redwood--he'll let it all slide. I wish I'd been with you when it happened. There'd have been a row. There will some day, too."

All which was very consoling to me and helped me to sleep soundly.

But the surprise of surprises happened next morning when I encountered the captain's fag at the door before breakfast with a letter in his hand.

"Here you are," said he, thrusting the document on me. "I don't see why you can't come and fetch your own things instead of me having to run after you."

"You can walk," said I, "I suppose."

I meant to be conciliatory, but he was highly offended and began to kick, and it took some little time to pacify him and induce him to return to the bosom of his house.

When he had gone, I opened the envelope with some little curiosity. What was my astonishment when I found it enclosed one hundred lines written out in a bold clear hand, which it was easy to guess was that of the captain himself!

There was no letter or message; but the explanation was clear enough. Redwood having got me into my row, had, like a gentleman, paid the penalty; and as I realised this I could have kicked myself for the unworthy thoughts I had indulged about him.

I only wished Jarman, to whom in due time I handed the precious document, could have known its history.

He evidently gave me credit for being an excellent writer, and perhaps for having an unusual acquaintance, for a boy of my age, with the works of the Immortal Bard. For Redwood had grimly selected the following passage to write out over and over again for the police-master's benefit: "It is excellent to have a giant's strength; but it is tyrannous to use it like a giant."

I fear the satire was lost on its victim, and that he meekly concluded I had selected the passage because it happened to be in my lesson for the day, and was probably the first to come to hand.

Tempest laughed when I told him.

"It's all very well," said he, "but it's encouraging the enemy. Redwood's a dear old chap, but he's too much of an anything-for-a-quiet- life fellow for captain. By the way, has Crofter replied to your polite letter?"

"No," said I, "not a word, and I haven't seen him."

"Well, take my advice, kid. If he wants to kick you, consider yourself lucky. If he's extra civil, cut him like mischief. Some day you may thank me for the tip."

It seemed queer advice at the time, but I had occasion to call it to mind later on, as the reader will discover.

By the end of my first week I was pretty well domesticated at Low Heath. My chief regret was that I saw so little of Dicky Brown; and when we did meet the only thing we had in common was our lessons, which were not always congenial topics of conversation.

Dicky was fully imbued with the superiority of the town-boy over the house boy, and irritated me sometimes by his repeated regret that I was not eligible for the junior Urbans.

"What do you do?" I inquired.

"Oh, hosts of things. We go in for geology, and part songs, and antiquities, and all that sort of thing; and have excursions--at least, we're going to have one soon--to look for remains."

"Ah! it's a pity you couldn't come to our picnic next week. It's to be no end of a spree."

"Oh, we've heard all about that," said Dicky, with a grin. "*Mens sano in corpore sanae*--you should hear some of our chaps yell about that."

"I'm sure it's not a bad motto," ventured I.

"I don't know about that. But it's not the motto, it's the grammar."

I wasn't quite pleased with Dicky for this. It seemed as if he thought he knew more than other people, which I held to be a reprehensible failing in any one--particularly a day boy. I flattered myself that, as an exhibitioner, he had hardly the right to talk to me about grammar. But it was Dicky's way, and I knew he couldn't help it.

For all that, I referred to the subject in the faggery that evening. My comrades were in high glee. Half a dozen subscriptions had come in, with requests to be allowed to join the picnic, and a considerable number of others had asked to be allowed at half price or on the deferred payment system.

"It's going like anything, Sarah," said Langrish, thumping me violently on the back.

"Where's the picnic to be?" I inquired.

"Wouldn't you like to know?" said the secretary.

I said I would, and, as president, considered I was entitled to the information.

"We're not as green as we look; are we, you chaps?" said Trimble. "Why, you don't suppose we're going to let out and give you a chance of blabbing to the day-boy cads, do you?"

"I'm not any more likely to blab than you are," said I, warmly.

"All serene. You keep your temper--you'll know time enough."

"Suppose I resigned," said I, feeling I must support my dignity.

"Resign away. We've got your subscription."

"I don't mean I shall," said I; "but--"

"Shut up, and don't disturb the committee meeting."

"If I'm president, I suppose I've a right to speak."

"Not till you're asked."

"All right," said I, playing my trump card desperately. "When you do ask me what's wrong with the grammar of your Latin motto, I sha'n't tell you. Ha, ha!-- *corpore sanae*. You should hear the fellows yell."

The effect of this announcement was electrical, Langrish turned white, and Trimble turned red. The others bit their nails in silence. It was a season of delicious triumph to me. I was master of the situation for once, and resolved to remain so as long as possible.

"Why, what's wrong with it?" said Warminster, presently.

"Wouldn't you like to know?" said I.

"*Corpore's* feminine, isn't it?" asked Coxhead.

"Common gender, I fancy," said Purkis; "depends on who the chap is."

"You mean if it was Sarah it would be feminine, and if it was one of us it would be masculine," said Langrish.

This was a nasty one for me, but I held my ground.

"You'd better look it up in the dictionary," said I.

This was diplomatic; for although I knew the motto was wrong I could not quite say what it should have been.

After much labour it was decided that *corpore* was neuter, and that the adjective in consequence must be *sanum*.

A resolution to that effect was proposed and seconded, but an amendment to the effect that as the document had gone out in the name of the president and every one knew it was his work, it was no business of the present company to help him out of the mess, was carried by a large majority.

With which delightful solution of the difficulty--delightful to every one but myself--we proceeded to the order of the day, which was to arrange the details of our picnic next half-holiday.

My colleagues remained obdurate on the question of revealing the place.

"If the day fellows get wind of it they'll be sure to try to do us," was the unfailing reply.

"Why shouldn't *I* know as well as you?" demanded I.

Whereupon it was explained that nobody knew where the place was to be yet--nor indeed was he likely to know till the morning of the day, when lots would be drawn.

Every member of the council would then be permitted to write the name of a place on a piece of paper, which would be shuffled in a hat and drawn for--the last paper drawn to be the place. I could not help admiring the elaborateness of the precautions, which had only this drawback, as far as I was concerned, that I did not yet know one place from another.

I casually asked Dicky one day if he knew any of the places round.

"What for, picnics and that sort of thing?" he demanded.

"Well--that sort of thing," said I, anxious not to betray my object too precisely.

"I don't know. I heard some chaps talking about Camp Hill Bottom--where the battle was, you know."

I did not know, but it sounded a likely place, and I made a mental note of it for the eventful day.

Meanwhile there was much to be decided. First, as to the applicants for admission on reduced terms, it was agreed if these brought their fair share of provender, and in consideration of their being taken on the cheap would undertake to row or tow the boats up stream, they might come. Then as to the bill of fare, it was resolved that no one should be allowed to take more than he could carry in his pockets--great-coat pockets not to be used.

Then as to the programme; this was drawn up with a view to combine entertainment and instruction in even quantities. For the entertainment was set down the President's "Inorgural"--the spelling was Langrish's-- address, a part song of the committee, and a public open-air debate or conservation on "Beauty." The credit of the last suggestion really belonged to Tempest, whom I unofficially consulted as to some good subjects for philosophical discussion. For the instructive part of the day's proceedings there was to be the dinner, a boat race, a tug of war, and, if funds permitted, a display of fireworks.

What concerned me chiefly in the arrangements was that I, as president, was held responsible for everything of a difficult or hazardous nature. For instance, I was sent down to select the two boats, and drive a bargain for their hire. Then again, when, owing to the prompt payment of two or three of the "paupers" (as the applicants for reduced terms were politely styled) rather than submit to the terms imposed, it was discovered that half-a-crown of the club funds remained unused, it was I who was sent into Low Heath to buy squibs and Roman candles; and it was I who was appointed to take charge of the explosives in my hat-box under my bed till the time arrived for letting them off.

I began to be anxious about my numerous responsibilities (to which, by the way, was added that of replying in the negative on the question of Beauty), for every day something fresh was put on my shoulders, and every day I found my school work falling into arrears.

Tempest and Pridgin both mildly hinted to me that I didn't seem to be knocking myself up with work, and succeeded in making me uncomfortable on that score. What concerned me still more was to find that Dicky Brown, although not an exhibitioner, kept steadily above me in class, and put me under frequent obligations by helping me out of difficulties.

Never mind, thought I, it will soon be all right--when once the Conversation Club picnic is over.

The morning of the eventful day dawned at last; fair on the whole, but not brilliant. The faggery was astir early, and before breakfast the solemn ceremony of drawing lots for the scene of our revels took place. I faithfully set down Camp Hill Bottom on my paper and committed it to the hat.

Tempest, who chanced to look in with an order for his fag, was requested as a favour to officiate as drawer, which he good-naturedly did. It was anxious work while he pulled out the first five papers and tossed them unopened into the fireplace. Then he drew the sixth and opened it.

"Camp Hill Botton," he read.

Every one seemed pleased, first, because every one had written it on his paper, and secondly, because it was the only really good place for a river picnic.

"There's one comfort about it," said Tempest, as we thanked him for his services, "we shall have a little quiet in this house for an hour or two. Take care of yourselves. Good-bye."

CHAPTER THIRTEEN.
THE PICNIC AT CAMP HILL BOTTOM.

Jorrocks, the school boatman, was a careful person, and suited his accommodation to his company. He knew something about the expeditions of "learned societies" to Camp Hill Bottom and elsewhere, and the conclusion he had evidently come to, was that the boats best suited for their purpose were craft broad in the beam and deep in draught, in which it would be possible to argue out any subject without danger to life or limb.

By a coincidence which afforded more pleasure to my fellow-voyagers than to me, one of the two boats reserved for the use of the Conversation Club was named the *Sarah*, the other rejoicing in the inappropriate name of *Firefly*. I was, of course, voted to a place of honour in the former, along with Langrish, Trimble, and seven other Philosophers of the same kidney; while Coxhead, Warminster, and Purkis took official charge of the *Firefly*, with an equal number of passengers.

It was noticeable, by the way, that at starting it was impossible for any two boys to sit close together, by reason of the stoutness of their pockets, which stood out on either side like rope buoys on the side of a penny steamer. Indeed, some of the party seemed to me to be exceeding the limits laid down by the committee; as, not only were they prominent on either side, but unusually stout in front, which led one to suspect that they had converted their entire waistcoats into pockets for the time being, and stowed the with provisions. But as the chief delinquents in this respect were the members of the executive committee, it was hardly for us to take official notice of it.

A hitch occurred at starting, owing to the uneven distribution of the "paupers" in the two boats. The *Sarah* boasted of six of these, whereas the *Firefly* only possessed one, who, when called upon to fulfil his part of the bargain and row the whole company up stream single-handed, showed an inclination to "rat." The crew of the *Firefly* also began to be concerned as to the length of the voyage under such conditions, and clamoured for at least two of our "paupers"; a claim which Trimble and Langrish indignantly repudiated. At length, however, after a little judicious splashing and a threat to go off on a picnic of their own, the point was yielded, and two of our "paupers" were ignominiously ejected to make room for an equal number of passengers.

This being done, the question arose as to whether we should row up stream or tow. It was decided to proceed by the latter method, at least until the towing-path became impracticable. Whereupon both bands of "paupers" were turned ashore and harnessed to the end of their respective rope, and the rest of us settled down to enjoy our well- earned leisure, and stimulate the exertions of our tugs with friendly exhortations.

I regret to say that the philosophy of our galley-slaves failed to sustain them in their arduous efforts. They began well. The *Sarah* led the way, the *Firefly* following close in our wake. As long as the friendly emulation between the two teams endured, we made fair progress. But when it was discovered that the *Firefly* had meanly hitched itself on to the stern of the *Sarah*, and was permitting our four "paupers" to pull the whole cavalcade, a difference of opinion arose. The *Firefly* tugs, having nothing to do, amused themselves by peppering the inoffensive crew of the *Sarah* with pebbles from the bank; while the outraged pullers of the *Sarah*, finding themselves tricked, struck work altogether, and alter pulling our head round into a bed of tall bulrushes, cast off the yoke and went for their fellow-"paupers." To add to the general confusion, a real barge, towed by a real horse, came down to meet us, threatening with its rope to decapitate the whole of our party, and, whether we liked it or not, to drag us back to Low Heath.

In the midst of all this trouble, I, as president, was loudly and angrily appealed to to "look out" and "make them shut up," and "port the helm, you lout," as if it was all my fault! I tried to explain that it wasn't, but nobody would trouble to listen to me. How we avoided the peril of the barge I really cannot tell. It lumbered past us in a very bad temper, deluging us as it did so with the splashing from its suddenly slackened rope, and indulging in remarks on things in general, and schoolboys in particular, which were not pleasant to listen to, and quite impossible to repeat.

However, as has been truly said, a common danger is often a common blessing. And it turned out so in the present case. The mutinous "paupers" brought their arguments on the bank to a close; and it was decided for the rest of the way to attach the *Firefly* officially to the *Sarah*, and allow the seven tugs to pull the lot. They were quite sufficiently alive to their own interests to see each pulled his fair share; and the progress we made, although not racing speed, was, compared at any rate with our bad quarter of an hour in the bulrushes, satisfactory.

No further adventure happened till Langrish pointed to a wooded hill a quarter of a mile further up stream, and said--

"That's Camp Hill. Jump in, you chaps, and row."

Whereupon the tugs, glad to be relieved, came on board, the two boats cast loose, and the oars were put out.

"Botheration," said Trimble; "there's a boat ahead of us."

"Only some fisherman--he won't hurt," said Langrish.

But as we approached the spot we perceived, not one boat only, but two, drawn up under the trees, and both empty. What was worse, they were Low Heath boats, and bore the name of Jorrocks on their sterns.

The committee looked glum as our party stepped ashore and proceeded to make fast our boats to the trees.

"Why can't Jorrocks send his excursionists somewhere else?" growled Langrish; "I shouldn't wonder if they've bagged the Bottom."

The Camp Hill Bottom was a curious dell among the trees, almost in the shape of a basin, with heather and gorse all round the top, and beautiful velvety grass in the hollow. For a picnic it was an ideal place: close to the water, sheltered from the wind, with plenty of room to sit round, and an expanse of delightful heath and wood behind and on either side.

It was on this heath, the legend went, that one of the most furious battles in the Wars of the Roses was fought, and the Camp Hill marked the place where Earl Warwick's standard waved during the engagement. The Bottom was popularly supposed to have been hollowed out by some monks, as a burial place for the slain; but their benevolent intention had been thwarted by the swoop of a band of marauders, who preferred robbing the slain to burying them, and left most of the monks dead in their own grave.

There is little sign now of this tragic story about the quiet grass- grown hollow, with its fringe of overhanging bushes and carpet of mossy velvet.

Just at present, however, as we made our way to the spot, we had something more important on our minds than Earl Warwick and the unlucky monks. What if the Bottom was already bagged by a crowd of common holidaymakers, and all our carefully planned picnic was to be spoiled by their unwelcome intrusion?

It was too true. As we advanced we could hear sounds of revelry and laughter, interspersed with singing and cheers. Who could it be? The voices sounded suspiciously youthful. Suppose--just suppose that the--

Yes! It was too true! As we reached the edge and looked down on the coveted dell the first sight which greeted our eyes was a party of Low Heathens, sporting the day boys' colours spread out luxuriously on one of the sloping banks, solacing themselves with provender and songs and leap-frog!

I never saw twenty Philosophers look more blank than we did when slowly we realised the horror of the situation. We were done! There could be no doubt that the enemy had got wind of our purpose and had deliberately forestalled us; and was now only waiting to enjoy our discomfiture, and make merry over our disappointment.

As to the possibility of their being as sick at the sight of us as we were at the sight of them, it never even occurred to one of us.

Our first impulse was to eject them by force. Our next was to expostulate. Our third was to ignore them.

"Come on, you chaps," said Langrish, leading the way to the bank facing that in the occupation of the enemy, "here's our place. Squat down and make yourselves comfortable."

The Philosophers followed the cue, and, apparently unaware of the presence of any strangers, took possession of their slope, and tried to be as jolly as possible.

"I wonder where the day-boy cads go for their tucks," said Trimble in an audible voice, evidently intended for the opposition. "Some one was saying they were trying to get up a kids' club; ha, ha! I'd like to see it."

"Such a joke, Quin," said a voice over the way, evidently pitched to carry across to us. "You know those kids in Sharpe's? they've started a society. What do you think their motto is? Oh my, it's a screamer!"

"What is it?" asked the voice of Quin.

"Keep it dark. I wouldn't like it to get out I told you. It's ***Mens sani in corpore sanorum***, or something like that. You should have seen Redwood yell over it."

"Now, you fellows, let's have our grub," said Langrish encouragingly. "Chaps must eat, you know. ***Corpore sanum*** is our motto, you know. Ha, ha! What do you think I heard one of the day louts call it? ***Corpore sanorum***!"

"Ha! ha! ha!" shrieked we.

"Ho! ho! ho!" shrieked the Urbans.

In the midst of which hilarities we produced our provender (greatly to the relief of our pockets), and fell to. The operation evidently did not pass unheeded by the other side.

"I say, Flitwick," cried some one, "do you know what Philosophers eat?"

"No; what?"

"I never knew till just now. Inky bread and cold bacon-fat sandwiches, or else sherbet, if their tongues are long enough to reach to the bottom of the bottles."

"Have some of this fizzing pork pie, Jones?" asked Coxhead ostentatiously.

"Thanks. You have some of my sardines," replied I.

"Rummy name for a chap, Sarah, isn't it?" said the voice of the captain's fag opposite. "There's a new chap in Sharpe's house this term, one of the biggest mules you ever saw--his name's Sarah."

"What," replied his friend--"is he an ugly little cad with a turn-up nose, and yellow kid gloves, that gets lines every day from the doctor, and can't kick a football as high as his own head? Rather! I know him."

It was impossible to go on much longer at this rate. The atmosphere was getting warm all round, and the storm evidently might break at any moment.

Fortunately for them, the Urbans, of their own accord, averted the peril.

"If you've done lunch," said Quin, "we'd better get to business. Our fellows go in for something besides tuck, don't they, Flitwick?"

"Rather," said Flitwick; "we haven't got a Latin motto that won't parse, but we meet to improve our minds, not stuff our bodies. I vote Mr Quin takes the chair."

"All serene," said Quin, perching himself on a hamper. "I now call upon Mr Brown iii. to read us his paper on 'Remains.'"

This was the first mention of my old comrade. During the interchange of courtesies during lunch he had kept steadily silent, anxious, no doubt, to spare my feelings. But now his chance was come. It was reserved to him to show off the Urbans on their intellectual side.

But before he could come to the front and clear his throat for action, Langrish had loudly called the Philosophers to order.

"Now, you fellows," said he, "we have our programme to get through, and we are not going to give it up, even if our place of meeting was swarming with day idiots. Mr President, you had better lead off."

Thus called upon, I loudly summoned Mr Philosopher Trimble to open the debate on the subject of "Beauty," venturing to add,--

"Some fellows, I've been told, discuss subjects they know nothing about, such as 'Remains,' and that sort of thing; but the Conversation Club makes a point of sticking to what they are familiar with, and that is why we speak to-day of Beauty."

It would not be easy to give a verbatim report of the proceedings which followed, for each party was evidently more attentive to what fell from the other side than to what fell from its own. And each speaker was evidently less concerned to impress his friends than his enemies.

But any one who had chanced to stand on the ridge above, half-way between the two parties, would have heard a medley somewhat of the following kind,--

"Gentlemen, in addressing you on the subject of remains--"

"--I need hardly explain what we mean when we speak of beauty--"

"--Remains are things dug up out of the earth where they--"

"--make a great mistake in calling things people eat, beautiful. In fact--"

"very few of them are to be found unless you know where they are, but--"

"When we talk of a beautiful face we mean a face that is--"

"--plastered over with mud and grime, and hardly recognisable till it is scraped clean, or--"

"people differ very much about it--what one person thinks beautiful, another--"

"generally digs for with spades and shovels, and may spend days--"

"--trying to look less ugly than they really are--"

"--some people find this quite impossible and have to employ persons to--"

"make personal remarks about their neighbours--"

"gentlemen,--"

"I need not remind you that among the Urbans--"

"are to be found some of the most hideous types of ugliness imaginable-- what we need is--"

"--a little common sense to enable us to tell the difference between shams--"

"--like ourselves and the baboons, which is not always easy. In conclusion, gentlemen, I beg to point to our--"

"--dirty hands and faces, which no one who is really interested in hunting for remains of his native--"

"--ugliness ought to be ashamed of."

And so on.

We were too busy cheering our own orator and listening to the enemy's to take in the full humour of the medley at the time. The opening speeches were evidently prepared beforehand (a good part of them possibly copied bodily out of some book). But, as soon as the chairman on either side declared the subject open for discussion, the interest thickened.

Flitwick led off on "Remains," whereas it fell to my lot to reply on "Beauty." By a little sharp practice, I got the lead, which, as it happened, turned out more to the enemy's profit than my own.

"Gentlemen," shouted I, for the breeze made it necessary to speak out, "I beg to disagree with all that the last speaker has said."

"Gentlemen," came the answering voice of Flitwick, "in consequence of a donkey braying somewhere near, I fear I shall find it difficult to make myself heard."

"When people have nothing to say," continued I, "the less they try to say the better."

"I will not imitate the idiots who call themselves Philosophers, and yet don't know what gender a simple Latin word like ***corpore*** is."

"It is sad to think how many afflicted ones there are, close to us, who cannot possibly be as big fools as they look, or look as big fools as they are."

"The one kind of remains you can't find are the remains of a Philosopher's lunch. 'Greedy' is a mild word to use for their sickening gluttony."

"If you want to look for beauty, gentlemen, you should look anywhere but straight in front of you." (Cheers.)

"Gentlemen, as I hear some geese quacking, as well as the donkey braying, I find it difficult to say what I want." (Laughter.)

"I deny that there is any beauty in the laugh of a pack of hyenas."

"If there was anybody here called Sarah," continued Flitwick, wandering farther and farther from his point, "who has been brought up in a girls' school, and wears tan boots and lavender gloves in school (loud and derisive shouts), and is well-known as the dunce of his house (hear, hear), I should advise him never to look in the looking-glass if he is afraid of chimpanzees."

This was too much for the pent-up feelings of the Philosophers--not that they particularly resented Flitwick's facetious allusions to myself--but in my capacity as President of the Club they felt called upon to support me.

"Shut up, cheap-jack!" cried Trimble defiantly. We had given ourselves away at last!

"Hullo," cried Flitwick, "there's somebody here! I wonder if those little cads of Sharpe's have found out our place?"

" *Your* place!" thundered Warminster. "You knew it was ours. And we mean to kick you out."

"Ho! ho! when are you going to begin?" shouted the twenty Urbans.

"Now," yelled the twenty Philosophers.

A battle now seemed imminent, as fierce and disastrous as that fought four centuries before on the adjoining heath. The blood of both parties was up, and I might even have found myself engaged in a hand-to-hand combat with my old chum Dicky, had not Tempest unexpectedly appeared on the scene, like a bolt out of the blue.

He was pushing along his bicycle, and had evidently been attracted to the Bottom by the noise.

"What's up?" he inquired, taking advantage of the temporary silence.

"Those day-boy cads have come and bagged our places and spoiled our fun," said we.

"No, it's your kids who have come and stopped ours," protested the enemy.

"And you're all going down into the middle to have a mill," said Tempest. "Just as you like. But why don't you try a tug of war across instead? You're pretty evenly matched, and I'll umpire!"

It was not a bad idea, and took beautifully. The only drawback was, that Tempest being a Sharper, was presumably prejudiced in favour of the Philosophers. However, he had the reputation of being addicted to fair play.

"The side that's pulled down," said he, "clears out, and goes somewhere else; and the side that wins I'll photograph in a group."

It was a tremendous prize to offer, and served to stimulate both teams to the uttermost. We had a rope with us which easily stretched across the dell, and admitted the twenty pairs of hands on either side to grasp it. Tempest carefully saw that neither side started with the least advantage, and waited till we were all ready before giving the signal.

A tug of war in which each side is ranged up the steep slope of a hollow is very different work from a tug on the level, as we soon found out. Indeed, as soon as the rope was stretched, those lowest down were hanging on to it by their finger tips, while those higher up were obliged to sit down to get within anything like reach. Under these circumstances the contest was short and sharp, and ended in a draw. For each side lost its footing the moment the strain was applied, and almost before Tempest had given the signal, the whole forty of us were sprawling in a confused heap on the grassy floor of the Bottom.

This abortive contest had the effect (which probably Tempest intended) of smoothing over, to some extent, the angry dispute which was on foot, and which was still further allayed by his undertaking to take a monster joint photograph of the two clubs, provided we stood or sat still for the process.

After that, he good-naturedly remained at our invitation, to officiate as judge in some impromptu sports, in which, once again, the rival parties proved most evenly matched. Finally, as evening was drawing on, he consented just to witness a hurried display of our joint fireworks, after which, he told us, we must at once take to our boats and repair home.

It was an imposing display. Twelve Roman candles were set up at regular distances round the hollow, with a fellow in charge of each. Two rockets were set in position, one on either side, and green and red lights alternately were planted on the banks above. At a given signal from Tempest, all were simultaneously lit, and in a perfect blaze of glory, accompanied by a babel of cheers, we concluded our programme.

At least, not quite. One unrehearsed incident was yet to come. For, as the smoke cleared off and the noise ceased, and our eyes once more grew accustomed to the twilight, we became aware of the presence of Mr Jarman, standing in our midst!

CHAPTER FOURTEEN.
EXTRA DRILL.

Mr Jarman must have felt flattered at the gloomy dead silence which fell on Philosophers and Urbans alike as we looked round and saw him. It was of course impossible to believe he had found us by accident, still less that he had come with any friendly purpose.

He advanced into the middle of the Bottom, watch in hand.

"This is contrary to rules," said he. "It is now a quarter-past six, and you are half an hour from Low Heath. In addition to which I have already said that fireworks are only to be had with leave. Tempest, you should have put an end to this. You will kindly send me in the name of every boy here. And each of you boys must attend an extra drill to- morrow and write out one hundred lines--except," added he, catching sight of me, "except Jones iv., whom I have already had to punish, and who must write two hundred lines."

It was a study to watch Tempest's face during this speech. It was all he could do to wait to the end.

"It's not fair," said he, with pale cheeks and angry brow. "It's a half-holiday, and boys always get half an hour's grace."

"That is not the rule," said the master.

"It's the practice, sir. Half these boys are in my house, and I have given them leave to stay. I also allowed the fireworks."

"Tempest, we will speak of this presently--"

"No, sir," blurted out Tempest, "the fellows have done nothing wrong; and if they have, I'm responsible to Dr England about it."

Mr Jarman was not the man to give himself away in a public discussion, and coolly walked off, observing--

"I shall expect the list of names to-night, Tempest."

Tempest's reply was a short, defiant laugh, which made the master turn a moment, as if about to notice it. But he departed silently, and left us to recover as well as we could from the surprise of the whole scene.

The general opinion was that the policeman had met his match at last in Tempest; and the more enthusiastic of us tried to express our feelings in words. But Tempest was by no means inclined to discuss the situation.

"Shut up," he replied angrily, when I ventured to applaud his courage. "Cut back to school at once, and don't speak to me."

This was a blow to some of the party, who had calculated on a general revolt, to be headed by the rock of Sharpe's house in person, and celebrated by general orgies on the spot.

"I sha'n't do my lines, shall you?" said Dicky, as we trotted down to the boats.

"Rather not. And I don't think our chaps will turn up for extra drill."

"Just like old Tempest," said Brown. "He enjoys a row of this kind."

"He didn't look as if he did," remarked I. "Perhaps that was because such a lot of day chaps are mixed up in it."

Brown looked a little glum at this.

"He needn't bother about us unless he likes," said he. "We can take care of ourselves, I fancy."

Luckily at this stage we reached the boats, and further discussion was interrupted.

The voyage home was comparatively uneventful. It was of course enlivened by a desultory race with the Urbans all the way, in which, I regret to say, Mr Jorrocks's boats received a few scratches, owing to the desire of each boat to take the water of its opponent before it was clear ahead. The town-boys unrighteously claimed in the end to have won by a quarter of a length, but as in passing our leader they had pulled away one of our bow oars and further turned the nose of the *Sarah* into the bank, we stoutly resisted their claim, and a very lively argument ensued, in which Mr Jorrocks lost a good deal of varnish, and most of the combatants became rather wet. However, we were back in school within half an hour of embarking, which on the whole was not a bad record.

Curiosity to know what Tempest would do prevented us from so much as thinking of our "lines." I took an early opportunity of presenting myself in Pridgin's study, feeling sure I should be likely to hear something of the matter there.

As it happened, Tempest and Wales were there too, in deep confabulation.

"Look here, old chap," Pridgin was saying, "don't spoil your term for a parcel of yelping young puppies like this kid here and his lot. They're not worth it."

"For all that," said Wales, "it's a question of whether the cock of a house is to be allowed his rights or not."

"It's more a question whether Jarman is to be allowed his rights," said Tempest. "I quite agree that these young muffs are a nuisance, and it's all the more aggravating to be dragged into a mess by them. But he'd no right to interfere."

"Strictly speaking, I suppose he was right," said Pridgin. "There is a rule about juniors being in by 6:30; although every one knows half an hour's grace is given on half-holidays. And I suppose he's right about the fireworks."

"You think I ought to cave in?" asked Tempest.

"I don't say that. But I'd let the matter alone."

"We shall never stop Jarman at that rate," said Wales. "I should say fight it out."

"All very well for you and me," said Pridgin, "who are comfortably out of it. But it means a big job for old Tempest. He'll have to bear the brunt of it."

"I can't well drop it when he's told me to give him a list of the youngsters present," said Tempest.

"You certainly are not called upon to give him a list of the day boys."

"Well, as I only know one of them, it wouldn't be easy. If he'd only lagged me, and given me extra drill and lines, it wouldn't have been so bad. But it was playing it low down to--"

Here came a knock at the door, and the school messenger entered with a letter.

"No answer," said he, handing it to Tempest.

It was plain to see by the flush on Tempest's face as he read it that it contained anything but pleasant news.

"It's from Jarman," said he, throwing it down on the table.

Wales took it up and read it.

"Mr Jarman informs Tempest that the list of names required in connection with this afternoon's incident will not be required, as Mr Jarman already has it. Tempest will please attend the extra drill with the other boys of his house to-morrow, as his conduct this afternoon was neither respectful nor a good example to others."

"Whew!" exclaimed Pridgin, rising, for a wonder, out of his chair; "that's a nasty one, if you like. He's taken you at your word, old man. Who's given the list of names? Did you, you young sweep?" he demanded of me.

"Oh no," said I, glad to be recognised under any term of endearment. "I wouldn't think of doing such a thing. But I'll tell you what I think."

"Really, Jones iv., it's nice to know you do think; but, if you don't mind, we would rather not hear. If you *know* anything, let us hear it, but spare us your thoughts."

Pridgin was rather crushing sometimes.

"I meant we were marked off by the porter at the lodge as we came in," said I. "Perhaps that's how he's got the names."

"Evidently," said Pridgin, "he's had you for once. Tempest. He guessed there'd be a bother about the list, and he has taken the wind out of your sails. You'll attend extra drill, of course."

"Certainly."

"So that," said Wales, "all you will score by the affair will be a public disgrace before the juniors."

Tempest's half dismal, half wrathful face was answer enough.

" *We* sha'n't consider it a disgrace," said I.

"Thank you very much, Jones iv. If that is so, we shall feel it was worth living for to have your approbation. Now you had better go and write out your lines."

"What?" said I. "I thought we were none of us going to do that."

"I have warned you once against the perils of thinking. It's a bad habit for little boys. Off you go, or you won't get your *poena* done in time."

"What am I to tell the others?" I inquired.

"You may tell them it's a fine evening. Cut--do you hear?"

It was a great come-down. The Philosophers thought so when I reported the case. Some were inclined to be angry with Tempest, others to pity him; and every one was unanimous, I do not know why, in expressing a burning desire to kick me.

The expectation of a general revolt, headed by Tempest in person, and rein-forced by the Urbans, faded dismally away as the company saw itself going down to "knock off" Mr Jarman's lines.

"This comes," said Langrish, rather illogically, I thought, "of getting mixed up with the day-boy cads. I knew it would land us in a mess, and so it has."

"Anyway, they're in the mess too," said Trimble.

"It's a little rough on Tempest having to show up for them as well as for us," said I.

"Shut up, and let a fellow write his lines, can't you?" growled Coxhead. "When we want Sarah's advice we'll ask for it."

The reader will gather from this that the Philosophers were in bad tempers, and that their president was in imminent danger of losing his.

At noon next day, when most of the school was turning out after morning class into the fields, a melancholy band might have been seen dropping in, in irregular order, at the door of the school gymnasium. All except one were juniors. Some looked as if they were used to the thing, other betrayed the shy and self-conscious embarrassment of the first delinquents. None looked cheerful, not a few looked savage. The exception in point of age was a well set-up, square-shouldered, proud-faced senior, who entered with an air of reckless disgust which was not comfortable to look at, and might be dangerous if provoked. None of us spoke to Tempest, and he vouchsafed no sign of recognition of us.

A squad of the school volunteers, chiefly composed of smart boys from Mr Sel-kirk's house, were concluding drill as we entered, and of course took stock of our dejected looks and of Tempest's unwonted appearance as they filed out.

"A row on, eh?" whispered one, as he passed us.

"It doesn't look like fun, does it?" snarled Langrish.

"Where does Tempest come in?" persisted the inquirer.

"By the door; and the sooner you get out by it the better."

"Ha, ha!--poor little naughty boys. An extra drill will do you good. Come on, you chaps. Let's leave them to enjoy themselves. They'll get used to it in time. Ho, ho!"

"Fall in!" called Mr Jarman.

And painfully conscious not only that a few of the volunteers were hanging about to look on, but that the school porter was at the moment conducting a party of visitors through the building, we obeyed listlessly and dismally. Tempest taking his place at the end of the line.

"Are these some of the volunteers?" we heard one of the lady spectators ask.

"No, madam. This is an extra drill for breach of rules," replied the official.

"Number from the right," cried Mr Jarman.

We numbered.

"Answer to your names," said the discipline master, producing a paper. We could not help noticing that Tempest's name was mixed in along with ours, and that no difference was made on account of his age or status. We were then formed into double rank, and fours, and open order, and put through a hideous series of extension exercises, irksome enough at any time, but under present circumstances specially so. I heard Dicky Brown beside me groan as he stood leaning over with his left knee bent, his right leg stretched out behind, and his two arms doubled up at his side.

"I wonder they don't all kick," he whispered.

"Not easy like this," said I.

"How Tempest must be enjoying it!" Dick murmured.

"Poor beggar! it's a nasty dose for him."

But if Mr Jarman counted on any protest or resistance from his senior victim, he was disappointed. Tempest went patiently and impassively through the drill with the rest of us; but, as we could see, with a blazing eye fixed all the while on the master. But I could guess the struggle that was going on in my friend's breast. Mr Jarman may have flattered himself he was "taking it out of him", Dicky and I knew better.

We all took our cue from Tempest that morning, and any inclination to rebel or mutiny was suppressed. We contented ourselves with glaring at our tormentor, and denying him the excuse he probably desired of prolonging the agony. My impression is that Mr Jarman was never so happy as when he realised that he was absolute master of the situation. The Roman emperors were not in it with him.

"Attention! Front!" said he at last, when the proceedings were becoming dull even to him. "Stand at ease! Attention! Stand at ease! Attention! Left turn! Dismiss! As you were! Dismiss!"

It was a prolonged insult, and we knew it. But Tempest stood it, and so, consequently, did we. But as we filed from the place we felt that Mr Jarman's turn would come some day.

Tempest, contrary to general expectation, evinced no haste to leave the scene of his tribulation. There was yet a quarter of an hour to next bell, and this he evidently decided to spend, as he had the right to do, where he was. Mr Jarman was evidently annoyed to find, not only that the senior was apparently unaffected by the humiliation through which he had passed, but that now the drill was over he evinced an entire unconcern in the master's presence.

Tempest was one of the best gymnasts in the school, and it was always worth while to watch him on the trapeze and horizontal bar. So the Philosophers and Urbans, by one consent, trooped back into the gymnasium to look on, and (what must have been particularly annoying to the master, because he had no authority to stop it) to cheer. How we did cheer, and what good it did us! Had Tempest been the meanest of performers, and done nothing but swing with his legs doubled up under him from one ring to the next, we should have applauded. But to-day his flights were terrific. No fellow was less given to show off, and he probably objected to our applause as much as Mr Jarman. But he was bound to relieve his feelings somehow, and the trapeze was just what he wanted.

When finally the bell rang, and we were hoarse with cheering (which was our way of relieving our feelings) he came to earth decidedly better for his exercise.

Mr Jarman evidently was impressed, and, to our surprise, even ventured on a compliment.

"You did that well, Tempest."

Tempest's reply was to walk away, putting on his coat as he went.

It was plain to see by the angry twitch of Mr Jarman's mouth that the shaft of this public snub had gone home, and we who looked on and witnessed it all had little need to tell ourselves that civil war had already been declared.

It is hardly necessary to state that the extraordinary meeting of the Conversation Club that evening was lively, and that there was no lack of a topic. Besides our own contingent, a few of the outsiders, including Muskett and Corderoy from Selkirk's house, and a few of the "paupers," dropped in. As the faggery would only conveniently hold six persons, and as at least twenty were present, it was considered advisable to adjourn to the shoe-room, where, in the dim light of a small candle, several particularly revolutionary motions were discussed, the company sitting on the floor for the purpose.

The meeting opened by my calling on Langrish to read the minutes, which he accordingly did.

"The inaugural picnic of the Ph.C.C. was held the other day. Present, all the usual lot and seven paupers. The president had chartered the *Sarah* and *Firefly*, two of the vilest crocks at Jorrocks's."

"He said they were the best they had got," I explained.

"Shut up, or you'll be kicked out, young Sarah."

"I've a right to speak."

"No, you haven't--unless you hold your tongue."

"If I held my tongue, I couldn't possibly speak," I explained.

"Turn him out!" cried the paupers. Whereat I subsided.

"The paupers," continued the minutes, "had beastly little go in them, and ought to have had a meal of hay before starting (interruption), and will be badly kicked if they don't shut up. The *Firefly* had the best of the race up." (Here there were most indignant protests from the crew of the gallant *Sarah*; and the question was argued out with some energy on the floor of the shoe-room before Langrish could proceed.)

"Nature was dressed in her most pristine colours, and the incandescent hues of the autumn leaves brought cries of enjoyment out of the mouths of the Ph.C.C, except the paupers, whose mouths were too full for utterance."

This paragraph was not likely to pass unchallenged. Coxhead impeached its grammar, Trimble its taste, and the paupers its accuracy, and a very heated argument ensued, at the end of which it was agreed to let the door stand open a few minutes to get rid of the dust.

"Arrived at Camp Hill, a flock of jibbering apes were discovered, headed by the president's arch-enemy. Brown iii."

"No, he's not my enemy," protested I. "I never said so."

"The minutes say so. They're more likely to be right than you."

"But I like Dicky Brown," said I.

"That sounds like poetry," said Warminster, "ho, ho!

"I like Dicky Brown,
 His cheek is so cool,
 And if I don't kick him
 You call me a fool."

"I can do that whether you kick him or not," said I, quite unmoved by this brilliant impromptu.

Here I was compelled to vacate the chair for a few moments, in order to discuss the matter further with Warminster. On order being restored, the minutes proceeded--

"The Philosophers soon made it too hot for these mules, and they were only allowed to stay on the ground as it amused us to see their idiotic sniggers. The paper on 'Beauty' was rot, and invoked well-deserved hisses."

"Say that again," ejaculated the outraged Trimble.

"*That*! there you are," said Langrish hurriedly. But Trimble had more to say on the subject, and once again the meeting became warm and dusty.

"Order, please; let's hear the rest," said I, when both had been brushed down by their friends.

"As for Sarah's speech in reply, it was the drivellingest balderdash you ever heard. It made the club blush."

"That speaks well for it," I suggested mildly.

The meeting did not seem to know how exactly to take this, but concluded it was meant to be complimentary, and contented themselves with ordering me to "shut up" if I didn't want to be kicked out.

"Tempest (loud cheers) turned up presently and backed us up (cheers). The baboons weren't in it in the sports. We pulled off the tug of war on our heads (cheers), and their speeches were even drivellinger than Trim's and Sarah's. (Interruption.) Just at the end a howling sneak and cad and outsider called Jarman came, and lagged us all, including Tempest. (Groans.) Our president behaved like a mutton-head throughout. Going home, the Philosophers led by several miles. The meeting then adjourned for extra drill in the gym. to-day, and mean to pay Jarman out." (Cheers.)

The patriotic sentiment with which the minutes concluded did away with any little difference arising earner is the evening, and they were carried unanimously.

It was then moved, seconded, thirded, fourthed, and fifthed, "that Jarman be, and is hereby, hung, and ought to be kicked."

It was further agreed, "that Tempest be elected an Honorary Philosopher, and be let off entrance fee."

Also, "that the town cads are about the biggest outsiders going."

Also, "that Trimble be requested to wash his face."

This last was not carried without some opposition, Trimble's amendment, "that you be hung," being lost only by a narrow minority. Finally it was resolved unanimously--

"That the Philosophers' Conversation Club make it hot all round for any one who doesn't want to kick Jarman or back up Tempest."

With which highly satisfactory piece of business accomplished, we adjourned to our own studies, and finally to bed.

CHAPTER FIFTEEN.
EXPLOSIVE MATERIAL.

It was plain to be seen that Tempest, although he had borne his humiliating penalty like a man, had been badly bruised by it. Not that he broke out into any wild rebellion, or tried to make for himself a party to avenge his wrongs; but he seemed to have either lost interest in his work as house captain, or to enjoy disturbing the sensibilities of his friends by a reckless indifference to its affairs.

The story of his "extra drill" had become public property in Low Heath. Most of the fellows sympathised with him, but could not understand why he had not appealed to the head master. A few, a very few, suggested that he had come badly out of the business; but no one particularly cared to discuss the matter with him.

To Pridgin and Wales he insisted that it was no use referring to Dr England. The Head was bound to support his policeman.

"Why not get Redwood to take it up?" suggested Pridgin.

"Redwood! He wouldn't go a yard out of his way. What does it matter to him--a day boy? No, old chap, we can take care of ourselves. There'll be a return match one day!"

It concerned me to hear my old friend talk like this; still more to notice how he began to lose grip in Sharpe's house. No news flies so fast in a school as that of a responsible head boy being slack or "out of collar." And when once it is known and admitted, it takes a good deal to keep the house from going slack and "out of collar" too.

In our particular department the relaxing of authority was specially apparent. It destroyed some of the interest in our philosophical extravagances; for the dread of coming across the powers that be lends a certain flavour to the routine of a junior boy. It also tended to substitute horseplay and rowdyism for mere fun--greatly to the detriment of our self-respect and enjoyment.

On the whole, then, Sharpe's house had a heavier grudge against Mr Jarman than it suspected.

The worst of the whole business was that Tempest himself seemed not to see the effect of his attitude on the house at large. He did not realise how much the juniors were impressed by what he said and how he looked, or how much his example counted with others of a less imitative turn. He looked upon his grievance as his own affair, and failed to give himself credit for all the influence he really possessed.

One curious result of the upset was that Crofter was now and then to be found in his fellow-seniors' rooms. He had blossomed out as an ardent anti-Jarmanite, and belonged to the party who not only vowed revenge, but was impatient at delay. Tempest's wrongs he seemed to feel as keenly as if they had been his own; and the insults put upon Sharpe's house he took to heart as warmly as any one.

Tempest could hardly help tolerating this effusively-offered sympathy, although he made no profession of liking it, and continued to warn me against having more to do than I could help with Crofter. Pridgin was even less cordial, but his laziness prevented his taking any active steps to cut the connection. Wales, on the other hand, though Tempest's chum, took more kindly to the new-comer, and amused himself now and again by defending him against his detractors.

"The wonder to me is," said Crofter, "Jarman has not caught it before now. We're not the only house he's insulted, although I don't think he's tried it on with any of the others as he has with us."

"Some day he'll find he's sailing a little too near the wind," said Tempest, with a pleasant confusion of metaphors; "and then he'll get bowled out."

"Upon my word, though," said Wales, "I think we've a right to get that extra drill of yours wiped out. It stands against you on the register, and it's a scandal to the house."

"They seem to think it so," observed Pridgin, as just then a loud chorus of war-whoops came up from the region of the faggery. "Somebody had better stop that row!"

"Jarman had better come and do it," said Tempest, laughing. "He's got charge of the morals of Sharpe's house now."

When in due time I returned, somewhat depressed by what I had overheard, to the faggery, I discovered that the particular occasion of the triumphal shout referred to had been a proposal by Langrish to celebrate the approaching Fifth of November by hanging, and, if possible, burning Mr Jarman in effigy, for which purpose an overcoat of mine had already been impounded. I had the greatest difficulty in rescuing it from the hands of the marauders, who represented to me that it was my duty to sacrifice something for the public good.

"Why don't you let them have **your** coat, then?" I asked.

"Because," was the insinuating reply, "it wouldn't burn as well."

"You won't have mine," I insisted. "But I tell you what; I've got an old hat and pair of boots I--I don't often wear--you can have them."

A shout of laughter greeted this ingenuous offer--but it saved my top- coat. And when in time my flat-topped pot-hat and tan boots were produced, there was general rejoicing. Each Philosopher present tried them on in turn, and finally I was compelled to wear them, as well as my top-coat, for the rest of the evening, and assist in a full-dress rehearsal of the proposed hanging of the discipline master, in which, greatly to my inconvenience, I was made to personate Mr Jarman.

The following day I was enjoying a little hard-earned solitude, and amusing myself by leaning over the bridge and watching the boats below, when a voice at my side startled me.

"Ah, my polite letter-writer, is that you? The very chap I want."

It was Crofter. My instinct at first, especially on the sly reference to my letter of apology, was to fly. On second thoughts it seemed to me wiser to remain. Crofter and Tempest were on better terms now. It would be best to be civil.

"What is it?" I asked.

"Can you steer a boat?"

"A little," said I.

"Does that mean you can run it into the bank every few yards?"

"Oh no, I've often steered Tempest and Pridgin."

"Come along, then; I'm going to have a spin up to Middle-weir."

If there was one thing I enjoyed it was steering a boat, and I was not long in accepting the invitation.

Crofter was not conferring a favour on me; only making a convenience of me. So that I was not in any way making up to him. Our relations were that of senior and fag only; and Tempest's and Pridgin's warnings to beware when he was particularly friendly (even if it had not already been cancelled by the fact that they now frequently had Crofter in their rooms) could hardly apply now.

For all that, I did not feel quite comfortable, and was glad, on the whole, that the embarkation did not take place under the eyes of my patrons.

For some time Crofter sculled on in silence, giving me directions now and again to keep in the stream, or take the boat well out at the corners--which I considered superfluous. Presently, however, when we were clear of Low Heath he slacked off and began to talk.

"I enjoyed that letter of yours," said he; "did you write it all yourself?"

"Yes," said I, feeling and looking very uncomfortable.

"You and Tempest must be quite old chums."

"Yes."

"It's very rough on him, all this business."

"Yes, isn't it?" said I, somewhat won over by this admission.

"The worst of it is, it makes the house run down. I expected we were going to do big things this term."

"It's not Tempest's fault if we don't," said I.

"Of course not. It's Jarman's. Every one knows that. It's rather a pity Tempest takes it so meekly, though. Fellows will think he's either afraid or doesn't care; and neither would be true."

"I should think not."

There was a pause, during which Crofter sculled on. Then he said,--

"Tempest and I don't hit it, somehow. He doesn't like me, does he?"

"Well--no, I don't fancy he does," I admitted.

"I dare say he advises you to fight shy of me, and that sort of thing, eh?"

This was awkward; but I could not well get out of it.

"Yes."

Crofter laughed sweetly.

"I wish he'd let me be friends. I hate to see a fellow coming to grief, and not be allowed to give him a leg-up."

"Tempest's not coming to grief," said I.

"Well, not perhaps that, only it's a pity he's adding to his other troubles by getting head-over-ears in debt. I hear he's been going it pretty well in the shops. You should give him a friendly tip."

This was a revelation to me. I had gathered some time ago, from what Pridgin had said, that there was some fear of it; but I had hoped I had made a mistake.

"Who told you?" said I.

"A good many people are talking about it; including some of the shopmen. It's just one of those things that a fellow himself never dreams anybody knows about till it's public property. That's why I wish I were on good enough terms to give him the tip."

"If he's owing anybody he'll pay," said I, feeling a great sinking in my heart.

"Look out for that stake in the water there; pull your left! Narrow shave that. Of course he means to pay. What I'm afraid of is, Jarman or England or any of them getting to hear of it. Ever since Sweeten last year got turned out of the headship of his house, and afterwards expelled, it's seemed to me to be a risky thing for a fellow to run into debt. These shopmen are such sneaks. If they can't get their money from the fellow, they send their bills in to the house master, and sometimes to the head master; and then it's a precious awkward thing. How are you getting on in your form?"

I had not much spirit to tell him, and if I had there was no time, for just then the swish of a pair of sculls came round the corner behind us, and presently a boat at almost racing speed appeared in sight.

"Pull your right!" said Crofter. "Hallo! it's one of our fellows. Looks like Tempest himself."

I wished myself at the bottom of the river then! What would he think of me if he saw me, and if he knew what I had been listening to?

In my perturbation I over-pulled my line and sent our boat into the bank. Tempest, who evidently was relieving himself with a spin of hard exercise after his fashion, and imagined he had the river to himself, was bearing down straight upon us.

"Hallo, there; keep her out!" shouted Crofter.

Tempest looked round in a startled way, and held water hard to avoid a collision. Then, as he suddenly took in who we were, his face lengthened, and he came to a halt alongside.

"You there, Jones iv.?"

"Yes, would you like me to come and steer you?" said I.

Considering the difficulty into which I had just landed my present boat, it was difficult to natter myself any one would exactly compete for my services. But Tempest answered shortly,--

"Come along."

"Hullo, I say," said Crofter suavely, but with a flush on his cheeks, "he's steering me, Tempest."

"He's doing no good. He's stuck you in the bank already. Come along, Jones."

"I haven't done with him yet," said Crofter, flushing still more deeply as his voice became sweeter. "I want him to stay with me."

"And I don't want him to stay with you," blurted out Tempest, losing his temper. "I've told him so already. He can do as he likes, though."

And he began to dip his sculls again in the water.

"No," said I, "I want to come in your boat, Tempest."

"Come along, then;" and he backed his stern up towards me.

Crofter made no further protest; but greeted my desertion with a mellifluous laugh, which made me more uncomfortable than a storm of objurgations.

Tempest said nothing, but dug his blades viciously in the water, and spun away with grim face and clenched teeth.

For a quarter of a mile he sculled on before he lay on his oars and exclaimed,--

"You young fool!"

"Why," pleaded I, "I didn't think you'd mind. He's been friendly enough to you lately."

"Bah! What do I care what he is to me? I told you to fight shy of the fellow, and there you go and give yourself away to him."

I did not quite like this. Tempest spoke to me as if I had not a soul of my own, and had no right to do anything without his leave.

"He was speaking quite kindly about you," persisted I.

Tempest checked the contemptuous exclamation which came to his lips, and said, more earnestly than I had heard him yet,--

"Look here, Jones; that fellow's a cad; and he'll make a cad of you, if you let him. Don't believe a word he says to you, unless he calls you a fool."

"I hope what he's been saying to-day will turn out to be Lies," said I oracularly.

To my disappointment Tempest evinced no curiosity as to my meaning, and relapsed into gloomy silence for the rest of the voyage.

For the first time in my life I felt out of humour with my old Dux. He had no right to treat me like a baby, or dictate to me whom I was to know and whom I was not to know in Low Heath. No doubt he thought he was doing me a good turn, and honestly thought ill of Crofter. But it did not follow he was not doing him an injustice, and demanding that I should join in it.

At any rate, I felt heartily miserable, and wished I had never put foot outside the faggery that day.

About a mile from home Tempest got out on the towing-path, and said he would trot to the school while I paddled the boat home. It was some relief to be left alone; a relief, however, which was considerably tempered by the fear of meeting Crofter, and having to explain matters to him. That difficulty fortunately did not occur, and I got back to the bosom of the Philosophers without further adventure.

In their sweet society I gradually recovered my spirits. Their enthusiasm for Tempest was still unabated, and their avowed contempt for his enemies all the world over was refreshing. A night's reflection further repaired my loyalty. After all, thought I, Tempest meant well by me, and was willing to make an enemy for my sake. He might be wrong, of course; but suppose he *was* right--

The result of all these inward musings was that I offered Trimble to do Tempest's fagging in his place next morning.

He seemed half to expect me, and the old friendly look was back in his face as he saw me enter.

"I'm sorry I offended you yesterday, Tempest," said I.

"I fancied it was I offended you," said he; "but I couldn't stand seeing you in that cad's clutches."

"Is he really a cad, then?" I asked.

"You don't suppose I asked you into my boat for fun, do you?" said he shortly.

I went on for some time with my work, and then said,--

"Would you like to know what he was saying about you?"

"Not a bit," said he, so decisively that I relapsed again into silence.

"Look here, kid," said he, presently, and with unwonted seriousness. "I'm not a saint, and don't profess to be. And I may not be able to manage my own affairs, to judge by what you and half a dozen other of the fellows seem to think; but I don't want to see you--well, come to grief--and that's what you're likely to do if you let that fellow get hold of you."

"He's not got hold of me," said I, feeling a little hurt once more. "Mayn't I be civil to a fellow, even? Why, he was saying if you--"

"Shut up! didn't I tell you I don't want to hear?" said he.

"Oh, all right."

If he had only vouchsafed to tell me why he disliked Crofter, or if he had given his counsel in a less authoritative way, it would have been different. He would not even let me repeat the friendly remarks Crofter had made about him; and was determined neither to say a good word for the fellow himself, nor let me say one.

The consequence was that our interview ended in my wishing once more I had confined myself to my own quarters and let ill alone.

My companions were not long in discovering that something was on my mind, and in their gentle way tried to cheer me up.

"What's the row--ear-ache?" demanded Trimble.

"He's blue because he's not had lines to-day," suggested Langrish.

"Perhaps his washerwoman has sent in her bill," said Coxhead.

"You'll get kicked out of here, if you look so jolly blue," said Warminster. "It's stale enough this term, without having a chap with a face like a boiled fish gaping at you."

"Look here," said I, resolved to be candid as far as I dare. "I'm in a jolly mess--"

"Never knew you out of it. What's up?" said Langrish.

"Really though, no larks," said I. "Tempest's down on me because I went out with Crofter, and Crofter's down on me because I cut him for Tempest. That's enough to give a chap blues, isn't it?"

"There seems to be a run on Sarah," said Trimble. "Anybody got a halfpenny?"

"What for?" I inquired, as the requisite coin was planked down on the table.

"Heads Tempest, tails Crofter," said Langrish.

It was heads, and I was solemnly ordered to adhere to Crofter.

"We'll square it with Tempest," said they. "He'll probably keep his shutters up for a day or two, but he'll soon get over it."

"But," said I, "I mean to stick to Tempest as well. The fact is, from what I hear,"--little I realised the fatal error I was making!--"he's in rather a bad way himself."

"How?"

"Well, don't tell; but he's owing a lot in the shops; and if he can't pay he'll get shown up."

There was a whistle of dismay at this. Sweeten's fate was still fresh in the memory of some of the faggery.

"We'll have to give him a leg-up," was the general verdict.

"Oh, don't let out I told you!" said I, beginning to get alarmed at the interest my revelation had evoked.

"Who's going to say a word about you? We can back up the cock of our own house, I suppose, without asking your precious leave. You go and black Crofter's boots. We'll see old Tempest through."

This was not at all what I wanted. I had at least hoped to be recognised as Tempest's leading champion in this company. Whereas, here was I coolly shunted, my revelation coolly appropriated, and my services unceremoniously dispensed with. I did not like it at all.

"This dodge about stringing up Jarman's guy," said Trimble, "ought to help our man a bit. It'll show we're taking the matter up. By the way, Sarah's not heard the latest--we're going to blow him up as well as hang him."

And they proceeded to explain that the guy was to be filled chock-full of fireworks and gunpowder, and his tongue to be made of touch-paper. Altogether, he was to be a most dangerous and explosive effigy; and I, as president of the Philosophical Conversation Club, was naturally selected to take charge of him.

I pleaded hard for a sub-committee to assist me, but they would not hear of it.

"It'll only be a day or two," said they, "to the Fifth of November. We'll have his stuffing all in to-morrow--there's almost enough fireworks left over from the picnic to load him. Then you can stow him away quiet somewhere till the day. Couldn't you stick him under your bed?"

"Oh no, he might go off, you know," said I; "or some one might see him. Besides, he'll be too stout to go under."

"Bother!--where can he go, then?"

"I vote we stick him in the lumber room under the gymnasium. Nobody ever goes there, and you can get into it any time by the area outside," said Coxhead.

This was voted an excellent idea. At any rate, if he was discovered or did go off there, the gymnasium was far enough away from Sharpe's.

So, with much rejoicing, the guy was duly loaded with his explosive internals, and clad in an old derelict overcoat of some late senior. My famous hat adorned his hideous head, and my unappreciated tan boots lent distinction to his somewhat incoherent legs. A train of touch-paper connected with a Roman candle was cunningly devised to protrude in the form of a tongue from his mouth, while ginger-beer bottles filled with gunpowder served as hands. And the whole work of art was one dark evening conveyed by me tenderly and deposited among a wilderness of broken forms, empty hampers, and old bottles in the lumber room under the school gymnasium, "to be called for" in a few days time.

CHAPTER SIXTEEN.
GUNPOWDER TREASON.

One result of my boating excursion was that Crofter ceased to frequent his fellow-seniors' studies. There was no declaration of war, or, indeed, any formal breaking off of relations. But Crofter had sense enough of his own dignity to feel that he had been slighted by Tempest: and Tempest and his friends had no inclination to heal the trouble, or assume an attitude of friendliness they did not feel.

As for me, I found it very hard to steer an even course between the competing parties. Crofter nodded and spoke to me just as usual, and was evidently amused by my panic lest these pacific overtures should be observed or misconstrued by Tempest. Tempest, on the other hand, did not refer again to the subject, but took a little more pains than before to look after me and help me in my work. And an evening or two later, much to my surprise, when I went as usual to "tidy up" in Pridgin's room while Tempest was there too, my lord and master said abruptly,--

"Let my things alone, kid. Tempest appreciates a mess in his place more than I do, so I've swopped you for Trimble."

"What?" said I, in tones of mingled amazement and pleasure. "Am I--"

"You're to go and fetch my blazer," said Tempest, "that I left on the parallel bars in the gymnasium this afternoon. Look alive, or I shall stick to Trimble."

I really began to think there must be something unusually desirable about me, that fellows should be so anxious to possess me. The Philosophers had with one accord sought me for president. Pridgin had wanted me. Crofter had wanted me. Even Redwood had wanted me. And now here was old Tempest putting in his claim! He should have me--I would not be so selfish as to deprive him of the coveted privilege.

In a somewhat "tilted" condition I went off on my errand, not even delaying to announce the great news to my fellow-Philosophers. It was a dark evening, and the gymnasium was some way off. But I knew the way by this time. I had daily walked past the area door and glanced down at the dangerous guy where it lay with its lolling tongue under the grating, to assure myself of its welfare. It was all right up till now, and in two days it would be off my hands.

The square was empty as I crossed it, and, to my satisfaction, I found the gymnasium door unlocked. I groped my way to the corner where the parallel bars stood, and there found the blazer, which I carried off in triumph.

As I emerged from the door and came down the steps, I became aware of two points of light in front of me, and a voice out of the darkness, which caused me to jump almost out of my skin,--

"Who is that?"

It was Mr Jarman's voice--and I could just discern his shadowy form accompanied by that of Mr Selkirk standing before me. The two masters were evidently taking an after-dinner turn with their cigars, and had heard my footsteps.

"Jones iv., sir; I came to fetch Tempest's blazer."

"Who gave you leave?"

"Tempest, sir."

"Take the blazer back where you found it, and tell Tempest if he leaves his things in the gymnasium he must fetch them at proper hours. This is the third time I have had to speak to you, Jones iv. You must attend an extra drill to-morrow, and learn fifty lines by heart. This constant irregularity must be stopped."

So saying, he took his companion's arm and strolled off.

I returned dismally into the dark gymnasium and flung the blazer on to the nearest seat; and then hurried back to report the result of my mission to Tempest.

As I guessed, our poor guy downstairs was likely to be nowhere in the explosion which this last insult called forth.

With clenched teeth Tempest sprang from his seat and snatched his cap.

"It's awfully dark," said I; "if you're going, you'd better take some matches."

"Fetch me some," said he, with a harsh, dry voice. I fled off, and returned with a box of fusees, which the Philosophers had laid in for the approaching celebration of Guy Fawkes' Day.

Tempest snatched them from my hand and strode off. I wished he had let me go with him. I heard his footsteps swing heavily across the quadrangle, as if challenging the notice of the enemy. Whether the enemy heard or answered the challenge I could not say. The steps died away into silence, and I listened in vain for further sign.

Presently I returned to the faggery, where the Philosophers were just preparing to obey the summons to bed.

Hurriedly I recited the event of the evening, and for once was honoured with their rapt and excited attention.

"My eye, what a shame we can't go out and see the fun!" cried Langrish.

"I hope he makes jelly of him," said Trimble. "I'm jolly glad I'm his fag."

This brought on a crisis I had rather feared.

"You're not," said I. "Pridgin has swopped me for you."

"What!" screamed Trimble, taking a running kick at my shins.

"I didn't do it. Shut up. Trim! that's my leg you're kicking. It was Pridgin. Go and kick him," said I.

But Trim was in no mood to listen to reason.

"I always said you were a sneak," snarled he; "now I know it. Come and kick the beast, you fellows. It's all a low dodge. Kick him, I say."

The company showed every disposition to respond to the appeal.

"Look here," said I, "it's not my fault--but if you kick me, I'll tell him about your precious guy, and you can look after him yourself; I shan't. There!"

This rather fetched them. As custodian of that illicit effigy I had my uses, and they hardly cared to dispense with me. So Trimble was ordered not to make an ass of himself, and the discussion went back to Tempest and his blazer.

"I tell you what," said Warminster. "I vote we hang about a bit and cheer him when he comes in. There's no one to lag us for not going to bed, and we may as well stay and back him up."

With which patriotic resolve we resumed our seats and occupied the interval with auditing the accounts of the club--a painful and tedious operation which gave rise to much dispute and recrimination, particularly when it was discovered that on paper we were 25 shillings to the good, whereas in the treasurer's pocket we were 6 shillings to the bad.

The treasurer had a bad quarter of an hour of it, till it was discovered that the auditors had accidentally forgotten to carry the total of one column to the top of the next, an oversight which nearly brought about the dissolution of the club, so fierce was the storm which raged over it.

More than half an hour was spent over these proceedings, and we began to wonder why Tempest had not come back. It was certain he must have been stopped by somebody, or he would have been back in ten minutes. Had he and Jarman had an encounter? Was Mr Jarman at that moment begging for quarter? or was our man answering for his riot to the head master?

Half an hour passed, three-quarters, an hour. Then, just as we were giving him up, hurried footsteps came across the quadrangle, and Tempest, with pale face and disordered guise, carrying his blazer on his arm, entered and passed rapidly to his room. His countenance was too forbidding for us to venture on our promised cheer. Something unusual had happened. How we longed to know what it was!

I was thrust forward to follow him to his study, on the chance of ascertaining, and was on the point of obeying, when a terrific sound broke the silence of the night, and sent us back with white, rigid faces in a heap into the faggery.

The sound proceeded from the direction of the gymnasium--first of all, a dull, spasmodic thunder; then a fierce burst, followed almost immediately by two tremendous reports which shook us to the soles of our boots.

It reminded me of that fearful night at Dangerfield, when Tempest--

I clung on to Langrish, who was next to me, in mute despair, and Langrish in turn embraced Trimble.

"Those," gasped the voice of Coxhead, "were the--ginger--beer--bottles. What--shall--we--do?"

"Cut to bed sharp!" said the resolute though quavering voice of Warminster, "and lie low."

"There won't be much of him left," whispered Trimble, "that's one good thing," as we huddled off our clothes in the dark in the dormitory.

It was a gleam of comfort, certainly. Effigies of that kind, when they do go off, leave few marks of identity behind them.

"Who let it off?" I ventured to ask. "No one knew about it except us."

"Look out! There's somebody coming!"

It was Mr Sharpe, who looked in, candle in hand, to see if any one had been disturbed by the noise. But every one was sleeping peacefully, blissfully unconscious that anything had happened.

"Narrow shave that," said Langrish, when the master had retired.

"I say," said Trimble. "I wonder if Tempest--"

Here he pulled up, but a muffled whistle of dismay took up his meaning.

"If he did, he must have found it out by himself. I never said a word to him," said I.

"You were bound to make a mess of it," said Coxhead. "Why ever couldn't you stick the thing where nobody could find it?"

"So I did; it was leaning up against the cellar wall; no one could possibly get at it."

"Why not? the area door's open."

"No, it ain't. I locked it, and hid the key," said I, triumphantly, "for fear of accident, under the scraper."

"Good old Sarah--that's lucky. But what about the grating in the gymnasium floor? Couldn't you twig it through that?"

"Not unless you were looking for it. And if you could, you couldn't get at it."

"Well," said Trimble, rather brutally, "I hope it's all right, for your sake. Fellows who keep guys must take the consequences. It would have been much safer if you'd kept it under your bed."

"You may keep the next," growled I. "I've done with it."

Considering the probable condition of the luckless effigy at that moment, nobody was inclined to contradict me; and the Philosophers relapsed into gloomy silence, and eventually fell asleep.

I was probably the last to reach that blissful stage. For hours I lay awake, a prey to the most dismal reflections. To do myself justice, my own peril afflicted me at the time--perhaps because I did not realise it--less than Tempest's. Whether he had blown up the guy or not, things would be sure to look black against him, and my recollection of the episode of Hector's death told me he would come out of it badly. How, if he had done it, he had contrived to get at the explosives, I could not fathom. I was sure, even with his grudge against Jarman, he was not the sort of fellow to take a revenge that was either mean or dastardly; and yet--and yet--and yet--

When with one accord we woke next morning it needed no special intimation to be aware that something had happened at Low Heath. Masters and school attendants were talking in groups in the quadrangle. Boys were flitting across in the direction of the gymnasium; and seniors in twos and threes were deferring their morning dip and hovering about in serious confabulation.

"Something up?" said Trimble, with ill-concealed artlessness. "I wonder what it is?"

"Looks like a row of some sort," said Langrish. "What are all the chaps going across to the gym. for, I wonder?"

"Let's go and see," said Coxhead.

"We needn't all go together," said Warminster, significantly. So one by one, casually, and at studied distances from our comrades, the Philosophers dropped into the crowd and made for the scene of last night's accident.

I felt terribly nervous. Suppose some one had been killed, or suppose the gymnasium had been burnt, and suspicion fell on any one, what a fix it would be!

In my distress I met Dicky Brown, full of news.

"Hullo, Jones, I say, have you heard? Some chap's been trying to blow up the gym. in the night, and there's a row and a half on. The front door is smashed, and the floor all knocked to bits. Come and have a look."

"Any one killed or hurt?"

"I've not heard. Didn't you hear the noise?"

"Yes. Our chaps heard a row in the night."

"We could hear it at our place," said Brown. "They say the chap's known who did it, too."

"Who?"

"How do I know? Some chap who's been extra drilled, most likely."

"There's plenty of them," suggested I.

"Well, yes. They say a lot of gunpowder had been stowed in the lumber room just under the door. There, do you see?"

We had reached the scene of the tragedy, and I was able to judge of the mischief which had been done. The door was broken, but whether by the explosion or ordinary violence it was hard to say. The floor and grating over the lumber room were broken away, and one or two windows were smashed. That was all. My first feeling was one of relief that the damage was so slight. I had pictured the whole building a wreck, and a row of mangled remains on stretchers all round. Compared with that, our poor guy had really made a very slight disturbance. Of him I was thankful to be able to observe no trace, except one tan boot and a fragment of a ginger-beer bottle in the area. That indeed was bad enough, but, I argued, the lumber room was full of old cast-off shoes and bottles, and these would probably be set down as fragments of the rubbish displaced by the explosion.

Brown, however, and others to whom I spoke, failed to share my view of the slightness of the damage.

"If the fellow's found, it will be a case of the police court for him."

The blood left my face as I heard the awful words. It had never occurred to me yet that the matter was one of more than school concern. Visions of penal servitude and a broken-hearted mother swam before my eyes. Oh, why had I ever left the tranquil seclusion of Fallowfield for this awful place?

As soon as possible I edged quietly out of the crowd, and made my way dismally back to Sharpe's, where I met not a few of our fellows, all eager for news.

I was too sick to give them much information, and sent them to inspect for themselves while I made my way dismally to Tempest's room.

He was up, reading.

"Hullo, youngster," said he, "what's all the row about? What was that noise in the quad, last night? were some of your lot fooling about with fireworks?"

"Don't you know?" gasped I, fairly taken aback with the question. "Why, some one's been trying to blow up the gymnasium!"

"What!" he exclaimed. "Why, *I* was there, not long before the noise. Who's done it?"

"That's what nobody knows. I'm afraid there'll be a row about it."

"Any fool could tell that," said Tempest, with troubled face.

"I wish you hadn't been there," said I; "they may think it was you."

"Let them," said he, with a laugh which was anything but merry. I was longing to hear what had happened to him last night, but he did not volunteer any information, and I did not care to question him.

Horribly uneasy, I was about to seek the questionable consolations of my comrades, when the school messenger entered with a long face.

"Master Tempest, the head master wants to see you at once."

"All right," said Tempest.

"He said I was to bring you."

"If you want to carry me, you may," said Tempest, with a short laugh; "if not, wait a moment and I'll come. Jones, tell Pridgin I want to speak to him--wait, I'll go to him."

The school messenger looked as if he felt it his duty to take the senior at his word. Had Tempest been a smaller boy, he might have done so. As it was, he repeated,--

"At once, please, sir."

Tempest took no notice, but went across the passage to his friend's room.

When he reappeared in a minute or two, Pridgin was with him, and without taking further notice of the messenger's presence the two walked arm-in- arm out of the house and across the quadrangle.

The news of the summons spread like wildfire. The Philosophers, when in due time they mustered in the faggery after their inspection of the scene of the outrage, were not slow in taking in the seriousness of the situation.

"Of course he's suspected. It's all your fault, you ass, for being such a muff and letting Jarman catch you. You can't do a thing without making a mess of it."

"How could I help it?" I pleaded.

"Couldn't you have fetched his blazer for him without running into that cad's way?"

"What I can't make out," said Langrish, "is how Tempest knew about the guy and was able to let it off."

"I don't believe he did," said I. "I'm sure he didn't."

"You'd believe anything. Things like that don't go off by themselves, do they?"

I was bound to admit they did not, but persisted in my belief that Tempest had nothing to do with it.

But the logic of the Philosophers was irresistible.

"Didn't we see him go over and come back? and didn't it blow up the moment he got into the house?" said Trimble.

"And didn't he go over on purpose to have it out with Jarman?" said Coxhead.

"And hadn't he got his blazer with him when he came back?--so he must have been in the gym.," said Warminster.

"Who else was likely to do it?" said Langrish. "I suppose you'll try to make out Jarman tried to blow himself up?"

"I never said so. All I said was that I'm positive Tempest never did it."

"And all we say is that you're about as big an ass as you look, and that's saving a good deal," chimed in the Philosophers.

How long the wrangle might have gone on I cannot say. For just then the school messenger appeared on the scene once more--this time in quest of me.

"Young Master Jones iv., you're to go to the head master at once."

"What for?" said I, feeling a cold shudder go down my spine.

"Ask a policeman," replied the ribald official. "You've had a short time and a merry one, my young gentleman; but it's over at last."

"But I never--"

"Sharp's the word!" interrupted he.

"You'd better cut," said the Philosophers. "We'll give you a lift if we can."

It was poor consolation, but such as it was I valued it. Never criminal walked to the gallows with as heavy a heart as I followed the school messenger across the quadrangle and past the fated gymnasium to the head master's study.

There I found four people waiting to see me. Tempest looking very sullen, the head master looking very grave, Mr Jarman looking very vicious, and a policeman looking very cheerful.

CHAPTER SEVENTEEN.
BEFORE THE "BEAK."

At the sight of the policeman I gave myself up for lost. The sins and errors of my youth all rose in a hideous procession before me. I recalled vividly the occasion when, years ago, I had borrowed Dicky Brown's "nicker" without acknowledgment, and lost it. I recalled a dismal series of assaults and libels in my guardian's office. I recollected with horror once travelling on a half-ticket two days after my twelfth birthday. Above all, the vision of that ill-favoured effigy under the grating rose gibbering and mocking me to my face, and claiming me for penal servitude, if not for the gallows itself.

How well I remember every detail of that scene as I entered the doctor's study! The bust of Minerva looking askance at me from above the book- case; the quill in the doctor's hand with its fringe all on end; Tempest's necktie crooked and showing the collar stud above; Mr Jarman's eye coldly fixed on me; and the policeman, helmet in hand, standing with his large boots on the hearthrug, the picture of content and prosperity.

"Jones," said the doctor, "we have sent for you to tell us what you did at the gymnasium last night. You were there, I understand, after dark?"

I looked first at the doctor, then at Tempest. I would have given worlds to be able to have two minutes' conversation with him, and ascertain what he wished me to say, if indeed he wished me to say anything at all. The memory of a similar dilemma at Dangerfield only served to confuse me more, and make it impossible to decide how I should act now; while the presence of the policeman drove from my head any ideas that were ever there. Would Tempest like me to say that I went there at his bidding, and if not, how could I explain the matter? I wished I only knew what had been said already, so that at least I might put my evidence on the right side.

"Yes, sir," said I, "I saw Mr Jarman there."

"What were you doing there, eh, young master?" said the policeman.

This was an unexpected attack from the flank of the battle for which I was wholly unprepared. I could have told the doctor, or even Mr Jarman. But to be questioned thus by a representative of the law was too much for my delicate nerves.

"Really, it wasn't me," said I. "I didn't do it, and don't know who did. I only went to get a blazer, and left it there directly Mr Jarman told me to do so."

"A blazer?" said the policeman, with the air of a man who has made a discovery. "What sort of a thing is that? A blazer? Was it alight?"

Here Tempest laughed irreverently, much to the displeasure of the policeman. I was, however, thankful for the cue.

"What," said I, "don't you know what a blazer is? Anybody knows that. It's what you have in the fields."

"Come, young gentleman," said the officer, whom Tempest's laugh had put on his dignity, "no prevaricating. What were you doing with that there blazer?"

"What was I doing with it? Fetching it."

The policeman was evidently puzzled. He wished he knew what a blazer was, but in the present distinguished company did not like to show his ignorance.

"That blazer must be produced," said he; "it'll be evidence."

I looked at Tempest, as the person best able to deal with the matter, and said,--

"I left it in the gym. Mr Jarman made me."

"How long was that before the explosion? Was it alight when you left it?"

"The blazer? Oh no."

"A blazer," explained the head master blandly, "is a flannel jacket. I don't see what use it can be as evidence."

"I suppose," said Tempest jauntily, who was evidently recovering his presence of mind, "he thought it was a lucifer match."

"You'll laugh on the wrong side of your face, young gentleman," said the policeman wrathfully; "this here matter will have to be gone into. There's been a party injured, and it'll be a matter for the magistrate. You'll have to come along with me."

"I tell you," said Tempest, becoming grave once more, "I've had no more to do with it than you have."

"And yet," said Mr Jarman, speaking for the first time, "the explosion took place immediately after you were there, and when it was impossible for any one else to be there."

"I say I know nothing at all about it," said Tempest shortly, "and I don't care what you think."

"Come, Tempest," said Dr England, "no good will be gained by losing temper. It is very necessary to get to the bottom of this business, especially as some one has been injured. It seems almost impossible the explosion could have happened by accident; at the same time, knowing what I do of you, I do not myself believe that you are the boy who would commit an outrage of this sort. As the policeman intends to report the affair to the magistrate, you had better go with him and let him investigate the matter. Don't do yourself injustice by losing your temper. Mr Jarman, your attendance will probably be necessary; and Jones had better go too, although so far he has not thrown very much light on the matter. Constable, if you will take my compliments to Captain Rymer and ask him when he can see us--"

"Beg pardon, sir," said the constable, evidently sore about the blazer, "the young gent must come along with me now. That's my duty, and I can't take no instructions contrary."

"Very well," said the doctor stiffly; "we will go to Captain Rymer at once."

"Hadn't you better handcuff me?" said Tempest, who appeared to be seized with a wild desire to exasperate the man of the law.

The policeman glared as if he was disposed to take him at his word.

"None of your imperence, I can tell you, my beauty!" said he. "I ain't a-going to stand it--straight. Come, stir yourself."

"It is not necessary," said the head master, "for you to come with us. I give my word that we shall be at the police court immediately. But I wish to avoid the public scandal of one of my boys going through the streets in charge."

"I ain't a-going to let him out of my sight," said the ruffled constable. "I know his style."

Tempest smiled provokingly.

"I'd sooner walk, sir," said he. "If the policeman holds me on one side and Mr

Jarman on the other--"

"Silence, sir," said the doctor sternly, while Mr Jarman raised his brows deprecatingly.

"Am I to come too?" said I.

"Yes."

"I should like Pridgin and some of the fellows to be there too, sir," said Tempest. "They saw me just before and just after the explosion."

"It does not seem necessary to have more boys," said Mr Jarman.

"Not to you!" said Tempest hotly; "the fewer *you* have the better. But if you choose to accuse me, I sha'n't ask you whom to have to speak for me."

"Tempest," said the head master, "you are only doing yourself harm by this. Jones, go and fetch Pridgin, and any of the others he speaks of, to the police court; and kindly do not say a word of what has passed here. How, constable, are you ready?"

The school was fortunately all within doors at the time, so that, except to the few who chanced to be gazing from the windows, the little procession, headed by the doctor and Mr Jarman, with the policeman and Tempest bringing up the rear, passed unobserved.

I was full of apprehensions. Whatever the result, I knew Tempest well enough to be sure that the effect on him would be bad, and would call out in him all that spirit of insubordination and defiance which had before now threatened to wreck his career. A strong sense of responsibility was all that had hitherto held it in check. If that were now shattered--and how could it help being upset by this charge?--it would break out badly and dangerously. I was not long in speeding over to Sharpe's, where I found Pridgin just going over to class.

He heard the doctor's message with a groan of weariness.

"What's the use of my going?--*I* can't tell them anything," said he.

"You can tell them Tempest never did it," said I.

"If they don't believe him, they won't me. Anyhow, I am coming." Thereupon I was inspired to tell him the secret history of the effigy of Mr Jarman, and my theory as to the cause of the explosion; namely, that Tempest might have dropped a match through the grating, not knowing on what it would fall, and that in the natural perversity of things it had lit on the projecting tongue of the guy.

"You'd better make a clean breast of that guy," said Pridgin, "if you want to get Tempest out of this mess. You'll probably get expelled or flogged, but Low Heath can spare you better than it can Tempest. It strikes me you'd better fetch down one or two of your lot to corroborate you. It sounds too neat a story as it is."

Whereupon I sought out Langrish and Trimble, and had the satisfaction of making their hair stand on end for once. At first they flatly refused to come, and reminded me that, as President of the Conversation Club, the entire responsibility for the guy rested on me.

"All serene," said I, "only come and let them know how Jarman brought it all on. The more we go for him, the better for our man."

They failed to see the force of my logic, but curiosity and love of adventure induced them to venture into the lion's den. On our way, moreover, we captured Dicky Brown, who, to do him credit, was only too eager to come with us and stand by his old Dux.

Contrary to our expectations, when we arrived, instead of finding a crowded court, we were ushered into the magistrate's parlour, where, to judge by appearances, a comfortable little party was going on.

The captain, a cheery old boy, familiar to all Low Heathens for his presence on speech day, sat at a table with his clerk beside him. The doctor and Mr Jarman were also sitting down, and Tempest was standing restlessly near the window. The lodge-keeper's son, with his head bound up (for he was the victim of the explosion, and I suppose, the prosecutor), was standing beside the policeman, cap in hand, on the mat.

At the sight of the three juniors the doctor frowned a little, and Mr Jarman scowled.

"What are these boys doing here?" said the former.

"Please, sir, we thought you wanted to hear how it went off," said Langrish.

"So we do," said the magistrate; "sit down, my lads. We'll hear what you have to say in time."

"Please, sir," said Tempest, "may I speak to Pridgin?"

"Certainly, my lad," said the captain again.

So the two friends hastily conferred together in the window, while we stared round with an awestruck, and apparently disconcerting, gaze at the gentlemen on

the doormat, who severally represented the majesty of the law and injured inno-
cence.

"Now, then," said the magistrate presently, "let us hear what this is all about.
One of your boys, doctor, I see, is charged with attempting to blow up part of the
school gymnasium last night, and injuring this poor fellow here. Who makes the
charge, by the way? Do you?"

"No," said the doctor, "I understand Mr Jarman does."

"Which is Mr Jarman?" said the captain, looking blandly round. "Ah, you.
Well, sir, this is a serious charge to make; *let* us hear what you have to say. This
is not a sworn examination, but what you say will be taken down, and the boy you
accuse will have a right to ask any question. Now, sir."

Mr Jarman, thereupon, with very bad grace, for he felt that the magistrate's
tone was not cordial, related how he was walking in the court at such and such an
hour, when he saw a boy attempting to enter the gymnasium. That he stopped him
and demanded his name. That the boy pushed past him and entered the gymnasium. Upon which Mr Jarman turned the key on the outside in order to detain him
there, by way of punishment. That the boy began to kick at the door, and after half
an hour broke it open and made his escape. That the boy was Tempest, and that
scarcely two minutes after he had left, and just after Mr Jarman, having stayed to
examine the damage to the door, had turned to go away, the explosion occurred;
that he heard a cry from young Sugden, the lodge-keeper's son, who was passing at
the time, and was thrown violently forward against the railings, cutting his head
badly.

"How do you know the boy was Tempest?" asked the magistrate.

"I recognised him in the dark," said Mr Jarman. "In fact, I expected him."

"Expected him?"

"Yes, he had sent his fag for a jacket just previously, and I had sent the fag
back."

"Why?"

"Boys are not allowed to enter the gymnasium after dark."

"Is that a rule of the school?"

"It is my rule."

"Does it apply to senior boys as well as juniors?" asked Tempest.

"I am responsible for the gymnasium, and--"

"That is not the question," said the magistrate. "Have you ever allowed senior boys in the gymnasium after dark?"

"I may have; but I forbade Tempest to enter last night."

"What harm was there in his fetching his coat, if it was not against rules?"

"It was against rules to go in when I told him not."

"Well, well," said Captain Rymer, "that is a matter that need not detain us. Have you any more questions, Mr Tempest?"

"Yes, please, sir. You said you were expecting me, Mr Jarman. What made you do that?"

"I expected, from my knowledge of your conduct, that you would come and try and get the blazer."

"When have I disobeyed you before?"

"You know as well as I do, Tempest."

"Yes, but I don't," said the magistrate. "Answer the question."

Mr Jarman thereupon gave his version of the affair at Camp Hill Bottom.

"The offence being," said the magistrate, "that the boys, Tempest among them, were out, on the afternoon of a holiday, half an hour from the school, with only a one quarter of an hour to get back. You punished the boys, I understand."

"Yes."

"And Tempest took his punishment with the rest."

"Yes."

"I suppose it is a special indignity to a senior boy, captain of his house, to be paraded for extra drill with a lot of small boys, eh, Dr England?"

"I should consider it so," said the doctor.

"I did not feel myself called upon to make any difference," said Mr Jarman.

"Apparently not. And on account of this affair, you say you expected Tempest would attempt to defy you last night?"

Mr Jarman bit his lips and did not reply.

Tempest resumed his questions with a coolness that surprised us.

"You were smoking, I think, Mr Jarman?"

"What if I was?"

"Nothing, only I wanted the magistrate to know it. And you locked me into the gymnasium for half an hour till I kicked myself out. I say you had no right to do that. What did you do while I was inside?"

"I walked up and down."

"Did you try to stop me when I got out?"

"No."

"Why?" asked Tempest, with a sneer that made us all contrast his broad shoulders with the master's slouch.

"I decided to deal with the matter to-day."

"How did you see what I had done to the door in the dark?"

"I saw by the light of a match."

"You say it was two minutes after I left that the explosion took place, and immediately after you left?"

"That's what I said."

"And you were striking matches during the interval?"

"Yes."

"And yet you suggest that it was I who blew the place up?"

"I say it was suspicious, knowing your frame of mind and the passion you were in at the time."

"How could I blow up the place without explosives?"

"There must have been some there already."

"He didn't know anything about that! That was our affair, wasn't it, you chaps?" blurted out Trimble.

"Rather," chimed in all of us.

The sensation in the court at this announcement may be better imagined than described.

The magistrate put on his glasses and stared at us. Mr Jarman looked startled. The doctor looked bewildered.

"You see, it was this way," said Trimble, who had been working himself up to the point all through the previous cross-examination. "We had--"

"Wait a moment, my boy," said the magistrate. But the witness was too eager to listen to the remark.

"It was this way. We had a guy belonging to the Ph.C.C, you know, and he was chock-full of fireworks. We were keeping him for Guy Fawkes' Day, you know.

You wouldn't have known he was Jarman (Mr Jarman, I mean), to look at him, but he was, and Sarah, being president, offered to look after him. It was too big to stick under the bed, so--"

"So," continued I, "I thought the safest place to stick him would be in the lumber room under the gym.; and I never thought any one would be dropping matches through the grating on his touch-paper tongue. Tempest didn't know anything about it, and--"

"You see," said Langrish, taking up the parable, "we meant to keep it dark, and only the Philosophers were in it; he had on Sarah's hat and boots, and a top-coat we found somewhere about. He'd have never gone off of himself, and he wouldn't have done any harm on the Fifth, when we should have hung and blown him up in the open. Tempest--"

"Tempest," broke in Dicky Brown, putting in his oar, "isn't the kind of chap to do a thing like that on purpose; and it must have been Mr Jarman blew him up by mistake, with one of his matches or the end of a cigar or something--"

"It was a mulish thing of Sarah to stick him there," said Trimble, "but he knows no better, and thought it was all right. So did we, and Pridgin says it was quite an accident, sir, and--"

"And if any one's to get in a row," said I, "we'd better, because he was our guy, and the mistake we made was letting his touch-paper tongue hang out so far. He'd have never blown up if it hadn't been for that."

Here there was a general pause for breath, and the magistrate, who evidently had a sense of humour, said,--

"And pray who is Sarah, my man?"

"That's what they call me when they're fooling; it's not my real name, really, sir. Jones iv. is my real name."

"That's right," said Trimble; "he's only called Sarah because he looks like it. He's not more in it than the rest of us, because he only had to take care of the guy because he was president. We're all sorry the tongue was made so long."

The magistrate did his best to look grave as he turned to Mr Jarman.

"Does this explanation help to clear up the mystery?"

Mr Jarman bit his lips and said,--

"If it is as they say, it may account for the explosion. I certainly dropped several matches through the grating."

"It is as we say, isn't it, you chaps?" said Langrish. "We wouldn't tell a cram about it."

"Rather not!" chimed we.

"Very well. Then I don't see that I can do much good," said the magistrate. "Dr England will know better how to deal with the matter. An accident is an accident after all; and if I may give an opinion, these boys have done quite properly in coming here and telling all about it. Little boys should not be allowed to play with explosives. At the same time, you must allow me to say, Mr Jarman, that it is unfortunate for a master to put himself in the position of being made the subject of an effigy. As for Tempest, there is absolutely nothing against him, unless according to the rules of the school it is an offence for a boy who is locked up in a dark room at night to do his best to get out. It is a great pity the matter was brought to me at all; but as it has been, my advice is to let it rest where it is. Meanwhile, this poor fellow who has been injured has some claim, and I dare say this sovereign will help get him the necessary bandages and plaster for his forehead. Good morning, Dr England; good morning, Mr Jarman. Good day, my lads. Let this be a lesson against touch-paper tongues." So ended the famous affair of Mr Jarman's guy.

CHAPTER EIGHTEEN.
GOING DOWN STREAM.

If any one supposed that Low Heath had heard the last of Mr Jarman's guy they little knew Mr Jarman, or Tempest, or the Philosophers. The ghost of that unhappy effigy was hardly likely to be laid by a simple magisterial decision.

Mr Jarman, it was rumoured, had a bad quarter of an hour with the doctor that evening, and went about his ordinary work for the next few days with a scowl which boded no good to any one who chanced to cross him, least of all to those of us who had contributed to his defeat.

Tempest, on the other hand, took his victory coolly. He talked it over with his chums, and came to the conclusion that they were quits with the enemy and could afford to leave him alone. But it was plain to see that he had suffered a jar, which found expression in his reckless unconcern for the duties of his position as head of his house, and an increased disinclination to make any exertion for the credit of a school which, he considered, had treated him ill. What troubled me most was to notice that his spirits had flagged, and that he was dropping slowly into the listless indifference which had made Pridgin only a term ago shirk his responsibilities to the school.

Towards us juniors he was utterly easy-going, perhaps in token of his gratitude for the assistance we had rendered him at a critical time; but chiefly, I fear, because he was slack to check anything which seemed to defy constituted authority or promised to give an uneasy time to the representatives of law and order.

To do us credit, we availed ourselves of his licence to the uttermost. Sharpe's rapidly became known as the "rowdy" house at Low Heath, and we grew almost proud of the distinction. Mr Sharpe, an amiable bookworm, made periodical mild expostulations, which were always most deferentially received, and most invariably neglected.

If any reader thinks (as we flattered ourselves at the time) that Mr Jarman was the cause of all this state of things, let me tell him he is as stupid as we young fools then were.

It's all very well to stand up for your rights, but the way to do it is not by letting everything go wrong. If poor old Tempest had taken a bigger view of things, he would have seen that the way to pay Jarman out was by making Sharpe's house the crack house of Low Heath in spite of him. But how hard it is to see just what the right thing is at the time! So I do not propose to throw stones at anybody, whatever the reader may do.

The Philosophers of course duly entered a record of the transactions just related in their minutes, the reading of which occupied the whole of one of the extraordinary general meetings of their club.

One could never say what line Langrish would take up; and I as president always had my qualms in calling upon him to read the minutes of the previous meeting.

On the present occasion our meeting was held one half-holiday late in the term, in mid-stream, on a barge which, in the course of a "scientific" ramble, we found in a forlorn condition, about a mile above Low Heath. It was empty, and neither horse nor man nor boy was there to betoken that it had an owner.

Being capacious, though dirty--for it was evidently in the habit of carrying coal--it struck us generally that in the interests of philosophy we should explore it. The result being satisfactory, it was moved and seconded and carried that the club hereby hold an extraordinary meeting.

Objection was taken to the proximity of our meeting-place to the bank--"in case some of the day louts should be fooling about," as Warminster explained. Thereupon, with herculean efforts, we shoved out the stern across stream, the prow being still tethered; and catching on to a stake, we had the satisfaction not only of feeling ourselves in an unassailable position, but of knowing that we were effectually blocking the river for any presumptuous wayfarer who wanted to go either up stream or down.

After exploring the bunks and lockers and hold of the unsavoury vessel, Trimble proposed that it would be best for the club to occupy seats on the floor of the barge, where, quite invisible to any one on shore or stream, we could hold our meeting undisturbed.

In a few introductory remarks, which were listened to with some impatience, I explained that things had reached a critical state at Low Heath. It was the duty of everybody to back up Tempest and make it hot for Jarman. (Cries of "Why don't you?" "What's the use of you?") We didn't intend to be interfered with by anybody, and if Coxhead didn't shut up shying bits of coal he'd get one for himself. (Derisive cheers from Coxhead, and more coal.)

Coxhead and I were both warm when, a quarter of an hour later, I resumed the chair and called upon our excellent secretary to read the minutes, which he accordingly did.

"Owing to the asinine mulishness of Sarah--" Here an interruption occurred.

"Look here," said I, "you've got to drop that, Langrish. I've told you already I'm not going to stand it."

"Stand what? Being called Sarah or an asinine mule?"

I explained that I was particularly referring to Sarah.

"Oh, all serene," said the secretary. "We'll start again."

"Owing to the asinine mulishness of S--H, and three between--"

"No--that won't do," said I, fiercely.

"Owing to the asinine mulishness of--" here the speaker pointed at me with his thumb--"of the asinine mule in the chair--"

I was weak enough to let this pass, and the applause with which it was received quite carried the secretary off his feet. When he got on them again he resumed,--

"Jarman's guy was mulled all through. Even Trimble couldn't have made a bigger mess of it."

Here Trimble mildly interposed, but Langrish, who had hooked one arm through a ring in the side of the vessel, and had a firm grip with his feet up against a rib in front of him, was inflexible.

"A bigger mess of it," he repeated, when at last he was free to proceed. "It was stuck just under the grating of the gym., and was neatly blown up by Jarman at 8:15 on November 2. The cost of the fireworks was four- and-six, which the asinine mule, as it was his fault, is going to hand over to the club, or know the reason why."

I said I would know the reason why. Whereupon a long Socratic argument ensued.

"Do you mean to say it wasn't your fault?" demanded Langrish.

"I couldn't tell Jarman would drop his cigar down."

"But if you'd tried you couldn't have stuck him in a better place."

"That's what I thought. What have you got to growl at?"

"You offered to put it in a safe place."

"No, I didn't. I didn't want to have it at all."

"But you did have it; you can't deny that."

"No--but--"

"Hold on. And you stuck it there under the grating."

"Well, and if I did--"

"And that's how Jarman's cigar got on to it."

"Yes--but--"

"And that's how it blew up, wasn't it? You haven't the cheek to say that wasn't the way it blew up?"

"Of course it was; only--"

"Therefore, if you hadn't stuck it there it wouldn't have blown up. You can't deny that?"

"I don't say that. What I say--"

"Therefore, it was you who blew it up; and it's you've got to pay for the fireworks, Q.E.D.; and if you don't shut up, young Sarah, you'll get your face washed."

I felt I was the victim of a very one-sided argument, but the popular verdict was so manifestly in favour of the secretary, that I was constrained to allow the point to pass.

"--reason why," resumed Langrish. "There was a bit of a row, and the doctor and some of the chaps were had up before the beak. We got on all serene till a howling chimpanzee whose name is Sarah--"

"There you are again," said I. "I'll pay you now."

"What are you talking about? I never mentioned you--did I, you chaps?"

"Rather not," chimed in the Philosophers assembled.

"Of course," said Langrish, "if whenever you hear of a howling chimpanzee you think you're being referred to, we can't help it, can we?"

The cheers which greeted this unanswerable proposition convinced me I had given myself away for once.

"--howling chimpanzee, whose name's Sarah, put in his oar and spoilt the whole thing."

"If it hadn't been for me," protested I, "you'd none of you have been there at all."

"The magistrate," proceeded Langrish, not heeding the interruption, "treated him with the contempt he deserved, and gave him a caution which he'll remember to the end of his days."

"I don't remember it now," I growled.

"Turn him out for interrupting," shouted the secretary.

"You'd better not try," snarled I, preparing to contest my seat. But Langrish, eager to continue, went on,--

"The rest of us pulled Tempest through easy. If Trim hadn't dropped his 'h's,' and--"

Here there was a real row. Trim rose majestic and outraged, and hurled himself on the secretary; and for a quarter of an hour at least, any casual passer-by glancing at the apparently empty barge in mid-stream, would have come to the conclusion that it was swaying from side to side rather more violently than the force of the current seemed to warrant.

Trimble's "h's" took a long time to avenge, and by the time it was done most of us were pretty much the colour of the coal-dust in which we had searched for them.

Langrish was about to proceed with his luckless minutes when Warminster, who had happened to peep above board for the sake of fresh air, exclaimed,--

"Hullo, we're adrift!"

Instantly all hands were on board, and we discovered that our gallant barge, probably during the last argument, had slipped her boathook at the stern, and that the rope which held our prow had evidently been slipped for us by a couple of youths wearing the town-boy ribbon, whom we could descry at that moment strolling innocently up the towing-path, apparently heedless of our existence.

The great lumbering barge was going down stream side on, about half-way between either bank, at the breakneck speed of a mile an hour. We had lost our boathook, and had nothing whatever to navigate our craft with. Worst of all, at the end of the long reach, coming to meet us, we could see another barge, towed by a horse, which could certainly never pass up in safety.

We were in for it, and had evidently nothing to do but peer, with our grimy faces over the gunwale, at our impending doom. About a hundred yards off the men in charge of the opposition barge became aware of our presence, and a hurried interchange of polite observations took place between the skipper at the helm and the driver on the tow-path, the result of which was that their tow-rope was cast off and hauled ashore; and man and horse, accompanied by a dangerous-looking dog, advanced at a quick pace to meet us.

The rope was hurriedly gathered up in a coil and thrown across our bows, and we were invited to hitch the loop at the end over the hook on our front thwart. The horse was then put in motion, and the downward career of our ark suffered an abrupt check, as we found ourselves rudely lugged in towards the bank.

The situation was an awkward one, for not only was the skipper of the opposition barge landed, and awaiting us with an uncomplimentary eagerness on the bank, but the driver, whip in hand, was standing beside him, and the dog, showing his teeth, beside him.

"Kotched yer, are we?" said the former, with a deplorable profuseness of unnecessary verbiage, as he jumped on board. "We tho't as much. Lend me that there whip, Bill."

"You tip 'em over, Tom; I'll make 'em jump."

Escape was impossible. Our exits were in the hands of the enemy. We made one feeble attempt to temporise.

"We're sorry," said I, in my capacity as spokesman. "We didn't know it was your boat, really."

"You knows it now," said the proprietor. "Over you go, or I'll 'elp yer."

What I was it a case of being pitched overboard? We looked round desperately for hope, but there was none. We might by a concerted action have tackled one man, but the other on the bank, with the whip and the dog, was a formidable second line to carry. It needed all our philosophy to sustain us in the emergency.

"Come, wake up," shouted the man. "'Ere, Tike, come!"

Whereupon, to our terror, the dog leapt up on to the barge, and jumped yapping in our midst.

"T'other side, if *you* please," said the bargee, as I prepared dismally to take my header on the near side. "Wake 'im up, Tike!"

I needed no waking up; and giving myself up for lost, bounded to the other side of the barge, and made a floundering jump overboard. Luckily for us the Low Heathens could swim to a man, and if all that we were in for was to swim round that hideous barge and get ashore, we should have been easily out of it. But we had yet to reckon with the man and the whip, who in his turn made every preparation to reckon with us.

I was the first to taste his mettle. He had me twice before I could get clear, and I seem to feel it as I write. One by one the luckless and dripping Philosophers ran the gauntlet of that fatal debarkation, which was by no means alleviated by the opprobrious hilarity of our two castigators and the delighted yappings of Tike.

At last it was all over, and, dripping and smarting, we collected our shattered forces a quarter of a mile down the towing-path, and hastily agreed that as a meeting-place for Philosophers a barge was not a desirable place. It was further agreed, that if we could catch the day boys who were the source of all our woes (for if our barge had not been let adrift, we could have sheered off in time), we would do to them as we had been done by.

By good or ill luck, we had scarcely arrived at this important decision when a defiant shout from a little hill among the trees close by apprised us that we were not the only occupants of the river bank; and worse still, that whoever the strangers were, they must have been witnesses of our recent misfortunes--a certainty which made us feel anything but friendly.

"Who are they?" said Langrish.

"Suppose it's those Urbans," said Coxhead. "I heard they were going to excavate somewhere this way."

"I vote we go and see," said Trimble, who was evidently smarting not a little.

So we went and saw, and it was even as Coxhead had surmised; for as we approached, shouts of--

"Who got licked with a whip?"

"What's the price of beauty?"

"Why don't you dry your clothes?" fell on our ears.

"Yah--we dare you to come down and have your noses pulled!" shouted we.

"We dare you to come up and have your hair curled!" shouted they.

We accepted the invitation, and stormed the hill. The battle was short and sharp. We were fifteen to ten, and had a grievance. I found myself engaged with Dicky Brown, who, though he did himself credit, was hampered by a scatheful of stones, which he fondly hoped might turn out to be fossils, on his back. I grieve to say I made mincemeat of Dicky on this occasion. In a few minutes the hill was ours, and the enemy in full retreat.

We remained a short time to celebrate our victory, and then adjourned to the school, a little solaced in our spirits.

The day's troubles, however, were not over, for at the door of Sharpe's house, reinforced by half a dozen recruits, stalked the Urbans, thirsting for reprisals, and longing to wipe out scores.

Then ensued a notable battle. We failed to dislodge the enemy by a forward attack, and for some time it seemed as if our flank movements would be equally unsuccessful. At length, by a great effort, we succeeded in cutting off a few of them from the main body, and were applying ourselves to the task of annihilating the rest when Tempest appeared on the scene.

He looked fagged and harassed, and was evidently not much interested in our battle. A row was now too common a thing in Sharpe's to be an event, and he allowed it to proceed with complete unconcern.

Just, however, as he was taming to enter the house, Mr Jarman came up.

It was almost the first time we had met officially since our encounter in the magistrate's room, and as with one accord we ceased hostilities and stared at him, one or two of the more audacious of our party indulged in a low hiss.

"Come in, you fellows, at once," said Tempest, turning on his heel.

"Wait, you boys," said Mr Jarman, taking out his pencil. "Wait, Tempest."

But Tempest did not wait, nor did we, but made a deliberate rush into our house, and in less than a minute were safely stowed away in our several studies, secure from all immediate arrest.

It was an act of open rebellion such as Sharpe's had not yet ventured on. There was no excuse that any of us had not heard the order. We had, and had disobeyed it. And in the present instance Tempest had headed us. What would be the consequence?

We were not destined to know till next morning, when a notice appeared on the board stating that Mr Sharpe's house having been reported for riotous conduct and disobedience to orders, the head master would meet the boys in the hall at eleven o'clock.

CHAPTER NINETEEN.
HALTING BETWEEN TWO OPINIONS.

There was no mistaking the doctor's meaning this time. Sharpe's had had a long rope, but had come to the end of it at last. I would not for the world have confessed it at the time, but I was half glad a crisis had come. My conscience had smitten me more than once about my work. I had fooled away the good chance with which I had entered Low Heath. Fellows far below me in scholarship had got ahead of me by force of steady plodding, while I was wasting my time. The good resolutions which I had brought up with me had one by one fallen overboard, and I had been content enough to take my place among the rowdies without an effort.

I had counted all through on Tempest's backing up. If he had been keen on the credit of the house, I felt I could have been so too. If he had been down on me for my neglect of work, I felt I should have stuck to it. As it was, slackness reigned supreme. Tempest was slack because he was out of humour. Pridgin was slack because he was lazy. Wales was slack because he wanted to be in the fashion. And all of us were slack because our betters set us the example. It needs no little courage for a single boy to attempt to stem the drift of slackness in a school house. A dull, dogged boy like Dicky Brown might have done it; but I could not afford to be peculiar, and therefore succumbed, against my judgment, to the prevalent dry rot.

Now that a crisis had come I hoped Tempest might, if not for his own sake, for ours, pull up, and take his house in hand, as he well could do if he chose. A short conversation I overheard as I was fagging in his study that morning, however, was not encouraging.

"What's it to be," said Wales, "a lecture or a row?"

"A row, I hope," said Tempest wearily.

"What's wrong, old chap?" asked Pridgin.

"Nothing. Out of curl, that's all," said Tempest, trying to assume a laugh.

"You're not going to cave in to Jarman at this time of day," said Wales, "are you?"

"Do you think it likely?" said Tempest.

"I tell you what I don't like," said Pridgin presently; "that's the way Crofter's lately taken to do the virtuous."

"That's not the worst of him," said Wales; "but he's been chumming up with Jarman. I've met them twice lately walking together."

"I suppose he's got his eye on the headship of the house," said Tempest, "when I get kicked out."

"Look here, old chap," responded Pridgin, looking really anxious, "it's not to come to that, surely. It would be intolerable to have him over us. Come what will, you must stick to us."

"All very well," said Tempest dismally; "that's England's affair more than mine. If knuckling under to Jarman is a condition, I'm out of it, and Crofter is welcome to it."

This was all; and it was bad enough. When the summons to assemble in hall came, I went there in a state of dejection, feeling that the fates were all against me, and that the new leaf I hoped for was several pages further on yet.

My fellow-Philosophers, I regret to say, neither shared in nor appreciated my forebodings.

"Look at that ass Sarah, trying to look virtuous," said Trimble. "Just like him, when there's a row on."

"I'm not trying to look virtuous," said I; "I'm sick of all these rows, though."

"Pity you aren't sick when you're getting us into them, instead of after. You know you've been at the bottom of every row there's been on this term."

This sweeping statement was not calculated to allay my discomfort.

"Don't tell lies," said I.

"No more we are. Who got us into that mess at Camp Hill Bottom? Sarah did. Who landed us in the row about Jarman's guy? Old Sarah. Who played the fool with that barge and got us all licked? Cad Sarah. Who started the shindy last night that's fetched us all in here? Lout Sarah. Who's going to be expelled? Howling

Sarah. And who'll be a jolly good riddance of bad rubbish? Chimpanzee Sarah. There you are. Make what you like of it, and don't talk to us."

This tirade took my breath away. I knew it said more than it meant. Still, it wasn't flattering, and it taxed my affection sorely to sit quietly and hear it out. But, somehow, to-day I was too anxious and worried to care much what anybody said.

Fortunately the entrance of the doctor, Mr Sharpe, and Mr Jarman, made further discussion for the time being unnecessary--and a gloomy silence fell over the assembly.

Dr England was evidently worried. Secretly, I believe, he was bored by the whole affair, and wished Mr Sharpe and his prefects could manage the affairs of their own house. Perhaps, too, the fact that Mr Jarman was once more the complainant had something to do with his lack of humour.

"Now, boys," said he, "this is an unusual and unpleasant interview, and I heartily wish it were not necessary. When a whole house is reported for rowdiness, it shows, I'm afraid, that the sense of duty to the school is in a bad way. This is not the first occasion this term on which this house has been reported, but I have previously refrained from interfering, in the hope that the good feeling of the boys themselves would assert itself and make any action of mine unnecessary. I am sorry it has not been so. As to the scrimmage in the quadrangle yesterday, I am not disposed to make too much of that; at any rate, that weighs less with me than what I understand to have been a deliberate act of disobedience to the master, who quite properly interfered to restore order; disobedience, I am sorry to say, encouraged, if not instigated, by the head boy of the house. I hope there may be some mistake about this. Will the boys who were engaged in the fight stand up?"

The Philosophers rose to a man, with a promptitude which was almost aggressive. Bother it all, why should we be backward in admitting that we had gone for those day boys, and "put them to bed" for once?

"I ask you boys to say whether you heard Mr Jarman tell you to wait till he spoke to you?"

"I did, sir," said Langrish.

"So did I," said Trimble.

"We all did," said I.

"And why did you not obey?"

"Tempest told us to come in, so we did," said I.

"That's right, sir," said Coxhead.

And the others assented.

"Very well," said the doctor. "Tempest, I ask you to say whether you heard Mr Jarman tell the boys to wait?"

"Yes, sir."

"And did you tell them, in spite of that, to come in?"

"Yes, sir."

"Why?"

"Because I'm head of the house, and I'm responsible for the order of my house."

"I am glad to hear you think so," said the doctor drily. "Have you always been equally jealous for the order of your house this term, Tempest?"

This was a "facer," as we all felt. Tempest flushed and glanced up at the head master.

"No, sir, I have not," he said.

The doctor was a chivalrous man, and did not try to rub in a sore. Tempest had made a damaging admission against himself, and might be left alone to his own sense of discomfort.

Unluckily, however, Mr Jarman stood by, and the matter could hardly be allowed to drop.

"As regards the incident last night," said the doctor, "you know quite well, all of you, that no boy, even the head of his house, has the right to set his authority against that of a master. Your conduct was an insult to him, and requires an apology. These small boys may have considered they were not doing wrong in obeying you. Tempest, but you can plead no such ignorance. I expect you to apologise to Mr Jarman."

A struggle evidently passed through Tempest's mind. His conscience had been roused by what the doctor had said, and his manner of saying it. Had the apology been demanded for any one else but Mr Jarman, he could have given it, and in one word have put himself on the side of duty. But apologise to Jarman! "If Mr Jarman wants me to tell a lie," said he, slowly, "I'll say I'm sorry. I can't apologise to him."

"Come, Tempest," said the doctor, evidently disconcerted at this threatened difficulty, "you must be aware of the consequences, if you refuse to do this."

"I know, sir, but I can't help it. I can't apologise to Mr Jarman."

Dead silence followed, broken only by the hard breathing of the Philosophers. The doctor twirled the tassel of his cap restlessly. Mr Sharpe looked straight before him through his glasses. Mr Jarman stroked his moustache and smiled. Tempest stood pale and determined, with his eyes on the floor.

"I shall not prolong this scene," said the doctor at last. "For the remaining week of this term the boys concerned in yesterday's disturbance are forbidden to appear in the playing fields. You, Tempest, will have a day to think over your determination. Come to me in my house this time to-morrow."

"I'd sooner it were settled now," said Tempest respectfully and dismally. "I cannot apologise."

"Come to me this time to-morrow," repeated the doctor. "As to the other boys of the house, I want you to understand that you are all concerned in the wellbeing of your house. If, as I fear, a spirit of insubordination is on foot, and your own proper spirit and loyalty to the school is not enough to stamp it out, I must use methods which I have never had to use yet in Low Heath. It may need courage and self- sacrifice in a boy to stand up against the prevailing tone, but I trust there is some of that left even in this misguided house. Now dismiss."

It had been a memorable interview. The doctor might have stormed and raged, and done nothing. As it was, he had talked like a quiet gentleman, and made us all thoroughly ashamed of ourselves.

And yet, as we all of us felt, everything now depended on Tempest. If he surrendered he might count on us to fall in line and make up to him for all he had sacrificed on our behalf. If he held out, and refused his chance, we *too* refused ours and went out with him! If only any one could have brought home to him how much depended on him!

Yet who could blame him for finding it impossible to apologise to Jarman, who had persecuted him all the term with a petty rancour which, so far from deserving apology, had to thank Tempest's moderation that it did not receive much rougher treatment than it had? He might go through the words of apology, but it would be a farce, and Tempest was too honest to be a hypocrite.

There was unwonted quiet in Sharpe's house that afternoon. Fellows were too eagerly speculating as to the fate in store for them to venture on a riot. The Philosophers, of course, stoutly advocated a policy of "no surrender"; but one or two of us, I happened to know, would have been unfeignedly glad to hear that Tempest had squared matters with his pride, and left himself free to take our reform in hand.

Tempest himself preserved a glum silence until after afternoon chapel, when he said to me,--

"Isn't this one of Redwood's evenings, youngster? I'll go with you if you're going."

The Redwoods had given me an open invitation to drop in any Thursday evening to tea and bring a friend. I had been several times with Dicky, and once, in great triumph, had taken Tempest as my guest. It had been a most successful experiment. Not only had Tempest taken the two little girls (and therefore their mother) by storm, but between him and Redwood had sprung up an unexpected friendship, born of mutual admiration and confidence. Since then he had once repeated the visit, and to-night, to my great satisfaction, proposed to go again.

To me it was a miniature triumph to carry off the hero of Sharpe's from under the eyes of his house, and on an occasion like the present, to a destination of which he and I alone knew the secret.

I flattered myself that, in spite of their mocking comments, the Philosophers were bursting with envy. It is always a rare luxury to be envied by a Philosopher; and I think I duly appreciated my blessings, and showed it in the swagger with which I marched my man under the faggery window.

Tempest was depressingly gloomy as we walked along, and my gentle reminder that we could not take the short cut across the playing fields, after the doctor's prohibition, but should have to walk round, did not tend to cheer him up. I half feared he would propose to walk over, in defiance of all consequences. Possibly, if he had been alone, he would have done so, but on my account he made a grudging concession to law and order.

At the Redwoods', however, he cheered up at once. He received a royal welcome from the little girls--in marked contrast to Miss Mamie's sulky reception of me as the destroyer of her nice sash. Redwood himself was delighted to see him, and the family tea was quite a merry one.

When we adjourned to the captain's "den" afterwards I was decidedly out of it.

Indeed, it was broadly hinted to me that the little girls downstairs were anxious for some one to teach them "consequences"; would I mind?

Considering there was no game I detested more than "consequences," and no young ladies less open to instruction than the Misses Redwood, I did not jump at the offer. It was evident, however, Tempest and Redwood wanted to talk, and with a vague sense that by leaving them to do so I was somehow acting for the benefit of Low Heath, I sacrificed myself, and sat down to assist in the usual composite stories; how, for instance, the square Dr England met the mealy-faced Sarah (the little girls knew my nickname as well as the Philosophers) up a tree. He said to her, "We must part for ever;" she (that is I) said to him, "My ma shall know of this;" the consequence was that there was a row, and the world said, "It's all up."

In present circumstances these occult narratives were full of serious meaning for me, and my thoughts were far more with the two seniors above than with the two exacting female juniors below. However, the time passed, and presently Tempest's "Come along, youngster," apprised me that the hour of release had come.

Redwood walked back with us, and from certain fragments of conversation which fell on my ears I was able to gather something of the result of the conference.

"If it were only yourself, you know," said Redwood, "I'd say stick out."

"But," said Tempest, "he knows I'm not sorry, even if I say so."

"It's a choice between humble pie and Low Heath losing you," said the captain.

"Not much loss."

"That's all you know. There's not a fellow we could spare less."

They walked on in silence; then Redwood said,--

"England ought to see that Jarman rots everything the way he goes on. We'll be in a better position to get it altered if you cave in this once."

"I vowed I wouldn't do it. He'll only chuckle," said Tempest, with a groan.

"Let him! Who cares whether Jarman chuckles or not?" retorted the captain. "Look here, old chap, don't you think he'd chuckle more if you got expelled? That would be the biggest score you could give him. Take my advice, and only give him the smallest."

"I don't know. I'll think about it," said Tempest.

"Of course you will, for the sake of Low Heath. Next term we'll go ahead, and the fellows will owe you more than they think."

Here, by an odd chance, just as we came to the school gate, we met Mr Jarman and Crofter walking out in deep confabulation.

I do not know if they saw us. If they did, they pretended not to have done so, and walked on, leaving us to proceed.

"Do you see that?" said Tempest.

"Rather. I know what it means too. It's an extra reason why you should swallow your pride for once, in order to sell them. I tell you they are probably counting on your sticking out, and nothing would disappoint them more."

"Well, old chap," said Tempest, as we came to our door, "it's not your fault if I don't do it. I know you're right, but--"

"But it's a jolly bitter pill, and I wish I could swallow it for you. Good night."

I had the sense for once to keep what I had heard to myself, and retired to bed more hopeful that all would turn out right than I had been for a day or two.

The next morning I was wandering about, aloof from my comrades, in the quadrangle, waiting for the bell to ring for first school, when Marple, the town bookseller, a tradesman familiar to most Low Heathens, accosted me. He was evidently not at home in the school precincts, and, with my usual modesty, I felt he had come to the right source for information.

"Do you belong to Mr Sharpe's house, young gentleman?" said he, with a respectful nod which quite captivated me.

"Yes. Who do you want?"

"I want to see Mr Tempest very particular."

"Oh, he's up in his room. Wait a bit till the bell rings, and he'll come out."

So Mr Marple and I stopped and chatted about the holidays, which were to begin in a day or two, and the football matches and the river.

"You know Mr Tempest pretty well?" said he.

"Rather; I'm his fag, you know."

"A nice gentleman, I fancy. Pretty well off, eh?"

"Oh no. He's a swell, but his people are poor, I know."

"Oh, indeed. Not likely to buy much in my way, eh?"

"Rather not. He's hard up as it is. It's not much good your trying to sell him anything," said I, remembering the rumour about my friend's indebtedness, and anxious to screen him from further debt.

"Ah, indeed--he's in debt, is he--all round?"

"How do you know that?" said I, bristling up. "I don't expect he owes you anything."

Mr Marple laughed.

"That's just what he does; that's why I've stepped over. I don't like showing young gents up, but--"

"Look here," cried I aghast, "for mercy's sake, don't show him up, Marple! It's as likely as not he's to be expelled as it is; this would finish him up."

"If he's likely to be expelled, all the more reason I should get my money before he goes."

"How much is it?" I gasped.

"A matter of two pounds," said the tradesman.

"Look here," said I, "I'll promise you shall be paid. Wait till the last day of the term, do, Marple."

Mr Marple stared at me. The security I fear was not good enough for him. On the other hand, he probably knew that it would not be good for trade if he were to show up a "Low Heathen."

He took an envelope from his pocket and handed it to me. It contained Tempest's bill for sundry stationery, magazines, books, postage stamps, and so on; headed "Fourth and final application." The envelope itself was addressed, "Dr England, with W. Marple's respectful compliments."

The bell rang just then, and I was so anxious to get Marple off the scene that I wildly promised anything to be rid of him, and was finally left, just in time, to meet Tempest unconsciously strolling across the quadrangle on his way to keep his appointment with the doctor.

CHAPTER TWENTY.
DEEPEST DEPTHS.

We did not see Tempest again till the afternoon. As we most of us surmised, he was relieving his feelings after his interview with the doctor by a spin on the river.

How, I wondered, had the interview gone? Had he agreed to the humiliating condition of apologising to Mr Jarman, or had his pride been too much for him after all? If so, this was probably his last spin on the river.

Had our house been Selkirk's, there would, no doubt, have been wagers on the event. As it was, the Philosophers contented themselves with bickering. The general impression seemed to be that he had refused to surrender. That being so, the game was up--there was no object in keeping up appearances.

A spirit of defiance seemed to get hold of us. We deliberately sat on the fence of the prohibited playing fields, in the hope that Mr Jarman or some one would see us. Trimble even went to the length of crossing it at one corner.

What made it more trying was the conduct of the day boys, who, with an acuteness which did them credit, seemed to have discovered our delicate situation, and resolved to make the most of it.

They paraded the field about twenty yards from our fence, jeering at us openly, and daring us to set foot on the turf.

"Look at them," said one, "hung up like a lot of washing on the palings. We'll make them cut. Let's have a scientific meeting. That'll clear them out."

Whereupon the Urbans ranged themselves on the grass under our noses, and called upon Mr Flitwick to address them on the "Treatment of Lunatics."

This was too much. We were few in number, and the palings were hard and uncomfortable. But if they thought they were going to frighten us away by this demonstration, they were mistaken.

Langrish, in a loud voice, called out "Chair," whereupon I, taking the cue, and assuming that the Philosophers were in congress, called upon Mr Trimble to favour us with his oration on "Mud."

"Oh, all serene," said Trimble, who till that moment had had as little notion of his subject as I had had. "Mud is dirty lumps of stuff lying about on the grass, like what you see in front of you. It has neither brains nor sense. It's a vile thing to look at, and worse to touch. If you--"

"--If you," here broke in Mr Flitwick, "want to see what lunatics really are, you should look on the palings of some of our school playing fields. If you happen to see a row of squinney-eyed, ill-dressed mules, with large boots and turn-up noses, and afraid of their lives to move off where they are, those are the prize lunatics. I have pleasure in exhibiting a few choice specimens collected from various sources. The one thing--"

"--The one thing about mud is, it daren't come within reach of you," continued Trimble, getting a little random in his statements, "for fear of getting one in the eye. If you want a sample--"

"--There's one," shouted Flitwick, interrupting our orator with a fragment of mother earth in his face.

Of course it was all up after that. Doctor or no doctor, we couldn't sit by and see our treasurer assaulted. So we hurled ourselves on the foe, regardless of consequences, and a deadly fight ensued. Some of the more cautious of our number were lucky enough to be able to drag their men off the prohibited field and engage them on the right side of the fence.

I was not so lucky--indeed, I was doubly unlucky. For not only was my adversary my dear friend Dicky Brown, whom I loved as a brother, but he edged further and further afield as the combat went on, so that at the last we were cut off from the main body and left to fight our duel conspicuously in the open.

Dicky was not a scientific pugilist, but he had an awkward way of closing in with you and getting you round the middle just at the moment that his left foot got round behind your right calf. And it grieves me to say that, although I boasted of far more talent in the exercise of the fistic art than he did, he had me on my back on the grass just as Mr Sharpe of all persons walked by.

"What are you two doing?" demanded the master, stopping short.

"Fighting, sir," said the stalwart Dicky, "and I licked him."

"Why are you fighting?"

"Because Flitwick shied mud at Trimble," said I.

The reason did not seem to appeal to Mr Sharpe, who replied,--

"You heard the doctor's orders yesterday, Jones iv., about keeping off the playing field?"

"Yes, sir," said I, realising for the first time that I was well out in the middle of the field, and that the rest of my comrades were looking on from a safe distance.

"Come to me after school for exemplary punishment. You are the most disorderly boy in the house, and it is evident a lenient punishment is no good in your case."

"Please, sir," said the loyal Dicky, "I lugged him on a good part of the way."

"No, you didn't," snarled I--taking this as a taunt, whereas it was intended as a "leg-up"--"I came of my own accord."

"Very well," said Mr Sharpe. "You will come to me, Jones iv., of my accord"-- and he walked away.

I was reckless and defiant, and deaf to Dicky's sympathy.

"I don't care," said I. "It was a good job for you he came up. I should have licked you hollow."

"No, you wouldn't, old chap; I had you over twice," said Dicky.

"Come outside and finish it out."

So we adjourned to the other side of the palings and finished it out in the presence of the assembled Urbans and Philosophers. And I grieve to say once more Dicky had me on my back.

The wrath of my comrades was even more grievous to bear than the rejoicings of the enemy. I was promptly withdrawn from the fray as a bad lot, and had it not been for the opportune bell, should probably have been kicked all round.

At any rate, I went in disgusted with myself, with Low Heath, with everybody. What was the use of keeping it up? Tempest, ten to one, was expelled. Dicky Brown, once my inferior, could put me on my back. The Philosophers hated me. Mr Sharpe had marked me down for exemplary punishment, and publicly denounced me as the worst boy in the house. And all this in a single term. What, I wondered, would it be like, if I remained, at the end of a second term?

I looked dismally into Tempest's study--he was not back. Pridgin was in, but did not want me. The faggery just now was impossible. I never felt more lonely and miserable in my life.

I was wandering down the passage, with my jacket flung over my shoulder and my shirt sleeves still tucked up, when the voice of Crofter stopped me.

"Look here," said he, "the contents of your pocket may be interesting to you, but we don't want them littered about the passage. Here, catch hold," and he held out a handful of loose letters. "Why, what's the matter? How blue you look! Has any one been hurting you?"

"Rather not. I've been licking a young cad, that's all."

"Well, you don't look as if you enjoyed it, anyhow. Has Tempest come back?"

"No--probably he's expelled," said I, determined to have things as miserable as possible.

"I sincerely hope not," said Crofter, in a tone which quite softened me to him. "He doesn't like me, but I'd be sorry if he left, all the same."

"He thinks you and Jarman would like to see him kicked out. That's the one reason why he might stay on."

Crofter laughed sweetly.

"What a notion! Why, I've had a good mind to go to England myself and stick up for him."

"It's a good job you haven't," said I.

"What I'm afraid is, that he is worried about other things. I hope, by the way, you never said anything about what I told you the other day."

"No," said I, not quite candidly. For I had tried to tell Tempest, but he would not let me.

"That's right. I hope he's cleared his debts off by now."

"I--I don't think he has," stammered I.

"Really! It's a pity. The doctor would be much more likely to be down on him for being in debt than--"

He pulled up suddenly, as Tempest at that moment walked up. He must have heard the last few words; and if it required looks of guilt and confusion on my part to convince him we had been speaking of him, I think I gave him proof positive.

He had apparently intended to summon me to his study. But, as he saw with whom I was conferring, and overheard the subject of our conversation, he thought better of it, and with lowering face stalked away.

I wished I was dead then! Something told me I had lost my friend, and that no amount of explanation could do away with the barrier which had suddenly been erected between us.

"Awkward," said Crofter. "It's a good job we were talking no harm of him."

"He won't fancy our talking about him at all," said I.

"I suppose we've as much right to talk about him as any one else."

"He'll be awfully down on me, I know," said I miserably.

"All I can say is, if he is, you're a young fool if you care two straws. Tempest's a good fellow; but he's rather a way of not allowing a fellow to have a soul of his own."

This failed to console me. I made one effort to see Tempest and explain, but he was occupied with his books, and did not even deign to notice my presence in his study.

Later on in the evening all speculation as to the result of the morning's interview was set at rest. An unusual summons came to Sharpe's to meet the doctor in our hall.

We assembled uncomfortably and with sore spirits. The worry of the whole business was telling on us, and we heartily hoped, while we clamoured for no surrender in words, that Tempest would disappoint us for once.

The doctor came presently, looking very grave, and accompanied by Mr Jarman. From the head master's face we concluded at once that all was up. But to our surprise he said,--

"I am glad to say, in reference to the matter I met you boys about yesterday, that Tempest has taken a proper sense of his duty, and has undertaken to apologise for his conduct to Mr Jarman. That being so, Tempest, you will please take this opportunity of expressing your regret."

Tempest flushed as he rose in obedience to the doctor's summons. It was evidently, as Redwood had said, "a bitter pill," and had he been a less brave fellow, he could hardly have swallowed it. As it was, even the knowledge that the welfare of the entire house was somehow dependent on his submission was scarcely able to break down his pride.

He advanced to Mr Jarman more like one who comes to administer a thrashing than ask for pardon, and after eyeing him almost fiercely for a moment, summoned his self-control sufficiently to say hoarsely,--

"I apologise, sir."

Mr Jarman bit his lips. It was not the triumph he had expected. Indeed the whole manner of it was such as to hurt instead of soothe his feelings.

"This is hardly an apology," said he to the doctor.

"I trust, Tempest, it means that you regret your action?"

It was an awkward question. Tempest had gone further than any one expected, and his silence now reminded the doctor what the cost had been.

"I think," said he, not waiting for a reply to his own question, "Tempest has fulfilled his pledged--not cordially, I am sorry to say, but sufficiently."

"Very well, sir," said Mr Jarman, "I accept his apology for what it is worth, which seems very little."

"Now, I regret to say," continued the head master, producing a letter which made my heart jump to my mouth, "I have a more serious matter to speak about. I wish heartily what we have just heard had been the end of this painful interview. But it is necessary to refer to something different--a very serious offence against rules. It concerns you, Tempest. Is it a fact that you are in debt to some of the tradesmen?"

Tempest changed colour again and replied,--

"Yes, sir, I am sorry to say I am."

I held on tight to my desk. This was a finishing touch surely, and I, if any one, felt myself the criminal.

"This letter, addressed to me, but containing a bill for more than two pounds owing by you, part of it since last term, has been left at my house--I presume by the tradesman to whom it is due. Come here and look at it, Tempest."

Tempest obeyed.

"Is it a fact that you are in debt to this extent?"

"Yes, sir--more."

"You are aware--"

Here I could stand it no longer, but sprang to my feet and shouted,--

"Please, sir, it's my fault!"

Everybody turned to me in amazement, as well they might.

"Your fault, Jones iv.?--come forward and explain."

"I mean," said or rather shouted I, speaking while I walked up the room, "it's my fault you got that bill, sir. I don't know how you got it, but it wasn't meant to get to you, really. I must have dropped it. I--I-- was going--to try--to get it paid for him, sir. Really--"

Tempest gave me a glare that knocked all the spirit out of me. What business had I, it seemed to demand, to meddle in his private affairs?

I felt I had done him a real bad turn by my clumsiness, but had not the wit to avoid making bad worse.

"Yes, sir, I told Marple--"

"I purposely refrained from mentioning names, Jones iv.; why can you not do so too?"

"I told him to keep it dark, and got him to give it to me. I--I knew Tempest hadn't enough money to pay it--and--and--"

An exclamation of anger from Tempest cut me short, and I was sent ignominiously back to my place.

"Tempest," said the head master very sternly, "send me in a list of all you owe before you go to bed to-night, and understand that, unless all is paid by Friday when we break up, you will not be allowed to return to Low Heath after the holidays. You must cease in any case to retain the headship of the house, even for the few days of the term that remain. You, I understand. Crofter, come next in form order; you will act as head boy in the meantime."

In the midst of my anguish I could see the look of meek resignation on Crofter's face, and that of quiet satisfaction on Mr Jarman's. At Tempest I dared not look, or at my fellow-Philosophers.

What had I done? What was to become of me? How could I get out of it? These were the three questions which set my poor brain spinning as I wandered off alone to the remotest corner of the quadrangle, and as, later on, I lay miserably awake in my bed.

I had done my friend about as much harm as I possibly could. I may not have meant it. But who cares what a fellow means, so long as he acts like a cad? As to what was to become of me, I had had a taste of that already. The faggery door had been locked against me, and a missive shoved under the bottom had apprised me of my fate in that quarter.

"To Beast Sarah.

"Take notice that you are kicked out of the Philosophers, and if you dare show your abominable face within a mile of them you'll get it all over with rulers. It has been resolved by Mr Langrish and seconded by Mr Trimble, and passed by all the lot, that you be and are hereby kicked whenever any one sees you. Any one not kicking you will be lammed. It is also resolved that the faggery be fumigated and disinfected during the holidays, and that any chap seen talking to you be refused to be let in till he has been vaccinated. You are about the lowest, meanest, vilest, abominablest, unmitigatedest sneak going. Three cheers for poor old Tempest, and down with girls' schools and washerwomen!"

This fiery document was formally signed by every Philosopher in the house, together with a particular word of opprobrium addressed to me by each of my former colleagues.

I was not long in realising that I was an outcast in Sharpe's. No one would look at me, still less speak to me. Pridgin ordered me off like a dog. Wales slammed his door in my face. When I appeared in the preparation hall, a long hiss saluted me, even though Mr Sharpe was present. Even outside fellows seemed to have heard of my crime, and looked askance or gave me a wide berth. I can truly say that I found myself the most miserable boy in Low Heath, and only longed for the end of the term to come, that I might shake the dust of the hateful place from my feet, and drop out of the sight of a school full of enemies.

Indeed, as I lay awake that night I had serious thoughts of making off there and then. If I had only had my boots, I think I might have done so; but they were in the blacking-room; and my desperation drew the line at walking off in my bare feet.

I was sitting up in bed, half whimpering with headache and misery, when a light appeared at the end of the dormitory. It was Crofter, in his new capacity of head of the house, taking his rounds before turning in. The sight of him brought home to me the injury I had done, not only to Tempest, but the whole house. For it was my fault, and mine only, that Crofter was at this moment captain of Sharpe's.

To my surprise and alarm, when he came up to my bed he stopped short, and drawing a letter from his pocket, put it into my hand, saying--

"Put that under your pillow till the morning."

It was more than nature could do to sleep with a mystery like this on the top of my misery. I listened to the clock as it struck the hours through the night, and thought the day would never come. Indeed, the getting-up bell had sounded before the winter sun struggled in through the dormitory window.

Then by the light of a candle I seized the missive from under my pillow and tore it open.

A five-pound note fell out, and with it the following letter.

"You have made a nice mess of it, and ought to be happy. The least you can do is to try to make things right for Tempest. Call round on the following six tradesmen (giving the six names, one of which was Marple) early to-morrow, and pay Tempest's bill at each, and bring home the receipts. You needn't mention who sent you. Send the receipts to me, and if Tempest asks any questions, tell him you paid the money by request of a friend.

"W. Crofter."

CHAPTER TWENTY ONE.
I AM ADVISED TO LIE LOW.

My first impulse on reading Crofter's letter was to jump for joy. It meant that Tempest would stay at Low Heath, and that I was to be allowed to assist in keeping him there.

But my second thoughts were more of a surprise than pleasure. Crofter was a mystery to me. His fellow-seniors disliked him, and warned me against him. But, as far as I could see, he was not as bad as they made him out, and certainly never said anything as bad about them as they said about him.

What could be his object now if it was not a disinterested one? He would be permanent captain of the house if Tempest left, and yet he was doing the very thing that would keep Tempest at school. Tempest had openly insulted him during the term, and yet here he was helping his enemy out of a very tight place. I knew he was well off, so probably he could afford the L5; but at the end of the term pocket-money was not a plentiful commodity. He said nothing about being paid back, too; surely he did not mean to make Tempest a free gift of this magnificent amount! The more I thought it over the more I felt Crofter was a brick, and had been scandalously misunderstood. He seemed to me a true type of the virtuous man, who, when struck on one cheek, turns the other, and when robbed of his coat offers his cloak too. I only hoped Tempest might know what he owed him. In short, in the brief time it took me to dress, I had worked myself up into a state of enthusiasm on the subject of Crofter.

As to the mystery of Mr Marple's letter having got into the doctor's hands, no doubt I had been careless and dropped the compromising envelope, which some foolish but honest person (it did not occur to me at the time it might have been Crofter himself) had picked up and dropped in the head master's letter-box, supposing he was doing a very clever thing. Tempest would not be likely to allow me to explain, which was hard on me, and made it all the more virtuous on my part to assist now in putting things right for him. Luckily for him, he had friends at Low Heath in spite of himself.

When I encountered Crofter in the morning, I requested him, with a knowing look of intelligence, to give me an *exeat* into the town to do some shopping. It was probably the first recognition he had received of his temporary authority as head of the house, and he made no difficulty in granting my request.

I made my way first of all to Marple's.

"Oh, about that bill you gave me. How much was it?"

"Two pounds and sixpence, young gentleman."

"I said I'd see it paid for you, didn't I?"

"You did. I don't want to show up--"

"All right, you needn't. Here's the money; give me the change, please, and a receipt."

Mr Marple opened his eyes very wide at the sight of a five-pound note within three days of the end of term. "I--I hope it's all right," said he, hesitatingly. "You needn't have it if you don't want," said I, mounting my high horse.

"I'm sure I'm much obliged to you, young gentleman," said the tradesman, giving the note a professional twitch, and proceeding to count out the change from his till. "I shall always be pleased to attend to any little orders from Mr Tempest or you."

"You can make out the receipt to Tempest," said I; "I expect he won't get much more here."

"Don't say that. I'm sure no offence was meant."

It was a delicious sensation to feel myself master of the situation like this. I could have bullied Marple if I had liked, but I resolved not to be too hard on him.

"I'm sure I'm much obliged," said he, "for all your trouble. Have you seen these pretty little pencil-sharpers? They are quite new. I shall be pleased if you will accept one, young gentleman."

A pencil-sharpener was the very thing I wanted. All the term I had been wrestling with a blunt penknife, which no sooner uncovered the lead at the end of a pencil than it broke it off. So in a weak moment I accepted the gift, and forfeited my advantage.

From Marple's I proceeded to the confectioner's, where a score of nearly a pound stood against Tempest. Here, again, I experienced the sweets of being treated with distinguished consideration, and being asked to partake of a strawberry ice (how Rammage, by the way, continued to have strawberry ices in the middle of December I have never yet clearly understood) while the receipt was being made out.

Mr Winget, the hatter, rather disappointed me by offering me nothing more than his sincere thanks for the settlement of his little bill. He might at least, I thought, have offered me a mourning hatband or a new school ribbon. His bill, however, was only five shillings, so probably the profit did not permit of any gratuitous allowance in recognition of my distinguished services.

I was consoled, however, by Mr Ringstead, the games man, who presented me with a net-bag for holding tennis balls, and urged me, whenever I wanted any little thing in the way of repairs to bats, or fresh spikes to my running shoes, to let him know.

It was all very pleasant, and I grieve to say that the shady side of all this petty bribery and corruption never once occurred to my simple mind.

I returned to school covered with self-satisfaction, and virtuously clutching in my hand half-a-crown, the final change out of the "fiver." This in due course I put in an envelope, together with the batch of receipts, and laid on Crofter's table after morning school, with the laconic message under the flap, "All right, T.J. iv."

I was far too knowing to let out my secret to the Philosophers, whose agitation and indignation at Tempest's probable expulsion knew no bounds and somewhat amused me.

"Look here, Sarah," said Langrish, as I entered for the first time after my disgrace of the previous day--I knew my comrades well enough to be sure they would like to see me--"we all know you're about the beastliest, howlingest cad in Low Heath; so that's all right."

"I'm glad you think so."

"Yes, and you've been told to clear out, as it's your fault Tempest's expelled."

"Is it? That's all you know," said I.

"Yes, and you're kicked out of the Philosophers, and we're going to invite Dicky

Brown to join us. *He's* a decent chap."

This was rather a blow.

"I thought no town-boys were eligible."

"No cads are; that's why you're out of it."

"Look here--" said I.

"We're not going to look here. You can cut and go, and sit on the stairs. We don't want you in here, do we, you chaps?"

"Rather not, unless we've got our kicking boots on."

"All right," said I, feeling I must play one or two of my trumps. "I sha'n't tell you what I was going to."

"Pooh, we know all about it," said Coxhead. But it was plain by the way they had all pricked their ears they did not.

"Oh, if you know, it's all right. But you don't know the latest."

"We don't want to, unless it's that old Tempest has got off."

"That's just what it is," said I triumphantly.

"Good old Sarah! how do you know?"

"Never mind, it's a secret; but it's a fact, honour bright."

"What, has he paid all his bills?"

"They're all paid, I know that."

"I suppose," said Langrish, "as that motion about Sarah being kicked out wasn't properly seconded, it's off, isn't it?"

"Does any gentleman second the motion?" said Coxhead, glancing round the assembled Philosophers.

No one seconded it.

"Jolly lucky shave for you, young Sarah," said Coxhead.

"Thanks awfully," said I.

"We may as well divide up the pool now?" suggested Warminster.

With a generosity which was really touching, the Philosophers had clubbed together the shattered fragments of their term's pocket-money to assist Tempest in his financial troubles. They had done it ungrudgingly, nay enthusiastically, and it was not against them that the enthusiasm remained now as each one unexpectedly received back his Philosopher's mite from the depths of the kindly "pool."

It is all very well keeping a secret like mine for twenty-four hours. It was an effort, but I did it, and prevailed on my comrades to keep it too. It was even harder work to prevail upon them as a matter of policy to accept the temporary supremacy of Crofter in the house. Nothing would induce them to refrain from cheering Tempest (much to his displeasure) on every possible occasion. It made it awkward for me sometimes when this happened in Crofter's presence; for as things now were in Sharpe's, a cheer for the old captain meant a hoot at the new; and I felt that Crofter, did the fellows only know all, did not deserve their resentment.

After forty-eight hours I could not restrain myself any longer. It was not fair to myself, or Crofter, or Low Heath, that every one should suppose Tempest was to be expelled when he really was not. So, with some misgivings, I decided to put myself in his way and break the agreeable news to him, and so have everything cleared up before the end of term.

It was not difficult to find an excuse. I had not been to Tempest's rooms since our unlucky quarrel, and had been suffering inconvenience ever since by the fact that my Latin Gradus was there. On the last day but one of the term, therefore, I developed a burning desire to consult my missing handbook, and must needs go in search of it.

Tempest was sitting, miserably enough, before the fire, with his feet on the fender and his hands up to the back of his head as I entered. It was not till I was well in the room and had closed the door that he turned round and saw me.

I thought at first he meant to fly at me, his face clouded so angrily. But it changed to a look of contempt as he said,--

"Well?"

"Tempest, I'm awfully sorry, really I am, but--"

"Don't let us have any of that. If I thought you'd meant it, I should precious soon know what to do. You've done me about the worst turn a fellow could, and if you weren't a conceited young ass it would be some use thrashing you. As it is, somebody else may do that when I'm gone."

The wretchedness of his tone quite touched me. I forgot my anger and sense of resentment, and all the old affection and loyalty came back with a rush. How could I ever have imagined a fellow like Crofter was worthy to hold a candle to my old Dux?

"Really, Tempest," began I, losing my head and blundering I scarcely knew whither, "when you saw me talking to Crofter--" He uttered an angry exclamation.

"There, now, shut up about your friend Crofter. I don't want to hear about him."

"He's not my friend, Tempest; he's--he's yours."

He wheeled round in his chair and laughed bitterly.

"It's a queer time to joke," said he, with a laugh that cut me through.

"It's no joke, Tempest. You don't know what he's done for you."

"Don't I? I fancy I do."

"About the bills," said I, faltering, "you know."

"Ah I don't come here to tell me about that."

"It was all of his own accord he paid them."

"He what?" shouted Tempest, springing from his chair and facing round.

"Paid them, you know; at least, I paid them for him."

"You? Paid?" and he caught me by the collar and shook me like a puppy.

"You said you knew," gasped I.

"Paid my bills! You say that blackguard had the cheek to--"

"He got me to do it; it was his money, though."

He groaned as if some one had wounded him. A crimson flush of shame and mortification overspread his face, and for a moment he stared at me speechless.

Then he pulled himself together and strode out of the room. Utterly bewildered and half terrified, I followed him. What had I done to offend him? Had all the trouble of the term turned his head?

To my alarm he made straight for Crofter's study. No one was there. He turned and saw me.

"Tell Crofter I want him at once."

I departed with my heart in my mouth. At the foot of the staircase I met Crofter.

"Tempest wants to see you," said I; "he sent me to--to ask you to come."

"He doesn't know?" inquired Crofter.

"Yes--I told him--I--I thought I ought to let him know." Crofter laughed his sweet laugh.

"If I had wanted it known all over Low Heath," said he, "I could hardly have done better than tell you to keep it a secret. I'd much sooner he had not known. However--where is he?"

"In your study, I think."

I felt constrained to follow. Crofter evidently was expecting to be the recipient of an outburst of effusive gratitude. I had not the courage to disabuse him.

He walked pleasantly and graciously into his study, where Tempest stood, flushing and biting his lips, awaiting him. "Is this true what that youngster says, that you've had the--that you've paid bills of mine?"

"I'm sorry he told you, Tempest. I thought it might get you out of a difficulty, and I--"

"And you expect me to thank you! Take that, for daring to meddle in my affairs!"

And he struck Crofter on the cheek--not a hard blow, but one which sent the recipient reeling across the room with astonishment.

For a moment I expected a fight. Crofter, however, pale, but smiling still, declined the challenge.

"You'll be sorry, I'm sure," said he, as coolly as he could. "I only wanted to do you a good turn, and--"

"I'm sorry already," said Tempest, who had already gathered himself together. "I hoped you'd fight like a man. As you're afraid to, I'm sorry I touched you."

"I see nothing to fight about," said Crofter. "I don't see what there is to be angry about."

Tempest waited motionless for a few uncomfortable moments, in the hope that Crofter would pluck up spirit to accept the challenge. But, as Crofter only smiled, he turned on his heel and strode out of the room. As he passed me, he beckoned me imperiously to follow him. I did so in terror.

He put a piece of paper and a pen before me.

"Write down there an account of every bill you paid, and the amount."

I obeyed--my memory fortunately served me for the task.

"Now go. You've had the satisfaction of seeing me make an ass of myself in striking that cad--he's not worth it. You may go and tell him I'm sorry if you like. As for you, I don't want to see any more of you. Go to your captain, and leave me alone."

And he flung himself miserably into his chair, leaning forward with his head on his hands, and apparently indifferent whether I stayed or went.

I went, leaving him thus. And the memory of him sitting there haunted me all that night and for weeks to come.

When, next day, the news went round that Tempest had escaped expulsion, the general delight was tempered with amazement at the rumour which accompanied it, that he owed his escape to Crofter. No one but Crofter himself could have put the latter story into circulation, and to any one knowing the two seniors as well as I did, it was obvious that what had completed the humiliation of one had been the crowning triumph of the other.

Crofter could not have avenged himself for the insults of the term more effectively; and Tempest's proud nature could not have suffered a bitterer wound than to know that he had been put under an obligation in spite of himself, and without the possibility of preventing it, by his worst enemy.

The ordinary "Sharper" could hardly be expected to trouble himself about questions of motive. It was sufficient for him that his hero was saved, and that the credit of the popular act which saved him belonged to Crofter.

Consequently both were cheered equally when they appeared in public, and of the two Crofter accepted his popularity with a far better grace than his mortified adversary.

But it was all very miserable to me as I slunk home that afternoon in the train. All the hopes of the wonderful term had been disappointed. I was a recognised dunce and idler at Low Heath. I had lost my best friend and sold myself to his enemy. My self-respect was at a low ebb. I knew that in a post or two would come a report which would bring tears to my mother's eyes, and cause my guardian to grunt and say, "I expected as much." The worst of it was, I could not get it out of my head yet that I was rather a fine young fellow if only people knew it, and that my misfortunes were more to blame for the failure of the term than my faults.

To my relief a letter came early in the holidays from Dicky Brown's people, asking me to spend the last two weeks with them, I jumped at it, for in my present miserable frame of mind even home was dismal.

But when I found myself back at Low Heath, installed in Dicky's quiet little family circle, I was almost sorry I had come. For Dicky was all high spirits and jubilation. He had won a form prize; everything had gone swimmingly for him. The Urbans looked up to him; the head master had patted him on the back; the Redwoods had taken a fancy to him. No one thought of calling him by a feminine nickname.

"I think Low Heath's a ripping place," said he, as we strolled past the gate of the empty quadrangle in one of our holiday rambles. "I'm jolly glad we got kicked out of Dangerfield, ain't you?"

"Middling," said I; "the fact is, Dicky, you may as well know it, but I'm rather sick of this place."

"Hullo!" said he, looking at me, "why, I thought you were having such a high old time."

"I--I've come a bit of a howler, Dicky;" here I gulped ominously, much to Dicky's concern. "I've fooled things rather, you know." I was in for my confession now, and gave the penitent horse his head. "I'm jolly miserable, Dicky, that's all about it, and wish I was dead, don't you know, and that sort of thing."

"What's up, old chappie?" said Dicky, taking my arm, and evidently in a fright lest I should compromise myself by breaking down on the spot. "Come down by the willows; it's rather muddy, but it's quieter."

So we ploughed through the mud under the willows, and I let out on Dicky all that was in my heart. I'm sure he thought it a lot of bosh, but he was too kind to say so, and hung on to my arm, and never once contradicted me when I called myself a fool.

"You have rotted it a bit," remarked he, when the story was complete. "Never mind, old chap, it can't be helped. You'll worry through all right."

This was true comfort. If Dicky had been a prig like me, he would have tried to talk to me like a father, and driven me crazy. It made all the difference that he understood me, and yet believed in me a little.

"It strikes me," said he, with refreshing candour, "you fancy yourself a bit too much, Tommy. I'd advise you to lie low a bit, and it will all come round."

"That's just exactly what Tempest said to me the first day of term," said I, with a groan.

"There you are," said he; "bless you, you're not going to get done over one wretched term, are you? I wouldn't if I were you."

"But all the chaps are down on me."

"What do you care?" said he, with a snort. "Who cares twopence about the lot of them--chaps like them too? You're a cut better than that lot, I fancy--ought to be, anyhow."

What balm it all was to my wounds! What miles of mud we ploughed through that afternoon I and how, as the water gradually leaked into my boots, my heart rose out of them, and got back somehow to its proper place, and enabled me to look at things in their proper light. I think Dicky, little as he knew it, was sent by God to help me pull myself together, and I shall always think better of him for his blunt, genuine encouragement that day.

On our way back he pulled up at Redwood's door.

"Let's see if he's in," said he; "he won't mind."

"All right," said I, beginning to quail again a little, and yet determined to go through with the whole business.

Redwood was in, mending a pair of skates, in anticipation of a day or two's frost before the holidays were over.

"Look here, Redwood," said Dicky, determined to make things easy for me. "Old Jones minimus is in the blues. He's been fooling it rather this term, you know, but he's a bit sick of it, and we thought you'd like to know, didn't we, young Jones minimus?"

"Yes, if you don't mind, Redwood," said I.

"Wait a bit--tea's just ready. We'll have ours up here," said the captain.

Over tea Dicky trotted out my troubles second-hand to our host, appealing to me every now and then to confirm his statement that I'd rather "mucked" it over this and that, and so on.

Redwood nibbled away at his tea, looking up now and then with a friendly nod to show he agreed with all that was said about me.

When all was said, he remarked--

"I wouldn't worry, youngster, if I were you. It's been a poor show last term, but you'll pull yourself together right enough. Take my advice, and lie low a bit, that's the best thing for your complaint."

"Why," said I, "that's just exactly what Tempest said to me."

"There you are again," broke in Dicky, cutting himself a hunch of cake.

Presently Redwood began to "draw" me on the subject of Tempest, and looked rather blank when I told him of the dismal circumstances in which the term had closed at Sharpe's. However, he did not favour Dicky and me with much comment on the matter, and finally got us to help him sharpen his skates and talk about other things.

I went to bed that night at Dicky's more easy and hopeful than I had been for weeks, and felt half-impatient for term to begin again, so that I might put into practice the new and trebly-patent specific of lying low.

CHAPTER TWENTY TWO.
PUTTING ON THE BRAKE.

The holidays went by rapidly enough. I tore myself away from Dicky's consoling companionship three days from the end, and rushed home to see my mother. I wonder what she thought of the difference a couple of weeks had made in me? When I started to Dicky's I had been limp, dejected, and down on my luck. Now she found me chirpy, and with a stiff upper lip. She did not make remarks, but I could see how relieved she was.

My mother was not the person to take a mean advantage of me, or get me into a corner to lecture me. Rather not! She took me for what I was, and let me see how she loved me. That was the proper sort of help for me. In some ways she made less of me than usual, but I could see why she did that; she saw I wanted letting alone, and she did it, bless her! Only on the last evening, a Sunday, as we walked back from church, she said--

"Are you glad or sorry to be going back to-morrow, Tom?"

"Sorry for some things--glad for others. I fooled a bit last term, you know, mother."

"Ah, well, sonny, it's part of the lessons of school to find out our mistakes now and then. It was all new to you at first. I expect you tried to do too much, you know."

"I know--you mean I'd best lie low a bit, mother."

"Yes. I know what you mean," said she.

"There you are!" exclaimed I, staggered by this new coincidence, "that's what every chap has said. I'll do my best, really, mother; only it's jolly hard. Don't be awfully sorry if I don't get right all at once; I'll try, you know."

"You can't do more than your best, sonny dear."

"Redwood says," continued I, "that I shall probably tool about more or less to the end of my time. It's in my line, he says; but he rather backs me to pull myself together for all that."

"So do I, Tom. And the best friend you have does so too."

My journey next day was very different from the strange journey of a term ago. I had neither tan boots nor square-topped hat nor lavender gloves; and I could afford to smile with Langrish (who joined me *en route*) at some of the poor little greenhorns on their way to make their entry into Low Heath.

How different it was, too, to be hailed by half a dozen voices from the top of the omnibus at the station and told to hop up beside them! And how jolly to ride in triumph up Bridge Street, exchanging shouts with familiar passengers on the way, or uttering defiant war-whoops at the day boys!

And how jolly to tumble in at Sharpe's door once more, and slap one another on the back, and crowd up into the old familiar faggery, and hear all the old chaff and slang, interspersed with stories of the holidays, and second-hand Christmas jokes!

And how jolly to hear the organ again in the chapel, and the prayers, with friends all round you; and finally, when the day was over, tuck up again in the little cubicle, and hear your chum's voice across the partition droning more and more sleepily, till finally you and it dropped off together!

One of the last to arrive during the day was Tempest, who had run from the station, and came in flushed with exercise, but grave and tight about the lips. The ovation he received from the Philosophers scarcely drew a smile from him, and when he reached his own study he slammed the door ominously and cheerlessly behind him. We none of us liked it.

"What's it to be?" said Coxhead. "Is he to be cock of the house this term, or has he chucked it up?"

That was the question which was agitating us all. Till the form orders were posted to-morrow no one could tell. Crofter, we knew, had been doing all he knew to get ahead, and considering the slack way in which Tempest had let things go all last term, it seemed very much as if he might succeed.

If he did, our duty would be a difficult one. Crofter had a claim on us for having saved Tempest from being expelled, and we could hardly refuse to own him should he come out cock of the house. On the other hand. Tempest was the man of our heart, and our tender imagination failed to picture him in any secondary position in Sharpe's,--secondary to Crofter, above all other things.

The day closed with one curious incident.

Langrish came to me after supper in a state of wrathful perturbation.

"Look here, young Sarah," said he, "are you Tempest's fag or not? That's all about it."

"I don't know," said I; "I was, but he told me--"

"He told you he didn't want a cad like you hanging about his place. All very well--that doesn't follow I'm his fag as well as Crofter's. Here, catch hold; you've got to take this to Crofter. *I'm* not going to take it--it means a licking most likely, and I don't see why I'm to be let in for it."

He handed me an envelope, evidently containing coin, addressed "Crofter," in Tempest's well-known writing.

I did not relish the commission, for I had my guess as to the contents of the missive. Curiosity, however, prompted me to take it and proceed to Crofter's study.

"Well, youngster," said Crofter, "turned up again? Have you seen Tempest yet?"

"Yes--he sent this," said I.

Crofter took the envelope and opened it. Five sovereigns and a half- sovereign dropped out on the table. No letter accompanied the money, but its meaning was clear enough. Crofter's brow contracted, and his habitual smile deserted him for once.

"What is this? Some mistake," said he.

"It's what he owes you," suggested I.

"I suppose so; but that was only L4 17 shillings 6 pence."

"Perhaps the rest is something for yourself," I remarked, making myself scarce in time to escape the task of returning the change.

Bother it! Crofter must square this part of the business up with his enemy. *I* didn't want to be dragged any more into it.

There was a rush for the house board early next morning to learn our fate as to the captaincy of Sharpe's.

"Whew!" said Langrish, as we reached it; "bracketed."

So it was. Tempest's and Crofter's names were braced together at the head of the list.

"That's a nice go! I suppose they'll have to go halves. All the worse for us."

"I should think, as Tempest was captain last term, he'll go on again this," I said.

"He wasn't captain when term ended; Crofter was."

"I vote they fight it out," said Warminster. "Two to one on the winner."

"It would save trouble if they made Pridgin head; he's third man up."

"Pridgin!" The easy-going owner of the name was spared something by not being present to hear the amused contempt with which the suggestion was greeted.

An hour later the doctor came down to settle matters for us.

"Under the circumstances," said he, "it seems right that Crofter should take charge of the house. I understand that Tempest's debts, on account of which he was removed from the headship last term, are now all honourably settled. But as he was more than once reported for breaking rules last term, it is only fair that Crofter, whose marks are equal, and against whom no complaint was recorded, should captain the house."

That was all. Tempest, on the whole, looked relieved. Crofter smiled a satisfied smile. Pridgin and Wales looked blue; and the Philosophers took time to consider what they thought.

As for me, although Tempest had thrown me over, I could guess what a blow this was for him; not personally, for he would probably be glad to be rid of the responsibility, but as a public disgrace it was sure to wound him keenly.

I longed to be able to go and tell him how sorry I was; but after what had happened last term I dare not. In that respect, whether I liked it or not, I must "lie low."

The Philosophers were not long in formally exchanging opinions on the situation.

A meeting was summoned for the same evening to inaugurate things generally. I was a little doubtful what I ought to do. Last term philosophy had not tended to diligent work, and with my good resolutions in view I felt that I should be better out of it. The little tiff with my comrades before the holidays had almost solved the difficulty; but since then I had been formally re-admitted to the fold, and it would be almost treasonable to "scratch" now.

"I ***move*** and third, and old Trim seconds and fourths," announced Langrish, "that old Sal be, and is, president as before."

"And I carry that motion," said Warminster, who prided himself on his acquaintance with the procedure of public meetings.

"I move an amendment," said I.

"Shut up, or you'll be kicked out again," said the secretary.

"Shut up yourself, or you'll be kicked in," retorted I, feeling I must carry everything with a high hand if I was to carry them at all. "No. Look here, you chaps, I'm not so green as I look."

"Then you must look fearfully green," muttered Coxhead.

I took no heed of the interruption, which was not relevant, and proceeded,--

"It was all very well last term, but it won't wash this. What I say is, that if the cock of the school is the head boy in the school, and the cock of the house is the head boy in the house, the president of the Philosophers has got to be the chap highest up in the Philosophers, and that's not me. Now old Warminster is. ***He's*** a jolly clever chap, and got the form prize on his head, and he's a rattling good speaker, and a middling sprinter, and writes a fairly good hand! ***He's*** the sort of chap we want. We want some one who can keep the secretary, and treasurer, and auditor, and registrar, and all that lot, in their place, and doesn't mind telling them they're idiots when they are. I never could do it. It's rough on the club not to have a chap like Warminster," continued I, waxing warm, and undaunted by the murmurs of my audience. "He can make you all sit up. He's not the sort of chap to let the Philosophers go rotting about, talking what they know nothing about and all that. He'll see that the louts are kept out of it, and only fellows who've got a record of something are let in. Bless you, I used to let in any sort of bounder that asked! Look round you and see. That's the sort of lot I let in. It won't wash, though. Fancy having a lot of outsiders who can't translate a Latin motto, and make 'corpore' a feminine genitive! Now old Warminster's a nailer at Latin, and can put one or two of us to bed at Euclid. He'll keep us out of blunders of that sort, that make all the school grin at us. I therefore propose, fifth, fourth, third, and second, that Tip. Warminster is the president of the Philosophers, and that the secretary, treasurer, auditor, registrar, and all that lot, get a month's notice to jack it up unless they're on the front desk. There you are! Of course they won't like it--can't help that. No back-deskers for us. Front desk or nothing!"

This oration, the longest I ever delivered so far, and in all probability the longest I ever shall deliver, was listened to with a curious mixture of discomfort and attention. At first it was nearly howled down, but it took as it went on. Warminster, for whom I really did not feel quite so much admiration as my words seemed to imply, but who yet was the hard-working man of our lot--Warminster was wonderfully pleased with it. The others, one by one, dropped their noisy protests, and looked out of the window. Trimble attempted a little bravado, by sticking his tongue in his cheek; but my peroration was listened to with marked attention.

"Cuts down the club a bit," said Coxhead, who occupied a desk in class on the third row, "if it's only to be top-deskers."

"Cuts old Sal out, to begin with," said Langrish, who was just on the bench of honour.

"It'll cut you out next week, old hoss," said I.

"Me! What are you talking about?"

"You wait till the week's order is up: you'll see."

Langrish glared indignant.

"If you think an idiot like you is going to--"

"Look here," said Warminster, "I vote we go easy at first, and make it any one who's not gone down in order in a month."

"I say, nobody who's not gone up one in the term," suggested Langrish, glancing defiantly at me.

"All serene," said I, "that'll suit my book. It'll be roughish on you, though."

"Will it? See how you'll feel when you're chucked out neck and crop, my beauty!"

My main object had been to get out of being president. But, somehow, in doing it I had struck a note which made the Philosophers sit up. It was no credit to me it happened so, but it was one of those lucky flukes which sometimes turn out well and do a good stroke without the striker being aware of it.

Warminster was unanimously elected president, and bore his blushing honours with due meekness.

"Old Sal"--the Philosophers had taken to abbreviating my pet name this term,

I know not on what principle of familiarity--"Old Sal piles it on a bit," remarked he. "Of course he couldn't help rotting the club a bit last term. That's the way he's born. But considering what a rank outsider he was, I suppose he did his best." (Laughter, and cries of "What about Jarman's guy?") "Yes, that was a howling mess. I vote we keep out of that this term, or leave it to the louts. I tell you what," said he, "I vote we make a show up at the sports next month, and take some of the side out of those day-boy kids. They fancy themselves a jolly sight too much."

"Dicky Brown told me," said I, "they were sure of both the jumps and the Quarter-mile and the Tug--and that Selkirk's were going to pull off the others, all except the Half-mile Handicap; and we may get that, he says, because they'll probably give us fifty or sixty yards' lead."

"Howling cheek!" exclaimed every one in furious rage. The idea of being given sixty yards' start in a half-mile by a day boy was too much even for a Philosopher.

Whereupon we solemnly considered the list of events "under 15," and divided them out among ourselves, with a vow to eat our heads if we didn't pull off as many for Sharpe's as all the rest of the school put together.

We decided to postpone making our entries till the last moment, so as to delude the enemy into the impression that we were shirking the sports altogether. Then we would, as Warminster politely put it, "drop down and rot the lot."

Before we adjourned for the night the question of Tempest and Crofter came up, *a propos* of a report, which some one mentioned, that Tempest had entered for the Open Mile against Redwood, and was expected to prove a warm customer.

"Is Crofter in?"

"No--Pridgin is, but of course he won't come up to scratch, and Wales only enters for the show of the thing."

"Crofter couldn't look in at Tempest over the Mile," said Langrish, "but he ought to enter, for all that."

"Can he look in at Tempest over anything?" said I.

"Don't ask questions, and you won't be told no whoppers," astutely replied Trimble. "I wonder if he expects us to back him up?"

"I sha'n't," said one. "Nor shall I," said one or two others.

"I vote we let him alone," said Coxhead. "What's he got to do with us? When does he come across us? Only when there's a row on. He's got nothing at all to say to us at other times."

"You mean, if we want to let him alone we shall have to shut up rows?" inquired Langrish. "Rather rough, isn't it?"

"Not if he knows the reason," suggested I. "Let's send him a round- robin and let him know."

"Not half a bad idea."

Whereupon the following candid epistle was concocted and signed by all present:--

"To T. Crofter, Esquire, Captain Sharpe's *pro tem*., etcetera, etcetera, etcetera.

"Dear Crofter,--We the undersigned Philosophers wish to say we're going steady this term on our own hooks, and hope you will not think it's because of you. We don't want to be interfered with by any chap except old Tempest, who ought to be cock of Sharpe's, so we've decided to go steady, so as not to be interfered with, because we would rather not you interfered with us, because we're all serene and are backing up Tempest, and hope he'll pull off the Mile that you've not entered for. We aren't down on you, because you pulled Tempest through last term, but it's rough you're cock of the house instead of him, and therefore on that account we are going steady, so as not to give you the fag of interfering with us, which we don't mind Tempest doing because we consider he has more right to interfere with us than you. Hoping you are well and in good health, as this leaves us, Believe us, with kind regards to all at home, Yours very kindly and in alphabetical order, so that you needn't know who started this letter. Samuel Wilberforce Coxhead, Thomas Jones, Everard Langrish, Jonathan T. Purkis, Alfred James Remington Trimble, Percy Algernon Warminster, and others."

This important document, the writing of which, I grieve to say, necessitated frequent reference to the English Dictionary, Langrish, as Crofter's fag, undertook to deliver, and faithfully discharged his mission by leaving it on the captain's table when he was out of his study.

It was decided to resist the temptation of sending Mr Jarman a similar explanatory letter, for fear it might lead to a row which would call for interference. Nor was it deemed prudent under the circumstances to commit ourselves in writing to Tempest, whom we hoped to convince of our loyalty by cheering him on every possible occasion and otherwise making things pleasant for him.

How Crofter enjoyed his letter we none of us knew. He was inconsiderate enough to give no sign of having received it; and still more inconsiderate to allow himself on more than one occasion to be publicly complimented by the doctor and Mr Sharpe on the order of the house.

Meanwhile the Philosophers stuck to their new programme. I had the satisfaction of pulling down Langrish from his place on the top desk at the end of the first week, and he had the triumph of recovering his seat at the end of the week after. In the seclusion of the faggery we indulged in a few mild recriminations, which were the natural outcome of our rivalry; but they only served to blow off steam, and we were too keen to win our self-imposed battles in class to allow personal feeling to interfere much with our work.

Mr Sharpe was fairly astonished, and took off his glasses, and rubbed his mild eyes as he read over our really meritorious exercises and listened to our sometimes positively coherent feats of construing.

Secretly, too, but with great precaution, and in spots far removed from the detection of the day boys, we practised grimly at jumping and sprinting and record-breaking generally, and finally, as the critical time for making our entries approached, agreed upon the particular exploit which each of us was to undertake for the honour and glory of Sharpe's house in general and Philosophy in particular.

Before that time arrived, however, one awkward incident occurred, to remind me I had even yet not quite purged myself of the follies of last term. I stumbled against Crofter just outside his door.

"Come in," said he.

I obeyed, guessing that at last we were to hear something of our famous letter. I was disappointed, however. Crofter made no reference to it, but said--

"Those bills you paid for me last term, Jones iv.--did none of the people allow you any discount?"

"Discount," said I, "what's that? We haven't got to it yet in Syntax."

"Don't be a young ass. Did none of them give you any change?"

"Rather, all of them. I brought it back, or used it to pay the rest."

"What I mean is, you didn't make anything out of it for yourself, did you?"

"Me--oh!" the conscious blushes suddenly mounted as I grasped his meaning.

"Yes, you."

"Well, only, you see, it was--"

"Come, no lies. I know all about it. Did you or did you not?"

"Not from the hat man," said I.

"From all the others?"

"Only--"

"Yes or no, that's what I want to know."

"Yes, but--"

"That will do. Now I understand why you were so pleased with the job. It's a profitable thing to help a friend sometimes. Tempest will be amused when he hears."

"Oh, I say, don't--really I didn't fancy--"

"That will do, I say. Cut--do you hear? I only wanted to know whether I was right or not in what I told Tempest."

"Oh, but--" pleaded I, with a groan of misery.

"If you don't cut I'll lick you for disobedience."

This, after all my good resolutions and hopes that all was squared and that before long Tempest would believe in me again!

I slunk away in despair, and curled myself up in my bed that night, the most miserable boy in Low Heath.

CHAPTER TWENTY THREE.
PRETTY WARM ALL ROUND.

Dicky, old chap, I'm in a howling mess."

"The same old one, or a new one?"

"It's about those blessed bills of Tempest's--I wish I'd let them alone. You see, it was this way. How was I to know? I'm sure I never meant to do anything shady."

"I dare say not, but what *are* you talking about?"

"Why, I've been regularly let in. You see, I--"

"Look here, old chap, let's hear what it is," said the practical Dicky.

"Why, the fact is, most of the chaps wanted to stand me something when I squared up with them, and Crofter tries to make out I'm a thief, and he's going to show me up to Tempest."

"But you didn't let them?"

"Well, yes, one or two. You see, Marple gave me a pencil-sharpener, and Rammage a strawberry ice, and Ringstead a net-bag and spikes--jolly bad ones too, they all came out in a week."

"And does Crofter say you swindled him or Tempest?"

"I didn't think I was swindling anybody," said I evasively.

"You made a pretty good thing out of it, though."

"I know. I say, Dicky, what's to be done? I thought I was going to pull round all square this term--really I did--and now I'm in a regular fix."

Dicky pondered.

"It was a bit shady," said he, with his refreshing candour; "the sort of thing Ananias and--"

"Oh, for pity's sake, Dicky, if that's all you've got to say--"

"It's not. I think you'd best make it good somehow. Can't you give them back?"

"How can I give back the strawberry ice?"

This was a poser, certainly, and set Dicky thinking again.

"Have you got the other things?" asked he.

"No; the pencil-sharpener smashed first time I used it, and the net-bag got lost at home."

"Awkward. You'll have to buy new ones."

"Who for?"

"Tempest, of course. They were his bills."

"But it was Crofter's money."

"But Tempest has paid him back."

The result of this conversation was, that instead of practising for the Quarter-mile that afternoon I went down town with a bag, and expended five shillings of my term's pocket-money in the purchase of a pencil- sharpener, a strawberry ice, a net-bag, and a set of patent screw spikes.

Dicky, like a brick, undertook to convey these to Tempest, with the following letter, which I wrote at his suggestion.

"Dear Tempest,--I send you back the change I got out of the bills I got last term. I'm sorrier than I can say, and hope you won't hate me more than you do. Dicky will tell you how jolly blue I am, and how we all hope you'll win the Mile. We aren't backing up Crofter, and hope you'll soon be captain again. Please excuse me writing, but I don't like to come and tell you this, as you're so down on me.

"Yours truly,--

"T. Jones iv."

I also penned a further letter for Crofter:--

"Dear Crofter,--You needn't mind telling Tempest, as I've done so and paid him back. With thanks all the same,--

"Yours truly,--

"T.J. iv."

I felt vastly easier in my mind when this polite letter was at an end, and when I saw the faithful Dicky depart to execute his brotherly mission. My one fear was lest the strawberry ice should get warm before it reached its destination.

I waited in vain for any sign of response from Tempest. The Philosophers went down during the afternoon to watch him training for his race; but he vouchsafed us no regard, and, for all I knew, still put me down as a thief and a sharper. Dicky, whom I met later on, explained that he had failed to catch Tempest in his study, but had deposited the articles along with the letter on his table, so that, if he did not know of them yet, he soon would.

My anxiety was not at all allayed by a casual encounter with Crofter in the evening. He summoned me into his study, where I saw my *billet- doux* lying on the table.

"I suppose you wrote this?" said he.

"Yes."

"And you think everything's clear now, do you?"

"Isn't it?" said I.

"I dare say Dr England will be able to tell you. By the way, why did you only give me 2 shillings 6 pence change instead of 3 shillings 6 pence?"

"There was only 2 shillings 6 pence to give."

"Really? I thought so too till your clever management of the tips tempted me to look over the bills again. I see that what you paid only came to L4 16 shillings 6 pence, instead of L4 17 shillings 6 pence. I don't want the other shilling, but hope you bought yourself something nice with it. You must consider it a present from Tempest, not me."

I timed red and white in the sudden confusion of that announcement. I was positively certain 2 shillings 6 pence had been the change, and that if there was any mistake it must be on the part of the tradesmen, not me. But how was I likely to convince Crofter, or, for the matter of that, Tempest, that such was the case?

"I promise you," said I, "I only had 2 shillings 6 pence change. Really, Crofter, do believe me."

"I believe every word you say," said Crofter, with a smile. "I have every reason to, haven't I?"

"But, really and truly--"

"What's the use of saying any more? Of course, it's all really and truly. I've no doubt Tempest believes it too."

"Please let me see the bills," pleaded I; "I'll show you I'm right."

"Unfortunately Tempest has them. I dare say he will be delighted."

"You haven't told him about this, have you?" I gasped, in helpless misery.

"I'm going to; it's too good a joke to be kept to myself; I don't suppose he'll mind. Certainly he won't be surprised."

"Oh, Crofter, for goodness' sake, don't tell him this!" said I, blundering on into an appearance of guiltiness of which I was quite innocent. "I'm wanting so awfully to be friends with him again. I've given him back all I got out of the shops; and it will spoil everything if you tell him this, really--it isn't true either."

Crofter laughed pleasantly.

"It's rather likely I should shield you, isn't it? when all this term you and your friends have been insulting and defying me, and setting yourself to upset my authority as captain of the house."

"Oh, but we aren't!"

"What does this precious thing mean?" demanded he, producing the famous round-robin; "it's meant to be all politeness, I suppose."

"It only means," faltered I, "that we are sorry Tempest is not captain."

"Naturally. It's nice to have a captain one can swindle and rob, isn't it?"

I groaned miserably--it seemed no use trying to put myself right.

"If you chose to be civil and back me up, it would be different," said Crofter.

"But we are--we're going as steady as anything," said I.

"What do you mean by going to Pridgin and Wales and Tempest for *exeats* and special leave instead of to me?" he demanded.

This was a point I was unprepared for. It was true that the Philosophers, in their desire not to be interfered with by the new captain, had made a point of applying, as they were entitled to do, to any of the other prefects of the house in preference to Crofter for *exeats* and occasional leave to go without bounds. It had always been considered the prerogative of the captain of the house to grant these; but, strictly speaking, the other prefects had the right too. I tried to explain as much.

"Of course," said he, "it is a very neat way of ignoring my authority. I expect you to come to me. I shall not refuse any reasonable request, but I'm not going to be insulted in my own house."

"But--" said I.

"There is no 'but' about it. If you want to prevent your being shown up to your friend as an amiable young swindler, you can stop it by undertaking that you and your lot will do what I tell you. If not, it is your own look-out, that's all."

Luckily the school bell enabled me to get away without giving any pledge. Fool as I was, I knew what all this meant. It was an attempt to buy us all over at the cost of that unlucky shilling, and with it to secure Crofter in the authority which he so dearly coveted, but so far so imperfectly enjoyed.

The Philosophers, as might be expected, waxed very indignant when I made a clean breast of the whole matter. With their usual frankness they quite admitted that I might have pilfered the shilling. That sort of thing, they remarked, was quite in my line, and in keeping with my character generally; and they hoped to live to see me hung. But as to caving in to Crofter as the cost of my shelter, they drew the line at that. He had no right to impose new rules, or take away the immemorial privileges of the "Sharpers." Besides, if they gave in on this point, they would immediately have to go and ask his leave to practise for the Sports in Callow Meadow, which was just out of bounds, and where, in strict seclusion, diligent practice had been going on for a week, with most promising results.

I was thereupon ordered to write a laconic rejoinder to the tempting offer, the Philosophers promising to back me up in the matter of the shilling and see me through it.

With a heavy heart, therefore, I sat down and penned the following brief epistle, which was approved by the faggery and ordered to be laid on Crofter's table before bed-time.

"Dear Crofter,--We all think it's not good enough. It's all a lie about the shilling. Yours sincerely, T.J. iv."

Some of the Philosophers demurred to the sentence about the shilling, which appeared to commit them to an opinion they did not hold. But I had my way for once, and retired to bed, when all was done, wondering whenever peace would come, and I and my friend should rejoice to see one another again as of old.

I do not know how soon I fell asleep. It must have been pretty soon; for I can remember seeing Crofter come into the dormitory and turn out the gas; and I can remember in the general stillness hearing voices and the noise of poking the fire in Mr Sharpe's room downstairs. After that I forgot everything, until suddenly I discovered myself awake again.

Things seemed strange as I slowly turned my head on the pillow and blinked up with half-opened eyes. The dormitory seemed hot and stuffy; somebody or something was making a noise, and I wished they would stop. I could see nothing, except the hazy outline of my shirt hanging on the back of the chair, and even that seemed to come and go as I watched it. I was indisposed to move, and my mind was half asleep still. The one thing I did long for was for the noise to stop and some one to open a window. It was simply choking; I could hardly breathe, and--

Suddenly my shirt seemed to turn red, and by the lurid light it emitted I could see smoke coming over the top of the door. Then the side of the room grew red too, and seemed to close in on me, getting redder and redder as it did so, till finally by a frantic effort I raised myself in my bed and yelled--

"Fire!"

The answer was a great volume of smoke, which leapt out at me like a savage beast and sent me back on to the pillow; a deafening roar outside, and a sudden blaze, which half-blinded me and stifled the cry that was on my lips.

That is all I can remember distinctly. I was vaguely conscious of hearing my name called, of seeing my door move, of everything whirling round and round, and finally of falling, or getting, or being dragged out of bed.

The next thing I was aware of was that I was lying in a strange bed, with a headache, but otherwise tolerably comfortable, though awfully thirsty, and as weak as a mouse.

"Water, please," I remarked at large.

Instantly a face bent over me--a strangely familiar face, which after a moment's reflection I told myself was my mother's.

It was such a surprise that I forgot about the water, and took a nap instead.

In due time I must have woke again, this time by candlelight.

"Mother, are you there?"

"Yes, darling; what is it?"

"My shirt caught fire, and--"

"Hush, dear. Don't try to talk."

I didn't quite see why. I was really curious about several things. In fact, I thirsted for information.

"Why mayn't I talk, mother?"

"Because you've been ill."

"Did I get doctor's leave?"

"Yes, dear."

"Mother?"

"Well, sonny darling."

"How did you get here?"

"They sent and told me you--"

"You didn't believe about that shilling? Really there was only 2 shillings 6 pence change."

"Yes, yes, dear. Hush now, there's a good boy."

"Mother?"

"Well, Tommy dear."

"Was there a fire last night?"

"It was a week ago, sonny."

"Who was the fellow called me? Was he riled at me for not answering?"

"Oh no--you were almost suffocated."

"Where shall I sleep now? Have they mended my cubicle?"

"You'll sleep here, dear. All the boys are over here."

"Was all the dormitory on fire, then?"

"Yes; but thank God every one was saved."

"Is Langrish all right?"

"Oh yes, all of them are."

"Will he be game for the High Jump?"

"Surely, surely--but you're talking too much, sonny."

"Mother?"

"What is it, darling?"

"Does Tempest know I've been ill?"

"Yes," and her eyes seemed to fill with tears as she bent over me.

"Will you tell him about the shilling?"

"Yes, if you like."

"Mother, why are you crying? Is Tempest ill too?"

"No, dear--but--"

"Tell us, mother."

"If it had not been for Tempest," said she, "I should have had no boy to-day."

"Did he get me out, then?" said I, getting thoroughly aroused.

"Yes, Heaven bless him for it!" she replied, kissing my forehead.

"That'll be a score for him," said I; "I'm so glad."

My mother evidently did not quite understand this point of view, and concluded I had been talking more than was good for me, and once more implored me to be silent.

But I had no notion of giving up my inquiries at this stage.

"Did he get hurt doing it?" I asked.

"Only his hand a little."

"How did he get at me?"

"Every one thought you were safe out of the burning room with the others. When it was found you were not, Tempest rushed back before any one could stop him, and carried you out. He had not got outside with you more than a second or two when the roof and staircase and all fell in."

Here she shuddered as once more she bent over me and kissed me.

This was all I wanted to hear at present, and I closed my eyes in order to think it over the better.

My chief sensation was one of exultation that Tempest should risk his life for me. It meant that I had won him back in spite of myself. Then when I recalled the frightful blaze and noise of that night, I began to realise what my rescue must have meant to any one. No one but a fellow utterly scornful of danger, and utterly determined to save a life in peril at all cost, could have ventured into that place. *He* would have done it for any one, I knew; but to come deliberately after me, who had ruined his chances last term, and whom he despised as a pilferer and a sneak--this was an act of heroism which it baffled me to contemplate, and in the contemplation of which consequently I succumbed once more to sleep and forgot everything.

As I slowly got better (and, after all, I was not much damaged, as soon as I had got over the effects of the suffocation and terror of that awful night) I heard more about the fire. Permission was given me to see one friend a day for ten minutes at a time, and the reader may imagine the wild excitement of those ten minutes.

I naturally called for Dicky Brown as my first man. He came, looking rather scared, and was evidently relieved to find I was something better than a mass of burns, and able to do my share in the conversation.

"It was a close shave for you, I can tell you," he said. "All the other fellows hopped out long before the fire got bad, and no one fancied you weren't out too. You must have been sleeping jolly sound. All of a sudden one of your lot yelled out that you were missing. It was so hot then the fellows were all standing back, but old Tempest, almost before the chap had shouted, nipped into the middle of it, and made a dash for your cubicle. My word! I wish I'd been there to see it! You were as good as done for when he collared you and hauled you out. He fell with you half-way down the stairs, but Sharpe and Pridgin and one or two others caught him and fished him out with you over his shoulder. He swears he's not damaged, but he's got his hand in a sling. I say, old chap, it's no use blubbing; it's all right how."

"I wasn't blubbing," said I. "When you've got a cold in your head your eyes water sometimes, don't they?"

"Rather, buckets," said the magnanimous Dicky.

Langrish was my next interviewer; and his account as an eye-witness was graphic, and not calculated entirely to cure my "cold in the head."

"You see, it's this way," said he. "Jarman was smoking in Sharpe's room, and chucked his cigar into the waste-paper basket or somewhere by mistake, and while he and Sharpe toddled across the quad, the thing flared up and went up the curtains, and when old Sharpe came back the whole place was in a blaze. I twigged it pretty sharp, and so did Trim, and there was a regular stampede. No one ever supposed you'd go snoring all through it. Crofter and Wales were first outside, looking as white as milk. Bless you, it was such a rush and shindy, no one could see anybody. Of course we made sure you were all serene. Think of you sleeping through it!"

"I was in the end cubicle, you see," said I.

"For all that, you might have stuck your head out to see what the fun was about," said Langrish, in rather an aggrieved tone. "Sharpe turned up presently, with his face all grimy with smoke, and yelled, 'Is every one here?' 'Yes,' said Crofter--silly ass, how could he tell? Then Coxhead said to me, 'Where's Sarah got to?' That made me look round, and I can tell you I was pretty sick when I couldn't see you. Just fancy a chap sleeping away through it all! Why, the ant and the sluggard," said Langrish, getting a little mixed in his proverbs, "weren't in it with you. So I yelled 'Sarah!' with all my might. You should have seen the chaps sit up when they heard your name. Then old Tempest, with his mouth shut and looking middling pasty about the face, broke through the scrimmage and sent us right and left, and made a regular header into the place. Sharpe yelled to him to come back; some tried to yell, but couldn't for lumps in their throats, and we all closed up. I can tell you it was a hot place. The smoke rolled out and got in our eyes, and the wood and stuff cracked and blazed, and sounded like the waves at Dover. We never expected to see him or you come back. The stairs were going to bits as fast as they could, and great bits of burning wood were tumbling off the roof. Then the smoke shifted somehow, and we heard Sharpe yell, 'Heavens!' Then there was a dull row like something tumbling, and Pridgin and Sharpe dashed in. We got kept back, or we'd have given you a leg-up too. Then you strolled in, fast asleep still--I never saw such a snoozer!--on Tempest's arm. He was pretty well done, and couldn't have pulled it off if Sharpe and Pridgin hadn't hiked him out. Even then he couldn't stand. So I hope you're jolly well pleased with yourself. I hope it will be a lesson to you, young Sarah, to keep one eye open while you're asleep. We were jolly glad you got canted out, though you *are* a bit of a mule. But it would have been rough on you to miss the Sports. They say Tempest's burned his hand pretty bad, but he means to have a shot at the Mile. I say, Redwood was asking after you. Jarman's jolly sick that it was his fault about the fire. He's been quite civil, and been to ask about you every day. Look sharp and get right, I say, or it'll rot the Sports if you don't. Hullo, there comes your *mater*. Ta, ta, old hoss. It's rather ripping you scraped through all right."

He was a good sort, Langrish. He did not tell me, what I heard later, that at the time of the fire he had to be held back by main force from following Tempest in quest of me; and that he had rather a "cold in his head" when he saw me hauled out safe and sound.

CHAPTER TWENTY FOUR.
"SMALL AND EARLY" IN THE SANATORIUM.

My recovery was far too rapid to please me. I never had such a jolly time in all my life. My mother was in and out all day; there were no lessons. I was allowed to summon any chum I liked to my bedside. I was receiving messages daily from masters and seniors, and, best of all, I had nothing the matter with me except, a strong disinclination to exert myself, and an occasional headache or dizziness when I sat up.

I had come up to Low Heath that term with the honest determination to "lie low." I little expected, however, that I should find myself quite so literally adhering to my resolution.

My one trouble was that all this time I had not seen Tempest. I did not like to send for him, in case he should not appreciate the compliment. And he, as I guessed, would not care to come of his own accord for the uncomfortable ceremony of receiving my thanks. My mother told me he had often asked about me; but when she asked him to come and see me he had replied,--"I'll see him as soon as he gets about again." When she inquired about his hand he had replied airily that it was all right, and he was only keeping it in the sling to get it right for the Sports. "But," said my mother, "I wish he would let the doctor see it, or give up running till it is well."

"But," said I, "he's a chance of winning off Redwood." This argument, which in ninety-nine cases out of one hundred in Low Heath would have been absolutely conclusive, failed to impress my mother in the least. She attached no importance to "winning off Redwood" compared with a boy's health, and obdurately protested that if she were Tempest's mother she would not allow him to think of running.

It was only my agitated appeals to her not to interpose that prevented her speaking to Dr England about the matter, and so knocking the race on the head altogether.

I took it as a compliment to myself that the Sports had been put off a fortnight in consequence of the fire. That warm event had so upset everything and monopolised so much attention that Low Heath would not have come up to scratch at all on the day originally fixed. And whereas the new date permitted of my being present to assist--though, alas I not to compete--in the day's proceedings, I felt specially satisfied with the alteration.

I had naturally heard a good deal of Philosophical gossip during my convalescence. On my last evening in hospital especially, there was quite a symposium.

My mother, in an innocent moment, had remarked, "I should so like to have one or two of your friends to tea, sonny, before I go home. The doctor says it will not do you any harm--and we can have them in here, as you are the only invalid in hospital."

"That'll be ten, with you and me," said I.

"Do you want quite so many?" asked she, beginning to get a little concerned.

"Must have the lot or none," said I decisively. "We can cut out Rackstraw and Walsh, if you like--they're paupers."

"Oh, Tommy!" said the dear, tender-hearted one, "if they are not as well off as--"

"Oh, that's not it. They can shell out as well as anybody; only they got on our club for nothing on condition of towing the boats, cleaning up, and that sort of thing."

"At any rate, let us have them," said my mother.

"All serene. Will you write the invitations? I say, mother, do you mind writing as well as you can? Our chaps are rather particular, you know, and I wouldn't like them to snuff up at you."

My poor dear mother began, I think, to repent of her hospitable offer, but decided to go through with it now.

So she got eight nice little sheets of scented invitation note, with envelopes to match, and wrote,--

"Mrs Jones requests the pleasure of Mr Alfred James Remington Trimble's company to tea in the Sanatorium parlour this evening at 6 p.m.;" and so on, in each case.

My suggestion to add "R.S.V.P." and "Evening dress *de rigueur*" she thought it best to decline. But her kind leniency was thrown away, for within half an hour eight notes dropped in upon us, couched in the politest phraseology.

Here was Langrish's, for instance:--

"Everard Langrish, Esquire, begs to thank Mrs Jones for asking him to tea at six sharp, when he will be very pleased to fall in with her wishes and be of service in any other way her better feelings may dictate."

Langrish told me afterwards he cribbed this last sentence out of a story he had read in a weekly newspaper. He rather fancied it was "on the spot."

Trimble's was less romantic:--

"Dear Madam,--I accept with thanks. Sarah gets rather outside sometimes, but we do what we can for him. Till then,--

"I am yours affectionately,--

"A.J.R. Trimble."

Warminster's was, no doubt, meant to be impressive:--"The President of the Philosophical Conversation Club presents his compliments to Mrs Jones, and desires to inform her of his intention to wait upon her at the hour named in her letter. He trusts that Mrs Jones is in good health, and that her ailing child will be spared to her a little longer. Having several matters to attend to, the President of the Philosophical Conversation Club must now abruptly terminate, namely, Percy Algernon Warminster."

The ending seemed to me decidedly weak compared with the rest. I will only give one more--that of Coxhead:--

"Dear Mrs Jones, I'll come to tea;
At six o'clock you shall me see.
I'm sorry Sarah's been laid up
And drinks his physic from a cup.
Unless unto the contrary I hear.
My Eton suit I think I'll wear.
And now 'farewell,' as great John Knox said.
Yours truly, Samuel Wilberforce Coxhead."

This effusion struck me as rather like cheek; but my mother seemed to like it.

As evening approached I began to grow very nervous, and have to confess that my mother was the cause of my concern. I was so afraid she was not properly impressed with the gravity of the occasion--that perhaps she would not be dressed at her best--or that the tea might not be up to the mark--or that for any cause the fellows should consider they had been "done." I'm sure I wearied the life out of her by my inquiries as to the nature of the jam, as to whether the cake would go round twice, whether any of the teacups were cracked, whether the nine chairs ranged round the little room were all sound on their legs, who would open the door to let them in, whether my mother would mind not proposing juvenile games like table-turning, or clumps, and whether when the time came for them to go she would mind not looking at her watch or yawning, for fear they should think it a hint.

All which points the dear soul faithfully promised should be borne in mind and attended to, with a little quiet banter at my expense, which helped to remind me that, after all, one's mother may be trusted not to disgrace a fellow, if left to herself.

In due time she presented herself in her Sunday dress, looking very pretty and smart--quite creditable, in fact. The tea also, as it appeared laid out on the sideboard--I had urged, by the way, that it should be served in party style, and not partaken of round a table-- looked a well-found meal for the most exacting of Philosophers. I myself reposed in state in bed, arrayed in my Eton jacket and best collar and choker. The fire in the hearth was both cheerful and adequate, and the knowledge that the Sanatorium maid was downstairs in her cap and clean apron, to show the young gentlemen up, finally relieved my anxiety.

In due time there was a ring, and a sound of the funereal tramp of eighteen feet on the staircase, and I knew that Mrs Jones's party had begun.

They all trooped in together, looking very grave and shy, and spick and span in their full-dress, and evidently on their good behaviour. My mother shook hands with each in unexceptionable style, repeating his name as I announced it from the bed, and expressing her pleasure at making his acquaintance.

The sight of me propped up on my pillows, somewhat pale still, and as shy as themselves, seemed to impress them a good deal, and added to the funereal character of the entertainment. A long pause ensued, broken only by the entrance of the maid with the teapot, and Langrish's remark to Trimble that it was a fine day.

Then my mother had the wit to observe that she hoped it would be equally fine on the day of the Sports, and she was so sorry she would miss them, as she understood Mr Sharpe's house was likely to win a good many of the events, and of course her sympathies were entirely that way.

This went down beautifully, and drew from Coxhead the remark,--

"It's a pity Sar--I mean Jones iv.--is out of it. He might have got the Quarter-mile."

"Are the names down yet?" I asked.

"Yes. We stuck them down to-day," said Langrish.

"Any one else in for the Senior Mile?"

"No; only Tempest and Redwood."

Another pause--everybody evidently meditating what my mother would like to hear next.

My mother meanwhile moved to the sideboard and began to pour out tea.

"Do you take cream and sugar?" she said, with a pleasant smile, to Langrish. How relieved I was she did not call him "Everard" or "dear!"

"Yes, please--can I pass round?" he replied.

It was admirable. I had been in terror lest he would have collared the first cup and stuck to it.

"Thank you, if you will, please. I see they are beginning to get your old house ready for rebuilding."

"It won't be ready this term, though," said Warminster; "it will take--a slice of cake, thanks."

"No sugar for me, thanks," said Coxhead. "I wonder if Jarman will have to pay for it?"

"Does your *mater* take cream and sugar?" said Purkis to me, in an aside.

"I shouldn't think so," said Langrish, "because he didn't do it on purpose, you know."

"Thank you very much. Do you mind putting it down there? And won't you sit down?" said my mother, setting the example.

"I expect he'd better give up smoking, as he's always setting things on fire," ventured I. "Mother knows about the guy last term, don't you, mother?"

"Yes, indeed," said she, with a laugh, which won over the Philosophers in a body. "That was a lucky escape for everybody. I was horrified."

"Well, old Sar--I mean Jones iv.--"

"I think he understands his nickname better than his real name," said my clever parent.

"Old Sarah," said Langrish, getting rapidly at his ease, "let us in for that. You see (cake up, please), it was this way--"

And he launched forth into an account of that famous adventure, into which the company one by one cut, at my expense, of course, and highly to the diversion of my mother.

Meanwhile the teapot was kept busy, and the jam went its rounds--some of it on to Coxhead's shirt-front--and by the end of it all the Philosophers found themselves comfortably at home.

"I say," said I, when a break came, "how's the club getting on? Anything fresh?"

Langrish glanced round at my mother.

"I've got the minute-book," he said, "would she--"

"Oh, do!" said she. "Is it an account of your meetings? I would like to hear it immensely. Debating societies are such capital things, I think."

"It's a bit down on Sarah, though," said the secretary, dubiously.

"Why, I wasn't there," said I.

"Weren't you? that's all."

"Let's hear it," said my mother, "I dare say he deserves it."

I forgave the dear traitress for giving me away like this, for I felt sure the minutes would save our evening.

"You see," said Trimble, "we try to keep it fair, so it's down on some of the others too. But Sarah gets it a little the hottest."

"I'm used to getting things hot by now," said I; "forge ahead, and sit where I can shy the pillow at you."

Whereupon Langrish moved his chair to a conspicuous place, and read,--

"'A meeting of the Ph.C.C. was held in dormitory on February 1, at 9 p.m.'"

"Why, that's when the fire was," said Trimble.

"Shut--I mean what's that got to do with it?" retorted the secretary.

"Well?" said my mother, taking a stitch or two at her needlework.

"'Owing to the side put on by the ex-president, who was lately, kicked out for being a howling cad, and because he was down in form order--'"

"What a cram!" I interposed; "I was on the second desk, and should have had you down weeks ago if I hadn't been laid up."

"Ha, ha, I like that--you! Did your *mater* ever hear about *corpore* being the ablative masculine, eh?"

"No, I never heard about that," said my mother.

"All right--Sarah will tell you--where was I, oh--down in form order, though he's not quite such a crock as Coxhead, who is champion dunce in Low Heath--"

"Me?" exclaimed Coxhead, warm with tea and indignation.

"There you are," said Langrish, "anybody but a champion dunce would have said 'I.' You ask Sarah's *mater* if they wouldn't."

"Well, *you*, if you like," said Coxhead; "what about it--"

"Look here, how can I read the minutes when--here we are--'crock as Cox-head, who is champion dunce in Low Heath.'"

"What happened then?" said my mother, looking a little mixed.

"'He was shunted to an outside berth, and was out of it.'"

"I rather think I was in it," said I; "never mind."

"Oh, if you think so, all right. The minutes say you were out of it. 'He'd not begun to snore many minutes with deafening effect, when, as might be expected, Jarman set fire to the show to stop the noise.'"

"Do you think that's why he did it, really?" asked Warminster.

"Look here, young Warminster. I don't *think*, I--"

"Pity you don't now and then," remarked the newly-elected president.

Langrish looked hard at his colleague, and then glanced at my mother, whose face was bent over her work. Whereupon the secretary threw the minute-book at the president's head, and observed,--

"Look out, Warminster; hand up that book, can't you--it's not yours."

My mother looked up, and Warminster meekly surrendered the book.

"'--Stop the noise. The club then adjourned, all except Sarah, who hung on, contrary to the rules, and is hereby fined 2 shillings 6 pence.'"

"Oh, I say," protested I, "that's rather rough, isn't it?"

"'But,'" proceeded Langrish, "'owing to his mother coming up to buy him off, he is hereby let off with a fie-- I mean a warning.'"

"Thank you so much," said my mother, gratefully.

"'When we thought he was pretty well warmed up, we sent Tempest in to fish him out, which he accordingly did, and is hereby elected honorary porter to the club, and is backed to win the Mile.'"

"That's the least he deserves, surely," said my mother, with feeling.

"'Sarah, owing to this unprincipled conduct, has been suspended for a month, and the club hereby hopes some day not far off to see him sus--' no, that's wrong--I mean--"

"Hung," suggested Trimble, in an audible whisper.

"Order--turn him out for saying hung, instead of hanged," said the president.

"Shut up, can't you?" said the secretary, "can't you let me finish the sentence? '--See him sus--susceptible of better emotions.'"

"Hear, hear," said the club, breathing again to see the corner turned.

"I hope that's not all," said my mother.

"That's as far as we've got; but we'll let him down easy in the next," said Langrish.

"The next will have the account of the Sports, I suppose," said my mother.

"If our men win," said Warminster. "We're bound to win the High Jump if Langrish keeps on his form; he did 4 feet 1 and a half inches this afternoon."

"You needn't talk--you're all right for the 100 Yards," said the modest Langrish; "there's no one in, except young Brown of the day cads, who can touch you; and he's sure to go a mucker on the day."

"Don't be too sure of that," said I. "Dicky Brown doesn't go muckers if he can help it."

"There you are--backing the town cads now. I move, and Mrs Jones seconds, that Sarah be, and is hereby, kic--I mean sat upon by the club."

"Oh, don't, please," said my mother, "the bed is not strong enough."

"All right--it's lucky for Sarah. If you were half a chap you'd see we didn't lose the Quarter-mile. Rackstraw will have a look in at it, but it'll puzzle him to beat Flitwick. Walsh is going to cut out for him. So we may just do it; but it'll be a go-- eh, paupers?"

Rackstraw and Walsh both protested there would be no difficulty about it if only the track was in good order, and their wind held out, and Flitwick muddled his start, and finished a yard or two behind. We were all prepared to stake the glory of Sharpe's on these trifling conditions.

Presently the preparation bell began to toll, and the party broke up with a cordiality and cheerfulness which contrasted strangely with the solemnity with which it had begun. My mother was politely requested to become an honorary member of the club, and as politely consented, expressing a hope that she might meet with its honourable members many times again.

When they had gone she told me how much she had enjoyed the evening, and how she liked every one of them, and hoped they wouldn't think her rude to have laughed now and then, but really, she said, not being used to it, she could not help it.

Next day she left, and, dismally enough, I made the first use of my liberty to accompany her in the fly to the station. She talked to me, as only she could, about the future, and the spirit in which she thought I would take up once more the work of the term and the thankfulness which she the widow, and I the orphan, could not help feeling to the Heavenly Father, who had saved us both from such peril and sorrow in the past. She urged me to show my gratitude for my escape, by seeking to follow more closely in the footsteps of that Saviour to whom she had so often taught me to look for help and guidance, and at the same time she urged me to pray for the guidance of the Holy Spirit. Her goodness only made my sorrow at parting the greater; and more than any time since I had entered Low Heath, the pangs of home-sickness fell upon me as I saw her into her carriage.

Just before the train started I felt my heart beat suddenly, and the blood rush to my cheeks, as I saw a figure, with one hand in a sling, running up the platform, looking into one carriage after another.

"Mother, here's Tempest!"

Next moment he saw us, and ran up.

"I heard you were going by this train," said he, "and I thought I would like to say good-bye."

"Good-bye, my dear boy, and God bless you once more!"

"The youngster's all right again, I see," said he, putting his hand on my arm.

"I'll see he takes care of himself--good-bye."

And the train steamed off, leaving us two on the platform.

"I hope your hand's not awfully bad," said I, breaking a silence of nearly three months in the only way which occurred for the moment.

"Rather not. We'd better cab it back--you're not up to walking yet."

"Thanks awfully, Tempest, for saving--"

"Look here, don't let's get on to that," said he.

"I say," said I, "I was afraid you believed what Crofter said, and thought--"

"You were an ass, Tommy--you always were--I ought to have remembered it. Of course I never believed a word Crofter said--I saw his game. But I was idiot enough to get riled at you for giving yourself away to him. I'm sorry. Now let's forget it. After all, it was the best thing for me that all that row about my bills came out when it did. You did me a better turn than you meant to do. Just like you--if you try to do things the right way, it's all up with everybody. But if you do them your own way, they manage to come round somehow."

"But Crofter's done you out of the captaincy."

"So much the better--I didn't deserve it. I'll get it back some day perhaps, and work it better. Come in to me to tea. Redwood's coming, and old Dicky, too."

"But you're against Redwood for the Mile," said I.

"That's no reason why I shouldn't give him a cup of tea, is it, you young mule?"

The way he said it, and the grip of his hand on my arm, satisfied me that all was square once more between me and my dear old Dux.

CHAPTER TWENTY FIVE.
A DEAD HEAT.

The few weeks during which I had been laid up had witnessed some curious changes in Low Heath--at least, they seemed curious to me, dropping, as I did, suddenly into them.

First of all, we poor "Sharpers" were all burnt out. The faggery was no more, nor was the hall, or the dormitory. We were being put up temporarily in a town house just outside the school gates, a good deal to the wrath of some of our number, who felt it was putting them down to the level of the day boys. However, the sight of the scaffolding round our old quarters, and the cheery clink of the trowel, reminded us that out exile was not for long, and that in a brand-new faggery, on brand- new chairs, and round a brand-new table, we should shortly resume our pleasant discussions on the deepest questions with which the human mind can occupy itself.

Somehow, apart from the fire, things weren't going exactly as I had left them. Pridgin was reported to be working hard--a most alarming symptom. It was commonly surmised that he could not stand playing second or third fiddle to Crofter; and as Tempest was apparently content to be second, Pridgin had come to the painful conclusion that the only comfortable place for him in Sharpe's was Number One. It was extremely inconvenient all round; for it made it necessary for Crofter to bestir himself, while of course it seemed to threaten Tempest's chance of recovering his place.

A few of the shrewdest held that Pridgin was merely forcing the pace in order to punish Crofter for his usurpation. It may have been so; but, whatever the motive, it quite upset the normal flow of things at Sharpe's.

Another change was a marked reaction of public opinion in favour of Tempest and against Crofter. This was probably due, in the first place, to Tempest's exploit in rescuing me from the fire; and secondly, to Crofter's caution in declining to enter for the Mile race at the coming Sports. A few weeks had dispelled the little glamour which the latter had derived from his apparently public-spirited conduct last term, and the attitude of the Philosophers had effectually deprived him of any opportunity of exercising his authority, and left him to the enjoyment of an altogether barren honour.

One other change was that Tempest's necessity to live very economically in order to repay his grandfather for advances made, had produced a coolness between him and Wales, who had now retired from the triumvirate, and attached himself to the cause of Crofter.

Lastly, Mr Jarman had suffered a shock, and taken on badly about his accidental part in the recent fire. It had knocked all the vice out of him, for the time being at any rate, and left him quite meek and limp.

Just now, however, the only topic about which any one cared was, as I speedily discovered, the Sports.

Unusual keenness was being displayed everywhere. The seniors were deeply concerned in the issue of the Mile. Would Redwood, who had hitherto held his own easily, save his laurels this time? Would Tempest, with his damaged hand, be able to run his hardest? Would any dark horse, at the last moment, enter to divide the interest? And so on.

Among the middle boys considerable excitement was afoot, especially in Selkirk's house, where it was reported a boy of fifteen and a half was going to beat the senior record in the Jump, and perhaps run the public school record very close.

But the chief excitement was among us juniors. We had modestly set before ourselves the task of winning every event under fifteen for Sharpe's house, to say nothing of pulling the day boys over the chalk in the Tug of War, and generally bringing the Philosophers well before the public notice. The secret of our intention had been well-kept till within a week of the day. We had been taunted with shirking our sports, with being "mugs" and "crocks" and "cripples," with exercising the better part of valour, with being afraid of being laughed at, and so forth. But we heard all with a conscious wink, and went on with our practice round the corner. Then, a week from the day, we literally pelted the list with our names.

Langrish put down for the High Jump, Cricket Ball, Broad Jump, and Hurdles. Warminster set down his name under Dicky Brown's for the Hundred Yards, and next to Griswold's for the Hurdles. Coxhead entered for the Cricket Ball against the crack thrower in Selkirk's, and Rackstraw and Walsh, noble pair of "paupers," put in for the Quarter- mile, which I was to have run against the fleet-footed Flitwick. Altogether it was a big order, and made the other houses look a little blue, as we hoped it would.

The great day came at last--a perfect Sports day, with a light breeze blowing, the track like elastic, the takes-off clean and sharp, and the field crammed with visitors and friends. I had my work cut out for me that day. It would have been far less exertion to run the Quarter-mile. I was to be coat-minder, time-keeper, rubber-down, straight-tipper, clapper-on-the-back, and bottle-holder to the Conversation Club at large, a sort of mixture of parent, footman, and retriever dog, which, flattering as it undoubtedly was to my sense of my own importance, promised no little anxiety and exercise before the day was done.

As I strolled down somewhat early, charged with the pleasing commission of "bagging nine seats in the middle of the front row of the stand and seeing no one collared them," I met Redwood, fresh as a daisy, just returning from a final inspection of the ground.

"Hullo, youngster, you're not running, I hear. What a pity!"

"It doesn't matter," said I. "Do you mind my not backing you for the Mile?"

He laughed, and said he should have thought poorly of me if I had not backed my own man.

"Is his hand all right now?" he asked.

"He says so," said I. "It's worth six yards to you, though."

"You think so, do you?" said he. "By the way, will you do a job for me? My two young sisters awfully want to be on the ground, and they've got leave if some one will look after them. I can't. How would you like to?"

Here was a thunderbolt! I had a fair day's work mapped out for myself as it was. Now I was to be saddled with a pair of teasing young female fidgets, and held responsible for their good behaviour and general comfort! What did people take me for? Why, the Mile itself wouldn't take it out of me half as much.

"All right," said I, "where are they?"

"I'm going home; I'll send them down sharp before the crowd comes. Thanks awfully, youngster."

And off he went, leaving me pretty full up with the cares of this deceitful world.

I proceeded to bag the nine best seats on the stand, which, as nobody else had yet put in an appearance, was easy enough without the trying necessity of sitting on them all at the same time. When the crowd arrived, it would be time enough to consider how I should then have to act.

I had not been long in possession when two dainty little figures in pink bore down hand-in-hand upon me, presumably under the protection of a nurse, who, however, was not in it when it came to racing.

"There's horrid Sarah," remarked Mamie, "who tried to drown me."

"Never mind," said Gladys, "he was nearly burned to death to punish him for being wicked."

"I hate him because he never gives us sweeties," said Mamie.

"Never mind," said Gladys; "Bobby says it's not his fault that he's a mule. I don't like mules though, do you?"

"I hate them," said the uncompromising Mamie.

"Please, Master Jones," said the nurse, "the mistress says will you see the young ladies behave nicely and don't dirty their frocks? Be good girls now," she added, by way of final admonition, as she departed.

I watched her go with the helpless despair of a man on a spar who watches the lifeboat put off with its last load for the shore. The young ladies, almost before nurse was gone, began to run along the rows of chairs, falling down once in twelve, and rapidly toning down the pretty pink of their frocks to a sombre brick hue. I was thankful when the crowd began to drop in, and I was able, by threats of taking them home before the races began, to reduce them at least to the nine seats for which I was responsible. How I wished I had some sweets, in order to reduce them to only three!

By good luck Dicky Brown hove in sight just as I was giving way to despair.

"Dicky, old chap," said I, "if you love me, get sixpennyworth of bulls'- eyes or something. I'd be grateful to you as long as I live."

Dicky looked at me anxiously--evidently concerned for my health. But a jerk of my head in the direction of the two little vixens, who were just then trying to pull a solemn-looking day boy off one of the chairs by main force, satisfied him that the case was an urgent one, and, like a brick, he flew off to the rescue.

The solemn day boy stood his persecution as long as he could, and then rounded sharply on his persecutors.

"Bother you, go away!" he growled.

Whereupon in floods of tears, the Misses Redwood made for me, and insisted on being taken up one on each knee and "cosseted" because of what the big ugly boy had done.

I complied with the energy of despair, conscious that in so doing I was allowing the reserved seats one by one to be usurped, and was at the same time rendering myself a spectacle of contempt to at least eight young persons, whom, in the gap left between the two wet faces which clung to my either cheek, I could see advancing in a body, clad in running drawers and blazers, in our direction.

It was vain for me to try to escape from my false position. The nearer the Philosophers approached, the more maudlin and effusive these unprincipled young females became, flinging their arms tragically round my neck, and bedaubing my face with their dewy kisses.

"Sarah *can* go it a bit when he likes," said Langrish, with a cheerful guffaw, standing in a conspicuous place, and calling public attention to me in a way which only added to my sorrows.

"Rather. I wondered why he went down so early," said Coxhead.

"Birds of a feather," said the sententious Trimble, "play the fool together. I say, what about our seats, though?"

"They are bagged," said I, getting my face clear for a moment. "I couldn't keep them."

"I dare say. You mean you were so busy spooning about with girls you never thought of it. All right, Miss Molly," said Warminster.

"I think we could squash up a bit here," said I meekly.

"Looks as if *you* could," said Langrish. "Squash away then." And, to the wrath and indignation of the whole stand, the Philosophers crowded in, in a solid phalanx, and proceeded to accommodate their eight persons in the space usually allotted to two. It took some time for the other seat-holders to appreciate the humour of the manoeuvre, and before then the bell had rung for the first race, and Dicky had returned with the brandy-balls, which he deftly smuggled into my hand as he trotted past.

It was now easy to "square" the Misses Redwood, who for a blessed half- hour cried truce. It was in vain that I suggested that they had better not plaster their faces and frocks more than could be helped with the sticky substance of their succulent pabulum. They contemptuously ignored my right to make any suggestion of the kind, and I finally abandoned them to their fate.

The first few events were trial heats, in which we as a body were not specially interested; but when the bell rang up for the Hundred Yards under fifteen, the Sports had begun for us in earnest.

Leaving the two Daughters of Eve with the bag of brandy-balls between them, I clambered out of my place to perform the last rites for Warminster, who was to carry the colours of Sharpe's against Dicky Brown of the day boys, Muskett of Selkirk's, and another outsider.

It went a little to my heart to be rubbing down somebody else's calves but Dicky's on an occasion like this. But such is life. Patriotism goes before friendship, and times do come when one must wish confusion to one's dearest brother.

So I rubbed down one of Warminster's calves while Trimble rubbed the other, and Langrish gave him a word of advice about his start, and Coxhead arranged to call on him for his spurt twenty yards from the finish. With the exception of the other evening when he arrived at my mother's party I had never seen Warminster so meek and nervous. He behaved exactly as if we were taking a last farewell, and would, I think, have embraced us had we encouraged him to do so.

"Now then," said Langrish, "give us your blazer. Bend well over your toes for the start, and do it all in a breath."

"Run straight on your track, and don't try to take the other chaps' water," said Trimble.

"Don't look round at me when I yell, but bucket all you can," said Coxhead.

"Don't pull up till after the pistol has gone," said I. Then we left him to his work.

And well enough he did it. He and Dicky went off at the start as if they'd been shot out of a double-barrelled gun, Dicky with his head down, our man with his head up. That was what saved him; half-way over Dicky had to get his chin up, and it lost him a sixteenth of a second, and that meant six inches. Selkirk's man made an ugly rush thirty yards from home, but he began it too soon. Warminster wisely waited till he heard Coxhead's shrill "Gee-up" in his ear. Then he laid on and made his six inches eight, and his eight ten, and landed so much in front of Dicky amid cheers which, if the clouds had been a little lower, would have assuredly brought on a shower.

One score to us! I was sorry for Dicky, but it couldn't be helped. "It's your fault," said he, "the brandy-balls did it. I took one, you know; never mind. I say, look at your kids!"

The "kids" in question had finished the brandy-balls, and, resenting my desertion, had decided to follow me into the open. As I had reached it by swarming over the front of the stand and dropping a foot or so on to the earth, they naturally selected that route as most suitable for them. They had half accomplished it, to the extent of getting over the edge of the low parapet and beginning to lower themselves on the outside, when Mamie's frock caught in a nail, which suspended her between heaven and earth, while Gladys, in her uncertainty whether to scream or assist, had toppled to the ground all of a heap, and solved the difficulty that way. Their screeches almost put our loyal cheers to the blush, and when I rushed up to extricate the one and pick up the other, I was in the centre of a hullaballoo which almost threatened to wreck the Sports. How they quieted down I know not. I believe it was my announced determination to walk them straight home which did it. At any rate, it was clear to me there was no more rubbing down of Sharpe's calves for me that day. I must remain, like Casabianca, on deck, even though it cost us all the events of the day.

It was a thankless task. First of all there was the usual ceremony of "cosseting" and drying tears. Then with a pin I had to mend the rent in Mamie's frock. Then I had to kiss both of Gladys's elbows to make them well, and finally I had to stand a fusillade of chaff and jeers from the Philosophers, which made life a heavier burden that it was already.

At last, to my joy, the bell rang up for the High Jump under fifteen, and public attention was diverted from my lamentable case.

As everybody who knew anything had anticipated, Langrish won this, metaphorically speaking, "on his head." He knocked out the second man (a Selkirker) at 4 feet and half an inch, and went on gamely 2 inches higher, clearing the bar as prettily and daintily as Wales himself might have done in the open event. It was not at all certain he could not have gone higher against an opponent; but having no such spur, he grew careless, and after barely shaking down the bar twice at 4 feet 3 inches, kicked it off awkwardly the third time, and so retired an easy victor, and quite overcome by the applause of the now crowded field.

Then came the event of the day--the Open Mile, for which Tempest and Redwood were the only combatants. I felt myself growing as nervous as if I were running myself.

For my instinct told me that the welfare of Sharpe's more or less hung on the issue. Could Tempest but win, there would be no doubt that he would return to the headship of the house with an eclat which even Crofter would have to yield to. If not, Crofter might still hang on to the reins and claim his doubtful rights.

A complication of an unexpected kind arose now. The Misses Redwood were quite sufficiently *au fait* with the etiquette of a race-course to know that if their brother ran he must win, and that everybody else must wish him to win. In an unguarded moment I joined in the cheer which greeted Tempest as he appeared stripped for action on his way to the starting- post. This was taken up as a grievous personal affront. The young ladies repudiated and flung me from them with an energy and disgust which quite astonished me. They loudly clamoured for my removal, and failing that, made a concerted retreat from my detested vicinity.

"Nasty horrid Sarah, go away!" they shouted.

Then spying Dicky Brown in the distance, they shrieked on him to deliver them.

"Want to go *to Dicky*--dear Dicky. Get away from Sarah."

And suiting the action to the word they swarmed over the back of the bench, and started in full cry for the enviable Dicky.

Richard, however, was an old bird for his years, and did not, or pretended not to hear their siren voices, and sheered off into the open just in the nick of time. Whereupon the Misses Redwood redoubled their clamour, and could only be allured back to the shelter of my fatigued wing by my going to them and audibly bawling in their faces, "Bravo, Redwood! go it, Redwood!"

On these terms they surrendered, and the difficulty, at the cost indeed of my reputation as a loyal "Sharper" was temporarily tided over.

It was noticed that Tempest, though cool as ever, was pale, and carried his left hand, while he stood waiting, in the opening of his waistcoat. I saw Redwood go to him and say something, pointing as he did so to the hand. Tempest's reply was a flush and a laugh as he removed his hand from its resting-place, and waved it about at his side.

I did not like it. But it was too late now. Mr Jarman stood ready with his pistol up, the noise of the field suddenly changed to silence, and the two athletes, with arms out, stood straining on the line.

Off! It was a good start, and the pace was startling for a mile. Tempest had the inside track. He seemed to have the advantage in lightness of step, while Redwood's strength was more in length of stride. The first of the four laps was run almost inch for inch. Perhaps Tempest, thanks to his berth, had a foot to the good as they entered on the second. Here our man forged ahead slowly, and gradually drew to a clear lead. But we trembled as we saw it. Would he stay? Apparently he ran as lightly as before, but Redwood, as he lay on at his heels, seemed to be going even easier. However, the half-mile saw Tempest three yards ahead and still going. Then, to our concern, we saw Redwood's stride lengthen a little, and watched inch after inch of the interval shrink, until at the end of the third lap there was scarcely more difference than there had been at the end of the first. Yet our man was still to the front.

And now it was almost difficult for us onlookers to breathe, for the tug was at hand. The fourth lap had scarcely begun when a wild yell called attention to the fact that Tempest was once more "putting it on." What was still more satisfactory was that he was going as well as ever, although in that respect so was Redwood. The gap opened again, the foot grew to a yard, and the yard to half a dozen, and the half-dozen to-- At last! It was but two hundred yards from home when Redwood's stride once more lengthened out, and a new shout told us all that the chasm was once more being filled up, inch by inch and foot by foot. Tempest heard the shout and knew what it meant. He, *too*, lengthened his stride, and seemed as if he was going to answer rush for rush. But our hearts stood still and our tongues clave to the roofs of our mouths as we perceived that it would not come off. He could barely keep up his present pace. Would it see him through? Perhaps half the distance was passed, and Redwood had only recovered a third of his lead. Then the yells broke out. Every one wished he could lend his man an inch, or the hundredth part of an inch. Redwood's rush increased, and the vanishing inches struck panic into our philosophic breasts. Could Tempest but hold out these few yards, we were safe. He would! No! Yes! No, they're all but level another six yards. Then suddenly we saw Tempest fling his hand behind and reel forward with a blind stagger over the tape, and as the simultaneous report proclaimed a dead heat, fall sprawling and helpless on the ground.

The cheers died on our lips, for it was surely something more than exhaustion or broken wind. Redwood was beside him in a moment, and drew his head on his knee. It was a dead faint--not from fatigue, but from pain.

His burned and blistered hand, which he had so carefully concealed from everybody, and of which he had made so little, betrayed the secret plainly enough.

For once his pride and determination had overrated his physical strength. He had calculated on just being able to win the race. All he had done was just to save it, at a price which, as it turned out, was to cost him weeks of illness, and even threaten the loss of a hand.

The news of his calamity spread like wildfire, and put an end, as far as I at least was concerned, to the sports for the day.

We heard later in the day that he was in the Sanatorium in a high fever. Next day he was delirious, and the notice on the board told us that the doctor considered his condition dangerous. The next day, his old grandfather, the only relative he had, came down, and the next, summoned by my urgent message, my dear mother. Then for a day or two we were kept in suspense, till one happy afternoon the bulletin reported a change for the better, and presently the welcome news came that all danger was past.

For me at least that was the happiest day of my life, except perhaps that a week later when my mother as a special privilege allowed me to see him for a moment.

He was sitting up in bed, smiling but pale.

"Tell me," he said, "I've never heard yet, did I win the Mile?"

"Dead heat," said I.

"What time?"

"Four four and a half."

"A record, isn't it? It was worth the grind."

I had my doubts, but knew better than to say so.

CHAPTER TWENTY SIX.
A GOOD SHOW-UP ALL ROUND.

It was the last day but one of the Summer term, and the Philosophers were in a ferment. The lists were to be out in the afternoon, and a score of events were to be decided by them. Was I to get on to the top form of my division, and if so, was it Langrish or Purkis who was to be displaced? Or was I, after all my grind, to yield a place to the truculent Coxhead?

More than that, was Warminster to be beaten after all by a day boy called Dicky Brown, who, amid all the changes and distractions of the term, had stuck doggedly to his work, and was reported a hot man for the head place in the junior division?

All this was exciting enough, but it was as nothing to the tussle at the head of the school.

Pridgin's alarming burst of work in the Easter term had, contrary to all expectation, not died out. Every one prophesied he would sicken of it. Wales laughed at him. Crofter smiled sweetly. Tempest inquired frequently after his health, and even Redwood knocked off some of his extra cricket to keep pace with it.

"What are you trying to do?" asked Tempest one day, as his friend looked in.

"Nothing, my dear fellow, only amusing myself, I assure you."

"You have a queer idea of fun. Do you know, I've hardly been out on the river all the term, owing to you."

"Don't let me prevent you, old chap. The exercise will do you good."

Tempest laughed.

"I hope yours will do you good. But two can play at your game."

"Two! Half a dozen.--I've not got my knife into *you*, though."

"Who? Crofter?"

"Rather. I see no other way of taking it out of him. He shirks sports, and takes his pound of flesh out of the captaincy, although he knows he's no right to it, and no one, not even the rowdies in the faggery, respects him."

"That's why we're going steady," said I, "just to rile him."

"The only way to take it out of him is to make him sit up, and harry him," said the amiable Pridgin. "I only hope, though, it won't land me head of the house. I'm depending on you to beat me. But I'm not going to play second fiddle to Crofter."

"It will serve you right if it does land you head," responded Tempest. "If it does, we'll have to keep you up to the mark and see you don't shirk."

"Don't say that, old chap, or I shall jack it up," said Pridgin, putting his feet upon the window-ledge. "Besides, does it occur to you that Redwood's leaving, and that the second man up, if he's one of us, is left not only captain of Sharpe's but captain of Low Heath?"

"I know," said Tempest quietly, "but they say Leslie of Selkirk's is in the running for that."

"Stuff and nonsense!" retorted Pridgin. "Tempest of Sharpe's is the man for my money."

Tempest laughed again; but it was a sort of laugh which did not bode well for Leslie of Selkirk's.

This talk had been a fortnight ago. Since then the examinations had come and gone. The Philosophers, sobered and perspiring, had been spread out at two-desk intervals on three fatal days in the large hall, with day boys to right of them and Selkirkers to left, writing for their lives, and groaning over questions which only a fiend could have devised, and only a double-first could have answered. How I had got on, I could no more tell than the man in the moon. My comrades, when we compared notes afterwards, cheerfully assured me that, out of some fifty questions on the three days, I had possibly got half a question right, but that that was doubtful, and depended on the particular crib the examiner swore by. Redwood, to whom I confided some of my answers, thought rather more hopefully of my case, and told me to keep my spirits up. Tempest said that if he were to cuff me for every discreditable blunder I had made, I should have ear-ache for a month. Dicky, on the other hand, confessed that he wished he could believe he had done as well as I.

As for the other Philosophers, general discouragement was the order of the day. It was moved and seconded that Coxhead be kicked for having made "amnis" feminine, and having translated the French "impasse" as "instep." And Trimble was temporarily suspended from the service of the Conversation Club because he had put a decimal dot in the wrong place. Public feeling ran so high that any departure from the rules of syntax or algebra was regarded as treason against the house, and dealt with accordingly.

On the whole, therefore, we were glad when the time of suspense came to an end.

How matters had gone with the seniors it was even more difficult to surmise than it had been in our case. The day after the end of their exams., Redwood and Tempest, with Pridgin to cox, rowed twelve miles down stream and back, and returned cheerful and serene, and even jocular. Leslie of Selkirk's also spent a pleasant afternoon in the school laboratory, whistling to himself as he mixed up his acids. Crofter and Wales mooned about under the trees in the field somewhat limply, but showed no outward signs of distress. Altogether, speculation was baffled, and it was almost irritating to find the chief actors in the drama refusing to take the momentous question seriously.

"How did you get on?" I asked Tempest.

"You'll hear to-morrow," said he; "so shall I."

"Do you think you'll beat Leslie?"

"Either that, or he'll beat me, or it'll be a dead heat," said he.

There was no dealing with frivolity of this kind; and Tempest, ever since his recovery last term, had been rapidly regaining all his old frivolity and lightheartedness.

It was a trying ordeal on "Result" day, sitting patiently in hall till the doctor made up his mind to appear. All the school was there. There was an unusual spirit of orderliness afoot. The few irresponsible ones, who, with nothing to lose, tried to get up a disturbance, were promptly squashed by the grim, anxious competitors to whom the coming results meant so much. We Philosophers huddled together for comfort, but not a joke travelled down the line. We sat and drummed our fingers on the desk before us, and wondered why on earth the doctor, on a day like this, should take such an unearthly time to put on his cap and gown.

At last he appeared, paper in hand, and glasses on nose. I could see Dicky just in front of me catch a quick breath, and Tempest up in the front brush his hair back with his fingers; and there arose before my mind in horrible review all the palpable blunders of my own examination papers.

"Lower school," began the doctor in a hard, dry, unemotional voice. "Aggregate form order--out of a possible 1000 marks, Brown iii., day boy, and Jones iv., Mr Sharpe's, bracketed first with 853 marks."

What! me? bracketed top with Dicky? Go along with you! But a huge thump on the back from Warminster, followed by a huger from Langrish; the vision of Dicky's consciously blushing cheeks, as Flitwick performed the same office for him; and, above all, a nod across the room from Redwood, and a grin from Tempest, convinced me that there was something in it after all. Of course it was a mistake, and when the marks came to be counted again it would be put right. But while it lasted it wasn't bad. What was the doctor saying?

"A very good performance, both of you; and the result of honest hard work."

It was true then? There was no humbug about it? Oh, I must write to my mother this very afternoon.

"Warminster, Mr Sharpe's second, 836, good also; Corderoy, Mr Selkirk's, third, 815; Langrish, Mr Sharpe's, fourth, 807; Trimble, Mr Sharpe's, sixth, 796; Purkis, Mr Sharpe's, seventh, 771; Coxhead, Mr Sharpe's, eighth, 734--(Mr Sharpe's boys have worked excellently this term);--Quin, day boy, ninth, 699; Rackstraw, Mr Sharpe's, tenth, 678."

And so the list went on. I was too much lost in the wonder of my own success to appreciate all at once the glorious significance of the whole result. But as the Philosophers crowded in a little closer on one another, and the friendly nudge went round, it began to dawn on me. Every one of our men had given a good account of himself, even Coxhead and the "pauper" Rackstraw! Not one of the old gang but was eligible for the club; not one but had done something to "put the day boys and Selkirk's and everybody else to bed," as Langrish said.

"Just like your side," said the latter to me, "trying to make out you'd made a mess of it. You can only make a mess of it, young Sarah, when you try not to; when you do try you can't do it." And with another thump on the back our excellent secretary gave me to know he bore me no malice, but on the contrary was pleased to favour me with his general approbation.

But more was yet to come. Compared with the "aggregates," the details of how we had passed each examination were more or less tame, and we were impatient to get on to the senior results.

The middle school had to come first. As a rule we were not greatly concerned in them, except as belonging to the division into which some of us would probably be promoted next term. But such as they were, they kept up the credit of Sharpe's. A Selkirker did indeed head the list, but after him a string of four of our fellows followed; after them a day boy, and then two more "Sharpers."

More back patting, crowding up, conscious blushes, and congratulations.

Then the doctor put down one paper and took up another; and every one knew what was coming.

"Upper school," read the doctor in exactly the same voice, as if this announcement were of no more importance than any other. "Aggregate form order--out of a possible 1000 marks, Redwood, captain of the school, and day boy, 902."

We were obliged to interrupt a little here. There would not be many more chances of cheering old Redwood, and we couldn't afford to chuck them away. So we cheered, and gave the doctor time to polish up his glasses and take a sip of water.

"Your cheers," said he, when at last we had relieved ourselves, "are well-deserved. In addition to this capital result, Redwood takes the Low Heath scholarship to Trinity, where, I almost venture to prophesy, we shall hear even greater things of him some day."

More cheers. But we were too impatient to hear what came next to interpose too long a delay.

"Tempest, Mr Sharpe's, second, 888; all the more gratifying when we remember the causes which interrupted his school work for a time last term."

We fairly gave ourselves away now! Sharpe's had reached the top of the tide with a vengeance. There was an end to all uncertainty as to who would be its captain; and there was the glorious certainty that the captain of Sharpe's would also be captain of Low Heath. Three cheers! Rather.

But still we could not, till the rest of the list was read, give ourselves up to cheering for as long as we should have liked. So we allowed the doctor to proceed.

"Pridgin, Mr Sharpe's, third, 869--very close."

Good old Pridgin! All his discomfort had not been for nothing. He had "taken it out of" Crofter, after all. By how much?

"Leslie, Mr Selkirk's, fourth, 832. Wales, Mr Sharpe's, fifth, 801. Crofter, Mr Sharpe's, sixth, 769."

A cool hundred between them! We had the decency not to rub it in too hard. It was clear by the disconcerted look in the face of our so- called captain that he was more surprised than any one. He smiled, of course, and leant across to pat Pridgin on the back. But that was just his way--we knew well enough that it cloaked a bitter mortification, and why worry the poor beggar with letting him see we noticed it?

So we waited till we got outside, and then let ourselves loose on Tempest and Pridgin, and positively injured our voices with cheering.

That afternoon in the faggery our jubilant review of the situation was combined with a wind-up meeting of the Conversation Club for the term.

"Jolly good show for us," said Langrish. "Crofter's pretty sick, but it'll do him good. I move and third, and Sarah seconds and fourths, that we send him a resolution of condolence."

"Better let him alone," suggested I.

"Shut up, or you'll get jolly well kicked out of the club," said the secretary. "If you don't want to be civil, it's no reason why we shouldn't." I had imagined I was on the whole more concerned for Crofter's feelings than they, but, putting it in the way they did, I could hardly resist. So the following resolution was solemnly drawn up and ordered to be conveyed to "The late Mr Crofter."

"That this meeting of the Philosophical Conversation Club is hereby jolly glad to see Tempest cock of the house again, with Pridgin second man up. It hereby condoles with Crofter in the jolly back seat he has got to take, and is sorry he shirked the Mile. It begs to inform him that he is a hundred and eighteen marks behind Tempest, and trusts he will in future obey the house captain, to whom all applications for *exeats* and extra leave are to be addressed. Crofter need not trouble to reply, as the club only desires to have communication with the cock of the house."

This done, I was ordered to take the chair as the new president, and called upon the secretary to read the minutes.

These were short and to the point,--

"'A general meeting of the Conversation Club was held on Monday in the Examination Hall. With his usual mulishness, Sarah thought he'd have a cut in, and it was resolved to give him a chance. Thanks to the drivelling idiotcy of Warminster, who doesn't even know the feminine genitive of ***corpus***, he scraped through; and, as he couldn't do much worse than Coxhead, he did a shade better.'"

"All very well," growled Coxhead, "he did a jolly sight better than you."

"'Coxhead, who is hereby expelled for using slang, was, as usual, down with the paupers at the bottom. A town cad called Brown, who managed to conceal his cribs, came out first, and it was decided to tack Sarah on to him. Trimble, as might be expected, came a cropper in his English grammar--'"

"A cram! They never examined us in it!"

"There you are; you don't even know it when you see it--'came a cropper in his English grammar.'"

"I tell you I didn't," expostulated Trimble. "Shut up."

"Shut what up?"

"Yourself."

"Come and shut me."

A warm argument ensued, which knocked over the table, and was only composed by my reminding the club that we didn't want to disturb the peace of the new cock of the house on his first night.

"All right," said Langrish, "where was I?--'English grammar. Purkis, not having paid his subscription, naturally came out too low to be classed, but to give him a lift he was allowed to be stuck in between Trim and Coxhead, who being outsiders at the best of times, had plenty of room for another.'"

"All very well--what sort of howler did ***you*** come?" asked the outraged Purkis.

"'It being considered well to stick one Selkirker into the list, the hon. secretary made room for Corderoy, and is hereby thanked on his retirement.'"

"Hullo!" said I, "don't say that, Langrish."

"Fact is," said Langrish, dropping the minutes, "I've got to. I've gone down, you see."

"Oh, but you've worked like a cart-horse. I move, Trim seconds, Warminster thirds, Coxhead fourths, Purkis fifths, and the paupers sixth, that old Lang be and hereby is perpetual secretary of the Ph.C.C., and that it's all rot his retiring."

"Oh, all serene," said Langrish, evidently pleased. "That's your look-out. Where was I?--'thanked on his retirement, but as nobody else can read his writing, he is hereby asked to hang on, which he hereby does. The meeting then adjourned.'"

We decided to celebrate the evening by a state tea, as which the usual loyal and patriotic toasts were given; of which I will only trouble the reader with one, that delivered by Warminster, the late president.

"It's a sell, of course, getting down; but we all had a good look in, and Sal's come out best man this once. We aren't going to jack it up though, and he'll have to mind his eye (cheers). After all, what with the mess he made over Tempest's bills (loud cheers), and the shindy about the guy, and all that rot about the barge, he's shown he's fit for the job (laughter). But he'll have to make a good show-up for Sharpe's now, or we'll let him know. We've scored a bit of a record, and we don't want to fool it away (loud cheers), and any fellow who doesn't put it on doesn't deserve to be a Ph.C.C. or anything like (prolonged applause). Gentlemen, with these remarks I beg to give the health of 'the army and navy and reserve forces' (loud cheers)."

The "reserve forces" were the most striking feature, after all, about the wind-up of the Conversation Club that night.

Before I went to bed I looked in at Tempest's study, where, to my delight, I found Dicky Brown.

"Hullo, I was just coming to fetch you," said the new captain. "Don't you think this a pretty good show for old Plummer?"

"Rather," said Dicky. "I wonder how he's getting on!"

"And I wonder if the pond is full up again yet."

"By the way," said Tempest, "I've never hided you for collaring that pistol of mine. I may as well do it now."

"Fire away," said I; "I don't mind taking a licking from the captain of Low Heath."

"It sounds queer, doesn't it?" said Tempest, disarmed by this compliment. "Between you and me, kids, I think we ought to be able to make the thing work next term."

"Rather," said I, "only we shall have to keep sitting up to do it."

"So much the better," said they.

The Codes Of Hammurabi And Moses
W. W. Davies

The discovery of the Hammurabi Code is one of the greatest achievements of archaeology, and is of paramount interest, not only to the student of the Bible, but also to all those interested in ancient history...

Religion **ISBN:** *1-59462-338-4*

QTY

Pages:132
MSRP $12.95

The Theory of Moral Sentiments
Adam Smith

This work from 1749. contains original theories of conscience amd moral judgment and it is the foundation for systemof morals.

Philosophy **ISBN:** *1-59462-777-0*

QTY

Pages:536
MSRP $19.95

Jessica's First Prayer
Hesba Stretton

In a screened and secluded corner of one of the many railway-bridges which span the streets of London there could be seen a few years ago, from five o'clock every morning until half past eight, a tidily set-out coffee-stall, consisting of a trestle and board, upon which stood two large tin cans, with a small fire of charcoal burning under each so as to keep the coffee boiling during the early hours of the morning when the work-people were thronging into the city on their way to their daily toil...

Childrens **ISBN:** *1-59462-373-2*

QTY

Pages:84
MSRP $9.95

My Life and Work
Henry Ford

Henry Ford revolutionized the world with his implementation of mass production for the Model T automobile. Gain valuable business insight into his life and work with his own auto-biography... "We have only started on our development of our country we have not as yet, with all our talk of wonderful progress, done more than scratch the surface. The progress has been wonderful enough but..."

Biographies/ **ISBN:** *1-59462-198-5*

QTY

Pages:300
MSRP $21.95

www.bookjungle.com *email: sales@bookjungle.com fax: 630-214-0564 mail: Book Jungle PO Box 2226 Champaign, IL 61825*

The Art of Cross-Examination
Francis Wellman

QTY

I presume it is the experience of every author, after his first book is published upon an important subject, to be almost overwhelmed with a wealth of ideas and illustrations which could readily have been included in his book, and which to his own mind, at least, seem to make a second edition inevitable. Such certainly was the case with me; and when the first edition had reached its sixth impression in five months, I rejoiced to learn that it seemed to my publishers that the book had met with a sufficiently favorable reception to justify a second and considerably enlarged edition. ..

Pages:412

Reference   **ISBN:** *1-59462-647-2*   *MSRP $19.95*

On the Duty of Civil Disobedience
Henry David Thoreau

QTY

Thoreau wrote his famous essay, On the Duty of Civil Disobedience, as a protest against an unjust but popular war and the immoral but popular institution of slave-owning. He did more than write—he declined to pay his taxes, and was hauled off to gaol in consequence. Who can say how much this refusal of his hastened the end of the war and of slavery ?

Law   **ISBN:** *1-59462-747-9*   **Pages:48**

MSRP $7.45

Dream Psychology Psychoanalysis for Beginners
Sigmund Freud

QTY

Sigmund Freud, born Sigismund Schlomo Freud (May 6, 1856 - September 23, 1939), was a Jewish-Austrian neurologist and psychiatrist who co-founded the psychoanalytic school of psychology. Freud is best known for his theories of the unconscious mind, especially involving the mechanism of repression; his redefinition of sexual desire as mobile and directed towards a wide variety of objects; and his therapeutic techniques, especially his understanding of transference in the therapeutic relationship and the presumed value of dreams as sources of insight into unconscious desires.

Dream Psychology
Psychoanalysis for Beginners

Sigmund Freud

Pages:196

Psychology   **ISBN:** *1-59462-905-6*   *MSRP $15.45*

The Miracle of Right Thought
Orison Swett Marden

QTY

Believe with all of your heart that you will do what you were made to do. When the mind has once formed the habit of holding cheerful, happy, prosperous pictures, it will not be easy to form the opposite habit. It does not matter how improbable or how far away this realization may see, or how dark the prospects may be, if we visualize them as best we can, as vividly as possible, hold tenaciously to them and vigorously struggle to attain them, they will gradually become actualized, realized in the life. But a desire, a longing without endeavor, a yearning abandoned or held indifferently will vanish without realization.

Pages:360

Self Help   **ISBN:** *1-59462-644-8*   *MSRP $25.45*

The Rosicrucian Cosmo-Conception Mystic Christianity by *Max Heindel* ISBN: *1-59462-188-8* **$38.95**
The Rosicrucian Cosmo-conception is not dogmatic, neither does it appeal to any other authority than the reason of the student. It is: not controversial, but is: sent forth in the, hope that it may help to clear... New Age/Religion Pages 646

Abandonment To Divine Providence by *Jean-Pierre de Caussade* ISBN: *1-59462-228-0* **$25.95**
"The Rev. Jean Pierre de Caussade was one of the most remarkable spiritual writers of the Society of Jesus in France in the 18th Century. His death took place at Toulouse in 1751. His works have gone through many editions and have been republished... Inspirational/Religion Pages 400

Mental Chemistry by *Charles Haanel* ISBN: *1-59462-192-6* **$23.95**
Mental Chemistry allows the change of material conditions by combining and appropriately utilizing the power of the mind. Much like applied chemistry creates something new and unique out of careful combinations of chemicals the mastery of mental chemistry... New Age Pages 354

The Letters of Robert Browning and Elizabeth Barret Barrett 1845-1846 vol II ISBN: *1-59462-193-4* **$35.95**
by *Robert Browning* and *Elizabeth Barrett* Biographies Pages 596

Gleanings In Genesis (volume I) by *Arthur W. Pink* ISBN: *1-59462-130-6* **$27.45**
Appropriately has Genesis been termed "the seed plot of the Bible" for in it we have, in germ form, almost all of the great doctrines which are afterwards fully developed in the books of Scripture which follow... Religion/Inspirational Pages 420

The Master Key by *L. W. de Laurence* ISBN: *1-59462-001-6* **$30.95**
In no branch of human knowledge has there been a more lively increase of the spirit of research during the past few years than in the study of Psychology, Concentration and Mental Discipline. The requests for authentic lessons in Thought Control, Mental Discipline and... New Age/Business Pages 422

The Lesser Key Of Solomon Goetia by *L. W. de Laurence* ISBN: *1-59462-092-X* **$9.95**
This translation of the first book of the "Lernegton" which is now for the first time made accessible to students of Talismanic Magic was done, after careful collation and edition, from numerous Ancient Manuscripts in Hebrew, Latin, and French... New Age/Occult Pages 92

Rubaiyat Of Omar Khayyam by *Edward Fitzgerald* ISBN:*1-59462-332-5* **$13.95**
Edward Fitzgerald, whom the world has already learned, in spite of his own efforts to remain within the shadow of anonymity, to look upon as one of the rarest poets of the century, was born at Bredfield, in Suffolk, on the 31st of March, 1809. He was the third son of John Purcell... Music Pages 172

Ancient Law by *Henry Maine* ISBN: *1-59462-128-4* **$29.95**
The chief object of the following pages is to indicate some of the earliest ideas of mankind, as they are reflected in Ancient Law, and to point out the relation of those ideas to modern thought. Religion/History Pages 452

Far-Away Stories by *William J. Locke* ISBN: *1-59462-129-2* **$19.45**
"Good wine needs no bush, but a collection of mixed vintages does. And this book is just such a collection. Some of the stories I do not want to remain buried for ever in the museum files of dead magazine-numbers an author's not unpardonable vanity..." Fiction Pages 272

Life of David Crockett by *David Crockett* ISBN: *1-59462-250-7* **$27.45**
"Colonel David Crockett was one of the most remarkable men of the times in which he lived. Born in humble life, but gifted with a strong will, an indomitable courage, and unremitting perseverance... Biographies/New Age Pages 424

Lip-Reading by *Edward Nitchie* ISBN: *1-59462-206-X* **$25.95**
Edward B. Nitchie, founder of the New York School for the Hard of Hearing, now the Nitchie School of Lip-Reading, Inc, wrote "LIP-READING Principles and Practice". The development and perfecting of this meritorious work on lip-reading was an undertaking... How-to Pages 400

A Handbook of Suggestive Therapeutics, Applied Hypnotism, Psychic Science ISBN: *1-59462-214-0* **$24.95**
by *Henry Munro* Health/New Age/Health/Self-help Pages 376

A Doll's House: and Two Other Plays by *Henrik Ibsen* ISBN: *1-59462-112-8* **$19.95**
Henrik Ibsen created this classic when in revolutionary 1848 Rome. Introducing some striking concepts in playwriting for the realist genre, this play has been studied the world over. Fiction/Classics/Plays 308

The Light of Asia by *sir Edwin Arnold* ISBN: *1-59462-204-3* **$13.95**
In this poetic masterpiece, Edwin Arnold describes the life and teachings of Buddha. The man who was to become known as Buddha to the world was born as Prince Gautama of India but he rejected the worldly riches and abandoned the reigns of power when... Religion/History/Biographies Pages 170

The Complete Works of Guy de Maupassant by *Guy de Maupassant* ISBN: *1-59462-157-8* **$16.95**
"For days and days, nights and nights, I had dreamed of that first kiss which was to consecrate our engagement, and I knew not on what spot I should put my lips..." Fiction Classics Pages 240

The Art of Cross-Examination by *Francis L. Wellman* ISBN: *1-59462-309-0* **$26.95**
Written by a renowned trial lawyer, Wellman imparts his experience and uses case studies to explain how to use psychology to extract desired information through questioning. How-to/Science/Reference Pages 408

Answered or Unanswered? by *Louisa Vaughan* ISBN: *1-59462-248-5* **$10.95**
Miracles of Faith in China Religion Pages 112

The Edinburgh Lectures on Mental Science (1909) by *Thomas* ISBN: *1-59462-008-3* **$11.95**
This book contains the substance of a course of lectures recently given by the writer in the Queen Street Hall, Edinburgh. Its purpose is to indicate the Natural Principles governing the relation between Mental Action and Material Conditions... New Age/Psychology Pages 148

Ayesha by *H. Rider Haggard* ISBN: *1-59462-301-5* **$24.95**
Verily and indeed it is the unexpected that happens! Probably if there was one person upon the earth from whom the Editor of this, and of a certain previous history, did not expect to hear again... Classics Pages 380

Ayala's Angel by *Anthony Trollope* ISBN: *1-59462-352-X* **$29.95**
The two girls were both pretty, but Lucy who was twenty-one who supposed to be simple and comparatively unattractive, whereas Ayala was credited, as her Bombwhat romantic name might show, with poetic charm and a taste for romance. Ayala when her father died was nineteen... Fiction Pages 484

The American Commonwealth by *James Bryce* ISBN: *1-59462-286-8* **$34.45**
An interpretation of American democratic political theory. It examines political mechanics and society from the perspective of Scotsman James Bryce Politics Pages 572

Stories of the Pilgrims by *Margaret P. Pumphrey* ISBN: *1-59462-116-0* **$17.95**
This book explores pilgrims religious oppression in England as well as their escape to Holland and eventual crossing to America on the Mayflower, and their early days in New England... History Pages 268

QTY

The Fasting Cure *by Sinclair Upton*   ISBN: *1-59462-222-1*   **$13.95**
In the Cosmopolitan Magazine for May, 1910, and in the Contemporary Review (London) for April, 1910, I published an article dealing with my experiences in fasting. I have written a great many magazine articles, but never one which attracted so much attention... New Age/Self Help/Health Pages 164

Hebrew Astrology *by Sepharial*   ISBN: *1-59462-308-2*   **$13.45**
In these days of advanced thinking it is a matter of common observation that we have left many of the old landmarks behind and that we are now pressing forward to greater heights and to a wider horizon than that which represented the mind-content of our progenitors...   Astrology Pages 144

Thought Vibration or The Law of Attraction in the Thought World   ISBN: *1-59462-127-6*   **$12.95**

by William Walker Atkinson   Psychology/Religion Pages 144

Optimism *by Helen Keller*   ISBN: *1-59462-108-X*   **$15.95**
Helen Keller was blind, deaf, and mute since 19 months old, yet famously learned how to overcome these handicaps, communicate with the world, and spread her lectures promoting optimism. An inspiring read for everyone...   Biographies/Inspirational Pages 84

Sara Crewe *by Frances Burnett*   ISBN: *1-59462-360-0*   **$9.45**
In the first place, Miss Minchin lived in London. Her home was a large, dull, tall one, in a large, dull square, where all the houses were alike, and all the sparrows were alike, and where all the door-knockers made the same heavy sound...   Childrens/Classic Pages 88

The Autobiography of Benjamin Franklin *by Benjamin Franklin*   ISBN: *1-59462-135-7*   **$24.95**
The Autobiography of Benjamin Franklin has probably been more extensively read than any other American historical work, and no other book of its kind has had such ups and downs of fortune. Franklin lived for many years in England, where he was agent...   Biographies/History Pages 332

Name	
Email	
Telephone	
Address	
City, State ZIP	

☐ **Credit Card**   ☐ **Check / Money Order**

Credit Card Number	
Expiration Date	
Signature	

Please Mail to: Book Jungle
PO Box 2226
Champaign, IL 61825
or Fax to: 630-214-0564

ORDERING INFORMATION

web*: www.bookjungle.com*
email*: sales@bookjungle.com*
fax*: 630-214-0564*
mail*: Book Jungle PO Box 2226 Champaign, IL 61825*
or PayPal *to sales@bookjungle.com*

Please contact us for bulk discounts

DIRECT-ORDER TERMS

**20% Discount if You Order
Two or More Books**
Free Domestic Shipping!
Accepted: Master Card, Visa,
Discover, American Express